# TEMPTATION

K. LORAINE

*USA Today* BESTSELLING AUTHOR
MEG ANNE

ISBN: 978-1-951738-83-9 (Paperback Edition)

ISBN: 978-1-951738-82-2 (Hardback Edition)

Permission requests can be sent via email to: authors@themategames.com

Cover Design by CReya-tive Book Cover Design

Photographer: Wander Aguiar

Model: Andrew Biernat

Edited by Mo Sytsma of Comma Sutra Editorial

*For Mo, If you're going to Hell, so are we.*
*Save us a seat!*

"I can resist anything but temptation."

— OSCAR WILDE

# TEMPTATION

# AUTHOR'S NOTE

Temptation contains sexually explicit scenes, as well as mature and graphic content that is not suitable for all audiences. **Reader discretion is advised.**

Welcome to The Mate Games, a detailed list of content and trigger warnings is available on our website. For those of you who prefer to go in blind, keep reading.

# CHAPTER
# ONE
### CALEB

*Ireland, 1922*

"Amen."

I stood, my head swimming with the euphoric rush of all that came to pass this day. My congregation, perhaps small in number to some, had shown up in droves to welcome me back to the island. This time as their priest.

My eyes landed on the small statue of Christ behind the altar as I made the sign of the cross and turned to walk down the aisle. As I moved along, my hand passed lightly over the age-worn wood of the pews, smooth and cool beneath my palm. Once again, nostalgia slammed into me, memories crowding my mind. These were the same benches I'd sat on as a child, restless and eager to run about with my friends and siblings. Knowing if I set a toe out of line, I'd have to face the wrath of my mam and her wooden spoon. How times had changed.

As I passed through the arched doors, the bell chimed, signaling the top of the hour, and in this case, the sunset. I surveyed the grounds as I took my time, drinking it all in.

The garden was overrun, and the chapel had seen better days. The whitewashed clapboard was dark with mud and rotten in places from neglect. The many stained glass windows hadn't been washed in years, muting any sunlight that bravely attempted to trickle in.

But the people weren't to be blamed for the unkempt state of their church. Five years had passed since influenza had ravaged our island, taking many, my family included, not even sparing our pastor. There hadn't been a new one to care for this place since. The few surviving priests had been needed in the bigger cities where the parishioners were plentiful. This was the first time there'd been enough new clergy to meet the demands of the people. Which is why I was here now. It'd be my honor to restore this holy sanctuary to its once pristine glory.

I tilted my head back as the bell rang out with its final peal, my gaze traveling to the iron cross standing on the top of the steeple that my father had crafted over a decade ago.

It was good to be home.

Surveying the garden, I bent to pull a few of the weeds I could see in the dying light of day, already forming a plan to clean this up and help it thrive.

"Oh, Father Gallagher, you shouldn't be lowering yourself to dig in the dirt. Not after such a beautiful service today." Maureen O'Shanahan bustled her way down the stairs after locking the church doors. "I can arrange for a few of my children to come tend the garden in the morning. Lord knows they need something to keep their hands busy."

I smiled at the woman who'd already made herself invaluable to me. "Thank you, Maureen, but I'm perfectly capable of pulling weeds. After all, this is my home as much as it is yours. There's no job too low for one of God's servants. We are tasked with caring for all of His creations."

She beamed at me. "Look at you. Your mam would be so proud to know her eldest took after her. What a scandal that was. The would-be nun and the carpenter." Her eyes twinkled as she spoke of years-old gossip, but the light in her eyes dimmed as she turned to the small cottage on the hillside. "They were a beautiful pair. God rest their souls."

My heart sank as I followed her gaze. The windows of my family home, the one I'd helped my father build, were dark and cold now instead of filled with the glow of life and happiness. "This plague took so many and spared so few. We must do our best to be worthy in their absence."

Her lower lip trembled as she took in a ragged breath. "When I think of your wee brothers and sisters . . ."

I placed a gentle hand on her shoulder, forcing myself not to relive the moment I came out of my influenza-induced fever dreams and realized my whole family had died. "Let us not dwell on the past, but look to the future we are building."

She sniffled loudly. "Yes. You're right, of course." Pulling a hand-kerchief from her bag, she dabbed her eyes and then blew her nose. "We're blessed to have you."

"And I you."

Her sunny smile returned at that. "Well, I'll leave you to your settling, and I'll be back in the morning for confession." She batted her teary eyes at me. "Five years is a long time to go without. I hope you're ready, Father Gallagher. The people will be lined up around the church waiting to unburden themselves."

"I can't wait."

She snickered, lowering her voice conspiratorially. "Tell me, Father. Is the listening as exciting as I imagine it would be?"

I pretended to lock my lips, unable to keep the smile off my face.

"Good man, you are."

"Goodnight, Maureen."

She walked away, leaving me with the looming figure of the church as my only companion. I wasn't ready to end my day yet. It didn't seem possible to finally have something I'd worked for be real.

Not after everything had been taken from me. But God had His plan, and I was His humble servant. I had to follow where He led.

Pulling the heavy keys from my pocket, I returned to the church doors, wanting one final moment of quiet reflection before supper. I wasn't without options, thanks to my parishioners and their many generous offerings. If the housewives of this island were any indication, I'd be well-fed, and gluttony would be my first sin.

I walked silently, my footsteps barely more than a whisper over the weathered floorboards as I lit a few candles to cast the interior in a soft glow. When I reached the pulpit, I moved to stand behind it, glancing down at the notes from my earlier homily with amusement. What a pretentious arse I could be.

The creak of the door opening had me glancing up, a smile on my face. "Forget something, Maureen?"

Instead of the short but fiery redhead, I found a tall, statuesque woman staring me down, her skin an eerily pale white, eyes a shade of green I'd never seen before. Her long dark hair fell in wild, tumbling curls to her waist. Strange for the fashion of this village. Women here wore their hair pinned back, out of the way, because they needed to be able to work. This was an extravagance.

"My apologies. I thought you were my secretary."

She smiled, her beauty startling and unnerving all at once. I gripped the pulpit hard enough that my knuckles turned white.

"Father, I hope I'm not too late to make my confession."

Technically confession was at a set time every day to help prevent these impositions on my personal time, but I couldn't turn her away. These people had been without for so long; the least I could do was sit and offer her absolution.

"Of course not, my child. Please come in."

That smile again. As though she had a secret she'd never share with me. "Thank you."

"What is your name?"

"Aisling O'Connor. And you're Father Caleb Gallagher, the talk of the town. The prodigal son returned."

She practically glided across the floor as she approached me, ignoring the confessional booth, her focus trained on my eyes.

"Aisling . . . Shall we continue our conversation in the confessional?"

Her palm was on my chest before I could blink, alarm bells ringing in my head. "No, Father. I don't think so."

"What are you playing at?" I gripped her wrist, trying to keep her from touching me.

"Immortality." She licked her lower lip, then bared her teeth at me, fangs glinting in the candlelight.

This had to be a trick. A hallucination left over from the nightmares that plagued me since my illness.

"The only immortality I seek is given by the Lord Almighty."

"Aren't you precious," she breathed, her eyes taking on a feral glow. "I think I'm going to keep you. I've always wanted a priest for my collection."

I backed away, but she gripped my shirt, and try as I might, I couldn't break her hold. "Release me."

"I think not. My, my, I had no idea priests could be so . . . handsome. Tell me, Father, are you as hard everywhere?" She slid her free hand between my legs, cupping me, making my stomach turn.

"This is a house of God. You are not welcome here if you mean to defile it."

"I mean to defile *you*. Now you have one more chance to come willingly. I can make it feel so nice, Father. So nice indeed."

"No. Demon."

Her grin turned wicked, her eyes hardening. "Wrong answer. Now I'm going to make it hurt."

Before I could move, her eyes bore into mine, and I felt as if I was falling.

"Stand very still. I'm going to make you mine now, Caleb. And then you'll never tell me no again. But I'll punish you for that later."

I heard her words as if they were floating down through water. I didn't want to obey, but my body was locked in place. Held captive by her evil spell. Panic and fear raced through my blood as half-formed prayers flitted through my mind. *Father, please. Save me. Do not let her do this to me.*

With fingers cold as death, she traced the line of my collar. A sneer curled her upper lip as she tore the white band off my throat and tossed it to the floor. "I bet you're going to be the sweetest I've ever had. I can smell your virgin blood thrumming through your veins." She inhaled deeply and let out a shuddering, sensual moan. "I'll take that too. You'll be mine in every sense of the word."

"No," I whispered, fighting through whatever spell she'd put me under.

Her low chuckle was the last thing I heard before she struck. Fangs I'd tried to deny existed ripped through my flesh and sank deep into my neck.

I floated on a sea of pain and despair as darkness clouded my vision. I think I screamed, but I wasn't sure. I wasn't aware of much of anything outside the agony of her bite. Just as suddenly, she released me. I sagged to the ground, my legs incapable of keeping me upright after losing so much blood.

She followed me down, red smears obscenely decorating her face as she bit into her wrist and held it up to my lips. "Your turn."

I tried to turn my face away, my gaze landing on my collar, now splattered with crimson drops of my blood.

"Eternal life, Caleb. Exactly what your god promised you."

Everything around me went gray, the world turning cold as my life bled from me and into the old bones of the church. Then her blood slipped into my now open mouth, and all I knew was darkness.

It was still dark outside when I came to, the candles nearly spent, their white wax pooling on the floor.

"Oh, good. You're awake."

My eyes snapped to the creature sitting on the altar, her legs bared but crossed, the rest of her body exposed save for the parts covered by my purple stole.

"What did you do to me, demon?"

She laughed—a high, musical sound that I once would have enjoyed. Now, all I knew was rage and hunger. Such hunger.

"I'm not a demon, you silly man. I'm a vampire." She hopped down from the altar, her naked body on full display as she slipped the stole from her neck and ran it through her fingers. "And so are you."

Too distracted by her nakedness to make sense of her words, I spat, "Cover yourself."

She rolled her eyes. "Still going to play the chaste little virgin? Very well, play your games. I'll have you on this altar eventually. It's time for you to feed anyway."

"Feed?" Even the word had my stomach twisting with need. I was so fecking hungry. My throat burned with thirst. Sweet merciful Jesus, I'd never known this type of starvation.

"Yes, darling. Feed." She craned her neck, and a small figure appeared in the shadows. "Maureen, be a love and come out here, won't you?"

Horror flickered in the back of my mind, but I was consumed with the low thump of . . . was that her pulse? My eyes zeroed in on her neck as if I could make out the network of veins beneath the thin skin and knew exactly which one would provide the most sustenance. Jesus, what was wrong with me?

And then her earlier words came back to me. *Vampire.* She'd turned me into a monster like her. *Dear God, no.*

Maureen gave a little gasp, causing my attention to snap back to her, to the blood trickling from her throat where Aisling had cut her.

"Now, my wee darling, get on your knees for your priest. He's going to rid you of those pesky sins. You know how to begin your confession," Aisling said, shoving my secretary toward me.

Maureen did as she was bade, wide eyes staring up at me before

7

she dutifully bowed her head and began. "Forgive me, Father, for I have sinned . . ."

Fangs filled my mouth, and uncontrollable thirst took over. I was on her before she finished her sentence, drinking deep, sating my hunger, draining her.

Her body slumped forward with a dull thud. Somewhere in my brain, I was shouting my outrage at what I'd done, but as I licked the last of her blood from my lips, the voice faded away.

"Good boy. We'll make a proper monster out of you yet. Now, get some sleep, love. We have a busy night ahead of us."

"What do you mean?"

"You'll see."

I woke hours later to the sound of murmured voices, the darkened confessional booth serving to keep my blood-soaked existence hidden. Maureen's shadowy corpse was just visible through the panel between priest and penitent. I had only a second to mourn her death at my hands.

"Come out, Caleb. Your flock is waiting for you."

Once again, my throat burned. Gnawing emptiness filled my belly, but this time, I knew how to quench the thirst. I stepped out of the confessional and took in the filled pews as Aisling's plan became clear and horror batted at me. She wanted me to sate myself on the blood of the people I was here to nurture. Even as the realization took hold, a sick pleasure rose in its place. I couldn't stop myself. The monster took over, and tonight he would feast.

When there was nothing left but a church filled with bodies, Aisling unlocked the door. "Come, dearheart. You're not finished yet."

By the time we fled the island, not a single soul remained. The village that had survived a plague was razed to the ground by the one man sent to save them. And perhaps I still had. I'd sent their souls to Heaven, given them the salvation they'd been praying for. Just a little sooner than they had planned.

My gaze flicked to the evil beauty standing beside me, licking blood off her fingers. If she had her way, there'd be a lot more sent on their journey to the Almighty by the time she was done.

Dread settled in my stomach as a horrible truth flickered through my mind. It was already too late for me.

I was damned.

∼

*Alaska, Christmas Eve, 1997*

I TRUDGED THROUGH THE SNOW, numb to everything except for the bitterness and barely suppressed hunger that were ever-present. My life was a mockery of what it was supposed to be—a man of God now enslaved to a hellish creature. Murdering and perverting the masses at her command.

I had more blood on my hands than I could ever wipe clean. But where was I to go? She'd taught me nothing but how to kill, not how to survive this . . . existence. And every time I'd tried to run, she'd found me and tied the metaphorical noose around my neck even tighter. Seventy-five years seemed to pass in the blink of an eye, and I lost more of myself, sinking even deeper into the hellscape she'd damned me to.

Tonight, on what was once one of the holiest days I observed in my human life, I feared I'd lose hold of the last shred of decency I had left. I stared at the church on the snow-covered hill. This was a favorite game of hers, robbing people of faith of their belief. Watching the hope snuff out when they realized their savior wouldn't be coming for them. She told me once of the twisted pleasure she received as their pitiful cries for their God to save them stopped and the truth finally registered. They were as damned as us.

Nothing I'd believed was real. I'd dedicated myself to lies and stories. Because if God loved me, surely he wouldn't want me to suffer so. Or at the very least, would take offense at one of his servants tormenting so many innocents. What kind of God could allow evil such as this, such as me, to exist?

The organ began to play from inside the church, candles illuminating within as the parishioners settled in for their midnight mass, welcoming their savior. And I would be out here, lying in wait to send them to him . . . or rather, show them the truth.

Alaska was a perfect place for us during the winter. Dark, cold, filled with shadows and places to hide as we hunted.

Tonight was especially beautiful, an idyllic tableau—the snow falling in the dim light of a moon covered by clouds, hymns filling the air, prey lined up and ready for us to feast. If only those inside knew that the peaceful landscape they loved would serve as their slaughterhouse.

Pulling the heavy chain and padlock from the bag I'd brought, I readied myself to lock the door and ensure the churchgoers had only one way out of their prison. Through me.

The air around me rippled, and my senses went on high alert. Before I could finish scanning the horizon, light flared to life behind me, throwing my shadow onto the suddenly blinding snow.

"What a disappointment you've turned out to be, Father Gallagher." A smooth, slightly annoyed British voice filled the surroundings, sending my blood curdling.

I turned, one arm raised against the painful glow coming from the . . . fecking angel?

My mind struggled to make sense of the visage before me. It was like staring straight into the sun. He was every masterpiece ever painted come to life. Long flowing golden hair, eyes that blazed with holy righteousness, pure white robe, feathered wings of white and silver. I didn't know where to look.

And then he drew his sword, lit with gold flames. His eyes shone with the power to smite me where I stood. Thank God.

It wasn't all a lie. My faith hadn't been for nothing. God was real, and His messenger stood before me, ready to serve His great purpose.

10

"Who are you?" I whispered, falling to my knees. "The Angel of Death come to punish me? Go on, then. Smite me. End this torture. Do what I never had the strength to do."

His head tilted as if my words surprised him, and he studied me for a second before releasing a heavy breath. Lowering the sword, he planted the tip in the snow, banking the flames as he leaned on the pommel. His brow furrowed. "Well, that was easier than I expected."

I blinked. "Pardon?"

The light swelled to blinding intensity, forcing me to close my eyes. When it faded enough for me to reopen them, the angel was gone, replaced by the same man now dressed in black motorcycle leathers. I frowned.

"Is this some kind of trickery? Are you playing with my mind?"

"Basically, yes. But not in the way you mean. I thought I had to make a splash to get you to pay attention. Everyone is so caught up in angels and their robes and wings. We haven't dressed like that for close to a millennium. Well, except for a few holdouts, but we don't talk about them."

"Are you really an angel?"

He scoffed. "Did you not see with your own eyes? The wings? The flaming sword? The heavenly *glow*?"

"What is your name?"

Shoulders straight, chest puffed out, he took on a haughty air. "I am Gabriel, archangel, Messenger of God. And I am here to deliver unto you a . . . message." He frowned and muttered to himself, "Twice in one sentence? Have you learned nothing from all the books you've read?"

"Excuse me?"

He waved a hand. "Like I said, I have a message for you. A proposition of sorts."

"A proposition?" I felt like a fecking fool trying to follow the conversation. I was still caught up on the part where I was speaking to a bloody angel after spending the last seven decades certain my entire belief system had been a sham. If I had a heart, I'm pretty sure it would have stopped beating. As it was, I wasn't entirely sure I hadn't already passed out and this was some sort of hallucination.

"Will you stop speaking and just let me finish? Vampires are worse than children."

"Forgive me."

His lips twitched. "That's usually reserved for my Father, but I appreciate the sentiment. I hold in my hands your metaphorical soul. You vampires are so precious about those. We had plans for you, Caleb. Ones that did not involve you massacring your flock. Your soul was stolen by a vampire, your choice taken away. Tonight, I'm returning that choice to you. Tonight, you may choose between your soul and your death."

He'd barely finished speaking before the words left my lips. "I want my soul." Without it, death only led me one place, and it wasn't the pearly gates.

A full-on grin split his lips this time. "You haven't heard what you'll have to do to get it."

"I don't care."

"I'm still going to tell you. The Apocalypse is coming. War is already riding free and bringing with her the harbinger. You are tasked with stopping it."

Purpose I hadn't felt since I'd been turned burned through my veins. "Yes. Anything. I am at your service."

"You might not feel that way when the time comes, but I want you to remember this was your choice."

"There's nothing that matters more to me than this."

Gabriel smiled again, and this time I felt as though he was laughing *at* me. "Very well." He took a step forward and placed his hand on my head. As soon as he made contact with me, a searing pain suffused my body. I couldn't breathe. My spine arched and my eyes rolled back into my head as I convulsed beneath his touch.

"What did you do to me?" I panted, falling forward once he released me.

"I linked you to the seven seals. Now you will know the instant they are broken."

"How am I to know this?"

Gabriel's eyes took on a haunted cast. "You will feel it."

"So what do you want me to do to stop them? How will I know what breaks them?"

"You really do expect me to do everything for you, don't you? I don't have that information. If I did, I wouldn't need you, and you'd be nothing but a scorch mark on the snow." He stiffened, brows drawing together, tension radiating from him. "She is coming."

My chest caught fire, pain lancing me, burning with agonizing intensity. I tore my shirt off, trying to stop the flames, to save myself, but there was nothing. No fire. No smoke. Just a round brand on my skin, tender to the touch, red and angry.

Gabriel's gaze locked on mine. "The first seal has broken."

I glared at him. Feel it, he said. It bloody well cut me in half. "You don't say."

"Come with me. It's time you leave all this behind."

Getting to my feet on shaky legs, I did as the angel of God said. Then he placed a palm on my shoulder, and the world around me shifted before righting itself. I took in the Gothic estate, the wrought-iron fence, the scent of country air.

"Where are we?"

"Your new home, Professor Gallagher. Welcome to Ravenscroft University."

# TWO

## CALEB

*Somewhere over the Atlantic,*
*hours after abducting Sunday*

I'd done it. I'd fecking stolen her from them because I had no choice. Cashel Blackthorne would *not* get to be the conquering hero in this story. Not if it meant Sunday had to be at his mercy. I was the one tasked by God with dealing with the child, and I was the *only* one who would do everything in his power to protect Sunday while fulfilling my vow. No one else could be trusted.

If that made me the villain, well, I'd been a monster far longer than I'd ever been a man. She may hate me for stealing her away into the night, but I'd do it again. I'd face her wrath and welcome her anger. I liked her feisty anyway.

My eyes drifted across the plane and back into the private bedroom. She was curled on her side, sleeping peacefully. As she would until long after we arrived at our final destination. I hadn't wanted this outcome, but that doesn't mean I hadn't planned for it.

I'd been prepared for this moment from the second I'd learned where Noah was taking her.

She couldn't escape me. Too much hung in the balance. The world. My soul. Her life. Closing my eyes, I listened for the sound of her rhythmic breathing, the steady beat of her heart, and the rapid thrum of the child's pulse. It soothed something in me to know they were both safe, but with the sound of that persistent flutter also came a sense of pure dread. She'd never forgive me for what I was tasked to do. I'd lose her even if she survived.

I gritted my teeth and looked away, filled with resolution. So be it. Her life was more important than my happiness.

Standing, I pulled my bag from the overhead rack and rifled through the few belongings I'd packed in preparation. She needed a second dose of the sedative. But instead of finding the cool glass vial I'd stored in the side pocket, my fingers slid across something unexpected.

Parchment?

Removing the folded paper from the bag, I stared in utter confusion at the green wax stamped on the edges, sealing the letter addressed to me. My thumb brushed over the raised M surrounded by stars.

Moriarty's personal seal. Why? What did that toady man have to say that would require such secrecy?

Breaking the wax, I opened the letter and began to read.

CALEB,

FORGIVE THE INTRUSION OF YOUR PERSONAL BELONGINGS, BUT PROFESSOR SINESTRA HAD A VISION. SHE TOLD ME YOU'D HAVE NEED OF THIS IN THE DAYS TO COME. FOR THE LIFE OF ME, I CAN'T FIGURE OUT HOW SHE KNEW I HAD IT, BUT IF I'M COMPLETELY HONEST, SHE GIVES ME THE HEEBIE-JEEBIES, AND I WASN'T ABOUT TO ASK QUESTIONS. SHE HAS THE MOST UNNERVING EYES. I DO NOT ENVY YOU HER ATTENTIONS. I, FOR ONE, WOULD RATHER

NOT BE ON THE RECEIVING END OF ONE OF HER PROPHECIES. OH, LISTEN TO ME, RAMBLING ON LIKE I DON'T HAVE A WHOLE HOST OF THINGS TO ATTEND TO.

THE POINT IS, WHATEVER YOU'RE UP TO, THIS SHROUD IS SPELLED TO CLOAK YOU AND YOUR LOCATION FROM ANYONE WHO IS SEARCHING FOR YOU (BY MAGICAL OR MORE TRADITIONAL MEANS). FOR ALL INTENTS AND PURPOSES, YOU AND . . . WHOMEVER YOUR COMPANION MAY BE WILL CEASE TO EXIST. BUT WHAT AM I SAYING? OF COURSE YOU ALREADY KNOW ALL ABOUT IT. IT IS YOUR SPECIALTY, AFTER ALL.

TAKE CARE TO PLACE IT IN A SAFE SPOT. THE MAGIC IS POWERFUL. I'M LOATH TO PART WITH SUCH PROTECTION, BUT SHE ASSURED ME IT WAS OF THE UTMOST IMPORTANCE. THAT IT WAS MY WAY TO 'SERVE THE CAUSE,' WHAT-EVER THAT MEANS.

WE'VE NEVER BEEN CLOSE, BUT I'D HATE TO SEE YOU DEAD, AND SHE DID STRENUOUSLY IMPLY THAT WOULD BE THE OUTCOME IF I DID NOT FOLLOW HER INSTRUCTIONS TO THE LETTER.
TAKE CARE, CALEB. PLEASE DON'T DIE. I DO LOVE OUR CHATS.

~ EUGENE

"SWEET SUFFERING JESUS," I muttered, pulling the linen shroud from the bottom of my bag. How had I missed this? Moriarty was right. It was impossible to mistake it as anything but the relic it was.

I ran the fabric through my fingers, the rough texture of the dingy faded garment surprising. It was old, ancient even, with spots worn so thin I could see through the threadbare patches. But if I've learned anything in my years, it was that magic didn't need beauty or splendor. Magic was best served by items with significance.

I couldn't pretend to know what the Seer was up to, but if she'd

17

foreseen this outcome, if she knew I'd be needing such protection, I wasn't about to turn it down.

I'd already been resolved in my purpose, but knowing that I had this added layer of protection sent the last of my anxiety away. This was my path. I was doing my God-sworn duty. I could not afford a shred of doubt.

A soft chime signaled an incoming announcement before the pilot's voice crackled through the plane. "Please prepare yourself for final descent. We'll be arriving in Dublin shortly."

I rarely used my thrall these days, but I was thankful for the ability, as I'd been able to easily control the flight crew and have us set up with a private airfield outside of Dublin proper. It seemed of late I was more vampire than man, turning to skills I hadn't made use of since my time as Aisling's puppet. A small tendril of guilt wormed its way into my mind, but I pushed it aside. This was too important.

"Whatever it fecking takes," I said to Sunday's now restless form.

Shoving the cloak back into my bag, I pulled out the vial I'd originally been searching for, along with my seldom-used burner phone. There was only one contact.

Selecting it, I hit the call button as I stalked back toward the bed. "Hello?"

"It's time."

Silence met my announcement.

"You know what to do. I'll be seeing you soon."

I powered the phone off, tossing it onto the bed as I drove the needle into the bared column of Sunday's throat.

"Whatever it takes."

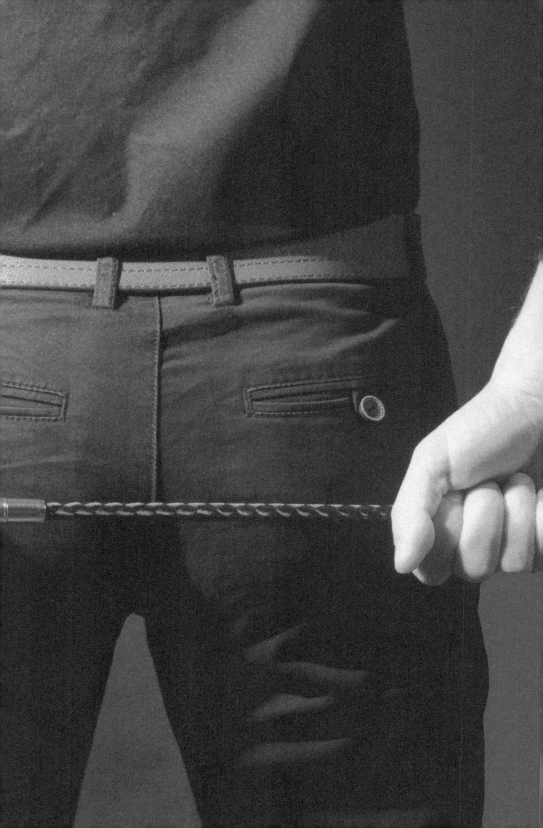

# THREE

## ALEK

"So you will kill the baby, and I . . ." Noah's acceptance of this plan sent protective fury burning through me.

I had to close my eyes against the rise of my berserker. But then Cashel spoke, and I lost my thread of control.

"Will attempt to turn your mate."

No one spoke as the words hung heavy between us. It was a battle for me to speak through the blind rage pumping through my veins.

"Absolutely not," I growled, my voice filled with quiet thunder.

"But if it's the only way," Noah started.

I leveled him with my stare. "You have no idea what it will do to her mixed blood. Your solution could be a death sentence. It is not your choice to make."

"If it means her dying anyway, I will try whatever I can to save her. You are a fool if you think I would just sit by and let her leave me . . ." His voice broke. "Leave *us*."

Knowing I only had one other ally in the room, I turned to Kingston. "You've been awfully quiet."

"I'm still trying to wade through the bullshit these two have been spewing for the last twenty minutes."

"Some protective Alpha you turned out to be." I clenched my fists and paced in front of the fireplace. "You can't be considering any of this. That's *our* child. Not some demon spawn from hell. And even if she *is* a monster, she's still ours."

Kingston's torn expression filled me with dread. "I don't know what to do. You heard Glinda. She's going to die, Alek."

The thread of panic in his voice helped me regain some of the control I'd lost. "It will kill her to lose the baby. You know that, right? If she survives, she'll never forgive you if you allow these two leeches to murder your child. The one you've been fighting to protect since the second you found out it existed." I took a heavy breath before continuing. "Are you going to risk that? Your child as well as the love of your mate?"

A shudder worked its way through his large frame, his wolf shining in his eyes when they met mine. "No. Never."

"Then this conversation is over. I will not agree to any plan that involves the murder of *any* child, but especially not one that involves mine. Are you coming?" I demanded, looking at the shifter as I started for the door.

Kingston nodded, jaw tense, eyes hard.

Even though he was part of the reason my berserker was rattling its chains, I couldn't leave without giving Noah a chance to change his mind. I owed it to him—and Sunday.

"And you?"

Noah swallowed, looking between his father and us. "I'm sorry," he whispered. But the words were not aimed at us.

Cashel's eyes flashed. "This is the only way to save her."

"We will find another way." Noah turned and walked to where Kingston and I were waiting at the door.

His father's panicked voice rang out. "If you leave this room, that's it. It's over. We will all die. The world will burn, and there will be nothing we can do to prevent it."

Noah's face drained of color, but he stood strong, not turning around as he strode through the door. "Then it burns."

I followed, Kingston not far behind, and the three of us went in search of our mate. We had to get her away from this place, hide her, protect her, and figure out how to save . . . everything.

It took mere moments to get to her room, yet every passing second felt like ages. The danger sat heavy, like a leaden blanket meant to suffocate me. The relief I hoped to feel vanished at the sight of Moira standing guard at the door.

"Stand aside, witch," I ordered, but the little spitfire crossed her arms over her chest and shook her head.

"No. She doesn't want to see you." She glanced behind me, looking at the others. "Any of you."

"Listen, Belladonna, I'm not here to play nice. My mate is in there, and she's upset . . . in danger. I need to get to her, and you won't stop me." Kingston's voice was a low, threatening growl.

"You'll have to go through me."

Noah sighed. "As you wish." His gaze flicked to me, conveying his meaning without saying a word.

Already of the same mind, I grasped Moira by the arms and lifted her out of the way. She let out a surprised gasp, kicking me in the shin when I set her down. I didn't mind. It was a small price to pay and likely wouldn't even bruise. Either way, the obstacle between Sunday and us had been removed.

Noah tried the door, but it didn't budge. "Locked? She never locks the door."

We exchanged uneasy glances.

"Break it down," Noah snarled. "Something isn't right."

Kingston got there before me, shouldering the wood and splintering it in one go. He stalked inside and we followed, fear instantly finding a home in my gut at the sight of the open balcony doors and the empty room.

"Sunshine?" Kingston called, his voice holding a frantic edge as he searched the adjoining bathroom. "It's empty. She's not here."

Noah stood inside the walk-in closet, staring down at his hands. "She left us."

"What the fuck are you talking about?" I looked at the vampire, unable to comprehend a word coming out of his mouth. After all she'd been through to get us together, why would she up and leave?

"Her bag. It's gone." He shook his head and locked eyes with me. "She fucking left us."

Moira sighed. "Of course she did. She overheard you idiots talking about killing the baby."

I rounded on her. "You knew?" Somehow containing my anger, I strode toward her, backing her into a corner. "You *knew*?"

"She told me everything. I can't believe you'd do this."

"Are you trying to get her bloody killed?" Noah snarled.

Moira tilted her chin up. "I was protecting her from *you*."

"Are you fucking stupid? You know how many people are after her. Regardless of your thoughts about us, you never should have let her go off on her own."

Moira wilted, though her voice still held a small tinge of defiance. "She was leaving no matter what. And I didn't let her just run off without protection. I cloaked her scent. No one who isn't here should even know she's left the house and be able to track her down."

"Next time help her by staying the fuck out of it or coming to get one of us," I said, my worry giving my voice a biting edge. My berserker was right there, just under the surface. I needed to keep a hold on my control for everyone's sake.

"Why? So you could lock her up until the time came? Sorry, no dice, boys. Tits before gits."

I gritted my teeth and fought the urge to shake her. "We would never harm her or the baby. *Never*."

"That's not what Sunday heard."

"Then she wasn't listening very closely, because we were quite clear in our position."

She swallowed. "Oh."

"Fuck this," Kingston said, shedding his clothes as he headed toward the balcony. "Someone get the priest." Then he jumped, transitioning from man to wolf in one seamless bound as he went over the railing.

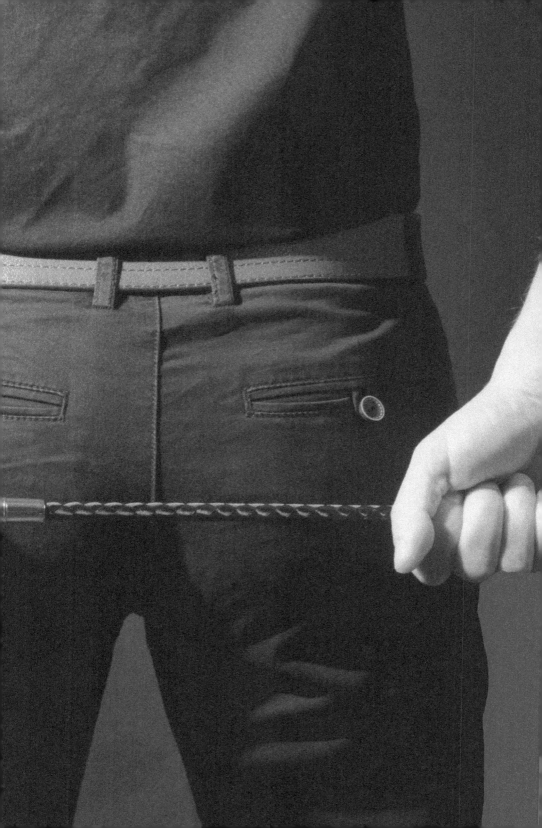

# FOUR

## KINGSTON

I caught the scent of her blood the second my paws hit the damp grass.

*Fuck, Sunshine. What did you do to yourself, baby?*

The distinct smell of Sunday was strongest on the trellis. Clearly my girl had cut herself up in her rush to get away from us. Guilt and pain hit hard. She'd wanted to escape us.

*Were you so desperate to get away you couldn't even wait for me? You know I'd run anywhere with you. That I'd die to protect you.*

But she was running *from* me. That was what hurt the most. She didn't trust that I'd provide for her. Care for her. She'd left me . . . after she promised never to do it again.

Shaking my head to clear the agony her abandonment planted right in my heart, I dropped my snout to the ground and caught the trail of her spilled blood heading away from the house and toward the gate.

*On foot, Sunshine? You didn't even steal a car?*

That worked in our favor, though. If she was on foot, unable to shift, I'd catch her. Then I'd remind her of exactly why we are her mates. We take care of her. End of story.

I came up short a few feet from the tall gate, her scent vanishing without a trace, the metaphorical breadcrumbs she'd left behind drying up and leaving me with nothing to give me any indication of which way she'd gone from here. For all intents and purposes, Sunday had disappeared.

*Why?* As soon as the question rang through my mind, the answer followed on its heels. I let out a deep growl of frustration, my wolf's voice echoing in the night.

*Fucking Moira. Why would your spell work at this point in her escape but not on the other droplets?*

But then I caught something else on the ground. Incense, self-loathing, shame . . . *Priest*. The clouds parted, moonlight pouring from the sky as though the goddess herself had sent me a beacon. A metallic glint in the grass caught my eye. A fucking syringe. Sunday's blood undeniably coated the needle, and a vile medicinal smell mixed with her aroma.

Relief flooded me for the barest hint of a second. If she was with him, she was safe. But why the drugs, then? Did she fight him? Try to resist when he attempted to reason with her? Seemed like something she would do, given their history. Fighting was basically their foreplay.

Still, I couldn't shake off the sense of low-grade panic curling in my belly.

Muzzle to the ground, I tracked his path through the grass, cutting back toward the house, then abruptly turning away. My stomach dropped further when I realized where I was heading. The trail ended right at the side door of the obscenely large garage.

*Motherfucking lying, cheating asshole.*

That's when I *knew*. He hadn't tried to save her. He'd stolen her. I was going to kill him.

I shifted into my human form as Thorne and Alek caught up to me. Blackthorne's brow seemed stuck in a permanent furrow, and tension radiated from the Novasgardian. I knew exactly how they both felt.

"Here," Thorne said, tossing me a set of clothes. "Figured you'd need those."

I was too furious to manage more than a nod of thanks, though the small act of kindness reminded me once again that while the bloodsucker and I weren't exactly best friends, we were pack.

"Caleb's gone. All his stuff, everything." Alek glanced around as I opened the garage door. "Why are we standing outside a garage?"

I pulled on the sweatpants Thorne had brought and let out a heavy sigh. "I know he's gone. He stole her from us. The fucker. This is where his trail goes cold."

"What? How do you know he took her?" Thorne asked, his eyes flaring in surprise.

Sure enough, one of the bays in the garage was empty, the scent of motor oil and exhaust still lingering.

"I found a syringe near the gate. It had her blood on it and smelled like ass. I think he drugged her."

Alek bared his teeth, his eyes flashing onyx. "He wouldn't dare."

"Oh, he dared."

Thorne's brows lowered as he worked through the possible explanations. I knew he was trying to justify the priest's actions, just as I initially had.

"Don't bother. There's no scenario where his drugging her was consensual. He must have been planning this for a while. Just waiting for his opportunity to get her alone."

"But to what end? It doesn't make any bloody sense." Thorne raked his fingers through his hair, tugging on the strands in frustration.

"I know. That bastard wants her all to himself. He always has."

Alek leaned against the open garage door frame. "No he hasn't. He likes to watch. This doesn't make sense. He has to have information we don't. Maybe he thought he was saving her from us? He wasn't in the library when Cashel mentioned his plans. What if he overheard us and mistook our intentions? What if she went to him?"

Thorne's eyes widened. "He's not far from our room. He had to have heard her talking with Moira. Bloody hell, I'm sure he thought the worst."

"Why are you making excuses for him? He. Fucking. Drugged. Her." I was going to lose my shit any second.

"Innocent until proven guilty, right? We can't immediately assume the worst. He's her mate. He's hardwired to protect her. Besides, if the situation was reversed, I'd at least hope one of you would try to understand my side. We're a family. We owe it to him."

I snarled at him. "You keep using the word family to explain away what's right in front of you. Have you already forgotten that your devotion to your *family* is the reason she left in the first place? Here. Let me make it easier for you." Without another word, I sprinted back the way I'd come, grabbed the syringe, and returned. I shoved the glass and steel in his face. "Explain this. Ignore this, you naive fucking prince."

His nostrils flared as he scented everything I'd already discovered. It was a lot harder to ignore the truth when it was in your damn nose.

"Would you drug her to get her to do what you wanted?" Alek asked Thorne.

He shut down, not answering, and then I realized the truth.

"Oh, my God. You would."

"If it meant saving her, yes. If I had to, I'd lock her away until she was out of danger."

"What medieval bullshit logic is this? You don't bully someone into doing what you want," I shouted.

"Don't you?" he asked coldly. "Isn't that exactly what you spent the last seven years trying to do?"

"Tell me when I fucking drugged her, motherfucker."

"Okay, stop," Alek said, moving between us. "We don't know what happened. The only one who can tell us is Caleb. So let's ask him before jumping to any more conclusions. Who has his number?"

We looked at each other blankly, each of us shrugging. I sighed heavily. "Are you fucking kidding me? No one knows how to contact the priest?" We were a regular bunch of Boy Scouts. Always prepared, except when it counted. "We need to start a goddamned phone tree."

Moira moved out of the shadows, her eyes solemn but lips tilted up in amusement. "You really are a useless bunch of swinging man meat, aren't you?" She sighed dramatically. "Leave it to the witch to have to come to your rescue. *Again.*"

"*You* have his number?" Thorne asked, eyebrows raised incredulously.

"Pfft. I don't have anything to confess. Why would I have his number? "

Alek crossed his arms. "So how do you propose to help us?"

It was her turn to look annoyed. "It must be hard having so little blood flowing to your brain all the time. Are you prone to fainting spells? Do you keep smelling salts in your purse?" Before he could answer, she gave a little huff. "If I can manage to find your ass across a different realm, I think I can do a basic locator spell. Easy peasy."

"Well, what the bloody hell are you waiting for? An invitation? Why are you just mentioning this now?"

Her gaze narrowed on Thorne's. "Jesus, do I have to do everything? I didn't think she'd have gotten that far on foot, and we didn't know the priest up and left until a couple minutes ago." She pulled a rosary out of her pocket. "Give a witch some credit."

"You stole his rosary?" Thorne's voice was filled with a strange sort of pride.

"He left it behind. I guess now that he's gone heathen, it doesn't really help."

"He went heathen a long time ago. Trust me. I saw it." I shuddered at the memory of the look in his eyes when he found me taking my mate during her heat. That was the first time I'd seen him stripped of the thin veneer of control and civility he hid behind. We just hadn't realized the truth yet. The priest was the biggest monster of us all.

Moira plopped herself right in the middle of the empty space, her eyes closing as she held the jet beads, the heavy silver crucifix swaying a little as she began murmuring. Then she frowned, her lips forming a pout I would've called cute if she wasn't holding Sunday's fate in her hands.

"I can't find him."

"What do you mean? He's not fucking dead. Find him, witch." I all but growled the words.

"He . . . oh, fuck." She blinked wide eyes at me, then looked at each of the others. "He's got to be with her."

"Tell me something I don't already know."

She bit her lip, giving me an apologetic glance. "The spell. It's cloaking him too."

"Well then, undo it."

"It doesn't work like that."

"Motherfucking witches," I muttered.

"There's only one way to find them, then," Thorne said, making all of us turn our attention to him.

"We're waiting," Alek urged.

"We search for her just like anyone else who's gone missing. The human way."

"What, with milk cartons and missing posters?" I snapped.

Thorne rolled his eyes. "They left some kind of trail. It might not be something we can track with magic, but people don't just up and disappear. Cameras, CCTV, credit cards, etcetera. Caleb might be a vampire, but he's not a superspy. He's hardly even computer literate. He left clues. We need to think like humans. Search like them."

"So you're saying she's lost forever." I dragged a hand through my hair, a frustrated growl rumbling in my chest.

"Noah is on to something, Kingston. Give me a few minutes to make a phone call. I know a guy," Moira said, standing.

"Great, the witch who can't even do magic right *knows a guy*."

"Give her a chance," Alek snapped.

"Fine. Who is this fucker?"

Her eyes gleamed as she pulled her phone from her pocket and dialed.

A tense voice grumbled over speakerphone, "Moira Belladonna, you fucking bitch. You'd better not be calling in that favor I owe you right now."

"Asher Henry. I'd say it's a pleasure, but we know that'd be a lie."

"What do you want?"

"I need you to do what you do best."

The line went silent, followed by the sound of rustling fabric, like the guy on the other end was sitting up and paying a lot more attention.

"I'm listening."

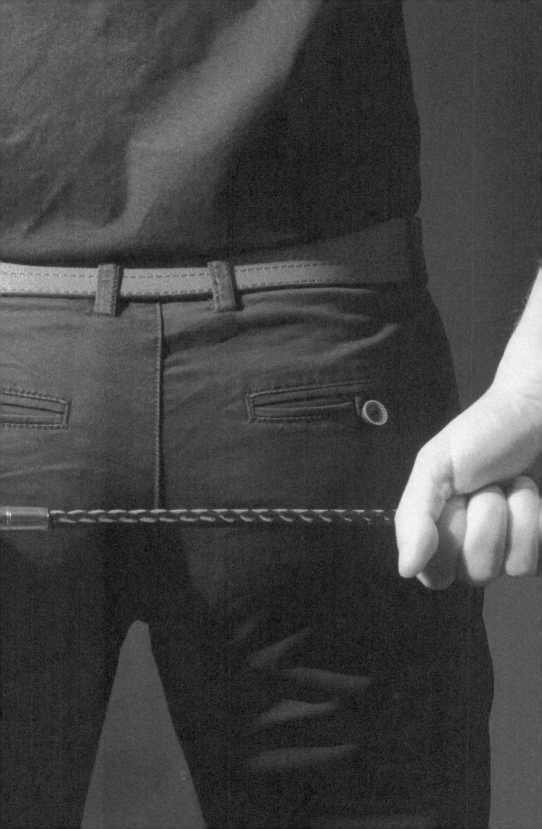

# FIVE

SUNDAY

"It's not you who has to die."

Caleb's words, delivered in that cold, calculated manner, sent fear surging through my veins. Even with the detached tone and the hollow look in his eyes, he was still devastatingly handsome.

"How could you do this? After everything you said to me? After our bond?"

"It was always supposed to lead to this."

Icy dread formed a pit in my stomach. He'd done it all to get here. None of it was real? Even the bond had been a means to an end. After what I overheard in the library, a part of me had hoped that while extreme, kidnapping me was Caleb's way of saving us. But if everything had been a lie, then it had just been a game. He was no better than they were.

I sat up, my protective instinct rearing as I placed a palm over my belly. "You're not going to touch her. I'll kill you first."

His lips curled in a cruel smile. "Wouldn't be the first time."

"I'll make it stick."

He canted his head to the side. "I don't think you will. You love me too much."

"Loved. Past tense. How could I love a monster who so clearly doesn't give a fuck about me?"

I searched his gaze for a flicker of something. Hurt, devastation, grief maybe. Anything to show he was mourning the loss of me and our relationship. I'd even accept guilt or regret that it had come to this. But there was nothing, no argument. Just a chilling detachment and acceptance that turned the man standing in front of me into a stranger.

"Thank you for proving my point."

The vampire—I couldn't see him as anything more than evil now —smirked before striding to the chair in the corner and sitting, legs spread, posture relaxed. So confident. I hated how much I responded to him even now. How my stomach tightened at the play of his muscles beneath his shirt, the fuller scruff lining his jaw, and the dark sweep of hair over his brow.

He was relaxed here. In his element more than he ever had been playing his role at the university. Here he was Caleb, not Father Gallagher. It scared me to see such a noticeable difference now that the truth of his betrayal was staring me in the face. Once upon a time, I would have loved this version of him. Now I wanted nothing more than to be free of his grip on me.

"You can't keep me here."

"I can, and I will."

"Fuck you, Caleb."

"That's one way we could pass the time." His hands dropped to his belt, and my traitorous eyes greedily tracked the movement of his fingers as he started to undo it. I knew he was taunting me, the bastard, and it was working.

I snapped my eyes back to his face, my hands curled into fists in my lap. "I'm not your plaything."

He cocked one dark brow. "Aren't you? What else is my *good girl* but a pretty thing for me to play with?"

Damn his dirty mouth. My thighs clenched on reflex.

My gaze finally left him for the sake of self-preservation, and a glimmer of hope unfurled in my heart at the sight of the front door, a straight shot from the bedroom. I stood, thankful I was dressed, unsure of what I was going to do next. If I had any chance of making a break for it, I needed to keep him from realizing what I was up to while I inched my way closer to freedom.

His next words sent my hope scattering.

"Don't even think about it, *a stor*."

"Don't call me that. You don't get to use sweet words with me anymore."

"There's nowhere for you to run."

"Anywhere is better than with you." Heart in my throat, I took two running steps toward the threshold only to be brought up short by a hand around my neck.

He reeled me back into the bedroom, forcefully shoving me against the open door and crowding into my space. His face was so close I could feel the brush of his stubble against my jaw. Fuck me, but I liked it. The scent of him, the anger radiating from his entire being.

"I said no." His admonishment was a sexy growl.

"I don't care what you said."

He ran his nose along mine, breathing me in. "Oh, you are a brat, aren't you? You've always known how to make me hard. But you already knew that, didn't you? You just can't help yourself."

"I hate you."

"You might, but your body doesn't." He rolled his hips, that thick length pressing into me. "I can smell how much you enjoy this game we play."

I spat in his face. Disgust washed over me. But I wasn't disgusted with him as much as with myself. I wanted him as much as I hated him. I was wet for him. And I ached.

He tsked, using his sleeve to wipe the spit off his cheek. "You know what happens to naughty girls. Is that what you want? To be punished? It can be arranged."

I sucked in a sharp breath; the shuddering inhalation had me betraying exactly how right he was. "Fuck. You."

"You have only to ask, little one." Those lips found his mark on my throat, and I despised myself for the needy moan that slipped out. The reaction was involuntary, but how could I keep it all in when pleasure shot straight to my clit at the contact?

"No."

He froze. "What?"

"I said no, Caleb. You don't get to kidnap me, break me, and then use me like this."

"You don't make the rules here, darling."

A small thrill zinged through me. I'd always loved breaking his rules. But not now. Not if he wanted me to. Then it hit me. He wanted this, wanted my body even if he didn't love me. That much, at least, hadn't been a lie. He was every bit a slave to this *thing* between us as I was. I had to use that to my advantage.

"My body, my rules."

He grinned, the hand at my throat flexing ever so slightly and making my breath hitch. The knuckles of his free hand skimmed the underside of my breast, my nipples tightening into sharp little points at the barely-there contact. He chuckled, low and soft, missing nothing.

"Seems like your body belongs to me."

"I don't belong to anyone."

"My mark would say otherwise."

He was right. All of them marked me; all of them owned me, just like I owned them. "Then my mark means the same. You're mine, even if you think you're not."

Unmitigated desire burst to life in his eyes. "I never said I wasn't."

I had to play this carefully. He was still bound to me, if only by lust. But if our connection was anything like the one Noah and I shared, he might be able to sense my thoughts or feelings. I wasn't sure to what degree, but to protect myself I'd have to block him, wear a mask to hide my intentions from him. I needed him to let down his guard, trust that I'd stay with him. That I was his.

Steeling myself, I slipped on the facade of his good girl. I didn't want to think about what it said about me that it was so easy. "Tell me the rules, Daddy."

His nostrils flared, and his eyes were all but black. "No harming yourself. I'm the only one who gets to mark this perfect skin." His thumb slid up the side of my neck, and his lips lifted when he felt my pulse's reaction to those words. "You'll eat and care for yourself. I don't mind your tantrums, but you will not take your anger towards me out on your body or your wellbeing."

I was surprised that he still cared enough to make such rules. It was easy enough to agree. I didn't have any intention of doing anything that would weaken me or hurt the baby. "Fine. Anything else?"

"You won't try to escape."

I had to school my features so Caleb wouldn't sense the massive mental eye roll that set off. If he really thought I would play the pretty little captive, he wasn't giving me enough credit. Then again, it might be why he was trying to make it one of his rules. Regardless, that's one rule I was absolutely going to break.

"I won't?"

"No, darling one, you won't. All that would serve to do is annoy me. This is my island. No one can access it except by my invitation, and no one is invited to join us at present. Or leave."

"They'll find me, Caleb. You have to know that."

He let out a low, dark chuckle. "No, I assure you, they won't. Ever."

"Don't be so sure about that. Have you met Kingston? And I doubt Alek or Noah are the kind of men to sit back and do nothing when someone steals their mate. Alek is a berserker, for Christ's sake. You have to know what they're going to do to you when they find us."

"Like I already told you. They aren't going to find us. The island is protected. Concealed by a spell—"

"Moira—"

He shook his head. "Not even your witch is strong enough to break through the protection. Heed my warning, Miss Fallon. You are alone here for as long as I want you to be. You will behave. You will follow my rules. You will be my good girl."

I gritted my teeth and fought back the urge to spit something hateful at him.

"Look at you, trying so hard to be good for your daddy. You can't help yourself, can you, darling? You want me to spank that pretty cunt."

I closed my eyes against the multitude of emotions hitting me at once. Desire, fury, hunger. No wonder hate sex was so popular. It was a potent cocktail. I might have given into the instinct if not for the panic. I was playing a game. I couldn't afford to forget what was at stake.

My freedom. My daughter's life.

"I'm trying, Daddy. For you."

Pleasure banked in his expression. He leaned his face in close and pressed a kiss to my forehead. "I know you are, *a stor.*"

Then he shocked me by releasing me. I thought for sure this was going to end up in his bed, but he turned away and left the bedroom. "Come. I need to feed you. You're going to need your strength for what's in store."

This was it. I'd been right. Caleb had to be reminded I was more than a task for him. He had to think I wasn't a threat, that I was his and wouldn't cause him any trouble. If he trusted me, I could get away.

But to buy myself the time I needed to escape, I'd have to kill him.

And I would. Nothing, not even my connection to him, would keep me hostage on this island.

Caleb Gallagher had to die.

# CHAPTER

# SIX

## CALEB

My eyes burned as the minutes ticked by, the sunrise palpable, making my blood sluggish and my body heavy. But there was no way I would allow myself to fall asleep with Sunday here. Not like this, when she was so clearly up to something.

I turned the page of the book I was pretending to read and cast my gaze at the woman across from me. She was draped on the sofa, her feet up, shoulders wrapped in one of my sweaters even though a fire roared in the hearth.

Never had I been more thankful I'd had the foresight to purchase this island. I'd known eventually I would need to come here, and the modern amenities had been sorely lacking. The first chance I got, I brought a crew out here to retrofit this place with plumbing, electricity, and as much insulation as was possible in an old home like this one. Thrall was a wonderful gift, though I used it sparingly. Sunday had no idea how much colder she would've been had I not taken care of these details.

I caught her running her nose along the knit wool and breathing in the scent of me. She might be playing at seduction, but she was still drawn to me.

I'd known what she was doing the second she'd given in to my demands. Sunday was many things. Sexy, tempting, arousing, maddening. But never compliant. She fought me tooth and nail even when she agreed with me. She loved pushing my buttons. There was nothing she could do to raise my suspicions faster than behave.

A little furrow between her brows had me on high alert. That wasn't confusion; it was discomfort. She let out a soft groan and pressed her palm to her belly.

"Are you all right?" Feck, I couldn't keep the concerned father out of my voice. My heart gave a pang at just the thought of something being amiss. How would I survive when I had to do my duty?

The only answer was that I wouldn't.

Sunday gave me a dubious glance. "You don't have to pretend you care. And I'm fine. Everly was just stretching and elbowed me in the ribcage."

"Everly?"

She blushed a little, like she hadn't meant to let that slip. Her answer, when it came, was defensive. "Just trying out names."

"You shouldn't name the child."

Hurt flickered in her eyes for just a moment, but it was there, and I'd been the fucking cause.

"Why? Because you're going to kill her?"

"It's bad luck."

"No, it's not."

"Babes die in the womb for all sorts of reasons."

"Maybe back when the dinosaurs roamed the earth, grandpa. Times have changed. We have this nifty thing called medicine now. Maybe you've heard of it? Science. Hospitals. It's truly miraculous."

"Oh, aye, medicine and hospitals on a remote island in Ireland. Miraculous, indeed. You forget, you aren't human, and your situation isn't normal."

She curled her arm around her belly as if she could hug the baby inside her. "Doc told me I have nothing to worry about until the birth itself."

That made my skin crawl. Part of me wanted to tell her she was right, but the other part knew she wouldn't survive this and that I'd be right behind her.

"You trust the word of a werewolf doctor who has no fecking clue what you're carrying?"

Defiance shone in her gaze. "Yes."

There she was, my contrary girl. "Fine. Have it your way. Name the child whatever you want. It doesn't matter anyway."

She tipped her chin up. "Elizabeth will be so happy to know one of her fathers cared so deeply."

"Stuck on the letter E, are you?"

"It feels right."

I stood, unable to continue sitting still. My eyelids were drooping, exhaustion taking over. If I didn't move, I'd drop like a stone. It was nearly impossible to keep my gaze off her as I began pacing the floor in an attempt to stay awake.

"And what is your little E's surname going to be?" I didn't know why I was asking. Morbid curiosity? A fantasy of some domestic life I'd never have?

"Fallon, obviously."

"You'd really name her after the pack that treated you so abominably?"

"Well, I'm not going to call her Gallagher. There's no way I'd give her the name of anyone who wanted to see her dead. And that's all of you at this point."

The blow landed straight in my heart, but I nodded. "Fair enough. So Elise Fallon, was it?"

Her lips twitched. "Elizabeth, but Elise has potential."

"And her middle name? Will you be naming her after anyone?"

"Mozart."

I blinked, certain my sun-addled brain misunderstood her. "Pardon?"

"Elizabeth Amadeus Fallon."

The laugh escaped before I could stop myself. "I didn't realize you were such a fan."

"I'm not. It's a Moira thing."

I shook my head. "Regardless, that is the most God-awful name I've ever heard."

"Well, it's a good thing you won't be around to hear it, then."

I stopped my pacing and leveled my focus on her. She'd gotten to her feet, her body clad in nothing but a thin tank and a pair of leggings, my sweater discarded carelessly on the floor. I hadn't let myself look at her—not in the way I wanted to—since spiriting her away from Blackthorne Manor. But now? It was impossible not to.

"And why won't I be around, Miss Fallon?" My words were carefully measured. Controlled. Dominant. She needed me to take charge and put her in her place. I could tell by the challenge in her blue eyes. My darling girl wanted a fight.

"I already told you why. I'm going to kill you."

I snorted. "No, you're not."

"You told me you brought me here to destroy my daughter. If I have to choose between her or you, I choose her. Every fucking time. So yes, Caleb. I'm going to murder *you* to save *her*."

Why was I so fecking hard from that threat? I should be livid. Instead, I wanted to push her against the wall, tear apart the sad excuse for pants she wore, and remind her why she called me Daddy.

"I'm your mate. You can't do it."

"You're a sad excuse for a mate. I deserve so much better."

I wasn't going to disagree with her. I was the first to admit she could do far better than the likes of me. If circumstances were different, if *I* were different, I'd be exactly the kind of man she deserved. But we'd already established that I wasn't a man and hadn't been for nearly a century.

"God has a way of giving us exactly what we deserve."

"I don't believe in your god."

"Fate, then. Either way, you're stuck with me."

"She's a cruel bitch."

"Aye, she is. Now bend over, Miss Fallon."

Her eyes widened. "What?"

"You heard me. You've been bad. Begging me to punish you. Do you think I'd let you get away with insulting me without doing something about it?"

"You've always been more talk than action, Priest. You love to start things you can't finish."

"Oh, I'm going to finish. It's you who'll be left unsatisfied. And I'm not a priest any longer, *a stor*. I'm a fecking monster."

"Ah, so you've decided to stop lying to yourself. Good, that's progress. And something we can agree on anyway." Her words were mocking, dripping with sarcasm. Even though I was the one who called myself a monster, hearing that she thought so too had my stomach churning.

I grabbed her by the shoulders, pulling her close as I inhaled her scent. My dick throbbed, begging for release. It had been too long since I'd had her.

"I said . . . Bend. Over."

I spun her around and gripped her nape before shoving her so her knees were on the sofa, right where she'd been seated earlier. She didn't fight; instead she presented her arse for me and gave a soft little whimper as she pressed her chest over the back of the couch.

Leaning forward, I ran my nose along her neck, breathing in deep and pressing my lips to her ear. "I may be a monster, but I am *your* monster. And I am done playing by the rules. If I'm going to burn anyway, I might as well enjoy myself."

She shivered at my rough whisper. "Prove it, then."

Ripping the leggings over her arse, I sucked in a sharp breath at the sight of her bare and perfect before me. That pretty pink cunt was already slightly on display, wet and glistening, begging for attention.

"Arch your back. I want to see all of you."

"Yes, Daddy."

She did as I commanded, and I couldn't stop myself from reaching out and tracing her lips, circling her clit once before retreating. Her moan of pleasure brought me back to the task at hand. Punishment. Our most sacred ritual.

I slid my fingers through the silk of her hair at her nape and grabbed a fistful before tugging her head back. "I want you to count. Out loud. If you forget, we start over." My other hand cracked against her tender skin, and the way she cried out had my balls aching.

"Oh, God . . . one."

"I thought you didn't believe in God, Miss Fallon." My lips curled up, pleasure and something that felt like peace racing through me. This. This was our communion. The way we always came back to each other. Everything else was noise. But here, we could be ourselves. No lies. Nothing but the truth of us and what we were to each other.

I spanked her again, this time twice in succession, loving the way my hand was imprinted on her pale flesh.

"I can't hear you, Miss Fallon."

"T-two . . . three." The words were nothing but moans, and her arousal dripped down her thighs.

"Two more. If you're good."

She wiggled her hips. "More. I need more."

I couldn't stand it. I pulled my cock free of my pants and stroked from base to crown, precum already beaded at the tip, my balls tight and full.

Releasing my length, I brought my palm down soundly against her sweet arse.

"Fou—oh, fuck."

I didn't give her a chance to finish saying four before I slapped her dripping center. Just the way she loved. She writhed against my hand, silently begging me for more.

"What was that, darling? I think I missed your count."

"Five . . . you asshole."

I let out a dark chuckle and sank two fingers inside her as she tilted her hips in search of something else from me. I pulled my fingers free and pressed my hips forward, sliding my length between her slick lips.

She groaned when the tip of my cock brushed against her swollen clit. "More," she begged.

"Shh, you're not in charge here. Don't make me gag you. Just take it."

"Christ."

"Isn't going to save you, Miss Fallon. But you can call me Daddy if you wish."

"Please, Daddy. I need you."

I wanted nothing more than to give her that pleasure she sought, but this wasn't a reward. She'd missed her last count. I'd had to remind her.

Canting my hips, I continued giving myself the delicious friction I knew *she* wanted. My hands roamed her body as I bent over her and layered kisses along her shoulder, palms finding the full weight of her breasts.

"I could sink inside you right now and give you everything you're begging for. Make you come screaming on my cock. Remind you why you're mine."

"Yes. Yes. Do that."

My breaths came in shuddering pulls as my orgasm neared. "I could fill you with my cum and watch it drip from you, make you wear it."

She moaned in response.

I positioned the tip of my cock at her soaked entrance, the fluttering of those muscles already trying to suck me in.

"Please, Caleb."

She was close to her own release from the feel of my length running along her clit and the words I teased her with. I pressed in the barest inch, her heat a temptation I knew all too well.

"Yes. I need it."

"I could . . . but I won't."

She moaned in protest as I drew out, pressing her back down with one hand, using her arousal and my other hand to shuttle along the length of my throbbing cock, chasing my own release.

"Sunday, good fucking Christ," I said on a ragged groan as the climax erupted from me, painting the pinkened skin of her arse white with stripes of my spend. I memorized the sight of her decorated in my adoration, taking a second to run my fingers through it and then back across her center, putting me where I truly belonged.

"I hate you," she panted, still on the edge of her own release.

"Not as much as I hate myself." Then I gave her clit a light tap, making her swear. "Time for bed."

"I'm not tired."

"I am."

"You're really going to leave me like this?"

"After everything else I've done, that's the part you're having trouble accepting?"

She glowered at me over her shoulder. "You really are a monster."

"Aye, but we've established that. However, I am a thoroughly satisfied monster, and you can spend the day thinking about what you've done."

"What do you mean?"

"Really, Sunday, plotting against me? Trying to seduce me as a means of escape? I saw right through your games and then used them on you. Quite effectively, I might add. I'm almost disappointed you didn't try harder. It's almost like you want to be my captive."

"You're pathetic. You know the only way you're ever going to be able to touch me again is by holding me hostage."

"You seemed quite willing, if the state of your cunt is any indication."

"You should be ashamed."

"Aye, I am. But not about this. Now be quiet, or I'll make good on my threat to gag you."

"Try to fall asleep, Father Gallagher. You know what a talker I am. I'll be shouting in your ear the entire time, waking you up whenever you drift off. You won't know a moment's peace with me near."

I huffed. "I haven't known a moment's peace since the day you were born." Gripping her chin, I forced her hate-filled gaze to meet mine. *"You will be quiet."*

She blinked at me. "What was that? Did you just try to *thrall* me?" She slammed her fist against my chest. "You asshole! How dare you use your vampy bullshit against me. To make me act against my will."

I stiffened, not anticipating she would be immune to it after I'd been able to calm her berserker the night Alek had been taken. Fecking hell. She was going to be impossible now. But I had to sleep, which meant I needed to figure out what to do with her—and fast. Everything in me hurt. If I didn't rest, she'd be able to best me soon. I couldn't give her the opportunity.

I took her by the wrist, dragging her into the bedroom. It was harder to keep hold of her than I cared to admit. My strength was leaving me fast as the sun drew higher in the sky. Spying my discarded belt on the floor, an idea came to me.

She could scream all she liked. I was going to be out the second my head hit the pillow. This way, at least, I could be assured she'd still be there when I woke.

With a gentle nudge, I pushed her toward the bathroom, knowing she'd have needs to take care of. If I was truly evil, I'd force her to bed without giving her the luxury, but I wouldn't do that to her. "Clean yourself up and get ready for bed."

She stomped inside, slamming the door behind her.

I used the time she was gone to prepare, ripping strips from a blanket and tying them to the bedposts on her side.

"What are you doing?" she demanded, glaring at me from the doorway.

"What does it bloody look like? I'm not risking you doing something stupid like getting yourself lost in the woods. Get on the bed."

"No."

Anger and frustration boiled just under the surface. "Get on the bed, or I'll put you on it."

"No."

"Saints preserve us, you are an infuriating woman."

"And you're a douchebag."

I blurred over to where she stood, using the last of my power to grab hold of her and toss her onto the mattress. Then I tied the bindings, and when I was sure she couldn't break free, I climbed onto the bed, narrowly avoiding the urge to add a gag.

"I despise you."

"So you've said," I mumbled, my body still humming from the remnants of my orgasm. I closed my eyes, the scent of Sunday filling my senses, and knew nothing more as merciful darkness claimed me.

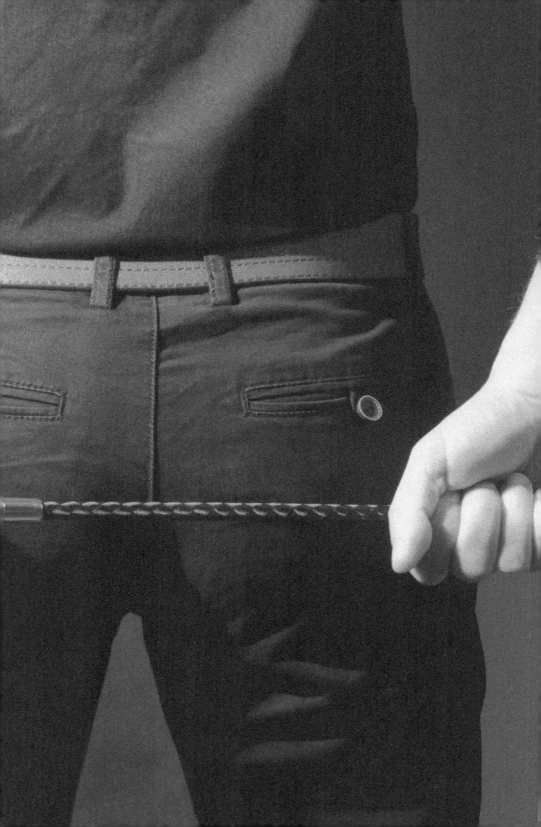

# SEVEN

W ell, that backfired.

*What the hell was that, Sunday? One smoldering look and a couple of filthy comments, and you're practically begging your kidnapper to fuck you. Okay, you* did *beg your kidnapper to fuck you.*

I glared over at Caleb. Furious with myself as much as I was at him.

The handsome asshole was already dead to the world, careless that I laid there next to him completely unsatisfied. He knew what he'd done. Left me horny as fuck, wide awake, and pissed the hell off. Knowing it was futile, I gave my bindings an investigatory tug. Nope. No way I was getting free until he untied me.

Even though I wanted nothing more than to cheerfully murder him in his sleep, I had to admit, I loved every moment of his dirty talk. I was a glutton for Caleb, even when he hurt me. Maybe more so then.

I was supposed to be angry with him, but it was impossible to get my heart and body on board with my mind. Logic was not in charge here. He had a hold on me I couldn't shake. Our bond did far more than mark my skin. It wove us together with chains that were as much bindings as they were links. There was no escaping him.

Letting out a grumpy huff, I tried to get comfortable, settling in for a miserable day of forcing myself to sleep and preparing for round two. So far the score was Sunday zero, Caleb one. And the bastard had the home team advantage. I had to even the playing field. Learn more about my surroundings. I needed him to loosen the reins enough that I didn't have to be tied down while he slept. These were key hours I should be using to my advantage. Which, of course, he knew—hence the bindings.

My first attempt at getting him on my side blew up in my face because he knew me too well. I'd been too sweet. I saw that now. Even when things were perfect between us, I was never that obedient. I needed to add a little more brat to the mix. In a word, I needed to be me.

Lesson learned.

After what felt like an eternity spent staring at the ceiling and plotting against him, I finally drifted off, dreaming of a time before all this, when Caleb was mine without betrayal and lies. I didn't have to admit he'd always been lying to me while I was dreaming. Or that my other three mates had been just as ready to break my heart as he had.

Over the next several hours, I tossed and turned as much as my bindings would allow. Every time my eyes closed, I was assaulted by dreams of one or more of my men, and each time I woke again, my cheeks were wet with tears and my chest heavy with loss. I may as well have stayed awake for as much actual rest as I got.

Finally, I gave up all hope of real sleep, waking to the scent of freshly baked bread wafting through the partially open door. I sat up, rubbing my face with my hands . . . my *free* hands. I was unbound. Of course I was. Caleb was awake. He wasn't worried about me killing him while he wasn't vulnerable.

A heaviness in my bladder let me know I had other matters to take care of before investigating what sort of meal a vampire thought would be appropriate for his mortal hostage. A few minutes later, I made my way to the kitchen, bathroom needs met, teeth brushed, and hair handled—as best it could be without a real hairbrush anyway. That was as much my fault as Caleb's. He'd left the bag I'd packed on the dresser for me, which meant I at least had fresh clothes to change into, but in all my preparation, it seemed I hadn't thought to pack so much as a damn comb.

"Are you coming out, then? Or do I need to bring your meal to you?" Caleb called from the other room.

I hated that his voice still skated across my skin in the form of tingles. "I'm coming."

Was I? I sure as shit hadn't yesterday. The Irish prick.

Caleb looked up as I entered, his lips quirking when he noted my disgruntled expression. "Sleep well?"

"Fuck off. You know I didn't."

"Actually, I don't, seeing as how I was fast asleep."

I growled low in my throat as I moved closer, but my annoyance dissipated as I noted the rich beef stew and rustic vegetables bubbling on the stove while Caleb put together a salad. A round of bread sat cooling on a rack, clearly just pulled from the oven.

"Look at you, Master Chef. Is all this for me?"

"Well, I'm certainly not going to eat it."

"You can't expect me to eat all of that."

"It'll keep. And you need a balanced diet. That's one thing I can ensure."

Suspicion took root as I glanced around the cabin. "How did you get all this fresh food anyway? There's not a grocery store on this island, is there?"

"No, there's not. I have my ways, sweetling."

I cocked a brow and assessed him. "As in, you have some person in your thrall, at your beck and call like Dracula?"

"Aye."

"Oh, my God, I was just kidding. Please tell me you don't actually have some poor unfortunate soul stashed away like some kind of slave."

His silence was damning.

"Well, I'm just learning all sorts of fun new things about you, Father Gallagher."

"She's being paid handsomely as well. And you'll be grateful once you taste your supper. Without her weekly visits, you'd starve. I'd be right as rain, but you . . . Well, I've seen starvation first hand. I wouldn't wish it on many."

"That's not how that expression goes. My worst enemy. Anyone. Not many."

"But I would wish it on my enemies."

"Caleb!"

"What? It's the truth."

"Here I thought you're supposed to be a godly man. A pillar of moral virtue. What's gotten into you?"

"The Apocalypse, darling. All bets are off when the world is ending." He winked. Fucking winked, and my insides did all sorts of things.

I shook my head but couldn't quite keep myself from smiling. I was sort of enjoying this new side of the good priest. Caleb as a bad boy was . . . irresistible.

Fuck me. I was so screwed.

"Well, you made this feast. Feed me, Daddy."

The flare of lust in his eyes made my belly flip. "Aye, I will. And then we are going for a stroll. We have months to wait out this baby, and you'll need to know how things work around here."

"What do you mean?"

"You'll need something to occupy your days. Might as well work the farm."

My mouth dropped open in shock.

"Close your mouth, or I'll give you something to put in it."

I fought the answering wave of desire that threat sent through me.

"Work *the farm*? I am not a little Irish housewife. I don't work farms."

"You do now. The garden is wild with weeds, and the soil will need tending if we're going to replant it."

"Do I look like a gardener to you?"

"It's that or chop wood, darling. Which would you prefer?"

I pressed my lips together, palms aching at the mere thought of hefting an ax.

"That's what I thought." He plated my dinner and set it on the table. "Some things need to be done in daylight hours, and sadly, due to my . . . aversion to sunlight, you'll have to take them on."

"This is bullshit," I grumbled as I sat in the chair he'd pulled out for me.

"It's not like you have anything else to do to pass the time. No phone. No computer. No TV. Might as well learn valuable new skills and expand your mind."

"Just when I was starting to like you again . . ."

That fucking smirk. I was trash for that smirk. "You can't help yourself." He tossed a tea towel over one shoulder before slicing a piece of bread and bringing it to me. "Now eat. You need your energy."

"For all that gardening," I muttered.

"I think you look your best a little dirty, *a stor*. Especially if I get to help clean you up."

Heat flooded my face, and it took everything in me to look away from him. Instead of saying something stupid, like asking him to get dirty with me, I shoved a steamy spoonful into my mouth. This was not going to plan. He was pushing all my buttons, acting more like Kingston than Caleb.

I wasn't prepared for a playful Caleb. I had no immunity against him. Not when he was grumpy and definitely not when he was . . . this.

He twirled the tea towel, plucking at it as he pulled it through his fingers. "How are you liking your meal?"

Oh, my God, was he fucking earnest? What the hell was I supposed to do with *that*?

"It's really good," I answered honestly, my eyes watering slightly from the temperature. It was still piping hot, but damn, it was fucking tasty.

"Good. That's good. It's been a while since I've had a reason to make something like this." I took another bite, almost spitting it back out when he added, "Save room for dessert, darling."

I gave him a questioning glance, wondering if he was referring to himself, but he wasn't even looking at me. "There's more?"

"Aye, I made a cobbler as well. It'll be coming out of the oven soon."

There was a soft roar in my ears as my brain tried to process Caleb the caretaker and chef. I had no idea he could be so domestic. It was doing funny things to my insides.

"What are we doing here, Caleb?"

"Eating."

"No, I mean, this. You kidnapped me. But now we're playing house?" I couldn't bring myself to address the other elephant in the room. The entire reason he'd taken me in the first place.

"No matter what end this has to take, I won't leave you uncared for."

"What do you mean, 'what end'? There's only one way this is going to go, isn't there?"

He looked away, his jaw set and stern daddy Caleb returning. "Aye. Only one."

I pushed my bowl away, the few bites I'd managed sitting heavy in my stomach.

"Eat."

"I did."

"Not nearly enough. Do not make me feed you like a petulant child, Sunday."

"Will you make airplane noises for me?"

"I prefer the train."

60

My eyebrows flew up. "As in chugga-chugga, choo-choo?"

He glared at me, unamused. "Eat. Now. You promised you'd look after yourself."

I gripped a hunk of bread and toyed with the idea of throwing it at him, but it was delicious and deserved better than to be used as a weapon. "Fine. But stop watching me. You're creeping me out."

When I still didn't pick up my spoon, he grabbed it in one hand, lifting my chin with the other. "All aboard, Miss Fallon."

I was too surprised to laugh. Instead I stared up at him and took the spoon. He lingered a few seconds longer, and I could feel his gaze as it traveled over me, but he eventually gave in and moved to clear the dishes while I finished my food.

I stood after I couldn't take another bite, stretching and groaning from being more full than I had in days. There was no way I could eat dessert. Not without being in serious pain after.

"Can we go on that walk now? I need to stretch my legs." Excitement hummed in my blood at the thought of getting outside, seeing the place he'd brought me to, and most of all, looking for a way out.

He nodded, tossing the towel he'd been using to wipe the counters into the sink and gesturing toward a coat rack near the front door. "Bundle up. It's cold outside."

I ran my gaze over the offerings, landing on a thin strip of faded black fabric. "I think you need a new scarf. This one looks a little . . . used."

Something in him tightened, his eyes narrowing slightly. "It's an heirloom. I don't wear it."

Feeling like I'd touched a nerve and accidentally insulted him by talking shit about a sentimental item, I shrugged and dropped the subject. Snagging a thick wool coat, I slipped it over my shoulders. I was still working on the buttons when Caleb placed a beanie on my head and started weaving a scarf around my neck.

I shoved him away when he tried to add a second coat. "Caleb, I'm not going to freeze. I have shifter blood, remember? We run hot."

He frowned, seeming uncertain, before spinning around and walking outside without a word.

"Cool. I'll just follow you, then," I snarked.

Stepping outside, I was immediately taken by the beautiful night that greeted us. The air was fresh and clean, crisp with the barest hint of winter still lingering. The thought immediately brought Alek to mind. Winter was his favorite season, and now that I'd been to Novasgard, I understood why.

A deep sadness made itself known, cracking through the walls in my heart. I hated this. Everything about it.

"Sunday, are you coming?" Caleb's voice was hesitant, tentative, and unlike the domineering man I'd come to know.

Taking a steadying breath, I pushed away thoughts of Alek and forced myself back into this moment. "Show me the fucking garden, Caleb."

His lips twitched, but he wisely remained silent. He offered me his arm, but I flinched away, not trusting myself to touch him.

"Suit yourself. The terrain is uneven. Be careful."

"I've been walking almost my whole life. I'm certain I'll manage just fine."

He led me around the cottage to the back, where a small iron fence did nothing to keep out the wilderness. In the absence of people, nature had reclaimed the space. Weeds came up to my hip, growing over the gate and choking any plants that had once called this place home.

"A little overgrown, huh?"

"I believe the phrase I used was 'wild with weeds.' Was I wrong?"

"No, you were absolutely right."

I shook my head. This little project of mine would take months. No wonder he'd assigned it to me. It would certainly keep me occupied. There was no way to get around it. It would be obvious if I didn't do the work, and I bet the bastard would check in on my progress and give me some sort of grade too.

"What else is there to do around here?" I asked, depression sinking in as my fate became clear.

"Fornicate."

My gaze snapped to his. "Caleb."

"Don't sound so scandalized, Miss Fallon. It's the truth. Why do you think the Irish are famous for having such big families?"

"But you chose the priesthood, remember?"

"As I reminded you again last night, I'm no longer a priest. I haven't been for a very long time. Especially not since you."

I didn't have anything to say to that as images of all the ways he and I could pass the time flitted through my brain. I also didn't know what it said about me that I was equal parts turned on and mad at myself for liking the idea. I needed to get us off this topic and fast before my libido took over and I jumped him right here in these weeds.

"So, you lived here when you were . . . uh, alive?"

He grinned. "Human. Yes."

"Right. Human. This was your childhood home?"

"I was born on this island, and I died here."

Even I wasn't stupid enough to continue down that line of questioning. "Seems like a nice place. You know, for a prison."

"It could be so much worse, and you know it."

I nodded my agreement, not paying attention to where I was going as I started walking toward a copse of trees off to the left. I took two steps at most before my ankle turned and I tumbled to the ground.

Caleb's hand caught my elbow and held fast. "I told you to watch your step." His words were more growl than anything, annoyance and frustration mixing with worry.

"It's dark."

"You're a shifter."

"Exactly. Not a vampire with crazy good vision. A shifter with moderately better sight than humans. My enhanced sense is smell. Some teacher you are."

He let out another rumble, waiting until he was sure I was steady before letting go of my arm and taking my hand.

"The village, or what's left of it, is down the path to the right."

I raised a brow. "What happened to it?"

"Plague, death, famine, war . . . take your pick."

"Sounds like the Apocalypse already happened."

"In a lot of ways, it did." Something about the hollowness of his tone and the hard set of his jaw warned me to tread carefully. There was more to this story, none of it pleasant.

Shuddering, I looked out in the direction he'd indicated, seeing little more than slightly darker shadows which must have been the structures.

"Lovely."

"It used to be. Would you like to see the church?"

Since my goal had been to learn as much as I could about my surroundings, there was only one answer. Still, I was playing a part. I couldn't be too obvious about my interest. "*Your* church?"

"Once upon a time."

"Then absolutely."

We walked hand in hand down a small incline, and the roar of the waves grew louder with each step. I didn't allow myself to think about how good it felt to have my palm pressed against his. I shouldn't like any part of this . . . of being with him. Then my thoughts drifted to all the other times we'd taken walks together in the moonlight when I'd hoped to do the same but had been denied.

*This is not a date, Sunday. No matter how much it feels like one.*

The church stood on the edge of a bluff. Small, simple, and perfect for Caleb. Though the stains of abandonment and disrepair were visible on the weather-worn siding and broken windows, I could picture him here, caring for his flock.

"My father made that cross," he said quietly, pointing at the steeple. "And my mother helped plant the community garden."

"Please don't put me in charge of that one too. One is enough."

He grinned, looking the slightest bit boyish and so charming it

64

hurt. "No, my darling one, you only have yourself to feed for now." His words were light, but his expression was haunted.

"Why do you look so sad?"

"The last time I was here, I lost everything, and I'm about to do the same all over again."

"You could have just asked me to come with you. You didn't have to steal me away."

He shook his head. "I promised myself I'd never come back. Not after what happened. But I had no choice. This was the only way."

I couldn't help myself. I reached up and ran my fingers through his hair. "What happened, Caleb?"

"Terrible things. I lost myself." His whispered confession wrapped itself around me, drawing me further under his spell. He caught my hand in his but held my palm to his lips as he brushed the softest of kisses to the center of it.

"And now?"

"You found me."

"Did I?"

He nodded, his eyes bright in the starlight. "Did you know that my mother was supposed to be a nun?"

"What stopped her?"

"She met my father. Fell in love. Left it all behind to have him."

"Ah, so it runs in the family."

His lips curled up, and he brushed a strand of hair off my cheek. "Aye, I suppose it does."

My breath caught as he leaned in. I could feel myself straining forward, every cell in my body desperate to be closer to him. A second before his lips could meet mine, I turned away, forcing his mouth to ghost over my cheek.

I couldn't do it. I couldn't kiss him. It was too intimate. Sex was one thing. It was primal, a release. But kissing? It spoke to deeper feelings. And I couldn't allow myself to get tangled up in those. It would only confuse me further.

"Fecking hell, Sunday," he whispered against my jaw. "The wanting is killing me."

"Wanting is one thing. Loving is another. You can't say you love me if you still plan to go through with it."

I didn't have to say what *it* was. We were both painfully aware.

He clenched his jaw, released me, and turned away, raking his hands through his hair. "Sweet suffering Jesus, you don't have any idea how hard this is for me. Do you think I want to see this through?"

"Yes."

"You're wrong. I tried for years to find another way. I nearly drove myself mad searching for another option until a few days ago when I finally had to admit defeat."

"Years?"

"I've been bound to you since the day you were born."

I shook my head, my gut churning with unease at the gravity of the bomb he just dropped. "So you've always known? And you made me fall in love with you anyway?"

He faltered, and I watched him try to walk it back, to put the cat in the bag again. "No. Not like you're thinking. I didn't know what we would be to each other. Only that I was tasked with putting a stop to . . . this."

I scoffed. "That's a pretty way of saying murder."

"I didn't know it would come to that. And once I did, I'd hoped for a different path. But now that it's inevitable, that this is what will come to be, all I want is to store up as many precious moments with you as I can before . . . " He paused and took a shuddering breath.

"Before what?"

"Before the only thing left in your eyes when you look at me is hate."

I wanted to say I could never hate him, but I didn't think that was true. Because if he went through with it, I would. There was no way I couldn't.

"I might be your prisoner, and I might be your mate, so you hold a power over me I can't ignore. But that doesn't mean I have to give you my heart. Know *that*, the next time you use our connection against me. It isn't love. It isn't real. It isn't *me*. When I give you my body, it's a means to an end. My way of scratching an itch, nothing more."

"Sunday . . ."

But I said everything I'd intended to say on the matter. Let him sit with that. Let him think about what he was losing by walking down this path.

I stormed away from him, heading toward the bluff and the glittering ocean below. Hope that had been shattered only moments before bloomed as my gaze lit on a dock at the shore. The only dock within sight.

That was how I'd escape. Caleb's servant. The next time they showed up with their supplies, I'd steal their boat, and the two of them could live out their days trapped on this island.

I should feel guilty about condemning an innocent to such a fate, but I didn't.

I was getting away. I had to.

# EIGHT

## THORNE

*The night Sunday disappeared*

I snatched the phone from Moira's grip, leaving it on speaker, but needing some sense of control in this maelstrom we never seemed free of. Staying close to the group, I scowled down at the screen. Asher Henry. Who the devil was he?

"Our mate has been taken. Find her," I barked.

"First of all, I'm good—the best, actually—but I'm going to need a hell of a lot more to go on than that. Second of all, who the fuck are you? Moira, did you put me on speaker without giving me a heads up? I've blacklisted people for less than that. You know the rules."

"Sorry, Asher. This isn't something I could have done privately." Moira glared at me. "I was going to tell you I wasn't alone, but *someone* got his knickers in a twist and stole my phone."

"If he hadn't done it, I would have," Kingston said.

"Me too. And I don't wear knickers," Alek added.

"What is this, a circus? How many fucking people are with you?"

Asher's voice dropped as he muttered to himself, "Fucking amateur hour."

"Not my circus, not my monkeys. But sort of. There are three other guys here. Noah, Kingston, Alek, meet Asher Henry. King of the Nerd Herd."

"Put some respect on my name, Belladonna," he growled. "It's you coming to me for a favor."

"Sorry, geez. I don't remember you being so uptight." Looking around at us, she explained, "Asher is what's known in the industry as a black hat."

"A hacker?" Kingston asked. "Do we really trust a guy known for snooping around in other people's business?"

He had a good point, but this was the only solution we could go with, and desperate times called for desperate measures. I had to get Sunday back. Everything was wrong without her.

"As a rule? No. But Asher and I go way back. He's not stupid enough to get on my bad side. He knows what I could do to him."

"Transmutation. My favorite," Alek said with his usual cocksure grin. He seemed to have gained control of his beast in the last few minutes. Having a plan of attack agreed with him. I only hoped it paid off.

"And how do the two of you know each other?" I asked.

Rosie burst through the open doorway, panic in her eyes. "What's wrong? I could sense your pain, Noah. What happened?"

"Good fucking God, how many more clowns are going to get out of this car, Moira?" Asher's voice was filled with pure annoyance.

I glanced at my sister and gave her a warning shake of my head. "It's fine. She's my sister. Rosie, Sunday's been taken. We're trying to find her."

She pressed her lips into a tight line, worry in her eyes. Then I turned my attention back to the phone in my hand.

"Moira, how do you know Asher?"

Asher cleared his throat over the line. "She helped make a pesky problem go away years ago."

"What kind of problem?"

"He was cursed by an angry witch. I bought him more time. He'd be dead right now if it weren't for me."

"But he's human, isn't he?" Generally we kept our existence secret. Humans had a tendency to die when they got mixed up in our world.

"Yeah, but you know how easy it is for norms to get too involved."

"Norms?" Alek repeated, his brows furrowed.

"Normals," I answered, just as Kingston said, "Humans."

Moira nodded as she continued with her explanation. "I swear he's legit. I wouldn't risk it otherwise. Asher is the last person to do anything that would bring attention to himself. He's as off the grid as you can get. Covert may as well be his middle name and all that. Seriously. The only reason I have his number is that he owes me, and I'm willing to bet this is only one of seven burner phones the dude has."

Asher chuckled. "Seven. That's cute."

"We need you to find Sunday. Now." My words were sharp and harsh, but I didn't have time to wait on this fuckwit. Every passing second took her farther away from me and made it that much harder for us to find her.

A scoff floated through the phone. "You should check a calendar. Generally Sunday comes after Saturday."

"In our world, Sunday comes first," Kingston muttered.

"Is everything a fucking joke with you?" I snapped.

"It's my defense mechanism, okay?"

"I get that things are tense over there," Asher said, sounding more serious than he had since I'd taken the phone, "but I need details, man. Sunday who? What does she look like? Any tats or easily identifiable markings? When did you last see her? Where are you? Give me some crumbs to go off of."

Taking long, slow breaths, I pulled myself together and gave him what he wanted. Everything I could think of, with help from the other guys. When we described Caleb, each of us tensed, and if my own righteous anger was any indication, we were each planning very specific ways to make the vampire suffer once we caught him.

"So . . . let me get this straight. Sunday has three mates?" Asher asked.

"Four," Moira corrected.

"No. We can't call Caleb her mate. Not when he drugged and stole her." Kingston's words were more snarl than anything.

"Why does it even matter how many mates she has? Can you find her or not?" I asked, nearly at my wit's end.

My question was met with frantic typing. "Yeah . . . yeah, this should get me started. Let me know if you think of anything else. Otherwise I'll be in touch when I get some answers."

The line went dead, and I instantly flicked my gaze to Moira. "Is he always that . . . short?"

Moira blew out a breath. "I'm shocked he was on the line for as long as he was. Asher may be a hermit, but he's a busy guy."

"If he's such a hermit, how'd he get on the bad side of a witch?" Alek asked.

Moira bit her lip. "Well, he made the wrong person disappear. You see, his specialty is helping people vanish. Poof. Like they never existed. New identities, documents, the works. The reason he's so good at his job is that he knows all the ways people can be found. But a while back, he ran into some trouble when one of his clients ended up being a witch hunter."

"And you helped him anyway?" I asked, surprised she'd willingly assist someone who'd worked with one of her mortal enemies.

"It was really good money. And an honest mistake. Asher is the kind of person you want on your side. You never know when having someone like him in your back pocket will come in handy." She waved her arm around. "Case in point."

Rosie gave a delicate little shiver pulling my attention.

"You should go inside, love. No need for you to get caught up in this mess."

"She's your mate, Noah. That makes her family. I'm already caught up."

My sweet sister, always trying to help. I hated that we'd be losing her to Gavin Donoghue in a matter of weeks.

"How long will it take him to find something we can go off of?" Alek asked, flickers of lightning back in his eyes.

Moira shrugged. "Minutes. Days. Weeks. Hard to say."

"We don't have weeks," Kingston growled.

"I don't think she's in any danger, you guys. Not from Caleb, anyway. Have you seen how he watches her when he thinks she isn't looking? He'd never hurt her."

I knew it the moment my father stepped in the doorway; I didn't even have to turn around. "I wouldn't be so sure about that."

"What are you talking about?" The harsh bite of Kingston's question would have been offensive if the situation had been different. My father would have had him pinned against a wall, fangs bared, ready to answer to such disrespect. As it stood, he glared at the wolf and held his composure.

"Caleb isn't who you think he is."

"You don't fucking say."

"Insolent pup."

Kingston sneered, eyes glowing. "Caleb's a lying sack of shit? What's new about that? My trust for vampires has never been very high, but it's been waning by the second since setting foot in your house. Maybe you drained her dry and set Caleb up to take the fall."

It didn't take an expert to see that Kingston was fighting against a full shift. Fur rippled beneath his skin, and his face had taken on a gaunt cast that looked more canine than human.

"Control yourself," Alek said, his voice low and filled with warning. It sounded like he was speaking from personal experience. "We won't get anywhere if you pick a fight you can't win."

"How do you know I won't win?"

My father laughed. "I will tear you to shreds so small your family won't have any way to identify you."

"Try it."

"Don't tempt me."

"Father," I interjected. "Please. Explain what you mean about Caleb."

"This is a conversation best done indoors. Come with me to the library. We can get out of this dank garage and think more clearly once the tale is told."

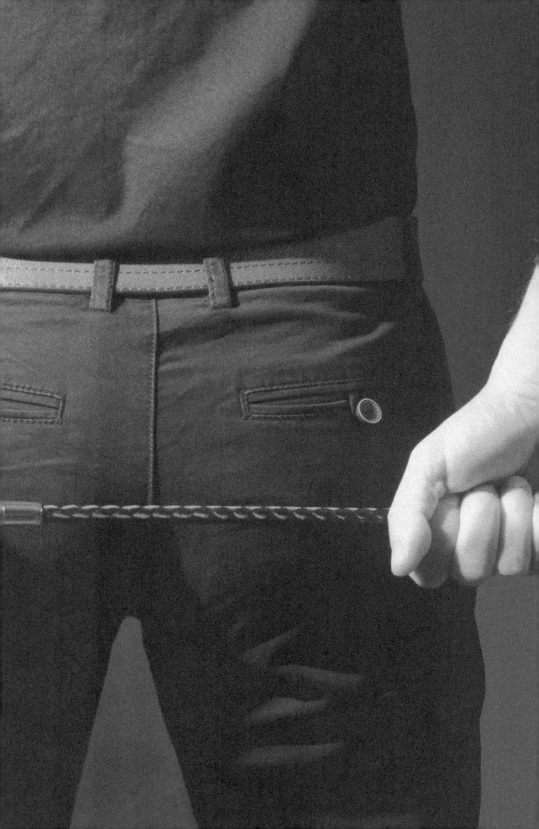

# CHAPTER
# NINE

## ALEK

This godsdamned library was becoming a permanent fixture in our lives. A place for all manner of bad news to be delivered. Kingston shoved past me as I headed toward the enormous fireplace, my gaze trained on the marred floor where our world had been turned upside down. A shudder ran through me before I could stop it. This was where life as I knew it ceased to exist. Nothing would ever be the same for me again after Natalie's revelation.

We hadn't just created a child; we'd all played our part in fucking Ragnarok. Or this realm's equivalent of it, anyway. How fitting that *I*, rather than my brother, would be one of the catalysts for the end times. They didn't call me the god of mischief for nothing, I supposed.

"Out of my way, Blackthorne. If you're dropping more bad news in our laps, I'm gonna need to be well lubricated. That means alcohol. Lots of it." Kingston's harsh words brought me back from my doom spiral. The berserker was rattling its chains, begging to be unleashed. Only my father's harsh lessons kept me from slipping into the bloodlust.

Kingston stood in front of Cashel, who blocked the decanters of spirits, wearing a sour expression on his face.

"Sit down, pup. We're all going to require something to take the edge off after I share with you one of my most well-kept secrets. I may never see the light of day again after this."

"Aren't you allergic to sunlight or some shit?" Kingston asked, glancing from him to Thorne. "You said you had magic sun blood. Doesn't the sun kill him?" Before Thorne could respond, Kingston returned his attention to the Blackthorne king.

"My wife ensures I'm able to walk in the light with her when I wish."

"I don't care what you do to your wife. I just need something to fucking drink. So move, or play bartender."

Cashel's shoulders stiffened, but to my surprise, he turned and began pouring heavy servings of a smoky amber liquid into crystal glasses. He passed one to each of us, then took a seat in a leather wingback chair. The rest of us joined him on the couches near the fireplace.

"It's like fucking Christmas Eve and we're all waiting on your daddy to tell us a story, Thorne."

"One more comment like that, and I'll be removing your jaw and shoving it up your arse, wolf. I've had just about all I can take out of you."

"Kinky," Kingston muttered before downing half the contents of his glass.

Out of all of us, it was Thorne who looked the most uneasy about whatever secrets his father was going to reveal. His sister was faring little better. She was perched beside Moira on one of the leather couches, her fingers digging into its padded surface. I couldn't blame them. It had been one hit after the other lately, and their sire seemed to be at the center of a lot of it. They were probably questioning everything right now.

"Father, enough of this posturing. Tell us what's going on."

The agony in Thorne's words echoed my own barely contained

misery. Each moment that passed was time wasted not searching for Sunny. My berserker stirred inside my chest, restless and on edge. It was a warning. If I didn't make progress in locating her soon, he would take matters into his own hands. Self-control be damned.

Ice-cold air whispered across my skin the moment before an apparition appeared in front of my face. "Boo."

I flinched, but I didn't jump back from the ghost of Callie Blackthorne this time. I'd grown accustomed to her and her pranks after our weeks here. At least to a point.

"Callie, now's not the time," Cashel chastised.

"I need Moira. You too, Rosie. Ash is awake and needs one of your herbal remedies. She said her headache is back."

Moira glanced at me, a plea in her eyes.

"Go to her. I will relay everything after we're finished here."

"Me too," Rosie insisted. "I'm part of this now."

The look Thorne tossed his sister was frustration tinged with gratitude. "We won't leave you out."

"You better not. I know where you sleep, Noah Blackthorne."

Rosie stood and brushed a kiss on her father's cheek before trailing out of the room behind Moira. Callie, damn her eternal soul, vanished while blowing me a kiss.

"Right, now to business," I said. "Explain the priest's role in all this."

"To understand Caleb, you must first understand the role of the Society."

Kingston made what I assumed was supposed to be a spooky ghost sound. "Ooooooh."

"Shut it, Casper."

Kingston grinned at me, then mouthed, "Boo," but didn't say anything further.

I was tempted to turn him into a hairless cat so I could call him a bald pussy, but managed to restrain the urge. Barely.

"What's the Society?" Thorne asked, ignoring both of us.

Cashel's frame was so tense my shoulders hurt to look at him.

"It's a group of creatures aligned with one goal. Maintain the balance of the world in which we exist."

"Caleb maintains the world's balance? We're fucked." Kingston was dead serious, and he wasn't wrong.

"Not alone, though he plays a crucial role. Thirteen of us were hand-selected to come together and aid this purpose."

"Who else is a member of your boys' club?" Kingston asked.

Cashel opened his mouth as if to answer and immediately looked like he sucked a lemon. Closing his mouth again, he shook his head. "The magic of the oath I swore precludes me from speaking their names."

"Convenient."

Over the next hour, Cashel filled us in on what he could. There were several false starts where his voice would fail, and he'd have to backtrack and mince words when he came too close to revealing information his oath deemed confidential. The long and short of it seemed to be that a bunch of rich, arrogant fucks shit the bed and now Sunday and our child were slated for extermination.

*Not on my watch.*

"So why is Caleb such a key player?" I asked.

Cashel leveled his gaze at me. "Because he stands to regain the one thing he'd betray even his God for."

Kingston sighed and rolled his eyes. "And that is . . ."

"His soul."

"What does he have to do to get it back, Father?" Thorne asked, but we all already knew the truth.

"End the Apocalypse. Kill the child before the gateway fully opens. It's the only way to stop this. He's been connected to her, waiting for her, all this time."

Thorne dragged a hand through his hair. "Fucking creep. He took advantage. He knew she was special and fucking stalked her."

"Pot meet kettle," Kingston muttered. "Don't think I didn't see you watching her every move when she first arrived at Ravenscroft."

"We all watched her," I pointed out. "We knew she was meant for us."

Thorne wasn't swayed by my logic. "Yes, but we aren't the ones who ran off with her, are we? We didn't know who she was or what we'd have to do. I'll have his balls for this."

"Not if she takes them first. Don't underestimate our girl. She's as bloodthirsty as we are. There's no way she's taking this lying down. It's not her way."

"I hope she makes him suffer," Kingston said, his smile more than a little deranged as he likely envisioned just how she'd go about it.

"He likes to suffer," Cashel reminded him.

"Fuck. You're right."

I blew out a breath, frustrated that Cashel's answers only seemed to create more questions. "So what do we do in the meantime? Moira couldn't locate them with her magic, and we can't just sit here and twiddle our thumbs while we wait for the human to finish his search. Where do we go from here?"

"To the Society," Thorne said, his voice cold and without emotion.

Kingston grinned. "To the motherfucking Society."

My berserker gave an approving roar, and I nodded, matching Kingston's grin with one of my own. I cracked my knuckles, eager for the opportunity to do the same to some heads. We'd go to them and get our answers. One way or another.

Cashel's brows rose. "I don't know if that's wise."

"I don't care what you think, Father. They know more about Sunday and her plight than anyone else. Take us to them. If you value family as much as you claim, you'll do this for me. She's my bonded mate. Just like Mother is yours. You can't honestly say that if this was her in Sunday's place you would just let her go." Thorne's hands dug into the armrest on his side of the sofa hard enough the leather cracked. "You would sacrifice the world for her, and you taught me well."

81

"That's what I'm afraid of."

"I'll go without your help. I *will* find her."

"We will," Kingston offered.

"Yes. We will find her. But your aid will help us do that sooner." I stood and crossed my arms over my chest, staring down the formidable vampire who held the only key to a lockbox full of answers.

Cashel took one look at the determined set of our faces before exhaling heavily. "If we're all going down in flames, it might as well be for love. I'll set it up."

"Thank you, Father."

His expression went grim. "Don't thank me yet. You have no idea what you're about to unleash. The truth is rarely what you expect, and even less often something you want to know."

Kingston stood next to me and clapped me on the shoulder. "We'll take our chances."

CHAPTER

# TEN

SUNDAY

"Stupid bossy vampire. Stupid garden. Stupid weeds," I grumbled as I pulled yet another bunch of unwelcome invaders from the soil and tossed them aside. My pile was huge, and I'd only managed to clean out the smallest corner of the space.

Thankfully Caleb had the foresight to ask his 'special helper' to bring gloves and tools that weren't from the turn of the century when she brought groceries, or this new little hobby of mine would have been even worse.

I snatched a particularly nasty-looking fellow and yanked, but the thick stock refused to budge, and I fell back on my ass into the dirt. "Fuck this shit. He can pull his own damned weeds."

It was nice being outside in the sunshine, though, even though the wind was still biting cold. After a few days of being confined indoors, unable to scratch *any* itch, today was the first time he'd given me a sort of freedom.

Freedom might be a stretch. I may not be in chains, but this island was as much of a prison as the cabin. The walls weren't made of brick and mortar. They were a wild and angry sea instead. Caleb

85

knew he had me trapped just as well as if I was in a dungeon. No matter how strong I was, I wouldn't survive the waves for long.

Back aching and tailbone likely bruised, I stood and dug my fingers into my lower back, kneading as hard as I could to alleviate some of the tension settled there. I was way too pregnant for this kind of manual labor.

I shook my head, Moira's voice ringing in my thoughts. *You're barely even halfway through your pregnancy. Stop being a whiny bitch, babycakes.*

Palm on my bump, I laughed. By my calculations, I really wasn't *that* pregnant. I could still wear baggy clothes and hide it if I really tried. But Kingston especially had babied me from the moment he found out I was knocked up. I'd been spoiled. No wonder Caleb thought I was a brat.

My heart twisted painfully. I missed my mates. I hated feeling this way after they'd just stood inside that library going along with Cashel's horrific plan. They didn't deserve my devotion. But love was rarely rational, and like it or not, I was still in love with all of them. Even stupid Caleb, though I refused to let him in on that particular secret.

I strode slowly down the dirt road that led to the church, needing a change of scenery, the ability to think, and to plan my next move. I'd never been very patient, but it seemed like all I could do these days was wait. Wait to give birth, wait for Caleb to sleep, wait for the boat to come.

If it was just my life on the line, I could afford to be reckless, but it wasn't. I had little Ellie to think of. I needed to time everything perfectly so when I made my escape, we would be far away from here by the time Caleb or the others could do anything about it.

I held no illusions that I could run forever. They'd find me eventually, but once our daughter was born and they could see for themselves that she wasn't the monstrosity Natalie had made her out to be, they'd come back around. I just had to wait it out.

As if sensing my thoughts, the baby shifted and pressed one of her little limbs outward, tickling my ribs and making me laugh. The sun broke through the clouds, a shaft of light hitting the rolling ocean waves and drawing my eyes straight to the dock. A sign. A sliver of hope.

My chest constricted as my gaze drifted from the water to the shore. A woman. There was a woman standing at the edge of the beach near the dock. There were people here? Caleb had made it seem like we were completely alone. Were they all under his thrall?

She must be one of his minions, waiting for the boat and its shipments.

Adrenaline surged through me, and I took off across the bluff, searching for a way down to the beach. I was hoping for stairs of some kind, but when I spotted a hill that had a gentle enough slope for me to walk down, I realized that was probably my best choice. Any stairs or path likely hadn't been well maintained and might give way beneath my weight.

Keeping my attention split between the woman on the shore and where I was walking, I half-ran, half-slid down the hill until I was running across the sand.

"Hey! Over here!" I nearly screamed for her to help me but thought better of it. If she was under his thrall, I had to play this right.

She turned her gaze from the water, her expression startled as I approached. I was sure I looked like a disaster in my dirt-covered sweatpants and one of Caleb's sweaters, with a scarf wrapped loosely around my throat. My hair was a wild mass, blowing every which way in the coastal wind.

"Hi!" I said, smiling too brightly. "I'm Sunday."

"That's an unusual name." Her voice was sweet and lyrical as she blinked up at me in surprise, a hand clutching the shawl wrapped around her slight frame. Her long fiery hair fell over her shoulder in a thick braid, soft curls framing her freckled face. She was a lot younger than I'd initially thought. Closer to a girl than a woman. Perhaps a teenager, though it was hard to know for sure. "I'm Kelly."

"What are you doing out here? Waiting for a boat?" The hope in my voice was ridiculous. She'd see right through me.

"No. They won't be returning for another four days. Once a week she delivers to the island."

"I'm just up there in the house on the hill. Where do you live?"

Kelly offered a ghost of a smile. "The village. We're all there."

*We?* My heart lurched. "How many people are on the island? I thought it was abandoned."

"Oh, we've always been here. So many of us."

*There's a whole damn village of people here? That fucking liar.*

"I didn't realize."

She grinned. "Well, miss, you've only been here a short while. You'll see. One day you'll be as much a part of Warg Island as the rest of us."

Something in her words sent a shiver of foreboding down my spine. "Warg Island? That's what this place is called?"

"Aye. Don't you know where you are? What a silly girl you are if you're in a place you aren't even knowing the name of." She gave a soft laugh and shook her head.

"It happened kind of fast."

"He is persuasive. Father Gallagher."

"You know him?" *Idiot, of course she knows him.*

She gave me another sidelong look. "Aye, we all know him. He's not one who's easy to forget."

The way she said that sent another tremor through me. "No. He leaves quite an impression." I heaved a frustrated sigh, not wanting to say too much but needing more information. "How do I get to the village from down here?"

Kelly pointed to my left, eyes not meeting mine.

I followed her gaze, seeing a bend in the rocky beach's shore. A hike. Lovely. "How far is that—" I started, but she was gone by the time I turned back to her, yards away in the distance, walking along the water's edge. "Okay then, bye. Nice talking to you."

With a huff, I started down the path she'd indicated and made my way toward the village. The wind picked up, catching my scarf and sending it flying down the beach before the tide swallowed it. I'd have to explain that to Caleb tonight, but I didn't think he'd care. It wasn't like the heirloom he kept sacred.

The walk didn't take as long as I feared, though the sun was a lot lower in the sky by the time I spied the three-foot stone with its smooth face proclaiming Warg Island had been established in 1819 with a population of 107.

I ran my fingers over the engraved text, wondering about the people who lived such isolated lives. Caleb had been one of them once upon a time.

"What kind of life did you have, Caleb?" I whispered into the silence.

The village loomed before me, small and run-down, with stone buildings lining a main street of dirt framed by rock walls. In the distance, plots of land divided by the same walls dotted the area. Homes. Farms. People.

Hope still burned inside me at the thought of humans I could talk to. People I could eventually convince to help me. As I slowly made my way through the town, an oppressive weight filled the air. Grief overshadowed everything around me. Bad things happened here; I knew that. Caleb had said as much.

This was like stepping back in time, but I supposed that was exactly right. Remote locales like this were often decades behind the rest of the world.

Still, I'd expected to find more signs of life. So far the locals were making themselves scarce. Other than a few shadows in the windows and twitchy curtains, I hadn't come across anyone else.

"I guess you aren't a fan of strangers here."

Kelly had been skittish and basically ran from me the second she could. I'd just have to keep coming around until the villagers got curious enough to confront me. Hopefully it wouldn't be with pitch-forks and torches.

When I reached the end of the main road, the cobblestone turned to dirt, though the trail continued onward. To my right, the tree line thickened, signaling the start of the woods, while the church loomed above me on the left. I could just make out the path I'd taken to the beach ahead of me, letting me know that I'd managed to circle back around in my wanderings.

I wasn't ready to go back and face him—or the weeds I'd left in the ground. Under the guise of wanting to explore my surroundings, I took a narrow, overgrown trail before the hill that led to the church. The light was fading quickly, casting the world around me in a gloomy violet hue. My road forked, and instead of heading toward the church, I turned and found myself standing outside an old cemetery. Vines curled around the rusted iron gate, pulling it open to suit their growth.

Curiosity piqued, I moved into the graveyard and its neat rows, drawn to the first of the stone markers despite myself. As soon as I reached it, I noticed that the roar of the ocean and wail of the wind were toned down. Hushed. Like even nature itself knew better than to interfere with the sleep of those that lay beneath the earth.

Nervous laughter bubbled out of me as I glanced around me, feeling very much not alone even though I was the only living soul in sight. "Get it together, Sunday."

I passed through rows of headstones, some so weathered they couldn't be read, others covered in moss. None of them looked recent. The oldest date I found was 1922, but with the state of some of the markers, it was impossible to know for certain if that was the last time anyone had been buried here.

My heart stuttered as a tall marker in the shape of a weeping angel caught my attention. Drawn to the figure, I approached, breath caught in my throat as I read the name etched into the base. *Gallagher.*

"Caleb," I whispered, an ache taking hold. I approached the large plot, which held far too many graves. All dead within a year of each other, some as young as a few months old. Was this his family? His mother, Siobhan? Nolan, his father? And the others, more siblings than my heart could bear to name. Not all of them died in the plague. Too many tiny graves were clearly stillborns or barely out of infancy. Life had been so much harder back then.

Poor Caleb . . .

My eyes shifted back toward his house, and my entire body went rigid when I noticed the soft glow of firelight in the windows.

*Shit. Fuck.* I'd been out here too long. Night had fallen while I'd been visiting with the dead, and he'd awakened.

I was in so much trouble.

# CHAPTER
# ELEVEN
## CALEB

"Where the fecking hell are you?" I muttered as I paced in front of the hearth, my nerves shot from the combined anxiety of Sunday not being here with me and the hunger I hadn't sated in days.

I used to be able to go without. To deny myself blood and starve for weeks—months even. But I'd fed on her too many times. Reawakened the demon inside me. Now there was no going without. I needed to quench my thirst like the monster I was. On this island, that meant hunting animals in the dense forest that made up the central part of the land. But I couldn't leave until she was secured in the house.

I could just go outside and demand she come in, but I was also attempting to give her some space. Despite her hateful diatribe the other night—most of which I deserved—I wasn't trying to imprison her.

When this was all over, if I succeeded, I wanted her to have a place to grieve and recover. A place that had become her sanctuary, if not her home. I'd leave her here with a little bit of me as a reminder that it wasn't all lies and deceit. It's why I wanted her to take ownership of the garden. To give her the opportunity to fall in love with the land. To forge her own place on this island so she wouldn't see it as just another metaphorical tower she'd been locked away in.

I loved her fierce independence, even though it often impeded my plans. Once I was gone, I'd at least be sure she was safe here. Even if she *wanted* me dead.

But I wasn't dead yet, and like it or not, I'd given her an order to be indoors by sundown. An order she'd disobeyed. I'd tried to be lenient. To allow her to do as she was bade and return to offer her apologies. I was tired of waiting. She needed to learn.

She needed to be punished.

My hand flexed with the rush of desire that singular word sent through me. Memories of my palm connecting with her round arse had my cock hard in an instant. Fuck. This would turn into much more than a punishment if my body's reaction was any indication.

All the better.

I tore open the front door and scanned the grounds, searching for my mate's familiar, beloved form. Walking around the house to the garden, I spied the pile of abandoned weeds with a slight smile. At least she'd done some work, though it seemed like the chore was not to her liking. The thought of her spiteful grumbling had my lips twitching with laughter. What I wouldn't give to have been there to witness it.

Lifting my gaze, I searched the rest of the property, not needing long to determine she'd wandered off.

"Oh, Miss Fallon, it's as if you're begging me to make an example of you."

Tilting my head back, I inhaled deeply, drawing the air into my lungs as I attempted to pick up her scent. The sharp aroma of pine. The salty tang of the sea. The damp earth. My brow furrowed in confusion. No Sunday.

"Where have you gone, sweetling?"

I strode toward the church, following the path I'd taken her down once before. It was the only other place she was familiar with on the island, so she must have come back for a closer inspection, but the lack of her essence on the wind was unsettling. As I approached the chapel, my gaze raked the surroundings, my senses on high alert.

"Come out, Miss Fallon. I'm not interested in playing hide and seek with you." If she was toying with me, there would be hell to pay.

Stalking the grounds, I came up empty-handed and finally found myself at the bluff's edge, staring down at the shore, the waves gently lapping against the sand. It seemed soft and almost romantic, but I knew the dangers of the sea. I'd seen this water pull a grown man under and drown him. My gut churned.

A dark shape caught my eye in the surf, a torn piece of fabric I recognized snagged on a piece of driftwood. My scarf. *Sunday's* scarf.

*No. She wouldn't be that stupid.*

Although . . . she was desperate to escape. Maybe she thought it was her only option.

My feet were moving before my brain registered the action, tapping into my power reservoir to blur myself down onto the beach below.

"Sunday, what have you done?" I whispered, my voice swallowed by the wind as I picked up the waterlogged cloth.

I held the scarf to my nose, trying to find even a hint of my mate from the fibers, but all I smelled was the briny scent of the ocean. Did she really hate me so much that she would choose such an end over captivity with me? But no . . . she couldn't have left me like this. She wouldn't. Not if she was trying to save the child.

It must be something more, something both innocent and sinister in the same breath. I could picture it so clearly. She could have been walking along the water's edge and been taken down by a rogue wave. Swept out to sea, calling for help with no one around to save her. Could God really be so cruel?

I knew the answer. Yes. Yes, He could.

Despair flooded me as sure as the tide filled the shore. He'd taken her from me because I didn't deserve even a stolen moment of happiness.

"Why?" I raged, shouting up at the sky. "You set me on this path. Why doom me at the last? Why make her suffer because of my failings?"

I spun in a circle, spewing my fury, chest heaving, eyes burning with unshed tears. I hadn't cried since the day my mother took her last breath.

What was the point of it all if Sunday was going to be taken by God in the end? Why had Gabriel toyed with me, dangling my salvation before my eyes like the proverbial carrot on a stick? Had it all been a sick and twisted game? Penance for the souls I'd claimed?

I fell to my knees, stricken with grief. "Gabriel! Messenger of God! Come to me, you fecking sadist!"

The roar of the waves was my only answer. I bowed my head, despondent. It was over. I lost my beautiful girl to a watery grave all because of my limits, my flaws. She'd died, and I'd done nothing to save her.

"Caleb?"

I stiffened, her voice whispering my name the cruelest punishment of all. My gaze lifted from the sand in search of the sound. She stood there on the bluff, hair blowing in the breeze but her scent not reaching me.

I blinked, hope the most painful punishment of all. "Is this a trick? Have they sent you to haunt me?"

"What the hell are you doing down there? Is this one of your priest things? Are you praying?"

A specter wouldn't be capable of such cheek . . . would it? Surely the afterlife would tame that sharp tongue of hers. Then again, if she was here to torture me, the bite of her sass would be the perfect implement.

"Sunday?"

She placed her hands on her hips, her face scrunching in annoyance. "Yes, Sunday. Who else would it be? Unless you're keeping some other helpless woman trapped on your other islands. What are you doing? I've been looking for you."

"Looking for me?" My voice was wooden, my brain numb with shock. I'd been so sure she'd been lost to me. Deep within my spiral of despair, I couldn't wrap my mind around the fact that she was still here.

"What is wrong with you? You sound weird."

That was it. I had to see if she was real. I blurred up the side of the bluff and had her in my arms before she could stop me. Tangible. Warm. Alive. I dipped my head and pressed my face into the crook of her neck, inhaling her, letting the distinct aroma of my mate overwhelm me.

For a single, blissful second, she relaxed into me, curling into my body. Then she stiffened and lifted her hands, pushing against my chest. "Caleb, what has gotten into you?"

"I thought . . . I thought you were lost to the sea." I shook my head, the gut-churning sensation of terror rearing as I spoke the words. "I found the scarf. You weren't home after sundown. I couldn't find you. Not a hint of your scent anywhere . . . the only explanation for that was if you'd been missing for hours."

Even in the darkness, I had no trouble identifying the wash of color in her cheeks. "Maybe not the only explanation. It's sort of Moira's fault. She did a spell to mask it."

"Why the bloody hell would she do that?"

"Because I asked her to? It was supposed to keep the others from tracking me when I ran away. I guess it's still working, though."

The harsh bark of laughter that escaped me was a mixture of relief and shock. "You conniving minx. I thought you were dead. I . . ."

A flicker of emotion crossed her face as she stared into my eyes. Was it love? I couldn't be certain, but I had to pull her into my arms fully once more, and there was nothing on this earth that would have stopped me from claiming her lips with mine. The kiss was brief but powerful. My dark heart beating only for her, existing only for her. She was my light in a world gone to hell.

She backed away, her posture tense. "Caleb, no. You don't get to . . . do that."

"What? Kiss you? Sunday, I thought you died. I thought my only reason for not meeting the sun was gone." Even in my darkest times, I'd never considered it, but at that moment, I knew if she was truly gone, nothing would stop me from following.

She shook her head, biting down on her lower lip as if she was at a loss for words. After a second, she swallowed and asked, "And now? Have your plans for me changed?"

Everything in me went still. "*A stor—*"

She took two more steps away from me, her eyes shuttering and locking me out. "If you're still going to insist on fulfilling your destiny or whatever, then you and I cannot pretend to be anything more than a means to an end. I already told you, Caleb. I won't give you my heart. Not even when it's broken."

"And I won't take your body without it."

Her chin tipped up in defiance. "You say that now, but I bet you'll be singing a different tune in a day or so. You've never been very good at resisting me."

"I resisted you when you were writhing on the bed, calling out for me in your sleep last night."

Cheeks burning pink, she cast her gaze away from mine.

"Oh, is that something you want, then? To wake up with me buried deep inside you?" I stepped closer. "I can smell how much you like that idea."

"I may have fantasized about it a time or two. So yes, it turns me on. What's your point? Do you want a cookie for keeping your cock to yourself? It wouldn't be the first time."

"Which is it, Miss Fallon? Am I unable to resist or skilled at it? You can't have it both ways."

"You're only good at it when I don't want you to be."

I lifted a lock of her hair, rubbing the silky strands between my fingers. "I've only ever resisted you to protect you. And when I gave in, it was because you made damn sure I knew where you stood. You've always given me your heart, *a stor.* Even when you didn't realize it. Play make-believe all you like, my darling one, but you can't simply turn off your love for me. Just as I can't stop my feelings for you, no matter how much I want to."

"The difference between you and me is I've walled my heart away. You don't have one."

That shut me up. Little did she know those four words could not have been less true, but the arrow hit its mark as though shot by an expert archer. I steeled myself, resuming the facade of the villain in her story. I'd let her see me vulnerable and lovesick. That was over.

"Right you are. Now get your stubborn arse inside. You need to eat and I have to shower. I took an unexpected swim this evening because of you."

She narrowed her gaze, remaining silent as she shot daggers at me with those blue eyes of hers. I expected a biting remark, some sort of reminder of how I'd wronged her. Instead she stalked down the path toward the house without another word, not looking back at me.

So it was the silent treatment, then. Just as well. I couldn't trust myself not to tell her my true feelings as it was.

All the blood in my body rushed south the moment I stepped through the door and saw her. She stood in front of the fireplace, stripping off the clothing that had become damp and chilled by contact with me. With each layer she removed, more of her creamy skin and luscious curves were revealed.

I let out a strangled curse. The bedroom was right bloody there. The woman knew exactly what she was doing. The tease.

"Do y—" My fecking voice cracked, and I had to clear my throat before I could start again. "Do you have an aversion to bedrooms now?"

She draped her sweater over the chair closest to the fire, casting a glance over her shoulder. "Not in particular."

"What's all this, then?"

"I have an aversion to you. You sleep there."

"Is that so?"

"Yes, Caleb." She slid her hands behind her back, staring me down as she unhooked her bra. "But from the looks of things, you sure don't have an aversion to me." She dropped her eyes purposefully to the bulge in my trousers.

"I never said I did. I've always been honest about wanting you."

She smirked, flinging her bra at me as she turned and headed into the bedroom. "How's it feel to want?" she called over her shoulder before slamming the door in my face.

I let out an agonized groan, scrubbing my hands over my face. "Like fucking hell."

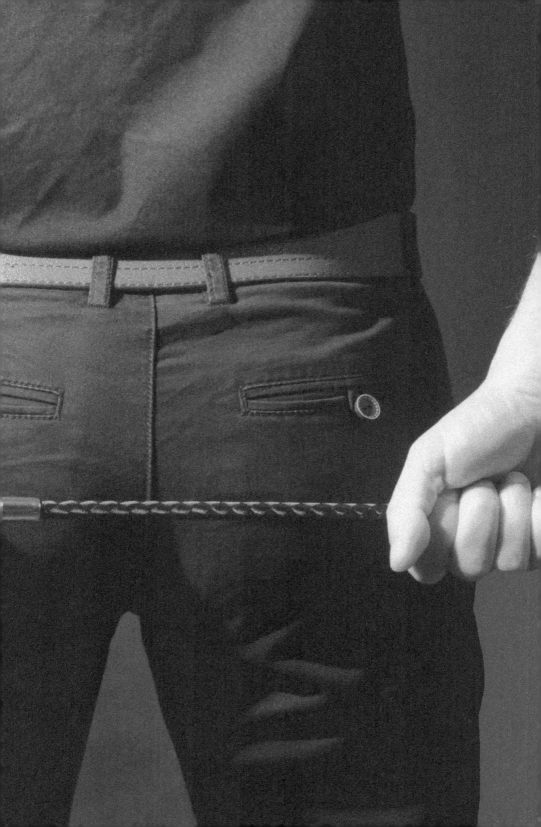

# CHAPTER
# TWELVE

## CALEB

Even in the dark of night, my homeland was beautiful. It always had been. But try as I might, staring out into the prison I'd created for us both couldn't ease the ache Sunday had caused in my body, my heart, my mind. Punctuated by another sort of pain.

Unsatisfied lust.

She knew exactly which buttons to press and when.

Though to be fair, when I was around her, lust always simmered just below the surface. There was very little she need do other than breathe to send desire careening through me. Part of me wondered if it was a mate thing. If the others felt this way when they were with her too. The rest of me didn't care. All my primal side focused on was sating the urge to be inside her, filling her, claiming her.

I let out a soft grunt as my cock throbbed. My fecking trousers were shamefully tented. I couldn't walk around the house like this. On display. Showing her exactly how she affected me. Reaching down, I adjusted myself until it was at least a little less obvious how hard I was.

The snick of the bedroom door unlocking had my shoulders tense and jaw tight. So she was coming out to play after all.

"Shower's all yours," she called, sailing past me and into the kitchen where the leftovers sat waiting for her. Yes, I'd already heated them for her. Yes, I was pathetic.

I debated going to her, pushing her down onto the table, spreading her legs and making a feast for myself out of her body. But she'd drawn the line between us, and I wasn't ready to surrender to her terms. Instead, stubborn arse that I was, I remained rigidly turned away, forcing myself to keep control.

"You're really going to ignore me?" she asked, her tone petulant.

"Aye."

She scoffed. The sound of a chair being pulled out followed by her soft sigh as she sat raked across my nerves. Everything about her called to me, luring me like a siren to my demise. I counted her breaths, savored her sighs. And with each passing second, I lost a little more of my fragile will. Not just to stop myself from fucking her, but to resist devouring her. My thirst for her was akin to a flame's unquenchable need for oxygen. Without her, I'd die.

I could hear the rush of blood through her veins with every beat of her heart. I was starving in more ways than one, and my fangs responded, lengthening in my mouth.

"Good. I needed some peace and quiet."

"Happy to give you what you want."

She let out a small huff of laughter. "That's a first."

My palm itched to crack against her round arse. She just couldn't help herself. "Perhaps you don't always know what you want, Miss Fallon."

"And you do? That's hilarious. You can barely admit to what you *need*. You're starving, and yet you still refuse to hunt."

"Tell me, who should I feed on?" I turned to face her then, giving in to my body's desperate desire to feel a connection with her. "You?"

I would have missed it if I hadn't been looking so intently at her, but her pupils flared and her breath hitched. She wanted me to drink from her. As if by its own will, her hand lifted, and she lightly stroked the mark I'd given her. My cock jerked as if the echo of the caress ran along its length.

Fecking hell. I had to get out of this room if I was going to save her from a ravaging she would hate me for come morning.

"Eat your dinner," I snapped, shoving my hands into my pockets and averting my gaze.

I didn't wait for her to respond. I couldn't. Instead, I stalked into the bedroom, heading straight for the steam-filled bathroom. Kicking the door shut behind me, I stripped out of clothes that suddenly felt too tight. Too rough against oversensitive skin.

But nudity provided me with no relief. As soon as I entered the bathroom, I was assaulted by the scent of her shampoo. She was everywhere.

Groaning, I cranked the cold water all the way up and stood beneath the icy spray, praying for some sort of pardon from my suffering. Even that provided little comfort. It was no use. The only thing that would satisfy me now was her.

Her hands on my body.

Her mouth pliant beneath mine.

Her warm, willing cunt.

"Fuck," I moaned, half in despair, half in pleasure.

I'd barely registered that I'd already taken myself in hand, my thick length pulsing. I should stop myself, not allow self-abuse with her right there in the other room. But I wasn't going to.

If the only way I could have her was in my fantasies, then I'd damn well make it worth my effort. I gave a cursory stroke, starting at the thick base and running my palm to the tip. A hissed breath escaped me, my balls already tight and full.

"Sunday, God in heaven, what you do to me," I rasped, thankful she couldn't hear me. Or could she? That thought sent a thrill straight to my dick and took me back to my nights of watching her in *Iniquity's* private room.

As if summoned from the depths of my most depraved imaginings, the visual of her, bound and presenting for me, raced through my mind. Her back arched, slick pink cunt on display, dripping for the only man in her vicinity.

Me.

I inhaled deeply, her musk mouthwatering and calling to me. I gave myself over, let the dream descend and draw me in. If I couldn't have her heart here and now, I'd have it in fiction of my own making.

"Miss Fallon, you seem to have forgotten your knickers."

She squirmed, cheeks flushing beautifully as her eyes met mine over her shoulder. "You told me not to wear any when I was with you."

A harsh pulse of pleasure had my cock jerking. "Aye, I did say that. Tell me, when did you start being my good girl?"

"I always try, Daddy."

Fuck. I had to stop stroking myself and pull my thoughts from the scene. I was already balancing on a knife's edge, nearly bursting. Taking a few deep breaths, I willed my orgasm away. I wasn't ready. I needed this to last.

When I'd gotten myself under control, I gave up on the cold water and turned the temperature as high as I could stand it. Then I closed my eyes and took my leave of reality once more.

"Such an obedient pet," I murmured, striding across the room to where she was waiting for me on the bed. "Slick and open and ready for me."

"Yes," she whispered, wiggling her hips.

"Did you touch yourself before I got here? If I taste your fingers, will they be coated in you?"

A guilty look flashed across her face.

"That's a yes, is it? You know the rules. You were instructed to keep your hands to yourself, my darling one. Let Daddy be the one to make you feel good."

She bit that lower lip and blinked at me a few times, then popped her arse back even farther, as though she was begging me for it.

"Punish me, Daddy. I've been such a bad girl."

"Do you remember your safe word?"

"Rosary."

Christ, my knees nearly gave out at the husky cast of her voice. I raked my gaze over the implements hanging along the wall. She tracked me with her eyes, giving a small whimper of encouragement when I selected my favorite riding crop.

She squirmed, testing her bonds as I padded closer.

"Do you know what this is?"

She nodded.

"Have you ever felt the sting of its kiss before?"

"No."

"Do you want to?"

"Yes." Her response was fervent and immediate. I could see how wet just the thought of it made her.

I ran the leather tip down her spine, giving the full globe of her sweet arse a swift strike. "And what are the rules when we play like this, my sweet one?"

"I c-count," she panted.

"And if you forget?"

"I don't get to come."

"And do you want to come?"

"Fuck yes. Please, Daddy, let me come for you."

My hand shot out to brace against the shower wall, the power of my imagination running away with me. I could make this a reality. I could storm out of this bathroom and grip her by the nape, give in to the raging need, and make her remember why I was bad for her in such a good way. Glancing down at my swollen, aching cock, I wasn't surprised to find it leaking with precum. She had me dripping for her.

No. I wouldn't let myself give her the hate fuck she so desperately wanted. If we were together, I needed more. I needed to feel her love surrounding me. But it was very likely I'd lost that forever. Except in my mind. I could write our story within the pages of my fantasies. And I would.

"Brace yourself, darling. This might hurt, but I promise the pleasure will be worth it."

"Do it."

Not needing further encouragement, I struck her with the crop, memorizing the bright pink stripe across her pale flesh.

She cried out, the sound beautifully ragged. "One."

"Can you stand more?"

"Yes. Please. Give me more."

I gave her the next two lashes in quick succession, spacing out my strikes so her marks were evenly placed along her back.

"Th-three," she moaned.

"More?"

"Y-yes."

"That's too bad, sweetling, because I need to feel you wrapped around my cock."

"Just one more, please, Daddy."

I grabbed her hair and yanked her head back. "You know I can never deny you when you beg so sweetly." And then I brought the crop down between her legs, the leather tip striking her directly on her clit.

She moaned long and loud, her cunt pulsing, begging for my cock. I'd give it to her . . . in a moment.

Turning the riding crop over in my hand, I held the tip, groaning at the wetness she'd left on that from a simple lash across her pussy. Then I slid the thicker base inside her, slowly, carefully, until she whispered she needed me. Until she was begging for her daddy to make the ache go away.

Pulling the hilt out of her, I sucked her arousal from the end before placing it on the bed. "So fecking sweet."

"I need you. Please, Caleb, fuck me."

"I'm Caleb now, am I?"

"What do you want me to call you?" she glanced over her shoulder, wide-eyed innocence in her gaze.

"Father Gallagher," I ground out before registering what I was saying.

"Please, Father Gallagher. Fuck me. Hard. I need you."

The taboo plea had my hand clenching tighter around my throbbing cock. I was seconds away from coming, but I wasn't ready for this to be over. Here, at least, I could have everything I ever wanted. Even that which I could barely admit to craving.

"Do you want my cum inside you, Sunday? Filling you. Leaking from your pretty, used cunt?"

She nodded, eyes shining with lust.

In this fantasy, she wasn't pregnant with some magical creature sent to doom us all. Here, she was mine to fill, to do with as I wished, to claim and mark and . . . breed.

I shoved my trousers down my thighs, freeing the straining cock I'd been hiding from her. Then, in measured movements, I positioned myself behind her, notching my leaking crown against her puffy lips.

Slowly, with control I didn't know I had, I pushed inside, the sensation nearly too much.

"God, you're so fecking tight."

She pushed her hips back, moaning as the shift made me slide deeper, stretching her. "You feel so good. It's been too long since you've been inside me, Father Gallagher."

A tremor worked its way down my body, and I involuntarily slammed the rest of the way inside her. Leaning forward and pressing my chest to her spine, I freed her and wrapped my arms around her torso, pulling her with me as I straightened. One of my hands kneaded her breast, the other pressed against her lower belly until I could feel myself inside her.

It did something to me. That feeling. I drew my hips out and then thrust quickly in just so I could enjoy the sensation against my palm.

"Yes. Like that," she breathed.

I dipped my chin down so my mouth was at her ear. "You're mine, Miss Fallon. Mine to take and fill."

"Yes."

"Do you want that? Do you want your professor to fuck you full of his cum?"

I thrust again, bottoming out and groaning in her ear as she shuddered and clenched around me.

"Yes. But . . . you should pull out."

A dark laugh escaped me. "Why would I do a silly thing like that?"

"I'm in heat. You could get me pregnant."

My balls tightened, pleasure racing up my shaft. "Which is exactly why I won't be wasting a drop of my spend outside your perfect cunt."

"Oh, God."

"No. Not God."

"Daddy," she moaned.

And I was lost. I came hard and nearly painfully, shouting her name with abandon. My toes curled from overwhelming pleasure as I shuddered out every pulse of my release.

Before the fantasy faded entirely, I allowed myself a last second of make-believe. In my world, my cum was dripping out of her after I pulled out, the evidence of what I'd done to her sliding down her thighs. We couldn't have that. I took two fingers and pushed my gift to her back inside where it belonged. Filling her just like I'd promised.

The water had run cold again by the time I finally opened my eyes. My breath still coming in shallow pants, my seed painted on the shower wall. Despite my earth-shattering climax, I was still hard and aching with need.

Fucking hell.

I shut off the water with a low growl, stunned to the core when the sudden silence was broken by a whimpered moan. I snapped my head to the door, eyes noting the shadow beneath it.

*Sunday.* She was on the other side. Pleasuring herself right along with me. I could smell it.

Blurring to the door, I reached for the knob, cock straining, body searching for my mate. She was in need, and I was hardwired to care for her. I could help her. And she could help me.

I pressed my palms against the wood, listening to her trying to swallow her cries.

"Caleb?" she whispered.

Feck. Did I answer her? Go to her?

"Sunday. Tell me you love me and I'll make you feel good." I was a glutton for her. She knew it as well as I did. "I'll replace those fingers of yours with my cock."

Her heartbeat picked up, breath catching as she leaned against the door, shifting the wood beneath my hands.

"You know I can't. Not until you give me what I need."

In my haze, I purposely misinterpreted her words. I'd give her exactly what she fucking needed.

Throwing open the door, I caught her as she fell into me. I lifted her easily, placing her on the counter.

"Caleb."

"Shut up. Let me give this to you."

Dropping to my knees, I took her soft leggings with me until the beautiful dripping cunt I'd been fantasizing about was right there. Begging me to eat it.

I buried my face between her thighs and made her come over and over until she ran like a fountain for me. I didn't take my time, draw it out. I gave her exactly what she needed. What we both needed, if I was being honest.

When I finished, and she was reduced to a quivering mess, I stood, wiping my lips with the back of my hand.

But my Sunday wouldn't meet my eyes. She allowed me to help her down from the vanity and right her clothing but pulled her hand from mine as soon as possible. Then, turning an icy stare on me, she said, "This doesn't change things between us, Caleb."

She left me and my pathetic heart in her wake, leaving us behind with all the grace of a queen.

I realized then how selfish of me it was to ask for her love when I was destined to destroy her. But I wanted it anyway. It was my only solace.

Because when this was finished between us, all I would have were my memories of our short time together. And my soul. But what good was a soul when your entire reason for being hated you? Besides, if Sunday was my temptation to resist, I'd fail and be damned all over again anyway.

That was the thing about sin. It was wrong and self-serving, but fuck, did it feel good.

At least for a little while.

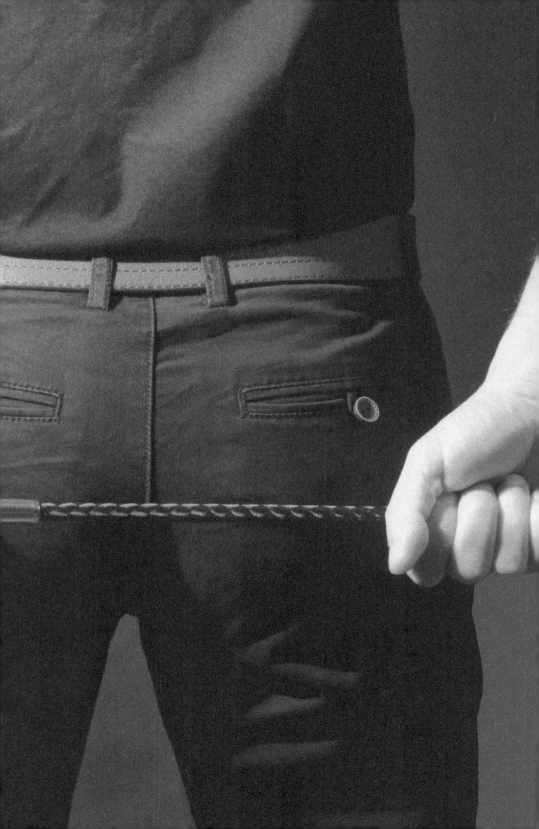

CHAPTER
# THIRTEEN
THORNE

*Three days since Sunday's abduction*

My blood hummed with anxious energy with every beat of my heart as I made yet another circle around the Blackthorne grounds. I felt caged. Restless. Too many variables sent me spiraling at the best of times, but now? Now I could barely stand to be in my own skin.

The Society meeting was scheduled, but we had to wait. The search for Sunday was underway, but we had to wait. I was so bloody tired of *waiting*.

The only time patience had ever been one of my virtues was during a hunt. And even then it was only because the ending was a foregone conclusion. Nothing about my current situation was known.

I wasn't handling it well.

A storm was brewing. I could feel it on the horizon, lurking. Ominous.

*Of course it is, you dolt. The Apocalypse is coming.*

My phone buzzed in my pocket, nearly sending me eight feet into the air. I'd been so in my head that I hadn't been prepared for its alert. Feeling foolish, I pulled it free and glanced at the screen.

*Unknown.*

My heart galloped, and my hands trembled as I answered the call.

"Sunday?" Desperation bled into that one word.

A soft huff of laughter—masculine laughter—sent ice through me. "Sorry to disappoint. It's your friendly neighborhood hacker."

"Asher? How did you get my number?" Suspicion worked its way to the forefront of my mind.

"What part of hacker are you having trouble with?"

"The part where it took you three pissing days to find anything out. I thought you were supposed to be the best. That hardly seems like an impressive turnaround. Mediocre perhaps. Crap more like."

There was a beat of silence before Asher's voice, hard and unamused, came through the tiny speaker. "Do you want my good news or not, *mate*?"

"Out with it then."

"I've got a lead on them. The last CCTV footage I found was at a private airfield in Dublin."

I gritted my teeth against the wave of rage his words caused. Ireland. Of course it was Ireland. The self-loathing arse just couldn't help himself. "And now? Where are they?"

"That's something I'm still working on. But I don't have the details yet."

"Why not?"

"Fuck, you vampires are so goddamned demanding. I like working with shifters so much better."

My answer was nothing more than a snarl. "Trust me, you'd be singing a different tune if Kingston was on the other end of the line."

"That's the Farrell kid, right?"

I stiffened. "How do you know that?"

His laugh had me clenching my jaw. "I like to look into the people I'm working for. Call it due diligence."

"Just because you've built a name for yourself sticking your nose where it doesn't belong doesn't give you the right to spy on us."

"Buddy, the reason I'm so good at what I do is that most people don't ever learn my name, let alone get direct access."

"Lucky me."

"Yes. Exactly. Glad we see eye to eye on this subject. Now we know she was in Dublin three days ago."

"She could be anywhere by now—"

"I'm working on tracking her whereabouts after that, but we have a jumping-off point. I'll be in touch."

"Wait a goddamn minute, you fucking bastard—"

He'd already hung up.

A steady stream of curses left my lips as I stalked back toward the house, intent on filling the others in on what I'd just learned. Before I could go in, I was brought up short, angling away from the front doors and rounding toward the yard on the other side when the faint sounds of a scuffle reached my ears. *Kingston and Alek must still be sparring.*

But my frustration shifted to unease as the sound of their practice grew louder, more frantic. Something wasn't right. That wasn't a friendly match.

I blurred closer, hoping against hope I was overreacting. That it was simply training, as they had been doing every night since we arrived. But soon the scent of blood filled the air, and the low growl of a wolf on the edge of the change made the hairs on the back of my neck rise.

"Viking, I need a bow!"

My sister's strident voice made my blood run cold. Rosie wasn't a fighter—until she needed to be.

Panic gave me an extra burst of speed, and I finally rounded the corner only to be met with utter chaos.

At least ten fae warriors swarmed the grounds. Alek was in full berserker mode, bodily ripping the one in front of him apart. His eyes were black orbs in his blood-soaked face. Kingston had shifted and was taking down another. Rosie, having found high ground, already pinned several others to the earth by loosing arrows with supernatural speed and precision. As I approached, she notched yet another arrow and let it fly, the deadly shot landing in the eye socket of a fae on the edge of our property.

A flare of pride barely had a chance to swell when I spotted the assassin heading toward her.

"Rosie!" I shouted, running full tilt toward her. As he brought down the blade meant to deal a killing blow, I crashed into her, taking the brunt of the attack.

Agony ripped through my shoulder as the silver met skin, but it wasn't a mortal wound. "That was your first mistake, mate," I growled, gripping him by the wrist until bones crunched under the force of my hand. "And it will be your last."

"Master Blackthorne—" Martin's inquiry was cut off as he peeked his head out the French doors and took in the carnage.

"Get my father," I shouted, dealing with my sister's would-be murderer.

As I pulled him closer and my fangs descended, he seemed to recognize death had come for him. The knowing was there in the dilation of his pupils. The soft draw of his breath. The racing terror of his pulse. It had been so long since I'd let my monstrous side come out and play. I grinned, my smile cruel and cold.

"One last look before I send you to hell. Let my family home be the last thing you see and the Blackthorne name be your final thought."

"P–please, d–don't. Please spare me."

Oh, how I loved it when they begged. "Hmm, I think not."

"Stop playing with your food and finish it, Noah," my sister snapped, notching her last arrow.

"Gladly."

Yanking the fae's head back, I brutally sank my fangs into his throat, employing none of my usual finesse. I wanted it to hurt. I wanted his last moments to be spent in fear and pain.

Once the frantic flutter of his pulse stopped and I'd drained him dry, I released his corpse, which fell to my feet with a familiar thud. My monster had missed his freedom.

Gaze sharpened from a fresh feeding, I took stock of the battle around me. A scant few remained alive, though two were missing extremities and wouldn't be long for this world. Kingston and Alek both stood covered in fae blood. My sister's arrows littered the bodies on the ground, and the one fae still standing tried to flee.

My father burst through the doors, eyes glowing, fangs on full view as he assessed the threat to his family. In one instant, he was in front of the running assailant, his hand around the man's throat.

"My, my, this didn't quite go to your plan, now did it?" He cocked his head and tutted at the fae. "Pity for you. But thank you for your service to the Blackthorne crown."

The man clawed at my father's fingers, trying to dislodge his hold. "I only serve my queen."

With a heavy sigh, Father tightened his grip until the fae turned purple. "Not anymore. Why are you here?"

"The . . . child . . . we . . ."

Kingston's wolf let out a growl that rattled my bones. If my father hadn't already claimed the fae bastard, Kingston would have ripped him in two.

"Oh, you thought you'd come take care of her, did you? Arrogant. So typically fae. No one touches my family and lives." But my father didn't kill him. Instead, he squeezed until the assassin lost consciousness and dropped him to the ground. "Martin!"

When our butler stuck his head through the open door, Father simply said, "Dungeon. We haven't had a fae donor in far too long. Make it last."

"Right away, sir."

Martin tossed the limp body over his shoulder as if he weighed nothing more than a sack of flour and disappeared back into the house.

"It seems this meeting cannot come fast enough," my father mused, looking somber now that the attack was over.

Well, almost over.

One of Alek's downed attackers let out a pitiful moan, and the berserker gazed down at him, ice-cold and unfeeling, before bringing his foot down on the poor bastard's face and putting him out of his misery.

I shuddered. Sometimes I forgot how terrifying we could be when given the proper incentive.

"Do you think your society knew about this?" Kingston asked, his voice retaining the gravel of his beast.

"No. They would never sanction such an attack. This is the work of an individual acting alone."

"Who?" Alek growled, death in his eyes.

"The Shadow Queen."

"Great, just what we need, more dramatic enemies," Kingston groused. "How many does that make now?"

"Why would the fae care about Sunday?" I asked, adrenaline still raging from the battle as I forced myself to ignore Kingston's jeer.

"Our realms are like two trees whose roots share the same soil. Faerie and Earth are so closely intertwined that if one dies, so too does the other."

"Like mates," Rosie breathed.

"Exactly."

"So this was just the beginning," Alek murmured.

"Well, I know what lengths I would go to save my mate. It stands to reason they will stop at nothing." I clenched my jaw as my words hung in the air.

Alek grunted, flickers of lightning shimmering in his black gaze. "We have to find her. Put a stop to this before they do."

"Don't forget that they aren't the only ones hunting her. The

Council will not cease its search either. More will come for her." My father's tone was deadly serious.

For once, Kingston's reply lacked a sarcastic bite. He sounded unexpectedly optimistic as he said, "You heard that guy. He still thought Sunday was with us. The only thing we have going for us is that no one realizes she's gone yet. At least if they focus their attacks here, we know she's safe somewhere out there."

"In what world do you think Sunday should be without us? Who knows what Caleb is doing with her? It's surely not what a mate should do for his partner. He's taken her against her will, hidden her from us, and if the Society's plot holds water, he's going to kill our child. You can't possibly think—"

"Whoa, slow down, Thorne. I never said anything about thinking she was better off on her own. Only that our enemies' ignorance is our advantage. We could use a silver lining right about now. That's all I was trying to do."

I clamped my mouth shut.

"He's right, son. We keep up the guise of protecting your mate until we know where to find her. Blackthorne Manor is well equipped to handle any foe. I'll talk to Knight and Logan, collect our army, and guard the walls. Let them come for us. We will welcome them with death."

"And in the meantime?" Alek asked.

"We go on as planned," I said, feeling calmer than I had in a long while. "We go to the meeting tomorrow night, and we find our way back to Sunday."

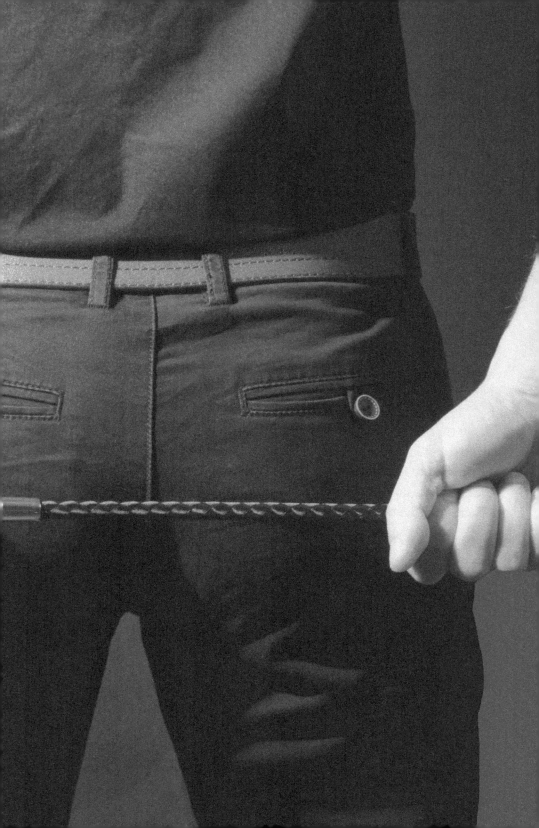

# CHAPTER
# FOURTEEN
## KINGSTON

"Why are we standing outside *Iniquity*, your royal leechness?" I almost laughed at my own joke, but Cashel wasn't amused.

"Because it's a sanctuary. If that word is too advanced for you, allow me to explain. Sanctuary means it offers certain neutrality and protections unavailable elsewhere." The look he speared me with was dripping with disdain. As if I should know something so obvious. Which I did, but I just thought of this place as a sex club. Its political uses were barely more than an afterthought.

"Brings a whole new meaning to the phrase safe sex." Alek's rumbled chuckle had a niggle of jealousy worming its way through my head. I was the funny one. Not him.

"Come along, children," Cashel said with the air of an ever-suffering parent.

"Your dad looks like he needs to get laid, Thorne."

The vampire prince had me shoved up against the wall before I was finished speaking.

"Don't."

Cashel cut me a glance. "You're not wrong."

Thorne shuddered. "Stop. I beg you."

"Your mother is a beautiful cre—"

"No. God, please."

I shook with laughter beneath his hold, loving every second of his tormented expression. No one enjoyed thinking about their parents bumping uglies. I could almost pity the poor bastard if I wasn't so entertained by his suffering.

"Bloody hell, are you lot coming in or not? I'm not a doorstop." A smooth British voice filtered from the open doorway, annoyance clear in his tone.

As one, our heads turned in his direction. "And who the hell are you?" I asked, not recognizing the fae man who absolutely radiated coiled power.

And call me crazy, but I didn't exactly trust the faerie bastards right now. And this guy? He oozed danger. My wolf paced, desperate for me to let him free so he could neutralize the threat in front of us. But I pushed him back, forcing my animalistic side to come to heel. It wouldn't get a damn thing done if I went into the meeting covered in fae blood with a body count trailing behind me.

"He's my pet," Lilith purred from the darkness behind the dark-haired fae, her hand curling around to press against his chest. "You may call him Rufus. It's his new name this week."

"That is not my name." His silver eyes flashed a dangerous gray.

I flicked my gaze to Alek, who was unusually tense and staring at the man with a suspicious gleam in his eyes. We'd come back to *that* later.

She tugged on a thin gold chain that hung from her wrist connecting to the collar around Rufus's throat. Hmm, kinky. That tracked.

"It is if I say it is."

He growled, and the sound was echoed by ominous thunder rolling through the clouds above.

"Temper. Temper. You know what happens to naughty boys."

I had to palm my growing erection. Fuck, but that succubus

knew how to turn it on. I wasn't interested in her one bit, but there was no way to deny her power. From the look on her toy's face, he agreed with me.

"I didn't realize you had a faerie kink, Lil. But where are the wings, Tinkerbell?"

Rufus bared his teeth, his eyes narrowed and brimming with disdain.

"Jesus, Kingston," Thorne muttered. "Do you never bloody learn?"

"Lil-ith, pup. No one calls me Lil and lives. I'll give you a pass this once because you're so cute."

Fuck. She was scary too. It was easy to forget she was the original demon, her true age and the extent of her power unknown. I needed to remember to tread more carefully around her. Too bad my mouth didn't seem to get the memo.

"So did you enslave him for his pixie dust? You got your happy thoughts on standby so he can help you fly?"

Rufus snorted. "I'm not a pixie, you dolt. I'm fae roya—"

Lilith stopped him with a swift kick to his shin. "He's my problem, not yours. What I do with him is of no matter to you, Kingston. Now follow me. There's a meeting specially gathered at the request of Blackthorne. That can only mean one thing. It's time for the truth to be told."

That statement sat between us all, a bomb about to detonate. What more was there? The Apocalypse was pretty fucking big.

Dread was a goddamned rock in my gut as I followed behind Lilith and her pet. She took us to the bowels of *Iniquity*, down a darkened set of stairs to a hallway I'd never seen before. Just how big was this fucking club?

"You will be quiet when you enter, or you answer to me."

Her tone was stern, and I almost instinctively responded with a soft, "Yes, Mommy," but stopped myself. Especially when I realized she was talking to Rufus.

"What can you possibly do to me that you haven't already?"

"Oh, you sweet summer child, I have all manner of wicked delights in store for you. We've barely scratched the surface."

There was an almost inaudible growl, followed by Lilith's tinkling laughter.

"Stop acting like you aren't living for every moment of being owned by me, Prince. You know what you stand to gain. Serve your sentence like a good boy, and then you'll have everything you need."

I wasn't so sure we should be here for this, but damn, did I want to keep watching.

"Why is this so hot?" Alek whispered in my ear.

"Because she's a succubus." In four words, Cashel proved just how sharp vampire hearing was. "Everything she does is with seduction in mind. She's feeding on all of us right now."

Lilith let out that bell-like laugh again. "You got me. But you're just such easy prey. Especially since most of you are pent up and in need of release. How sad that your little mate is missing. Let's see what we can do to help ease your pain, shall we? I could send you each one of my girls after the meeting. Kingston, we have a few new brunettes who resemble her well enough."

My wolf growled, low and deep, the sound bouncing off the walls.

"I'll take that as a no." She winked, then waved a hand in front of the double doors, her blood-red nails looking more like claws than they had a right to.

A flash of those talons raking down her pet's back and leaving bright red marks on his skin hit me hard. She must've sent that thought to the rest of them as well because every man in our group reacted. Their sharp grunts of surprise mirrored my own.

"Can you please shut that off? I really don't think it's appropriate to walk into a meeting this serious with a raging erection." Thorne snapped, his voice edged with tension.

She pouted, batting her long lashes at us. "Spoilsport. Just like your daddy."

"We're mated men, Lilith," Cashel said, clearly annoyed. "Play your tricks elsewhere. We do not belong to you."

"That doesn't mean you're dead."

"Technically . . ." I didn't finish my sentence because the vampires in our group weren't amused by my badly timed joke. "Jeez, I was just trying to lighten this shit up a little."

"Not now," Thorne bit out. "Are you going to let us in or continue to sexually assault us with your mind?"

Lilith's pouty lips fell open, and then her eyes flashed with anger so intense my wolf cowered. "I take consent *very* seriously, Blackthorne. You know the rules of my club. When you walk through its doors, you provide your consent for me to feed. If you don't like it, go elsewhere. But do not, under any circumstances, accuse me of taking advantage."

Rufus snickered. "Idiots."

She jerked the chain around his collar. "Quiet."

"Yes, Mistress."

The doors opened, revealing—surprise, surprise—another dark room. This place needed a good electrician to help install more lights. Fuck.

"Go ahead, boys. We'll be in shortly."

"Oh, goody," Rufus muttered, leaning against a wall with his arms crossed as we filed past.

"So pouty. It's adorable." She reached out and squeezed his cheeks before licking the tip of his nose. "I do so love a brat prince."

I had to force myself to step inside the room before I did something foolish like stay and watch her work. I wanted to take notes for Sunday so we could reenact the scene later. Maybe I could ask Lilith for some suggestions . . .

*No. Focus, Kingston.*

Shaking myself, I practically jumped across the threshold, my steps a little uncoordinated as I broke through the lusty spell she'd been weaving.

My gaze raked the large space, walls free of all adornments, nothing like what I'd have expected from Lilith. She screamed of leather and lace. Rich fabrics and darkness. Not concrete and bare-bulbed light fixtures. But here we were. There was also a suspicious drain in the floor. I shuddered. What kinds of things did they get up to in these meetings?

Some creatures filled the chairs positioned in a semi-circle, while others stood in conversation together, and another hid in the shadows.

The hair on the back of my neck stood on end when I found the familiar green gaze of my father staring at me. "Dad? What are you..."

And then I started placing the other faces. Tor and—

I growled when I recognized the gray-haired man seated by himself. "Fallon."

"Leash your mutt, Ronin. Before I put him down," Niall Fallon snarled.

"He's petulant. Can't be contained, Niall. It's why we sent him to the school in the first place." My father crossed his arms over his chest and chuckled. "Can't stand up to a pup? Are you that old?"

"There's only one way to deal with a petulant child. You should have locked him up until he learned his lesson."

"Like you did with Sunday?" I snapped, lunging forward without conscious thought.

I was brought up short. Thorne's hand fisted in the back of my shirt as he reeled me in with one sharp tug. Fucking vampire strength.

"Let me go."

"This is not the time or place. We'll deal with him. But not today."

I jerked out of his hold, huffing out my frustration, shooting daggers and whatever other weapons I could from my eyes as I stalked along the back of the chairs, seeking one as far away from that prick as possible.

"Brother?" Alek's question drew my focus to Tor, sitting in a chair, regal as if he was the King of fucking . . . well, Novasgard.

"Father sent me in his stead. I'm as clueless about this as you are. One moment I was rolling in the sheets with a valkyrie, the next, I had a summons to this place."

"Great. You'll be so fucking useful," I muttered.

"Oh, good, I see introductions are underway." Lilith peered around the room as if she was counting heads on a school bus. "Farrell, Fallon, Nordson, Blackthorne . . . all the in-laws in one place. All we're missing is the bride, and it could be a wedding."

"Enough, Lilith." A tall biker dude with a face way too pretty for the clothes he wore stepped out of the shadows. The light reflecting off his golden hair made it look like he had a freaking halo.

"Always ruining my fun, Gabriel. Bloody angels are such downers."

I stiffened. *Angels?* Motherfucker, this really was apocalyptic shit. I don't know what I expected, but it wasn't coming face to face with one of the winged fucks. Who and what were the rest of these people? Because not one of them was human.

"Can we get to the blessed point, please? I have a full moon ritual to prepare for with my coven, and this meeting was *not* on my calendar." An older woman with steel gray hair and eyes I knew glared at me. Her name hit me before I could stop the thought. *Belladonna.* She had to be Moira's relative. The closer I looked, the more she resembled the little witch.

The last figure remaining in the shadows emerged, and my gut churned in response. Professor Sinistra, meek and soft-spoken but eerie as fuck, stared at us. "We are waiting for Antoinette. Then we may begin."

Antoinette? "Wait, the headmistress?"

"Of course."

We were closely connected to nearly every person in this damned Society. They'd been pulling the strings all along. Manipulating things so we'd all end up together.

Those motherfuckers were playing with us like we were no more than pawns on a chessboard.

"You're all in on it." My accusation was a harsh growl, the need to shift burning through my veins. My eyes found my father. "All of you."

"And the penny finally drops. These boys are thick-skulled, aren't they?" Rufus said, his voice snide.

"How long has this been going on?" Alek asked, completely ignoring Lilith's pet.

"Long before you were born," Gabriel's smooth voice didn't hold any hint of his emotions. He was unaffected by all of it.

"But why?" Thorne asked.

"We didn't know which of you would fulfill the prophecy. Little did we realize it would be *all* of you. Father always does work in mysterious ways."

"Magical baby batter. Who knew the Apocalypse would be started by a gang bang?" If someone didn't shut that fae asshole up, I was going to do it.

"Can you *please* keep Crombie quiet?" A tall man snapped from his position in the center of the chairs. "Surely that pact of yours allows you to muzzle him?"

The Novasgardians stiffened, their heads snapping in the direction of Lilith's plaything. "Crombie? I knew it," Alek breathed beside me.

"Father never said a word," Tor whispered to himself.

They shared a look deep with unspoken meaning. Clearly Crombie and the Novasgardians had a history. That was *another* person in this room connected to us somehow.

Rufus . . . no, Crombie snorted. "Oh, Finbar, it must be so trying to be last choice to your Shadow Queen. Are you always the end of the train? Should we call you the caboose?"

So this fucker was from the Shadow Court? I added him to my list of revenge kills. The tally was getting longer by the minute.

"Shut your mouth, or I will do it for you. Permanently."

"Promises, promises. I would love to see you try."

"Hush now, poppet," Lilith whispered, her soft command belied by the sharp yank she gave the chain. "You're here to observe. Let the important people talk."

"Waiting on me? My apologies. There were matters at the school that required my undivided attention." The headmistress swooped in from the still-open doors and breezed past us like we didn't even exist. "What's the rush? I am in the middle of a murder investigation, as you well know."

"Murder investigation? Who died?" I asked.

She looked my way with a slight lift of her brow. As if she was surprised to see me here.

*That makes two of us, lady.*

"Eugene Moriarty."

"Professor Moriarty was murdered?" Thorne's voice was filled with shock.

"Did I stutter?"

"What happened?"

"What part of the word investigation is escaping you, Mr. Blackthorne? He was found dead in the great hall. Magical foul play suspected. Honestly, if you don't even understand basic vocabulary, I have no clue how you were accepted at Ravenscroft."

"Do not speak to my son in that tone."

The headmistress sniffed. "Don't bark at me, Cashel. You're the ones who have failed in properly educating your children. I'm just filling in the gaps."

"Bloody hell, can we move this along? I know I'm not technically a member of this backwards council, but I have punishments to receive," Crombie groaned.

"The pet is right." Gabriel acknowledged Crombie with a slight nod of his head. "The reason, Cashel."

"Sunday is missing," Thorne said, answering in place of his father.

The room went still, the air thick with tension.

MEG ANNE & K. LORAINE

"What do you mean, *missing*?" Antoinette asked, her voice low.

"Now who doesn't understand basic vocabulary?" I asked.

She glared at me.

"The priest took her," Alek added.

"Caleb is involved in this?" Gabriel said, looking thoughtful. "Then I don't see the problem. All is going according to plan."

"Plan? What fucking plan?" I was going to murder someone, and there wouldn't be a need for any goddamned investigation.

"Stop the Apocalypse. You know this already," Thorne muttered.

"Oh, you mean that stupid idea you all have to kill an innocent baby?"

My dad stood and glared at me. "It's not a child, Kingston. It's the end of the world."

Hurt stabbed me in the chest. "What are you talking about? You saw the ultrasound. There was a baby. Heart beating, little tiny arms moving. Sure, she looked more like a tadpole than a person, but she was there."

"Evil can take many forms, son."

"That's my fucking child you're talking about. Not some name-less, faceless being."

"No, Kingston. You need to stop thinking about it like it's a real child."

"Maybe you need to *start* thinking about your real child. How could you be part of something that would do this to me? To my mate?"

"Because you're not my only fucking child. I am responsible for an entire pack. Start thinking like an Alpha, and stop thinking with your dick. This is so much bigger than one person."

"She's *my* person."

"Ours," Thorne said, stepping up to my side.

"Yes, ours." Alek took up position on my right.

"Fools. The lot of you," the headmistress grumbled. "It doesn't matter because the damned priest has her, and if he doesn't do his job, the world ends. From the way he looks at her, I'd say it's highly likely we're all doomed."

"Isn't it your job to give us a heads up about these sorts of things?" Finbar snapped at Professor Sinistra.

"Fate speaks as she wills. I cannot control what I See. You know this."

"Some Seer you are. What good are you if you can't enlighten us? I could've locked her up and thrown away the key when they came to visit." My dad's snide voice sent my temper spiking.

"Pot, meet kettle. You're not doing a very good job with your titles either." I couldn't keep the words from leaving my lips.

"What the hell is that supposed to mean?"

"You know exactly what it means, *Dad.*"

"We need to find Caleb so we can get to Sunday." Thorne stepped forward, his hands balled into tight fists.

"Why would we help you if Caleb already has her and will see out our plan? Gabriel, you're confident he will follow through?" The witch cast her gaze on the . . . fucking biker angel.

He shook his head. "He has free will, Blaire. His connection to Sunday is stronger than any of us thought possible. He knows what hangs in the balance."

"Would he really choose his dick over his soul?"

Crombie snorted. "Why wouldn't he?"

Blaire rolled her eyes. "Men."

"Is there any possibility this child isn't the bringer of end times?" Tor asked, surprising us all with the intensity of his question. It was impossible to know whose side he was on as he demanded an answer from the Seer.

"No."

The lone word was damning. But I refused to believe it. No matter who or what she was.

"*That* you're certain of, but nothing else. What a gift you have, Seer." Niall Fallon's voice was mocking and just as cutting as my father's had been.

She went still. "If you're going to keep insisting on belittling me, perhaps you'd prefer to weather the storm without me." She swept out of the room without a backward glance.

Antoinette moved to follow her, but Gabriel gave a jerk of his chin. "Leave her. I'll deal with her later."

Blaire let out a heavy sigh. "If there's a possibility Caleb won't go through with the ritual, we have to try and find Sunday. The rest can be sorted out once that is done."

"So how do we do that? Moira already tried." I hated the tightness in my throat.

"She did?" Blaire's eyes flashed with concern. "Is she all right?"

"She's fine. Safe back at Blackthorne Manor," Alek said. "She mentioned the spell she placed on Sunday concealing her scent must be hiding Caleb from us as well. She tried to break it but failed."

"My granddaughter always was too strong for her own good. You'll need an entire coven to pierce that veil." She nodded decisively as if reaching some sort of conclusion. "You'll come to us. Bring Moira and that friend of hers. We'll see what we can do after our ritual is complete."

I nodded, knowing the others would agree to a fragile truce between the Society and us. Once we found Sunday, however, all bets were off.

"If that's all, I think I hear heaven calling." Gabriel vanished before anyone else could respond, and the room darkened just a bit. So he *was* fucking glowing.

The rest of the members dispersed slowly, trickling out of the room until it was just me, my father, and my friends.

"Give us a minute," I said, never taking my eyes off my dad.

"You sure? We can stay," Alek offered.

"This is between us."

"We'll be just outside," Thorne said, his gaze filled with understanding.

"Son, I know you think this is the worst thing that could happen, but—"

"Yeah, I fucking do. What if this was mom? One of us? Would you have killed me to stop the Apocalypse?"

He clenched his jaw. "That's not fair. You can't ask me to make a choice based on those circumstances. This isn't a real baby, son. You're being fooled. Tell me, what kind of baby is made by four fathers?"

My heart hammered, pulse roaring in my ears. "She's real."

"Maybe it's real, but it's not natural. It's the result of some kind of evil magic. I'm telling you, that *thing* you're calling a child has no soul. It's a vessel of destruction, nothing more. Would you really risk everything to protect it when the result is losing everything and everyone else you love? Me, your mama, your sisters? Your pack? You tell me I'm failing as Alpha, yet you're the one placing everything above the people you're supposed to protect. What kind of man does that make you, Kingston?"

"A better one than you."

"It makes you selfish. I'm ashamed to be your father right now."

"You're not my father. Not anymore. I renounce all claim to the Farrell pack."

He sucked in a breath. "Kingston."

"No. We're done here. I never want to see you again. You're dead to me."

I walked out of the room, my heart pounding and something that felt an awful lot like grief swirling inside my chest. I was angrier than I'd ever been, but instead of feeling any of that heat, I just felt . . . empty.

"You okay?" Thorne asked.

"I won't be okay until we get our mate back."

He nodded, placing a hand on my shoulder, stopping me before I could brush by him. He didn't say anything, just held my gaze, reading whatever he could find there. Finally he squeezed my shoulder and released me. "So let's go find her."

As we started down the hall, a sharp cry echoed ahead of us. I locked eyes with each of my companions, and we ran toward the place where the sound came from.

Rounding a corner, we found her crumpled in a pool of blood, a jewel-encrusted dagger sticking out of her chest.

The Seer was dead.

Before anyone else could speak, Crombie's cool voice filled the hallway. "Well . . . I guess she didn't see that one coming."

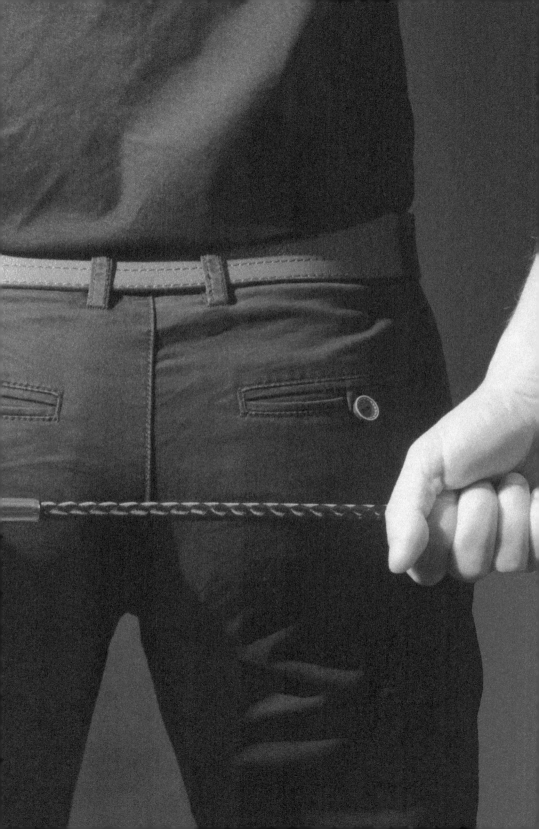

# FIFTEEN

## SUNDAY

I *can hear you muttering to yourself, you stupid kidnapping bastard.* I tightened my grip on the knife and sliced my apple in half with more force than necessary, smiling tightly at the sound of the blade hitting the butcher's block.

Caleb hadn't spoken a word to me since our little chat in the bathroom last night, and a small part of me hated the silence. The rest of me welcomed it because it was too easy to be pulled into his web. They'd all pulled me in, if I was being honest with myself.

I'd forced my thoughts away from my men as a means of self-preservation since Caleb had taken me. I'd had to. It hurt too much to let down those walls and think of the love I'd lost.

I'd been in survival mode since the second I climbed out the window at Blackthorne Manor. Focusing on each moment as it came, trying not to think too many steps ahead, because all that waited for me was an endless stretch of loneliness.

Tears pricked my eyes, which only fueled my anger. I did not want to cry over a bunch of men who had turned their backs on me. They didn't deserve it. But my heart didn't care. I missed them. All of them.

It was the scent of freshly cut apple that sent me over the edge. "Fuck you, Kingston. You and your damn pie-making skills. Of course you'd be the one to make me cry first." But even as I said the words, Alek infiltrated my memories. The wide smile on his face when I'd presented his favorite dessert to him on Thanksgiving flashed in my mind. The way he'd taken my face in his hands and kissed me until I could hardly breathe right there in front of everyone.

I couldn't stop the tidal wave of moments anymore. Noah's arms wrapped around me, holding me through the night, kissing my shoulder and the mark on my neck. Whispers of adoration and devotion that all turned out to be lies.

Even the soft murmur of Caleb's voice sweetly reciting our bedtime story when I'd been too anxious from my nightmares to fall back asleep.

All of them had duped me. Made me believe they truly loved me. That they'd always be there for me. That we belonged to each other.

*Thunk.* Another chunk of apple went flying as I cut into the ripe flesh entirely too hard. Alek would have taken over by now, his skills with a blade much better than mine. The man could peel an entire apple in one long strip, leaving a pretty curl of red skin coiled on the cutting board.

A deep ache took hold in my heart, the empty raw parts where they should still be, now finally allowed to feel the agony of losing them.

My lower lip quivered as my battle against the tears was lost. Vision blurry, I knew I should have stopped slicing the fruit, but I couldn't make myself. There was something cathartic about the slam of the blade against the board with each painful bout of memories.

The door to the bedroom opened, startling me, and the knife bit into my thumb, the burn of a fresh wound radiating through my hand and making me hiss.

"Ow. Fuck." I lifted my thumb to my lips, sucking hard to stop the bleeding.

Caleb stood transfixed in the doorway, his eyes laser-focused on the digit in my mouth. Hunger raged in his expression. How had I not noticed? He bore the classic signs I'd seen in Noah. Dark circles ringing his eyes, skin more ashen than usual, even his lips were pale. He looked . . . haggard. Starved.

And I was bleeding

A lamb at his altar.

Caleb blinked, reopening his eyes slowly. Appearing like a man lost in a dream.

"I need to hunt," he said, his words distracted. "I'll be back before sunrise."

I stared at him, not sure what to say. Happy hunting seemed inappropriate. Enjoy the mindless slaughter of animals? Too rude. Before I could come up with anything to break the swelling silence between us, he was gone. Leaving me alone with my thoughts and poor mutilated apple.

I frowned down at the terribly sliced pieces of fruit that were supposed to serve as a midnight snack. One blood-stained, the others strewn across the counter. Now I wasn't even hungry. I was heartsick.

If Moira was here, she'd witch up some of her special tea and magic us some ice cream. But she wasn't. No one was. I was well and truly alone.

Just like I would always be.

I might as well sit down and write a farewell letter while wearing all black and staring morosely out the window.

Sighing, I shook my head as I pictured my favorite angsty teenager, Lydia Deetz from *Beetlejuice*. That girl was my emo soul sister when I was twelve.

"Yet another pop culture reference that would leave you scratching your head, Noah," I grumbled.

Fuck. Now I was talking to them even when they weren't here. I had to get out of this place. It was making me a victim. And Sunday Fallon wasn't anyone's goddamned victim.

If Kingston were here, I knew what he'd say. "All right, Sunshine.

So do something about it. If you don't want to catch a case of Stockholm's, you need to get your pretty ass off this island."

My imitation paled compared to his sexy voice, but it was the best I could do.

"I've done all I can. There's no way off until the boat comes, and Caleb won't let me go."

"Have you really, dove? Have you planned out your escape? How will you get away from him once the boat comes? Do you have a bag packed to take with you? Supplies to last until you reach your new sanctuary? Escape is only the first part of a plan."

Wow, my British accent wasn't so bad. If I changed my name and identity when I got free of Caleb, maybe I'd do the same for my accent.

"Bag. Right. Pack a bag. Fuck. I need money. And maybe a phone. Does Caleb even have a phone?"

"He must have something on hand. He's sneaky, not stupid. Find it. Tear up the floorboards if you have to, Sunny. He's hidden it away, and you need everything you can find to get you away from him."

I didn't quite match Alek's Novasgardian accent, but there was no one here to judge me, so we were going with it.

There was something about pretending they were here, that we were doing this together, that soothed the jagged pieces of my broken heart.

"You won't be getting away from me, my darling. I'll find you. I'll hunt you down to the ends of the earth and make you mine. You'll beg for my palm on your arse after I get you back."

"Shut up, Caleb. You're not invited to this party."

"You'll have to kill me if you want to truly escape."

*Fuck.*

I'd wandered into the living room while participating in this little tea party with my imaginary friends. They'd had some good ideas.

Searching the house.

Checking for anything Caleb might be keeping from me.

Killing him.

*Thanks for the suggestion, Father Gallagher.*

The thought of killing Caleb didn't sit quite as easily as it had the first time it came to me. Probably because I knew now that we were talking about the permanent kind of death. I couldn't just break his neck and risk him coming back before I made it off the island. I needed to end him. Forever.

Sooner rather than later. Because if last night proved anything, it was just how weak I was against him. Caleb was temptation itself.

The baby rolled in my belly, giving me a sharp jab in the ribs with her elbow—or was that a foot? But that was all it took to remind me of the stakes. This wasn't just my freedom. It was my future.

I glanced at the clock, noting two hours had passed since Caleb left. I didn't know how long it would take him to hunt, but if I was going to get ready to escape him, I had to take the advice of my imaginary boyfriends. Pack a bag. Prepare myself to run. Kill Caleb.

A sick twist of guilt gripped my stomach, but I pushed it aside. Painful? Yes. But it was my only way to break free. If the choice was between my daughter and the men I loved, it would be her every time. There was no choice. I could live with a broken heart. I couldn't live without her.

Over the next two and a half hours, I'd managed to pry up some floorboards and hide a packed bag, easily covering my work with the rug in the living room. Unless Caleb inspected underneath the carpet, he'd have no idea. If he was still alive to take a good look. Now I was outside, roaming the grounds in search of anything I could use to help me take the last step toward escape.

I knelt by the wood and wire fence around the garden, wondering if the post might make a good stake, when I caught something out of the corner of my eye. Boards, mostly covered by rogue weeds, leaning against the back of the house.

It only took a second for my brain to register their use. They were to cover the windows during a storm.

That's when the first flickers of a plan sparked to life in my mind.

I didn't need a stake. And honestly, if I had to get close to him, I knew I'd fail. If Caleb looked into my eyes when I was driving a stake through his heart, I wouldn't be able to go through with it. But there was one surefire way to deal with all made vampires, and it didn't require me to do a damn thing.

The sun.

I just needed to make certain Caleb was stuck outside once the sun came up. These little beauties would ensure he couldn't just break a window and crawl in. And I could easily push furniture in front of the door and pray he wasn't strong enough to breach my protections.

My chest tightened with anxiety at the thought of what I was plotting, but when it was all said and done, I didn't have any other options. He'd taken them all away the moment he agreed to go through with this.

"Yeah, Caleb. This is all your fault," I muttered to my imaginary captor.

"Aye, *a stor*. It doesn't make you any less of a killer."

"Well, you should have thought about that before you brought me to murder island, you psychopath."

"What's the saying? It takes one to know one?"

"Sure. Make fun of the girl who's talking to herself to stay sane. Nice move."

"You're the one talking for me. You're doing it to yourself."

"Go sit on a cactus, Caleb."

Jesus, I was losing it. "Get it together, Fallon. We have work to do."

I was careful not to leave drag marks as I brought the panels inside. It didn't take me long, and bonus, Caleb wouldn't have any heads up about my betrayal. I winced but didn't stop. The train had left the station. This was happening.

The boards fit perfectly in the windows, and when I found a stack of 2x4s stored in a closet, custom cut to fit in the brackets on either side of each window, I let out a sigh of relief. The extra barricading would help keep him out. Hopefully long enough.

Once that was done, I took a deep breath and stared at the door, eyeing it like a monster was about to jump out and bite me.

*Are you really doing this?* The question was a nervous whisper in my mind. The part of me that looked at Caleb and saw only the man I loved. The part that couldn't imagine a life without him. But on the heels of that uncertainty came the reminder that he'd brought me here for one reason. And it wasn't to live happily ever after.

"It's her or him, Sunday."

Steeling my shoulders, I took the few steps forward and slid the lock into place. The heavy click sent a shiver down my spine.

"And now we wait."

# CHAPTER
# SIXTEEN
## CALEB

C ome to an isolated island with no fecking animals to feed on, Caleb. Bloody brilliant.

I'd already broken my other rules, but I wouldn't break this one. It had to be animal blood. Nothing else.

Any woodland creature I found was so small the nourishment they provided was non-existent. At this rate, I'd be out here until sunrise. Not only that, I'd starve long before the child was born. I'd have to make sure blood bags were on the list of supplies for the next shipment.

I sighed. That meant I'd have to pull out my burner phone and hide my call from Sunday. I wasn't going to kid myself that she'd simply accepted her lot in life. She was plotting silently. I knew her too well to think otherwise.

*Can you blame her? She knows what you're about now. She hates you.*

My thoughts drifted to the end of my fantasy session in the shower. To the taste of her cunt. To how close I'd been to sinking my fangs into her inner thigh and feeding while she came around my fingers. Nothing would compare to the satisfaction I got when I fed from my mate.

*Fecking hell. Stop it.*

I knew my search was futile, but I couldn't bear the thought of going back to the house before sunrise and sitting in more of that damned silence. All I wanted was to hold her. To claim her over and over again until our bodies were slick with sweat and my cum was inside her. Where it fucking belonged.

But that wasn't going to happen, and the sun was close. I could feel it in the weight of my limbs and the imperceptible lightening of the sky. I couldn't hide out here forever. It was time to return.

With sluggish steps, I trudged out of the patch of forest, starving in more ways than one, and panic laced my veins. I'd waited too long. The clouds were pink tufts of candy floss. Beautiful. Deadly. The house was in sight, close enough I'd make it if I was quick. It had been decades since I'd stayed out this long, and I'd felt the burn of the sun's rays once before. I didn't want to meet it now.

I moved as fast as I was able, willing my body to the door that stood between me and safety. If I'd been stronger, well-fed at the very least, the drain wouldn't be nearly as bad. But my propensity for self-flagellation and punishment had gotten the better of me this time. I was a fool to think it somehow made me stronger to fight the urge to feed, to bring myself to the brink of collapse so I could stay awake during the daylight hours with Sunday. That wasn't strength. That was stupidity.

What was my abstinence proving? That I was a bloody idiot. That's what.

My skin buzzed with the first brush of the sun's rays. Huffing out a relieved breath, I reached for the knob and twisted.

It didn't budge.

I blinked at it in my sun-dazed stupor, not registering that it was locked. I shoved again, but the fecking thing wouldn't move.

She'd locked it? Why? For protection, most likely, but I was the only one who'd ever dare to come inside.

"Sunday," I said, as loud as I could. "Sunday, let me in, love."

She didn't respond, but I could feel her. My heart beat with hers.

"Please, *a stor*. I need to come inside."

Still no answer.

Pulling every ounce of strength I had left, I went to the window, thinking to open it and climb inside to the safety of the dark. The move brought me into direct range of the sun, and the sizzle of my burning skin made me cringe against the pain. Not even my clothing offered protection.

"Feck. Sunday, please." I wasn't above begging. Not if it meant surviving to have her in my arms again. I slammed my fist against the glass, but it was a pathetic blow at best, barely rattling the panes. I was as weak as a newborn colt. The sun drained me exponentially faster with each second I stood outside.

It wasn't until I made out her muffled whimper that I realized this was intentional.

She'd locked me out on purpose. She meant to kill me.

"Don't do this, *a stor*. You don't want me to die. Not even with how much you hate me now."

I was so fecking weak as I crawled to the stoop and crouched in what little shade the roof offered. "Please, darling. I'm at the door. Let me in."

It wouldn't matter soon. This house bore the brunt of direct sunlight. It was why my da had chosen this location. Good for crops and warmth. My mam always said she wanted every window to have light streaming in because the sun was good for the soul.

A bitter laugh escaped at the irony of it all. Good for the soul, terrible for the soulless.

Sunday wasn't going to come to my aid. And why would she? I'd betrayed her. I deserved this. I just hoped someone found her and cared for her. The rest of her men, perhaps. She needed looking after even if she wouldn't admit it.

For the first time in almost a century, I watched the sun take its place in the sky, and when the harsh beam of light finally reached me, I closed my eyes and whispered one final prayer.

"Sunday."

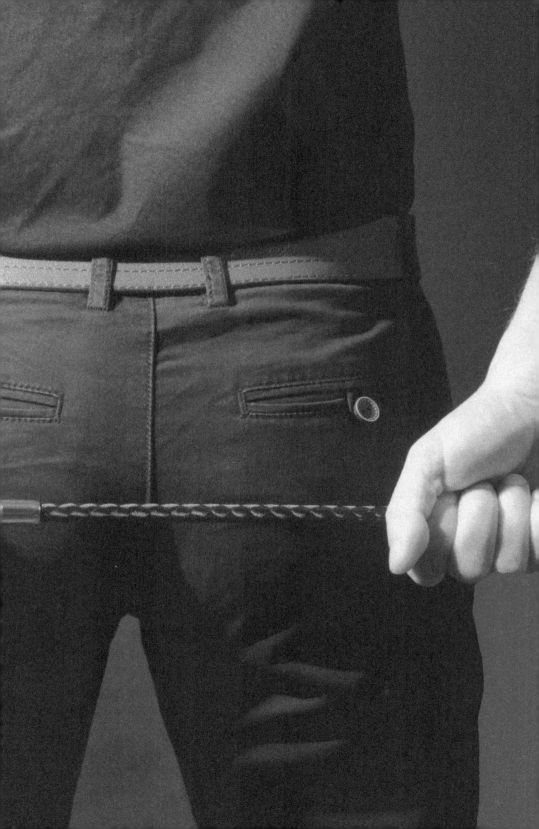

# CHAPTER
# SEVENTEEN
## SUNDAY

The instant the doorknob rattled, my blood ran cold. The urge to go to him, save him from this fate, keep him close even though he wanted to do the worst, hummed in every single cell. I took a few stumbling steps backward until I collided with the wall and slid down, curling my arms around my knees and ducking my head.

I knew it was going to be hard, but I hadn't been prepared for the way my very heart seemed to rebel against what was happening.

The wood shuddered as he shoved against the bolted entrance.

"Sunday. Sunday, let me in, love." His voice was rough, tired, and pained.

I bit down on my lip, swallowing back my reply as I fought against the soul-deep instinct to obey.

"Please, *a stor*. I need to come inside."

I could make out his footsteps as he moved away from the door and went to the window. My heart was a restless bird in its cage, fluttering against my ribs, begging me to put a stop to this. To keep him safe.

"Feck. Sunday, please." He was desperate now. Pleading. I'd

never heard him this vulnerable. Caleb was the strong one. My port in the storm. And I was his siren. But right now he was destroying me every bit as much as I was him.

I couldn't stop myself from letting out a whimper as I dropped my head and gripped my hair at the root, tugging to help me focus on the pain in my scalp rather than the ache his pleas shot through me.

"Don't do this, *a stor*. You don't want me to die. Not even with how much you hate me now."

A tear slid down my cheek as I glanced up at the clock, at the second hand slowly moving.

Tick.

Tick.

Tick.

It wouldn't be long now. It would be terrible and I'd never get over this, but I had to be brave.

"Please, darling. I'm at the door. Let me in."

I was crying openly now. Hating myself and him and God—especially God—for putting us in this situation. When I'd been the one begging, he hadn't budged. Still, I couldn't keep myself from straightening and tentatively walking toward the door. Reaching it, I pressed my palm flat against the wood, wishing it was him instead.

*You're doing it for baby Emilia*, I reminded myself. *So that she has a chance to live and be free.* But even that excuse was falling flat. How was this any different from what Caleb was doing? I couldn't sink to his level. I couldn't be the monster in this story. There had to be a different way. One that would save us all.

The soft slide of his form down the front door was like a nail in my heart. But then he whispered an almost prayerful, "Sunday."

I couldn't do it.

A sob stuck in my throat, my stomach churning with guilt and grief and fear I was too late. I lifted the barricade from the door and threw back the lock. He fell inside the instant I opened it, skin an angry red, smoke rising from his too-still form in ominous curls.

"Caleb?"

He shuddered, and instant relief washed over me. "Shut . . . the fecking . . . door," he rasped.

I grasped him beneath his shoulders and dragged him back, pulling an agonized groan from him as he slid against the hardwood floor. Then I jumped up as quickly as my pregnant form allowed and slammed the door closed, locking it again for good measure. As if that could somehow undo the damage I'd helped to cause.

"Caleb . . ."

"You . . . tried . . . to kill . . ." His labored words were barely audible, his body going limp as his eyes rolled back in his head.

Oh, God. Was I too late? He should be healing, shouldn't he? Dropping to my knees beside him and his still smoldering clothes, I gingerly touched his shoulder, one unmarred spot on an otherwise burned exterior. I hated the sight of the deep burns covering him where his shirt had already caught fire before I opened the door.

"Why aren't you healing? You should be getting better."

His lips moved, but no sound came out. I leaned close, resting my ear above his mouth, only just catching his thready, "Forgive me."

Those two words unraveled the last of any resentment buried inside of me. This was *my* Caleb.

I knew what he needed. I'd given it to him before when he'd hovered on the brink of death. Blood.

Instead of wasting time to go grab a knife, I called on my wolf and shifted as much as my pregnancy allowed. My nails sharpened into claws.

"For once in your damn life, don't you dare argue."

Then I slid the deadly tip of my claw along the mark he'd given me, barely feeling the pain as blood welled to the surface.

"Drink, Caleb. Drink and live. For me. You have to live."

Any protest he might have had was lost as my blood flowed into his mouth. I could feel the feather-soft touch of his lips moving against my neck and then the shuddering exhale of his breath as he gave in. When his hand fisted in my hair and held me in place, I nearly wept with relief.

He let out a groan before sinking his fangs into my throat and tightening his hold, feeding from me in deep pulls.

"I'm sorry. I'm so sorry."

Another rough grunt came from him, and pleasure began tingling in my core. God, I hadn't felt this in so long, that nearly orgasmic experience of a mate bond during feeding. I could feel his pleasure spurring on mine, a dull throb pulsing between my thighs. I knew if I reached down, I'd find him equally needy.

"God, Caleb." I was nothing more than moans and sighs, and he'd barely touched me. But our bond, that mark, it was just further proof I'd never have been able to go through with my plan.

He lifted his other hand and wrapped his arm around me, his large palm pressing between my shoulder blades, holding me tight to him. Then he sat up, still latched to my throat. It seemed so effortless, but only moments ago he'd been a wreck of a man. I don't know how he did it, but in one smooth movement, we'd traded places and I was on the floor, his broad frame caging me under him.

He licked my wound, lapping up the last of my blood as he sealed it. The soft kiss he pressed to my neck had shivers of pleasure racing straight to my clit. And I moaned like a cat in heat as he rocked his hard length against my pussy. Pulling back slightly, he cupped my cheeks in his hands, one of his thumbs dragging over my bottom lip and pressing into my mouth.

"Tell me what you need."

I rolled my hips up, searching for him again. "You know what I need."

"Tell. Me." His hard stare shot arousal through me.

"I need my Daddy. I need to know I'm still your good girl."

His eyes darkened with desire, the stain of my blood painting his lips red. He looked feral. Dangerous. "Oh, but you're not my good girl, are you? You've been very, very naughty. You tried to kill me."

Somehow he made the words sound like sex instead of the condemnation they were. Like he was proud I could be so brazen.

"I let you inside, didn't I?"

"Aye, that you did, my wee darling. And for that, I'll give you one special request before I punish you."

"Fuck, Caleb."

His wicked smirk had me whimpering.

"Is that what you're wanting, then?"

"I want you to own me." I needed the balance between us restored. I needed to know he still wanted—loved—me despite what I'd done.

"Give me your safe word, Miss Fallon. Because you'll be telling me to stop when you don't mean it before I'm through."

*Oh. Shit.* The fact that he was asking now, after everything we've already done, told me just how intense this was going to be. It only made me wetter.

I licked my lips, the tip of my tongue sliding over his finger. "Rosary."

He sucked in a sharp breath, his eyes widening before a sexy smirk curled his lips. "You've always been a dirty heathen."

"And you a terrible priest."

"I'm not a priest, Miss Fallon. I'm your professor."

That did *things* to me.

"And here I thought you were my *confessor.*"

He leaned down, his lips hovering over mine. "That too. I know all your sins, darling one. And I'm going to make you pay for each and every one. Starting now. When I'm done, there's not a part of you I won't have claimed. I will own all of you."

"Please, Daddy. Take me."

He backed away, and my body mourned the loss of his. As he got to his feet, I saw the pristine skin through his tattered clothing. He was fully healed. By me. Right there in the living room, he shed his clothes, cock hard and jutting forward, begging for me to touch and taste.

"On your knees for me, Miss Fallon."

I moved into position, my knees already aching with the memory of the first time I'd done this for him. Ninety minutes of his dominance left my cunt wet and aching.

"What is it about the sight of me on my knees that gets you so hard, Father Gallagher?" I hit the G hard, purposely mispronouncing his name.

His eyes sparked with wicked delight. "Oh, Miss Fallon. I'm going to put that smart mouth of yours to good use. Open up, and when we're done, you'll remember exactly how to say my name."

I pressed my thighs together, already eagerly anticipating all the ways he was going to keep that promise.

"Hands behind your back."

I debated not doing it, just to see how he'd react, but some resilient sense of self-preservation wouldn't let me.

"Remember, if this is too strenuous for you, use your safe word. And . . . when your mouth is full, because it will be, shake your head three times and I'll stop."

I swallowed, already anticipating the taste of him on my tongue. I wanted to be used. To know that I could push back and still be desired—still be loved—despite everything. Caleb, more than anybody else in my life, gave me the security of unconditional love. I felt safe enough with him to push every button he had, knowing in the end, he'd never stop wanting me.

My hands slid to the front of my body without my permission, resting on my thighs, and he offered me one cocked brow in response. I blinked, lowering my gaze. "Sorry, Daddy."

"Arms up," he ordered. "Now."

I did as he said, and in one quick motion, my shirt was over my head and my torso was bared to him, nipples pebbling in the cool air.

"Feck, I love it when you don't wear a bra. Those perfect tits of yours would have made me break my vows if not for your heat."

"They're bigger now. After . . ." I glanced down at my belly, afraid to say the word.

"After I filled you with a child. Aye, they are. That makes me fucking hard."

My heart stumbled. I hadn't realized I'd needed to hear him say that. That I needed someone, anyone, but especially one of my mates, to acknowledge the life we'd created as something other than an abomination.

"They're sensitive too," I whispered. "I'm pretty sure I could come just by you playing with my nipples."

"Oh? Should we test your theory, Miss Fallon?"

"I want you to fuck my tits."

His gaze returned to the swell of my pregnancy, then lifted to my eyes. "Logistics say that wouldn't work, but one day, sweetling . . . I absolutely will."

He held out a hand and waited for me to take his offered palm. "I thought you wanted me on my knees."

"I did as well, but how will I suck those pert nipples if they're so far away from my lips?"

"Good question, Father Gallagher."

He smirked and reached down, grabbing me by the waist. My arms wrapped around his shoulders as my legs followed suit around his hips. If it weren't for these pesky leggings, his dick would already be sheathed inside me. I was soaking wet, practically in heat for him.

"What are you doing?"

"Making you mine again."

"Caleb," I groaned, the sound tinged with exasperation. "I've been yours since the first time you got me on my knees."

"No, darling one. You were mine long before that."

I laughed, the sound breathless and disbelieving. I pressed my lips to the center of his tattoo. "Okay, Caleb. If you say so."

He stopped walking, his breath hitching the second my mouth touched his skin. Then with a tenderness I'd only dreamed of since we arrived, he sat on the bed and tucked my hair behind my ear before kissing my forehead.

"I got that mark the day you were born, *a stor*. You may not believe that you've always been mine, but I've been bound to you since before you drew your first breath. This mark is proof."

I traced the circles with my fingertip, then placed my hand over his chest. The insistent thump of his heart against my palm told me it was true. That the revelation cost him.

"One ring for each seal that was broken. Each a reminder that I was failing in my duty to protect you. And one in particular of my own making."

I swallowed, worried my thoughtless action had just cost us everything, but when I straightened and my eyes met his, my worry fled.

"I know now that I couldn't have prevented a single moment that came to pass. Not when we were written in the stars. We were meant to be. You and I, Sunday Fallon, were inevitable. You were my calling. And I do not regret a single second of being yours."

"And your duty?" I couldn't stop myself from asking the question. "The reason you brought me here?"

Pain flickered across his face, followed by iron-clad resolve. "There's something I need you to know before we take this any further."

"What? Are you secretly a vampire king or something?"

He chuckled, my joke providing the right amount of levity for a serious conversation. "No, sadly, I can't offer you the kingdom Noah can."

The mention of Noah brought another ache to the forefront, but I pushed it away. This was about Caleb, not anyone else. "What do you need to tell me?"

"These marks. They're not some random happenstance that connected us."

"I figured that. Coincidences don't exist, Caleb."

"You don't believe in the God I devoted my humanity to, but I know He is real."

"Okay . . ."

"He sent the angel Gabriel to me. Offered me my soul if I would be theirs. All I had to do was stop the Apocalypse. It seemed an easy enough agreement at the time. Serve the Society, save the world."

"Society?"

"A group of individuals who each had a vested interest in the outcome. Your grandfather among them."

I couldn't help but flinch at that. I shouldn't be surprised by the depths Niall Fallon would sink to, but it still hurt. Then again, I guess it explained his hatred all these years. How could you love something you were destined to destroy?

Caleb continued, "Little did I know what the true cost would be."

"And now . . ."

"And now I would gladly surrender my soul to ensure your happiness. A soul is a little thing in comparison to the love of a woman who's become your entire reason for being."

"It seems cruel to put you in my path only to take it all away in the end."

"Isn't that what fate does? Cruelly snatch everything from us and laugh as she takes it all?"

"I don't want you to have to choose, Caleb. It's not fair."

He smiled, the look tender, if not a hint sad. "Nothing is fair in a game where mates are on the line. Happiness costs everything, and it's worth every penny to know the touch of true love. To look into the eyes of the one being created solely for you and know you are loved despite every flaw. To know, with utter certainty, that you have found your place in the world. There is no price I wouldn't pay, Sunday, to be right here, right now, with you. To be yours."

"To get your soul, you have to . . ."

He cupped my belly and pressed his forehead to mine. "It's what they've charged me with carrying out. And I thought I could, if it meant you'd have a life after. Even if it wasn't with me. But God help me, I can't. I hear her heart. I feel her there. She's real. She can't be born evil. Not if she's made from someone as good as you."

A weight lifted from my shoulders the moment he said those

words. That was what I'd been longing for. "I love you. God, I tried not to, but I can't stop."

"Never stop." He held me close, kissing my shoulder, my collarbone, my neck, my mark. "Please never stop. I can't . . . I can't leave this world without feeling your love."

"I couldn't if I wanted to, Caleb. Even when you made me hate you, I still loved you. I've always loved you."

"Aye, *a stor*. It's the same for me." A tear slipped from his cheek as he locked gazes with me. "If the world ends, so be it. I want to be holding you in my arms as I meet my maker."

Tears pricked my eyes as I ran my fingers through his hair. "So hold me."

His smile was slow and sent warmth curling in my belly. "The world isn't ending right now, love. Tonight . . . tonight I plan to show you just how much I love you."

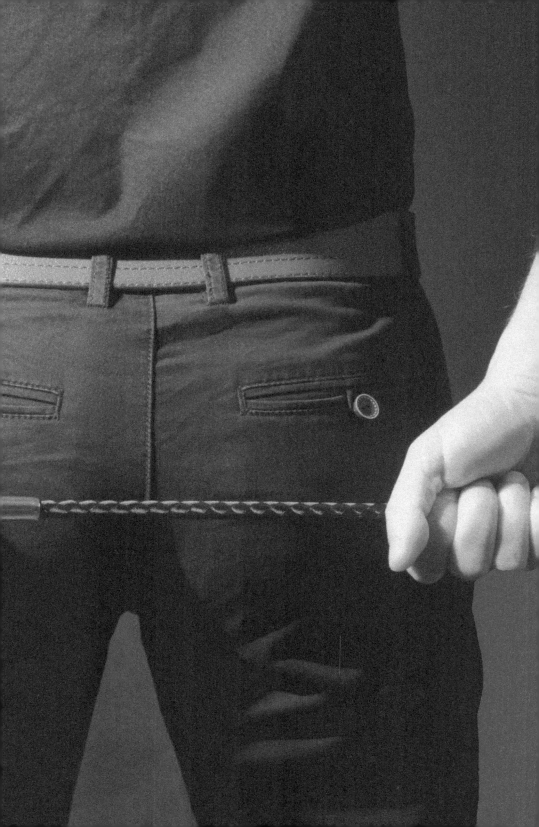

CHAPTER

# EIGHTEEN

CALEB

Nothing on this earth could have prepared me for Sunday's admission of love and the look in her eyes when I bared my empty soul to her. We might not have long together, but I'd make every last second count. Every beat of my heart was hers. I'd love her until the light left my eyes and I'd go to hell with her name on my lips.

But if this was one of the last times I had to make her mine, I wanted to do it with nothing but the truth between us. I wanted to make amends for all the ways I'd let her down. I'd failed every single person I'd been sworn to serve. I would not fail her.

Not now. Not ever again.

"Lie back, sweetling. Let me love you."

"I thought I was going to be punished."

My laugh bubbled up without conscious thought. "We'll get to that. For now, let me prove that I deserve to be yours."

She smiled up at me with all the innocence of a virgin and all the knowledge of a succubus. That had my cock jerking, desperate to be inside her.

"Okay, Daddy."

163

Could I claim her if I spent my seed right here and now? Sunday Fallon was the one creature able to bring me to my knees with something as simple as two words.

"I said, lie back. Let me make you come."

Her breath hitched as she did as she was told, and the sight of her, naked from the waist up, carrying my child, had me palming my cock and fighting the urge to drive deep inside her. She was full and beautiful, an erotic picture of a woman nearing the end of her journey to motherhood. I allowed myself one moment to dwell on the fact that she shouldn't appear this far along by human standards. But I was hardly an expert, and who knew what the standard was for a child like this?

She shifted restlessly on the blanket, pulling me from my thoughts.

"What's wrong?"

"You said you were going to make me come."

"I am."

"But I'm still wearing pants."

"You think that's going to stop me from keeping my promise?"

She was slower to respond this time. "Well . . . no."

I laughed, making easy work of her leggings as I tore them in two. "Better?"

Her pupils were blown wide, her cheeks flushed. "Much."

"No touching yourself, Miss Fallon. Grasp the bar above your head."

She squirmed but obeyed, hands clasping the headboard as she spread her legs wide.

But I had no intention of touching her there. At least not yet. I was still intent on proving her theory. Taking one rosy nipple in my mouth, I sucked. Hard.

Her back bowed off the bed, her breath escaping her in a strangled moan. "Caleb!"

"I did promise you'd never forget my name by the time I was

done with ya, lass. Now hush and take it, darling one. For I'm seeking to ruin you with pleasure."

"Careful, Caleb, your Irish is showing."

Fecking hell, I loved her teasing me. "Aye, it is. And before long, you'll have some Irish in you and be begging for more."

Her blush deepened. "Stop making promises and do something about them."

"Be careful what you wish for, darling."

I was done playing with her. I needed to prove to myself I could make her come like this. I wanted to use our mate bond to feel everything she experienced. "Close your eyes and let me in."

She did, not needing further instruction to open her mind in a way only mates could. Then I pulled that same tight bud into my mouth and sucked, nipping her with my teeth, rolling the sensitive flesh with my tongue, making her writhe under me.

I could feel each pull of my mouth over her like it was a stroke along my straining cock. *Christ on the cross.* It didn't take long before I was rocking my hips into her in time with my mouth while my hand mercilessly plucked and pulled at the furled peak of her other breast.

"Caleb, fuck, I'm so close."

*God in heaven, so am I.*

I pinched the nipple not in my mouth, hard enough she cried out in delicious pain. My sweet girl loved the bite of pain along with her pleasure. Tingles shot down my spine, building at the base, a familiar warning of what was about to happen. I needed her orgasm so I could have my own. I wanted to paint her belly with my seed. Mark every part of her.

I was certain I could get her there with solely my lips and tongue on her nipples, but I wouldn't last long enough for that. Needing to speed her along, I slid two fingers into her soaked core.

Her grunt was low and primal. "More, Caleb. I need more."

Taking her nipple between my teeth, I bit down and slid a third finger inside her, followed by a fourth. My balls were heavy and tight, aching with the need to release. Fuck, I'd put my entire hand inside her if it meant she'd come. But my thumb was busy, needed for more important stimulation. As I curled my fingers upward, I cupped her mound, pressing and rolling my thumb over her swollen clit.

"OhmyGodI'mgonnacome."

"Come for me, Sunday," I ordered as I released her nipple with a wet pop.

Her inner muscles clamped down, squeezing my fingers hard as her orgasm reached its pinnacle. Fluid rushed out of her, coating my fingers, running down her ass and onto the sheets as she cried out and bucked her hips, riding out the wave of her release.

There was nothing more beautiful than the sight of my mate enjoying what I did to her.

I didn't follow her. I maintained control and kept my climax at bay. But I was going to fuck her long and deep now. There was no question.

I lifted my head to look down at her flushed cheeks.

Instead of floating on a cloud of pleasure, she wore confusion and worry on her beautiful face. "Caleb . . . did I . . . uh . . . did I pee?"

I laughed, unable to stop myself before I reined in the bemusement her question caused. "No. You did not. I forget how innocent you are, no matter what your romantic life suggests. That was . . . um . . . female ejaculation is the technical term."

Her cheeks went bright red. "Oh, my God. I squirted?"

"I take it that hasn't happened before."

"Uh, no, Caleb. That has *not* happened before."

That made me incredibly proud. "You're welcome?"

She grabbed a pillow and smacked the side of my face with it. "Shut up."

"Should I grab a towel next time?"

She hit me again. "I swear to God, Caleb, shut up, or I will never let you inside me again."

"Pretty liar, we both know that's not true."

Her gaze flared with arousal and warning all at the same time. "I thought my water broke. Don't make fun of me."

Tenderness rushed through me. I reached out and ran my palm over her belly. "No, *a stor*. The baby is safe and warm, right where she should be." Then I trailed that hand up until I cupped a full breast again, squeezing as I made my way back to the nipple I'd been sucking.

"Fuck, that feels good. It . . . tingles. Everything sort of aches. Keep touching me, Caleb."

"Gladly. You taste delicious. A berry, ripe for the picking."

She glanced down, her cheeks crimson, her body stiff.

"What's wrong?"

"Um . . ."

I followed her gaze to the pearl of milky liquid beading from her other breast. I didn't say a fucking word, just smirked as I licked the evidence of her impending motherhood from her tit. The answering growl of need that came from her had my neglected orgasm rearing its head once again.

"Fuck, *a stor*, I need to be inside you."

"Yes, you fucking do," she breathed, writhing beneath me.

Positioning myself between her thighs, I gripped her hips and slid home. She was wetter than I'd ever thought possible. Even when she was in heat, she hadn't felt like this.

Everything hit me at once as our bodies joined in the most intimate way we could. This was the very scene we'd played out at *Iniquity* the night I served her as she rode out her heat. Only this time there was nothing holding me back. It was real. Sunday was in my home, my bed, my fucking heart.

She was mine.

I moved in her, the words I wanted to say but couldn't bubbling up in my chest each time I sank inside. She was the most heavenly creature I'd ever known as she arched her back and cried my name, her hands fisting the sheets, perfect pink cunt clamping down on my cock with the echoes of her orgasm still rolling through her.

This could very well be the last time I ever felt her clenching around me. I couldn't lose this moment. It may be my only chance.

I whispered, hoarse and desperate, "Sunday, I need you . . . will you . . . fuck."

She reached up, weaving her fingers through my hair, her desire-darkened eyes pinning mine. "What do you need, my love?"

"Marry me. Be my wife. I need to know, I need you . . . I need to know you're mine. That not even death can come between us."

"Caleb . . ."

"Please, *a stor*. The world is ending. We may never get another chance. If I'm going to die tomorrow, I need to know that I made you mine in every possible way. In front of God Himself."

She froze beneath me, but instead of growing cold and distant, she seemed to be suspended on a breath. Her eyes searched mine. "Okay," she breathed, stunning me.

"Okay?"

"Okay. Yes. I'll marry you."

I leaned down, careful of her belly, and kissed her deeply, the euphoria of what we'd just done racing through me and chasing the pleasure I'd forced to heel. Her fingers in my hair, the soft moan she released against my lips as my tongue dipped inside, and the answering flood of arousal from her sent me over the edge. I came on a ragged groan, filling her, marking her, making her mine.

She was right there with me, clenching around me, milking me. Calling out my name to the heavens above.

I didn't care if she tried to take it back. Sunday Fallon had just agreed to be my wife. And not even the Apocalypse itself would stop me from cashing in on that promise.

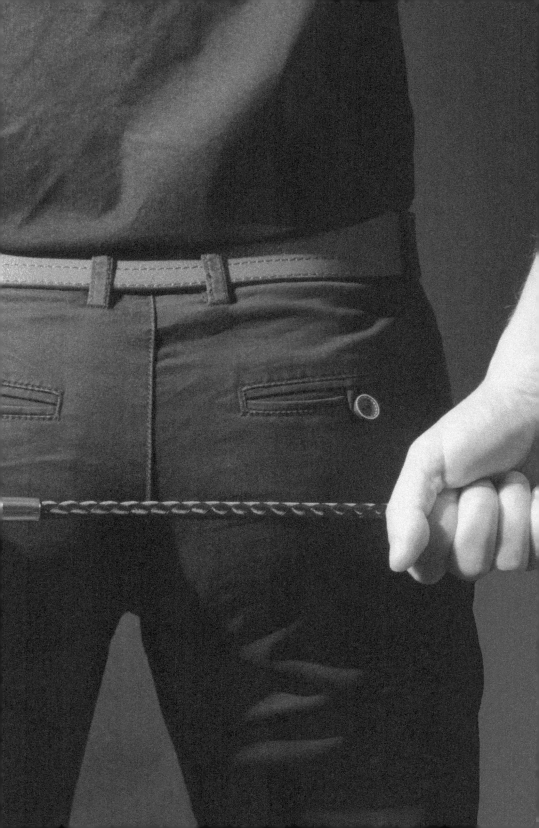

# CHAPTER
# NINETEEN
## MOIRA

*Six days since Sunday's abduction*

If the world wasn't freaking ending, I might have been a little happy to see my childhood home. Sure, things were tense for reasons I didn't like to dwell on, but it was still a place where lots of good memories lived.

The guys were still unloading the car while Ash and I stared up at my grandmother's colossal Cape Cod-style house. Every single window was lit with a warm glow that somehow still didn't make me feel welcome.

Ash slipped her hand into mine, giving it a warm squeeze. "Everything's going to be all right. She wouldn't have invited us if she didn't think we'd be successful."

"I'm more worried about why she wants to be successful."

"She's not in control of what happens after we find Sunday. So her reasoning doesn't really matter, does it?" Ash raised her brow, showing an uncharacteristic hint of sass.

I liked it. "Well, well, it looks like I'm rubbing off on my girl."

Her lips twitched, and she flicked her gaze to the ground. "You certainly rubbed something this morning."

"And I'll do it again tonight just to spite them."

Her blush deepened and she started to let go of my hand, but I gripped hers harder, refusing to release her. "Nuh-uh. You're my girl-friend. If they can't accept that, then fuck 'em. I'm done pretending to be somebody else for them, Ash. We're a team. Period. There are plenty of same-sex couples in the coven. The rules shouldn't be different for me just because I'm a Belladonna."

"We can figure out how to have a baby if you want. Smooth things over by giving your grandmother the heir she's after. You know that, right?"

My stomach churned. "I'm not ready to talk about anything that life-changing. Let's get Sunday through delivering *her* spawn first, okay?"

A soft chuckle left Ash as she nudged me with her shoulder. "I love you," she whispered, offering me a sweet smile. "No matter what. Kids, no kids. Magic, no magic. It doesn't matter to me. I just want you."

My heart somersaulted into my stomach as I stared at the woman who was far too good for me. I had to make sure she never figured it out. I was beyond lucky to have her. Pulling her in close, I kissed her. "Love you too, baby."

"Please tell me there's food in this house? I'm fucking starving," Kingston called from behind us, breaking the moment.

"I'm sure we can fry up some eye of newt for you, wolf boy," I teased as I stopped on the first step leading to the porch and turned to face them. "Oh, or maybe some dead man's toe."

Kingston gagged. "No thanks, I'll just go hunt some squirrels or teach myself how to fish."

Why did the thought of Kingston dressed in fisherman's gear give me the giggles?

"You idiot. Yes, there is food. Witches eat too. For fuck's sake," Alek grumbled. "Even the vampires fed us, or don't you remember?"

"I might have blocked out a lot of our time at that place. Nothing good happened there." Kingston's grin turned slightly evil as he shot Alek a sideways glance. "Except for hearing you scream like a little girl."

"Oh, I forgot to mention Belladonna house also has a ghost or two. Don't worry, Alek, they won't bother you."

I couldn't hide my smile as he paled. There was something so adorable about big strong Alek afraid of, well, anything.

"Honestly, a Viking scared of a non-corporeal being? Who would've guessed?" Thorne shoved his hands into his pockets and smirked. "They can't hurt you, Alek."

"Ever heard of a vengeful spirit? I promise you, they can hurt. They watch you when you don't know they're in the room, just waiting until you're naked."

"This sounds an awful lot like a book I once read," Kingston said.

"You know how to read?" Thorne drawled.

"Fuck off."

"What was the title of this book? *Goodnight Moon? The Gruffalo?*"

"I call it *Ghost Dick.* It's about this earl and a lady at an inn in a snowstorm."

Thorne's brows rose. "Are you telling me you not only read, but you read historical romance novels?"

Something about that warmed my heart a little.

"There's a reason I'm a better lover than you, Thorne. I not only read it, I take notes. Trust me, Sunday doesn't have any complaints."

Alek leaned closer to Kingston and murmured, "Can I borrow that book?"

"You sure it won't be too scary for you, big guy?"

Alek wrapped his arm around Kingston's neck and mercilessly ground his knuckles into his skull.

My laughter rang out in the night. I'd needed this small bit of light before we headed into the lion's den. The lion being my grand-mother and her expectations of me.

"Bugger," Thorne muttered.

The one word killed my amusement. "Everything okay?"

"Just got a text from our hacker. Trail's gone cold. We're on our own."

*Dammit, Asher. You were supposed to be my ringer.*

"So nothing's changed then," Kingston said.

"Well, it's a good thing we have a coven of witches to help." I pasted a smile on my face, trying to hide the nervous energy spiking through my veins.

"Are you coming inside, or do you plan to stay the night on my porch like a bunch of ill-mannered hooligans?" My grandmother's voice wiped the smile off my face.

Blaire Belladonna stood in the doorway; her long hair flowed in unkempt waves. Once dark as night, now the thick mass was so shot through with gray it was almost a solid color. She wore the same dressing gown she had since I was a child growing up in this house. Dark silk embroidered with ivy and all manner of jewel-toned birds and flowers. But I could tell she'd only just started her nighttime ritual because she still wore all her rings and several crystals hung around her neck.

"Grandmother, my, what big teeth you have."

She rolled her eyes, pushing the screen door open. "Some things never change."

I smirked, loving that I could get under her skin as easily as she did mine. That had always been our problem. We were the same. And when I'd come out, she'd taken it as some kind of personal insult. Not because she cared about who I was attracted to, but because my lifestyle would prevent me from carrying on the family bloodline or some bullshit. Her reaction only hurt because of how close we used to be.

"Come in, child. We have a great deal of work to do before this visit is over."

The five of us clambered into the old house, the scent of sage and lavender hitting me and making me feel more at home than anything else thus far.

"Moira, you know the way to your old room. You girls can bunk up there. Your bed's all made up for you two."

Ash and I exchanged a glance. The last few times we visited, she'd put us in separate rooms. I couldn't be sure if it was because of the extra company or not, but something told me she was making a point by placing us together. Was this the olive branch my heart wanted it to be? I was too afraid to ask.

"As for you three, we only have two other rooms, so you're going to have to double up. I'll let you decide who's sharing."

"I guess I call big spoon, Kingston," Alek said as Thorne raced up the stairs before anyone else.

Ash snorted.

Kingston grunted. "You try and cuddle me, Nordson, and I'll hump your leg, I fucking swear."

"Is that a promise? You wanna be a good dog and keep me warm by sleeping with me in your furry form?"

There was another hiccup of laughter from beside me.

"I hate you."

"I love you too, buddy."

Ash lost it at that, doubling over and gasping as tears of laughter streamed down her cheeks. I wasn't faring much better. These guys were ridiculous. If they couldn't see their bromance for what it was, nothing would show them. I couldn't resist joining in and goading them a little. "Alek, if he gets ahold of you, it's best to just let him finish."

"Oh, goddess, Moira," Ash panted, still wheezing as she wiped at her eyes.

Alek shot me a wicked smirk. "He won't have anything to finish with if he tries."

Kingston cupped his crotch. "Don't worry, Jake. I'll protect you."

"Which one is Jake?" my grandmother asked in a poor attempt at a whisper.

"You don't want to know."

"Oh. Well, then. I'll just pretend I didn't hear that." She swept her arm toward the staircase Thorne had already ascended. "The vampire didn't waste any time. The rest of you, follow me. We only have a few hours remaining until the coven arrives."

BY THE TIME the five of us joined my grandmother and the rest of the coven outside in the ritual clearing, the bonfire was burning brightly and women I'd spent my whole life casting alongside gathered together. But instead of happy chatter acting as the soundtrack to this meeting, a tense, heavy dread buzzed in the air. They knew we were up Shit Creek without a paddle.

"Join us, Moira and Ash. Gentlemen, take a seat. You can't participate in this," Grandmother said.

"You don't have to tell me twice," Kingston muttered.

"Afraid of a little magic?" I teased. "You're just as bad as Alek."

"Alek's scared of ghosts. I'm wary of anyone who can shrivel my dick with a spell. Which one of us has the healthier phobia?"

"You," Thorne said. "Definitely you."

Power crackled in Alek's eyes, and for a second, I thought the wolf and vamp were going to make a couple of cute toads, but he swallowed it back and accepted their teasing. He must be used to it, being a twin and all.

I stared at the men for a second longer, my heart warming at how far they'd come since Sunday brought them all together. Sure, I still thought they were neanderthals who loved to swing their dicks around simply because they had them. But things had changed. Their love for her had forged a new family for all of them, one where they were all welcome and equally valued. I wondered if they had any idea how special that was. How unique. Looking at the tense sets of their shoulders, the earnest hope in their eyes, I thought they did.

They truly loved my bestie.

Dammit. This was all my fault. It was past time to clean up my mess.

"Don't leave this space. The magic is strong, and you'll feel it if you step into the ritual clearing," I warned. "I mean it."

After they acknowledged me, I took Ash's hand, and the two of us joined the already formed circle of powerful witches.

*This should be easy. This much power should knock my silly spell back with no problems. We'll find her.*

There was something about needing an entire coven of witches to undo my casting that had me standing tall with pride. I wouldn't admit it. Not out loud. But I was more than a little impressed with myself. Too bad I inadvertently broke a cardinal rule. *Don't cast a spell you can't undo.* Then again, how was I supposed to know I wouldn't be able to? It had never been an issue before.

"Focus, wifey."

I grinned at Ash, loving hearing that nickname more than I expected to. We hadn't told anyone, but last night we decided to get married once this was over.

Releasing a breath as my grandmother began the invocation, I steeled myself. Locator spells were as basic as they came. This was going to be a cakewalk.

As one, the women around the fire took up my grandmother's low chant, our heads tipped back toward the sky, focusing on the swirls of smoke drifting off the fire and lending her our considerable strength.

But instead of easily lifting the veil of magic I'd draped over Sunday, we came up against a wall of nothing. So we pressed on harder, adding more power to the mix. My limbs shook as the chant continued, the pressure of heavy spell casting hurting my ears. It reminded me of the time I thought it would be fun to lie down at the bottom of a pool. My gaze found the woman across from me, a trickle of blood leaking from her nose.

Panic shot through me at the sight. Something was wrong. This wasn't my spell. This was something else.

Before I had a chance to give any sort of warning, the fire erupted upward, one massive pillar shooting into the sky. Cries rang out as we were thrown backward. I landed with a grunt, my head smacking against the ground with enough force to make my ears ring.

As fast as it had happened, the fire went out, leaving us in darkness. In its place, a harsh buzz filled the air, swirling above our clearing like one angry swarming mass and growing louder with each thud of my heart.

"What is that?" Ash asked, her voice sluggish as she pushed herself to a sitting position.

"Is this supposed to happen?" Alek asked, his voice wary.

"No," I said, my head still ringing like a gong. "Definitely not."

"Why is it spells never go to plan around you?" Thorne asked.

"It's not me. Something bad is attached to Sunday."

"No shit. The Apocalypse." Kingston's voice was full of annoyance.

"No . . . this is different. It's fighting back. Whatever is hiding her doesn't want her to be found—"

"Moira, look out!"

Ash's voice reached me just as hundreds of dark blurs flew at my face. The chittering sound intensified until I had to press my hands against my ears to drown it out.

"Are those . . . locusts?" Thorne asked, hunched over in a mirror of my position.

Locusts.

Fuck. Wasn't that one of the signs of the end times? I wasn't as up-to-date on my biblical references as I could be, but I was pretty sure that one was in there.

"Everybody down!" Alek shouted as another swarm came in, circling our gathering.

With a wave of his hand, the bugs glowed neon blue for a split second, lighting up the night sky with their sheer number before transforming into gently floating bubbles. Each one popped until every last locust was gone.

The witches of my coven slowly got to their feet, bloodied and scratched from the force of the attack mounted by the insects.

"What just happened? That wasn't normal," I asked, gaze locked on Grandmother.

She wiped the blood from under her nose. "The spell you cast doesn't exist, Moira. It's been long broken. This is something more powerful than I've ever encountered. We can't break it. She's hidden by a force only a deity could breach."

"Well, where the bloody hell do we find a deity? Do you happen to have any lying around?" Thorne asked, frustration coloring his words.

"The only god-boy I know is Thor over here," Kingston said, jerking his thumb at Alek.

"How many fucking times do I have to tell you, Tor is Thor-blessed. I'm the fun one."

"At least a few more, I suspect."

Alek punched Kingston in the arm.

"Ow, fucker."

"Maybe that will help you remember."

Not wanting them to dissolve into a full-on tumble in the grass, I asked, "Well, do you think you've got what it takes, hot stuff?"

He shook his head. "This is far beyond my understanding. I wouldn't know where to start trying to unravel whatever force is around her. Give me an enemy to fight, and I'll do it. But mystical forces? That's not my bag."

"What about that angel?" Kingston asked. "The biker dude? Can he help us?"

"Gabriel?" my grandmother mused. "Possibly. If you can find him. He's not exactly . . . available."

Kingston looked at me, then at the other guys. "I know exactly where we should go."

"And where's that?" Thorne raised one brow skeptically.

"To the only place we've ever seen him. *Iniquity*. Lilith is a demon, and still she works with Gabriel. I bet that angel's secretly got the hots for her. He'll come if she calls."

"But the question is, will she call?"

"There's only one way to find out." I walked toward my grandmother, working up the courage to tell her we weren't staying overnight now that things had changed, but Kingston's phone rang, stopping me as a sense of dread punched through my chest.

"Sorry, guys, it's my mom." He held the phone up to his ear. "Hey, Mama. Wha—" He stopped mid-sentence, and every ounce of bravado and cockiness left him as though a drain had been opened. He went pale as his eyes widened. "Wh-what do you mean, sick? I just saw him." Then his knees gave out, and he wobbled.

Alek shot to his side, wrapping an arm around the usually sturdy wolf and holding him up.

"Of . . . course. I-I'll be there as soon as I can."

The phone slipped from his hand, and he blinked, but I knew he wasn't really seeing any of us.

"Kingston, what's wrong? What happened?" I asked, going to him.

"My father . . . he's dead."

# TWENTY

I hadn't even fully stepped through the door before Trouble flung herself into my arms.

"It's awful." My little sister's muffled sobs were almost completely unintelligible as she clung to me.

I hugged her out of instinct, still too shocked by my mother's news to do more than go through the motions. "It's gonna be all right, Tessa."

"W-w-we t-t-t-tried—" Her entire body trembled as she gasped and worked to get her words out. It reminded me of when she was little and fought for every single thing she wanted to say.

"Shh, Tessa. It's okay. Take your time." I stroked her hair, my gaze traveling over her head and to the pack Sunday had created.

Alek, Thorne, Moira, and Ash stood a few steps from the porch, sympathy written on their faces. Our hastily packed bags lay at their feet.

"Sh–sh–sh–she's gone."

He. She meant *he*. Right? My gut churned. "Who's gone?"

"Phe."

The world dropped out from under me for the second time in as many days. "What? How?"

This couldn't be happening. Why did it feel like my family was under attack? Taken from me one after the other before I could do any-fucking-thing.

"The illness that got your dad took her as well." Doc's soft twang reached me.

"What illness? We don't get sick."

"Perhaps it's best if you and I speak in the other room. Alone."

"I need to see Mama."

He shook his head. "No. You need to come with me, Alpha."

The seriousness of his statement, the fact that he ordered me, his new Alpha, to do something, meant this was more than I'd been prepared for. I released Trouble and silently made eye contact with Alek, asking him without saying a word to take over for me. The Viking wouldn't be a threat to Tessa's wolf like a vampire.

"We've got her," Moira said, following Alek as they all entered the house.

Thorne stayed outside until I gave him a sharp nod. "You're pack. Come in."

The subtle tightening of his eyes and harsh clearing of his throat told me he understood exactly how big of a statement I'd just made. Not as the man of the house, but as the Alpha of the Farrell pack. For the first time in living memory, I'd just declared a vampire one of us.

Look at me, first day on the job, already making historic changes.

My grief was too raw for the thought to make me actually smile, but a part of me was relieved I was still the same asshole as ever. I'd get us through this. I had to. I just wished my Sunshine was here to help *me* through it.

Fuck. Thinking of her wasn't a good idea. A sharp pain tore through my heart, opening that barely protected wound, adding an additional layer of hurt.

I followed Doc into my dad's office. Shit, now it was mine. I had to swallow down the shards of glass that seemed to have filled my throat before I could speak. "What happened?"

Doc gave me a bewildered look, seeming to age before my eyes. He gave his bushy mustache a cursory stroke, his eyes wandering to the empty hearth. "I've never seen anything like it. By all accounts, it shouldn't have been possible. I saw your parents at church just the day before, and Ronin was as healthy as ever. He was dead by sundown the next day. Your sister followed him only hours after."

"I don't understand. Shifters don't get sick."

"We don't. But he did. So did she."

"Can I see them?"

His complexion went slightly green. "I don't think that's a good idea. This was . . . ugly. They don't even look like themselves."

*Oh, God.*

"Doc, I'm going to need more info so I'm able to make some sense out of this."

He blew out a breath, looking like he was trying to gather himself. "The only word I have for it is plague. The onset was immediate, the symptoms fatal"—he shuddered—"like something straight out of a horror film. Phe was with your father when it happened. She must have caught it from him."

"But where did *he* get it?"

Doc shook his head, baffled. "No clue. As far as I know, he was home. No telling when he could have gotten infected, how long it was incubating. I don't know shit all, Kingston, and I'm not too much of a man to admit that scares the ever-loving crap out of me. But that's not the worst part." He paused, licking his lips. "I didn't see your dad go. But I watched Phe slip away. She was delirious. We had to quarantine her, seal off the room and keep everyone out. But I stayed at the door and talked to her, offering what comfort I could."

Tears burned my eyes thinking of my sister dying like that.

"She said some things, Alpha. Things any God-fearing person would find alarming."

Icy dread raced down my spine. Locusts. Plague. And . . . we'd already fought a war with demons. Was it all related to Sunday? To us?

"Tell me."

"She was babbling by the end. Near incomprehensible. Mentioning things like boiling oceans and horsemen, and . . . a woman standing over your father's body, reaching out and touching her. But the part that made my blood run cold was when she started quoting scripture. From the book of Revelation."

The hair on my arms stood on end. Phe hadn't attended church a day in her life—much to Mama's chagrin. I don't even think she'd ever seen a bible. "Do you remember what she said?"

Stricken, he nodded. *"Then a great sign appeared in heaven: a woman clothed with the sun, with the moon under her feet . . . She was expecting a child, and she cried out in pain, in the agony of giving birth. She gave birth to a child, who is going to rule all the nations with a rod of iron. And the child was snatched away to God and to his throne."*

Shock took my knees out from under me, and I sat down on the desk, sending pens and books clattering to the ground. "Sunday." Her name was ripped from me. Disbelief and absolute fear turned my blood to ice.

"That's what I thought as well. Kingston, I don't know what you're involved in, but I have a bad feeling it's not going to end well for your mate or your child."

*Or for any of us.*

"Where's Mama? The girls? We need to get them out of here. Somewhere they can be looked after. What if they get sick?"

"I think the danger has passed. No one else has shown any signs. If they were infected, considering how fast Phe went, they would already be gone."

"How can we be sure? You already said you've never seen anything like this."

"You're right. I haven't, but I'm intimately familiar with the aftermath, and I already ran some tests. What was *in* them is not in the others. They're safe, Kingston. As safe as we can make them."

I barked out a harsh laugh. Safe? Who the fuck was safe anymore? The world was ending, and I'd helped usher it in. Now we were all going to pay the price.

I stood and started pacing, dragging my hands through my hair and pulling. "Is there anything else you need me to know? Anything more earth-shattering? What do I do?"

Doc lowered his gaze for just a moment, then matched my stare. "I'd start praying."

"I've got bad news for you, Doc. I don't think He's listening."

"Maybe not. But it sure as hell can't hurt."

"Thank you for being there for her. So she didn't die alone." That fucking broken glass was in my throat again. "She deserved so much better."

"So did he."

My conflicted emotions didn't know what to do with the words. I was still so angry at my father for his betrayal. Had all but fucking cursed him myself when I told him I never wanted to see him again. That he was dead to me.

*Looks like you got your wish, Kingston.*

Something slithered in my stomach, making me nauseated as a terrible possibility took root. *What if . . . No, there's no way. I couldn't be . . .*

But what if I was?

My thoughts were chasing each other, my mind too scared to even think the words, let alone say them out loud. Could I be responsible? Those horsemen my sister saw in her fever-induced dreams, could she have been referring to me? To Thorne and Caleb and Alek? We were dealing with Armageddon here. Signs of it were everywhere. Hell, even that witch said our baby would bring about the Apocalypse. If she was the Harbinger, had we been the Horsemen all along?

Fuck.

It was impossible, right? Crazy talk.

FUCK.

I tore out of the office, leaving Doc standing alone with his own grief as I headed out in search of the guys. They needed to know what Phe had said, how this was connected, before I could face my mom or sisters. But what I really needed was to hear Thorne and Alek tell me I was reaching with my theory. Because I couldn't be the reason my dad and sister died. I fucking couldn't. And if I was . . . I didn't know what I would do.

# TWENTY-ONE

## ALEK

"Well, if we are the Horsemen, clearly I'm War." I forced a smile as I let Kingston's words sink in. I didn't want to admit it could be true. How could I be something so nefarious and not know it? Then again, I *was* a berserker and didn't have a clue. But now, I couldn't deny that part of me. As if summoned by thought alone, a tremor worked through my hand, and I had to ball it into a fist to stop the involuntary movement. The beast was becoming harder to control with every passing moment I was without my mate.

"Who does that make me?" Thorne asked, his lips twitching.

"Death, obviously. And Caleb would be Famine. The bastard loves to deprive himself."

Thorne snickered. "Hilarious and oddly apt. There might be something to your theory after all, Kingston."

"Fucking Pestilence, of course. They died of a fucking plague right after I said he was dead to me." The wolf looked like he was about to be sick. He hung his head and braced his elbows on his knees, refusing to meet our gazes. For once, he wasn't the one cracking inappropriate jokes.

That sobered me more than anything else, and my smile slipped. "You aren't responsible for this," I said, lowering myself next to him on the couch and resting a hand on his shoulder. "Don't you think we'd know if we were somehow involved in all this chaos?"

"But we are involved. That baby exists because of us. Who's to say we aren't part of the rest of this too?"

"I haven't killed anyone I don't know about." Thorne's conviction bled from his words.

"Neither have I. And neither have you, King—"

"Would you guys shut up? We can't hear what they're saying." Tessa's words were uncharacteristically harsh as she gestured to the television. Moira, Ash, and Kingston's youngest sister were squeezed onto the room's second sofa, all wearing matching looks of shock as they read the scrolling headlines of the evening news.

As a unit, the three of us trained our focus on the news program on the screen. She raised the volume and turned on subtitles for good measure.

"This is Bill Williams reporting live from the shores of Lake Michigan, where scientists are still scratching their heads over this morning's baffling discovery. A spokesperson from the Department of Agriculture and Fish and Wildlife Service's joint task force has just confirmed the mysterious substance responsible for the change to the water is, in fact, blood rather than the suspected invasive algae. The CDC has not yet commented on these findings, likely awaiting their own results as samples from the lake were also sent to them for further research.

"So far, reports indicate the blood is human, and every sample has been linked to the same DNA source, which should be impossible given the sheer quantity. But as matters currently stand, the entirety of the lake seems to have been replaced with blood overnight.

"This strange development comes directly on the heels of two other events, now being called Acts of God. A massive underwater volcano erupted in the South Pacific Ocean with a nuclear blast force, triggering an earthquake measuring 9.1 on the Richter scale. The shock waves were felt at nearly maximum strength all the way up the west coast of the United States and into Canada. Currently, the entire coast is under a tsunami warning, and reports of catastrophic damage have begun filtering in.

"We don't know yet if this is connected to the wall of flames reported in the Red Sea, but to this lapsed Catholic, it all seems very biblical to me. Are we in the end times? I, for one, plan to dust off my rosary and head to confession. Back to you, Karen."

Tessa muted the TV, the remote falling from her now limp fingers. "Holy. Shit."

I swallowed through a thick throat. "Not it. I did not do any of that."

"Has someone said you did?" Moira asked, cocking a brow.

"End times. Destruction. Disasters. Apocalypse baby." I stared at the now muted screen as the news continued playing, showing the evidence of everything the reporter had mentioned. "That says Horsemen to me. Especially given what we know."

Moira gave me a slow blink and then shifted her attention to Kingston. "Wait, were you actually serious about that nonsense you were spewing? You really believe you four could be the *actual* Horsemen of the Apocalypse?" She snorted once and then again right on its heels, her fit of giggles turning into loud, body-shaking guffaws. "Oh. Oh, that's rich. Just how big is your ego? As if you are remotely powerful enough for something like *that*." She gestured to the TV, which was frozen on a static image of an ocean literally on fire.

"Wait, so Sunday can be the daughter of Lucifer—"

"Rumored daughter. It's never been proven," Moira interrupted.

Rolling my eyes, I continued, "I am a demigod, but *we* can't be the Horsemen?"

"Do you *want* to be a Horseman?"

"If I was, I could stop this."

"Men, always walking around with raging power boners," Moira muttered.

Ash snickered, and even Tessa seemed amused, though her smile didn't quite reach her grief-reddened eyes.

"Something is responsible for all of this. Not to mention the deaths we've been surrounded by," Ash offered, her expression pensive.

"Dad and Phe died of an inexplicable illness. No one did that," Tessa murmured.

"Has anyone noticed how many people tied to the Society have dropped dead recently? I think Ash is on to something." Thorne stood and began pacing in front of the TV. "How many is it now? Three? Four?"

"Ronin and the Seer. That's only two. One was stabbed, and Ronin got sick." I frowned as I tried to put it together the way he saw it.

"What about Moriarty?" Kingston asked.

"He wasn't related to the Society, at least as far as we know. Could be a coincidence," Thorne mused.

"I was taught never to believe in coincidence," I said, mostly under my breath, but Kingston caught my words and shot me a look filled with no little trepidation.

"But he *is* related to Ravenscroft. The Seer was a professor too. Your dad . . . he was on the board," Moira's voice was filled with discovery as she put pieces together I'd never have considered.

"You think the university is at the heart of this?" I asked.

"You have to admit, it's not the craziest conclusion—far less out there than Kingston's Horseman theory. Think about it. The headmistress is part of the Society as well, not to mention Caleb. All of this started when Sunday was sent there. Everything ties back to Ravenscroft."

"What is it, some sort of ancient burial ground? How can a place be tied to the Apocalypse?"

Thorne cocked a brow. "Well . . . it *was* the site of a battle between angels and demons long before the Blackthornes took possession of the land."

"Christ, we're all going to die," Kingston moaned, gripping his head between his hands.

"Y-you t-t-think o-one of these Horsemen killed Dad and Phe?" Tessa's question was the barest whisper but somehow shot through the room as if she'd screamed it.

"Doc called it a plague. Pestilence is sort of known for those."

She looked at her brother with terror in her eyes. "A-are w-we all going to d-d-die like that?"

"Not if I can fucking help it."

I could sense the Farrell siblings' panic building. I couldn't dismiss Kingston's theory outright. There were too many parallels to discount, but that didn't mean I wanted to watch his entire family spiral into hysteria. It was too soon to draw any conclusions. But I had one thing I could offer right now that would save them. The same thing I would give Sunday if I could.

"Let me take you to Novasgard. You'll be safe there. It's a completely different realm."

Kingston's eyes widened. "You . . . you'd do that for them?"

"Yes. Do you really think I'd just stand here and let you all die? You're family, Kingston. Which makes everyone in this house family too. Nothing is more important than family." It was a mantra my parents had instilled in me. Right along with family didn't always mean blood. Sometimes it was the people you choose, the ones who prove themselves vital to your existence in ways you can't even fathom at the first meeting. Because of Sunday, everyone here fit that bill. We were bound. Connected. I could not let harm come to a single one of them.

The wolf's jaw clenched as he fought his emotions.

"All it will take is Finley opening a portal for them. He's a call away."

"Do it," Kingston said.

"No. We won't leave the pack." Mrs. Farrell stood in the hallway between the kitchen and living room. There was no mistaking the matriarch of Kingston's family. "But the offer means more than you will ever know, Viking."

Kingston went to her without a word, wrapping his arms around the smaller woman but seeming like a child as she held him close. I saw it the moment he crumbled. I would've done the same were I in his place. As his shoulders shook, we all averted our attention elsewhere, giving him the moment he needed to fall apart.

We were no closer to our answers, but we wouldn't find them today anyway. Kingston and his family needed time to grieve. Thorne and I could give them that much while we did our best in the meantime to make sense of everything. Because if one thing was certain, this was just the beginning.

As if proving my point, Thorne's phone rang. Before he even spoke, my berserker rattled its chains, preparing to leap to our defense as a sense of ominous anticipation rolled through me.

*What the fuck had happened now?*

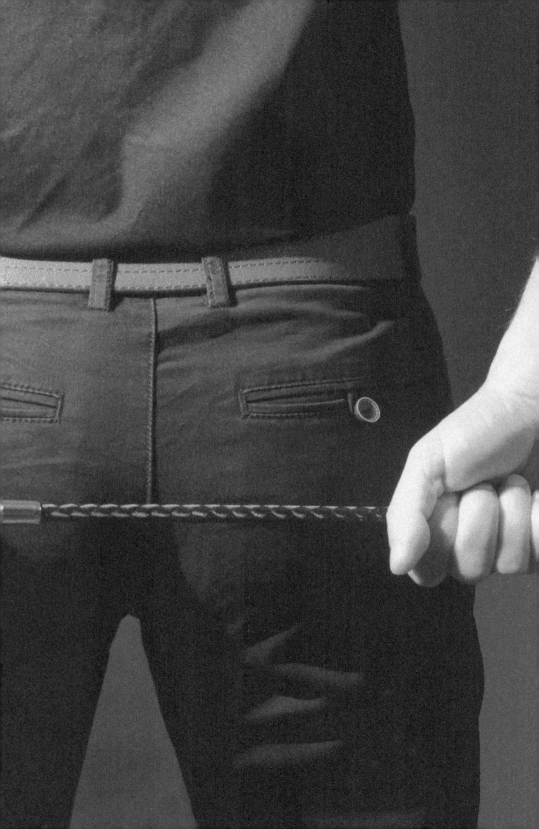

# TWENTY-TWO

## THORNE

"Father? What is it?" I couldn't keep my voice from shaking as apprehension wormed its way through me. It was one thing after another these days, to the point I couldn't believe something as innocuous as a phone call promised anything resembling good news.

"No, brother. It's me."

"West?" My younger brother never called me, and definitely not from my father's phone. "What's going on?"

I knew before he answered he'd tell me something that shattered my world. Who had *I* lost?

"The fae . . . they attacked early this morning. Most of the manor is gone. Burned to the foundation."

My head went fuzzy as my pulse roared in my ears. "How?"

"We don't know how the fire started yet, though we assume the bastards did it to draw us out. They got . . ." My brother swallowed, and my heart sank further. "Noah, it's Rosie. She didn't make it out. Martin eith—"

My hand clenched around my phone so tight I heard the plastic groan in protest. "You're lying."

"I'm not. She was in Aunt Callie's lab. No one could get to her. Father . . . he found her a pile of ashes."

"No, he must have been mistaken. It wasn't her."

"Noah, we found her necklace. The one you gave her. It *was* her."

His grief was more convincing than his words. Still I refused to believe it. Rosie couldn't be gone. I'd just seen her. Alive. Healthy.

"No," I whispered, deep in my denial. I could feel the intense gazes of Alek and the others on me. Kingston and his mother had left the room, but I knew it was only a matter of time before they'd be back. I should go, leave them to their grief before adding any of my own, but I couldn't seem to make myself move.

"There's more . . ."

"Please don't." If our mother or father were lost to this war against the Apocalypse as well, I would personally take it up with the entirety of the Shadow Court until they were nothing but a memory. Killing innocents did not further the goal of stopping what had been put into motion. What end did this serve but senseless destruction? What had Rosie ever done to deserve such a fate?

"Noah."

Steeling myself for what would surely be another blow, I gritted out, "Who else?"

"Mother."

My knees buckled, and I hit the floor hard, the jolt running up my thighs and knocking sense into me enough that I could process his statement. "How is that possible? Father would have gotten her out first. She couldn't defend herself against—"

"She's alive. In a manner of speaking."

Hope bloomed inside me. "He finally turned her?"

"Her injuries would have been fatal otherwise."

At least I wouldn't have to say goodbye to her as well. That was some comfort. But another thought unfurled, this one darkening my newly lit hopefulness. Our mother's blood was the reason we could walk in the sun. It was why she'd spent her life on the run until Father found her. But the magic inside her bloodline wasn't as strong in my brother or me because we'd turned. Now that Mother was a vampire, the only remaining person with the blood of the sun had been Rosie.

"Mother's bloodline is gone," I whispered.

"Yes."

"What happens if sun sickness returns?"

West let out a shuddering sigh. "I don't know."

"I need to come home."

"You can't."

"How can you say that? I need to be there. To help—"

"Noah, do not come back here. Not until I send for you," my father's voice filled my ear as he commandeered the phone. "You can't. It's . . . your mother . . . she's feral. She needs time to adjust."

I blew out a heavy breath, at war with myself. On the one hand, I couldn't stand the thought of being anywhere but with my family right now. On the other, I couldn't leave Kingston and Alek, not with everything going on. And it wouldn't be fair of me to ask Kingston to leave his family. How could I put my dead sister over his? And technically, he had me beat since he'd lost his father as well. The grisly thought did nothing to make me feel better.

What had my world come to where I was now counting dead family members to decide whose grief took precedence?

"Father, she won't hurt me."

"She tried to tear my throat out, son. I'm her bonded mate, and she nearly killed me. She needs time. A few more nights, at least. If you show up here with your friends in tow, you'll be bringing her an all-she-can-eat buffet. Nothing is going to change here in the next seventy-two hours. Your sister will still be gone. The manor will still be ruined. Please? I can't risk you as well."

Once again, it was the sound of his pain that convinced me.

"Fine. Seventy-two hours. Then I'm coming home."

"Good. That's good. That will allow me to settle things before we contact Gabriel."

"Gabriel?" I sat up straighter. I'd almost forgotten our plan to call on the angel for help locating Sunday. But what could my father want with him?

"Yes. Things are getting out of hand. I assume you've been watching the news?"

"Yes." I was slower to respond this time, uncertain what conclusions my father might have drawn and if I could handle any other bad news.

"Gabriel is our last resort, son. If we can't find your mate, these disasters won't be in our backyard. They will be constant and right on top of us. We won't be burying our dead. They will rise up and kill us. The end of the world is here. There's nothing we can do to keep it away, except . . ."

"Find Sunday."

"Right."

There was a weight to the word I didn't like. A finality akin to a dagger to the heart. How was it that our plan was exactly the same, but he made it seem like everything had changed? The truth was, we'd lost too many people we loved in a short time. It wasn't even days between deaths at this point, but mere hours. Who would be next? Someone in this room?

Yes, everything was the same, but in the ways that mattered, it would never be the same again.

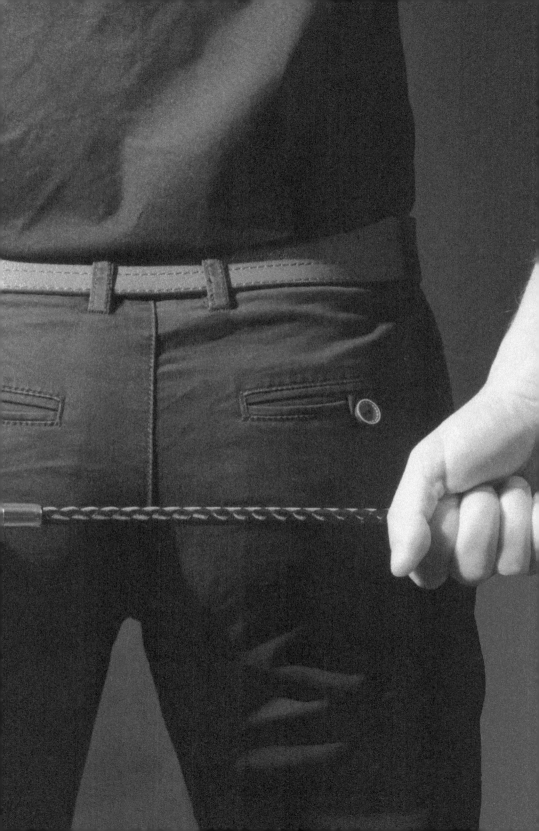

# TWENTY-THREE

SUNDAY

Thick fog blanketed the sparse, darkened forest, the cool mist coating my skin in a layer of damp I felt down to my bones. I could barely see my hand in front of my face as I forced myself to take one slow step after another, wading through the dense low-lying clouds. It was like walking through deep water, the weight causing me to use my arms to help move me through.

Without knowing *what* I was searching for, I knew instinctively that I *was* searching. There was something here in the fog, lying in wait for me. Something, or perhaps some*one*, I needed to find. Prickling at the back of my neck kept me wary. Watchful. Whatever I was hunting required me to remain on guard. Despite being the hunter, I was also the hunted.

Whispers floated in the air around me, indistinct enough I couldn't make out what they were saying, but I could tell at least two people were talking. People . . . or creatures.

Apprehension hummed through me, and I reached for the dagger Alek had given me. Surely I had it strapped to my thigh if I was out here alone, didn't I?

But where I expected to find the leather bound to my leg, I discovered smooth, silky material.

"What the fuck?" I stared down my body, only now realizing what I was wearing. A floor-length nightgown of thin, pale blue silk. But that was absurd. I was in a forest. Hunting. Why was I wearing my nightgown?

The answer rippled through my mind like the lapping of water. *Dream.* This wasn't real. My palm shot to my belly, fear gripping me as I found softly curved flesh, not the full swell I'd become so used to. Where was she?

Before I could chase away the panic spiraling through me at the discovery, the voices floated toward me once more. Drawing me forward as surely as a hook through my chest. I continued on my path, parting the mist with my arms as I went, hoping the fog would clear soon so I could see where I was, who I was with.

Light loomed in the distance, beckoning me with its warmth. It pierced through the particles of fog, illuminating the thousands of droplets until they shimmered like a veil. If I could reach the light, I'd break through the mist. I knew it.

My answer was on the other side.

I kept my steps slow and sure. My ears were on alert for the slightest shift, but other than the murmur of those voices, there was nothing else here but my thoughts and erratic heartbeat.

Until I heard them.

The muddied words suddenly came through, crisp and clear. One voice I knew; the other was a mystery to me.

"It wasn't time yet. They'll figure it out."

My mother's voice.

Dread shot through every cell, which only ratcheted higher when the other woman replied.

"I'm tired of waiting and playing these mortal games. Besides, I could not go another day choking on the scent of wet dog."

"You're the one who chose him. You could have had your pick."

"Right, because the options were just limitless. The succubus would have been more fun, but she wasn't exactly useful to our purpose, now was she?"

"She wasn't an option, and you know it."

I took one tentative step forward, needing to see who Mommy Dearest was talking to.

My mother's heavy sigh sounded much closer than before. I jerked backward. "Besides, we needed forms that would put us in the best position possible. Lilith is too well-connected. Gabriel would have sensed a change."

Lilith? What were they talking about?

"Regardless, I don't see how *that* body will serve you any . . . " My mother's voice lost its exasperated edge, and I could sense a newfound tension in her snapped words, "Leave me."

"But—"

"Now."

The oppressive atmosphere around me changed, shifting, the ethereal weight lessening but still holding an ominous sense of foreboding. I wanted to leave. This was dangerous. Something I shouldn't have found.

My blood ran ice-cold as the macabre silhouette of fingers stretched behind the veil. That one small thing took me right back to childhood. This was the boogeyman, come to steal me from my bed. I hadn't been this scared of a shadow since I'd been a four-year-old lonely girl whimpering beneath my blankets.

And when the fingers broke that misty wall, my heart clamored so hard beneath my ribs I thought they'd surely break. I jumped back, knowing it would be my death if those fingers brushed against me.

When I landed, I was no longer in my misty dreamland.

Harsh, gasping breaths burned my lungs as I stared ahead, the world around me returning to the four walls of Caleb's bedroom. The vampire slept peacefully beside me as I trembled, coated in sweat, heart thundering.

I hadn't had a dream like that . . . ever. It wasn't quite a nightmare, but it had climbed under my skin and grabbed hold of me just the same. I would never fall back asleep. Not with the memory of whatever *that* had been looping through my mind.

Restless. On edge. I needed to move. To remind myself of what was real and what was fantasy. My palm skated over the prominent swell of my belly as the baby kicked, and relief flooded my veins as that one thing grounded me.

I still couldn't shake the lingering sense of unease after a cool shower and fresh change of clothes which included another of Caleb's heavy sweaters. Needing some way to burn off this energy while he slept, I wandered outside, my feet leading me down the path to the beach.

"I wondered if I'd be seeing you again."

The unexpected voice, when I hadn't noticed another living soul so far, forced a shocked cry from my lips. I spun around, one hand curled protectively around my belly, the other clutching the amulet Natalie had given me. I hadn't taken the necklace off since she'd gifted it to me.

I eyed the young girl I'd met before. Kelly. She was wearing the same shawl and dress as the last time I'd seen her. "Jesus Christ, you need a fucking bell."

"I wasn't after scaring you, Sunday. I did wave as you passed by, but you seemed a fair bit lost in your thoughts. Is something the matter with you?"

"Just bad dreams."

"Oh, aye, I've had my share of those. It was always worse before a storm. Me Ma would tell me a story to send me off to sleep when the nightmares got especially bad."

*Yeah, well. My mom's the one who gives me nightmares, so . . .*

"Do you know when the supply boat is coming?" I asked, changing the subject. I didn't want to think about mothers or dreams anymore.

"Soon. The boatman should arrive any day now." She glanced at the horizon, her young face turning pensive as she eyed the gray clouds. "Though a storm is coming. Might be bad, from the looks of it."

Fucking great. I wondered if Caleb had prepared for something like this? Was there enough food if access to the island was cut off? If the boat was lost at sea? Or worse, the boatman in his thrall ended up dead?

What would Caleb do? Swim?

I let out a tight, nearly hysterical laugh as the image of Caleb swimming to the mainland hit me. He probably would, knowing that stubborn and determined man. And I'd be right there with him, clinging to his neck like a half-drowned backpack.

"Do you get storms often?" I turned my focus to Kelly, but she was gone again.

"You really need to work on your social skills!" I shouted down the beach. "These Irish goodbyes of yours leave a whole lot to be desired. No one likes standing around talking to themselves . . ."

Realizing I was doing just that and that it was only a small step above creating invisible boyfriends to talk to, I bit off a muttered curse and turned away from the water. In addition to the dark clouds looming, the afternoon sunlight had turned a dim, sickly green unlike anything I'd ever seen before.

My lower back ached as the unease from my dream flared up. The need to return to Caleb was a strong, insistent thrum in my veins. I knew he'd keep me safe from whatever threat headed our way. Storm or otherwise. Caleb had proven that he'd never let anything happen to me. Regardless of his abduction plot.

Instead of climbing the steep hill that would take me directly to my sleeping vampire, I opted for the more gentle slope which meandered through the village. I couldn't handle more than that. Not with this basketball belly making me waddle like a fucking duck. Because make no mistake, I was waddling.

I swore this baby had grown so much quicker than I thought she should. I'd seen pregnant women. Done my research. By my count, I shouldn't be this big. In the shower, I noticed my belly button had popped, and my skin was stretched tight over the taut dome of my pregnancy. I looked nearly full-term.

"There's only one of you in there, right?" As if she heard me, little Elvira fluttered.

Cradling my belly, I continued onward through the village. My breath came in labored huffs, and I was eyeing the last stretch of my hike with a growing sense of ire. What I needed was a golf cart. No. What I needed was to be far away from Ireland and its stupid rolling hills and rocky cliffs. Who thought bringing a pregnant woman to a place like this was a good idea? Oh, right. The sneaky fucking priest who wanted to make it impossible for her to run away. Criminal mastermind, that one. A real freaking genius.

My grumbled tirade amused me enough to spur me forward.

"I wouldn't go that way if I were you. It's not safe."

I swallowed back a scream for a second time that day. "What the hell is wrong with you people?"

A tall, spindly man wearing a pair of brown trousers and a cream shirt with dark suspenders tipped his hat at me in belated greeting. His beard was nearly to his collar, wild and bushy. If he'd been twenty years younger, I would have mistaken him for a hipster. "Apologies, miss. It's only that a storm is coming. You don't want to be caught out here without cover."

"I'm on my way home now."

"You're sure you don't want to come inside? You can wait out the storm by my fire. Nothing will happen to you."

"No, thanks. I'm good. My . . . fiancé is waiting for me." A wave of dizziness hit me from out of nowhere, and I had to sit down on the edge of the rock wall bordering the road.

Oh, shit. He'd proposed to me. I accepted. But I'd never said the word out loud. We hadn't talked about it again. I think part of me passed it off as something done in the heat of an emotional moment.

Caleb and I needed to talk about what me marrying him meant for the rest of my life. Surely he knew my heart was shared between all of them. Marrying him wouldn't change my connection to

Kingston, Noah, and Alek. If anything, it meant I'd be marrying each of them because there was no way any of my mates would let Caleb have something they didn't.

Well, I'd be marrying them if I didn't currently hate them.

A wave of crushing sadness swept through me, reminding me I didn't hate them. Not at all. I missed them. So fiercely that with each passing day it was harder to push them from my thoughts. I heard them talking to me, commenting on what I was doing as if they were right there in the room. I knew it wasn't healthy, but it was the only way I could have them in my life right now, and I'd take anything I could get. Any piece of the men who held me so tenderly and promised me the world.

But the truth was, nothing had changed. They still wanted to hurt us. I palmed my belly, a stab of agony accompanying that thought. It was why I was trying to leave them before Caleb took me. I couldn't help but wonder now if that had been the right choice. I'd managed to change Caleb's mind. Who's to say I wouldn't have been able to do the same with them? I hadn't even given them a chance. I'd just acted on pure protective instinct. Look where that got me.

"Are you well, miss? Come inside, please? Let me see to you."

The man reached for me, but every fiber of my being recoiled. I shook my head. "I'm fine. I'll just head home. Get there before the storm hits."

He looked troubled, his eyes hazy with some unnamed emotion. "Right. Well. Hurry then, miss."

I lumbered to my feet and lifted my hand in a wave. "See you around, I guess."

He waved before turning and heading inside. As I hustled as fast as I could up the hill to Caleb's house, unease prickled the back of my neck. Shadows loomed in the windows of every dwelling I passed. Why were these people watching me so intently?

The sky was nearly fully dark by the time I started up the hill that would lead me back to Caleb's land. I hadn't planned to be gone so long. The first fat raindrops fell from the clouds, landing on my exposed neck and sending a shiver rippling through me. My gaze traversed the path, a jolt of elation striking me at the sight of Caleb in the distance.

He met me halfway, his eyes blazing with concern. "What are you doing down here? It's dangerous."

"How is it dangerous? It's just a village. They're just people."

The man was looking at me like I was insane. "People? What are you on about? The island's deserted. There are no people."

"Caleb, there are people here. I just talked to two of them. I've seen Kelly on the beach twice now."

His eyes widened. "Kelly?"

"Yes, and the old fisherman."

He shook his head, palms clutching my shoulders, eyes locked on mine. "No, Sunday. You didn't. There's nothing but ghosts here."

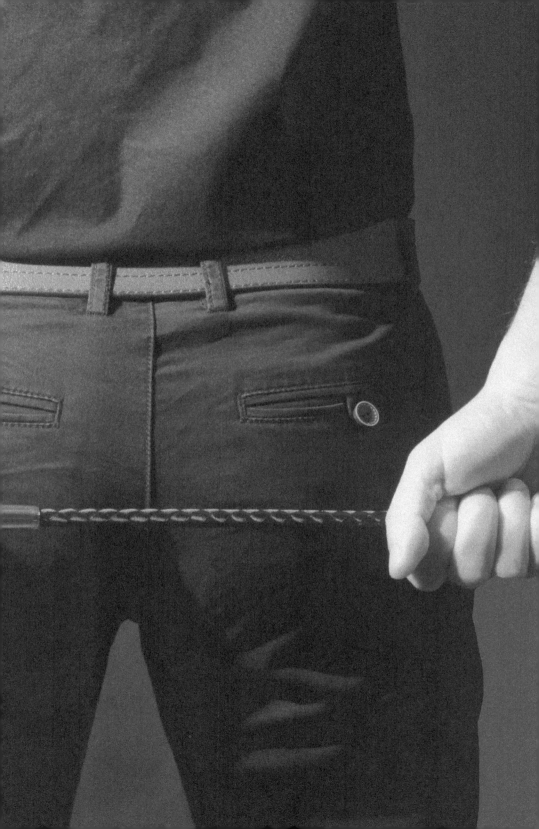

# CHAPTER
# TWENTY-FOUR
## CALEB

"Stop being so dramatic, Caleb." The way she laughed at my statement sent a chill up my spine.

"I'm not. There is no one on this island but the two of us. If you've seen anyone, they were most certainly not alive."

She laughed again, but it fizzled out when I didn't so much as crack a smile. "Caleb, I've seen my fair share of spirits, remember? Hell, I had a whole damn girl's night with Noah's Aunt Callie. I know the difference between a human and a fucking restless spirit."

"Do you?" I cocked a brow. "There are all sorts of ghosts, Miss Fallon. How can you be sure of what you saw?"

"I . . ." Her brow furrowed. "How do you know there's no one on this island?"

"Because I killed every last man, woman, and child the night I was turned. And I spent the last century ensuring no one set foot on this cursed land."

Her mouth fell open, all the color draining from her cheeks. "Wh—what? But, Kelly . . . she . . . and the fisherman . . ."

"Don't believe me? Here, I'll prove it to you." I grasped her wrist and yanked her harder than I probably should have, considering her condition, but my heart was racing, my confession sending me spiraling into a kind of self-loathing I hadn't experienced since I drained my flock dry.

She stumbled after me, the storm gathering strength as the drops fell faster from the sky. Thunder rumbled overhead as the wind picked up and whipped my too-long hair into my eyes. When we reached the edge of the village, I threw out my arm, gesturing to the row of darkened buildings. "Do these look like the kind of dwellings a mortal would reside in? Where's the light? The fire? The fecking noise?"

"But I . . . I saw him walking into that house." She pointed a trembling finger at a small stone cottage to our left.

"Aye, that belonged to Finnegan Killgariff, fisherman by trade, skirt chaser every other moment of his pathetic life, whether welcomed or not. I did the world a favor when I tore that drunkard's throat out."

She gasped and pulled her wrist free of my hold. "He tried to get me to go inside."

"Oh, I'm sure of it. A pretty lass like you all by her lonesome."

"It's not like he could have . . . done things to me . . . right?" She shuddered, biting down hard into the plump flesh of her lower lip.

"If the spirits are still here, there's no telling what kind of strength they've amassed over the years. A century is a long time, Sunday."

"But Kelly wasn't in the village. She . . ."

"Was on the beach?" Pain speared me at the mention of the O'Shanahan girl. I remembered her well. She'd been the final soul to be trapped here. Fitting, as her mother was the first. Her beloved daughter had been my last.

Sunday nodded.

"Aye. Because that's where she died. Where I drained her as she begged me to spare her."

"Caleb." Her voice was pleading but also confused. As if she wasn't entirely sure what she was asking me for.

"What's wrong, Miss Fallon? You no longer want to learn my truth. Do you think less of me now? I wouldn't blame you. Trust me, I hate myself more than you ever could."

"Don't fucking *Miss Fallon* me, Caleb. You're trying to make me see you as a monster. But the truth is, you don't want to face what you did."

I sputtered. "Don't want to face . . . Sunday, all I bloody do is reflect on the crimes I've committed. Make no mistake, I know *exactly* what kind of monster I am. Do *you*? Do you know who you've let in your bed? Inside that sweet cunt of yours?"

"Aren't we all monsters in the dark?"

"Not you. You're an angel sharing her light with me."

Her laugh was low and harsh. "I highly doubt an angel would have found herself knocked up by four different men at the same time and somehow ended up engaged to the man who kidnapped her. I'm just as fucked up as you are, Caleb. My sins just look a little different."

"They're the most beautiful sins I've ever heard. And even angels fall."

Her expression softened, her blue eyes piercing me with their earnest intensity. She took a step closer to me and rested her palm against my cheek. "And even good men are forced into situations out of their control. You need to forgive yourself, Caleb. If I can do it, so can you."

"The things I did . . ."

"Come with me," she said, threading our fingers and bringing my knuckles to her lips. "It's time for you to make your confession, Father Gallagher."

We walked silently toward the church, my mouth growing drier with each step. I hadn't set foot in there since the night I was turned. My very essence protested the thought of bringing my mate to the scene of my worst crimes. And yet there was a small part of me that wanted her to see it. To punish me. I deserved her hate more than I ever deserved her love.

"Sunday . . . I can't. The things I did . . ." I hated how my voice faltered as I repeated my protest, more for me than her.

"The things you did don't make you who you are now. A person is more than a series of moments. It is what they do after they fall down that defines them. They will always haunt you unless you lay yourself bare and face them head-on."

"I don't think I'm strong enough."

"You don't have to do it alone. We're stronger together, Caleb. I will see you through this. Be there for you like you've been there for me. That's what a wife is supposed to do, right?"

Her smile was teasing, the lift of her brow a challenge. I knew I was lost. I'd never been very good at denying her. And that one word coming from her lips. *Wife*. Christ, it ruined me. Shattered any resolve I might have clung to. I had no defense against her.

We may not be married in the eyes of God, but I wasn't even worthy of His gaze anyway. We may never make official vows. That didn't change the simple truth of it. She was still mine, and I was hers. We'd already promised ourselves to one another. That was enough for me.

"Lead the way, wife. I'll follow you into hell if you ask me to."

She smirked. "Careful, you might get your wish."

Together we pushed open the old wooden doors, the creak of rusty hinges echoing through the sanctuary. Flashes of that night hit me hard, but Sunday gripped my hand and reminded me she was there, holding me fast, keeping me grounded.

"I wasn't expecting it to be so dark in here. Aren't there supposed to be stained glass windows or something?"

"It's dark outside. No light coming through the clouds in this storm. Stay right there. I'll get the candles sorted."

I reached into my pocket, pulling out the lighter I kept on hand out of force of habit. In a few moments, I'd lit the dust-covered candles still lining the walls, stooping to pick up those that had fallen from their places in the candelabras. The heavy pillars smelled of wax and reminded me of the monthly deliveries I used to make to this very church before I became its pastor. Before this island was set up with electricity, we had to rely on firelight to get us through our nights. These thick candles were made to endure.

"So this was your parish?" Sunday asked as the glow lit the space. "Where's your confessional booth?" She flashed me a flirtatious grin, clearly thinking back to the last time we'd been seated in one together.

"Destroyed."

"By you?"

"No."

"Where will you make your confession, then?"

I shoved my hands in my pockets, feeling more uncomfortable in this space than I had since I was a lad. "I don't think it truly matters."

"Well then, I guess it's my turn to get you on your knees, Mr. Gallagher." She emphasized the title, putting me in my place as easily as if she'd shoved me to the floor herself.

I couldn't help myself; I growled low in my throat at the order. She would pay for that when we were finished here. I would enjoy every fecking second of it.

But first, I had ghosts to exorcise. That meant facing my demons. I slid into the nearest pew and settled on the kneeler. "Sunday, I'm not even sure where to begin."

"Haven't you ever seen that musical? You start at the very beginning. It's a very good place to start."

"I was only the priest on this island for one day . . ."

Sunday's playful teasing gave way to intense focus and profound empathy as she sat on the pew in front of me, her eyes glued to mine. For as reticent as I'd been about doing this, the words poured from me as soon as I started, desperate to be released. I hadn't realized how badly I'd needed this confession. It's one I'd offered up many times, but never to another living soul. Never to someone whose opinion mattered to me.

There wasn't a flicker of disgust or judgment in her eyes as I finished my tale. Then she leaned forward and kissed the seemingly permanent furrow between my brows. "You're forgiven, Caleb. And you're loved. So loved it's painful for me to see you like this. No one should despise themselves this much."

Tears burned in my eyes, and it was impossible to breathe as her hushed words sank deep into what was left of my blackened heart.

"What did I do to deserve a life with you? No matter how short," I looked up into her eyes and swallowed thickly. "I don't know how you can love a creature as undeserving and monstrous as me."

"I don't know why you can't see the truth. A monster wouldn't think twice about what he did. True evil has no remorse. You aren't the demon you think you are. You wouldn't be this upset if you were."

I sucked in a breath, feeling as though razor blades had taken up residence in my lungs. She cupped my face, sweetly kissing me.

"No more, Caleb. You cannot keep punishing yourself. I won't allow it. If you don't trust yourself to make that call, then trust me. I wouldn't give my heart to someone who wasn't worthy. And more than that, husband, how can you tell me you love me if you don't even know how to love yourself?"

I didn't have words to respond. Instead, I stood and exited my pew so I could stand in front of her. I needed more than her sweet voice. I needed her in my arms. "Come here to me, *a stor*." She nearly melted into my hold, letting me clutch her to my chest as I breathed in her scent and let her chase away all my ghosts. "I do not deserve you," I whispered against her lips.

"No. But thankfully fate saw fit to give me to you anyway." She grinned, her eyes flashing in the candlelight. "Are you ready for one of my confessions, Father Gallagher?"

My cock gave an appreciative twitch at the hunger in her voice. "What could you possibly have to confess?"

A wicked gleam lit her eyes. "I get dirty thoughts about you."

A surprised laugh escaped before I could stop it. "Do you, now? I would hope so, given the ones I have of you."

"No, I mean . . ." She licked her lips, her eyes darting to the altar beside us. "During class, when you'd be lecturing—"

"You mean to tell me you were daydreaming in my class, Miss Fallon?"

She nodded, her lips twitching. "Pretty much exclusively. I couldn't stop thinking about one thing in particular."

"Oh, and what's that?" My palm skated down her spine until I reached the swell of her backside. One hard squeeze had her moaning.

"You, fucking me on the altar. Taking me in every hole until I screamed."

What breath I had left stuttered out of me at her filthy words. The man I used to be would have been scandalized by the thought, but the creature I was now? He was hard and already weeping at the possibilities.

"Well then, let's make those dreams of yours come true. I won't have it said that I don't take care of my wife's every need."

Her tongue darted out to wet her lower lip.

"On your knees, Mrs. Gallagher. Before the altar. Clothing off, arse ready for my palm."

Her cheeks went rosy at my use of the name, need flaring to life in her eyes. But without a second request from me, she pulled her sweater—no, *my* sweater—over her head and dropped it on the floor, baring her delectable breasts as if offering them up as her tithe.

"Sweet suffering Jesus," I muttered under my breath, raking a hand through my hair as I forced myself not to lay her down and defile every inch of her right fecking now.

Then she slipped out of those flimsy little leggings she seemed so fond of, knickers going with them.

"I told you not to wear those any longer, Mrs. Gallagher."

She blinked up at me, looking both innocent and oh-so-naughty all at once. My hands itched to punish her, if only to hear her sweet cries and watch the flood of arousal it would surely cause. My girl did love to be punished.

"I forgot, Father Gallagher."

Gritting my teeth against the groan that swelled inside me, I palmed my aching cock and took a deep breath. "And you're still not on your knees. My, my, you are a bad girl, aren't you? One little proposal and you lose all your training. I'm going to have to start all over."

She clenched her thighs, her breaths coming in shallow little pants. "Yes, Daddy."

"Well . . . why are you still standing?"

Biting her lower lip and averting her gaze, she whispered, "It's just . . . it's hard to get on my knees like this."

"Like what?"

Bringing her eyes to meet mine, she gave a soft sigh. "I don't know if you've noticed, but I'm not as agile as I used to be." She waved a hand at her rounded belly.

Understanding dawned, and I immediately felt like an insensitive arse. "Here, let me help you."

I moved to her, cupping her cheek and feathering kisses over her forehead and eyelids as I held her close. And then I dropped my hand and tenderly rested it against the place where our child was safe and growing.

"Caleb," she moaned, though I was barely touching her.

"You are the most beautiful creature I've ever seen. Looking at you like this gets me so fecking hard. All the time. I can't believe I held off for as long as I did."

"I'm huge."

"You're so tempting. You were gorgeous before, but now? God in heaven, Sunday, knowing I helped put that baby inside you makes me want to do it again and again."

Tears misted her eyes, and she blinked a few times. "Well then . . . I don't think there's a whole lot we can do to make that happen right now. But we can practice if you want, so you'll be ready next time."

I grinned, taking her hand in mine, supporting her as she dropped to her knees. Fuck, I could smell her wet cunt, and my mouth watered. I wanted to feast on her until I made her squirt again. I needed to remind her that her changing body wasn't anything she should be ashamed of. That it was such a turn-on I could barely keep myself contained.

But first. There was the matter of her punishment to see to.

"Palms on your thighs. Eyes on me."

A devilish gleam sparked in her irises, but she did as I asked. Then, without taking my gaze from hers, I pulled out my stone-hard cock and placed the crown on her full lips. "Open."

Her tongue darted out, sweeping over my leaking tip and collecting the pearl of liquid I couldn't hide. A shiver tore through me at the wet heat of her mouth as she opened wide for me. She moved to grasp me with her hands, but I stopped her with my fingers in her hair.

"Don't. You're not in control here, Miss Fallon. You're not sucking me off. I'm fucking your face. Now be a good girl and take it." Just saying the words made my balls tighten and throb. I would spill myself all over her face here and now if I didn't get a grip.

From the looks of things, Sunday was in a similar predicament. Her pupils were blown, her cheeks flushed, her fingers digging into the tops of her thighs as she fought against her need to touch me.

Gripping myself at the base, squeezing hard and fighting back a groan, I slipped past her lips, guiding her head forward until I hit the back of her throat. Sunday moaned, the vibrations shooting through my cock and settling in my aching balls.

Christ, I wasn't going to last. I didn't want to come yet. I needed to make her feel just as good, to paint her with my spend, consecrate our bond with the evidence of what she did to me.

"Fuck." My harsh shout left me as her throat constricted, the involuntary movement pulling me deeper and driving me wild. I couldn't remain still. I rolled my hips, fucking her throat as her eyes streamed with tears and she met me thrust for thrust. Taking everything I had to give.

"Take my fucking cock. That's my good girl."

She groaned again, and I knew if I didn't stop, I'd be spilling down her throat in mere moments.

I pulled out, a line of her saliva connecting us from my crown to her swollen bottom lip. I ran my palm over the top of her head as we both fought for breath. I was pulsing. Seconds away from reaching my crest.

The image of her covered in my cum gave me an idea. Neither of us wanted this to be quick. And we both needed a second to come back from the edge.

"Stay. Do not move."

She whimpered but nodded. The look of absolute trust in her eyes had me wanting to praise her.

"You're doing so well. Daddy's proud of you, baby girl."

Her eyes fluttered, her reaction to my words primal and instinctive. "Thank you, Daddy."

I hid my grin, loving that I could make her squirm without even touching her. Then I stepped away, moving behind her to the tower of flickering candles by the altar. Grasping one, I lifted it free and returned to her.

"Do you remember your safe word?"

She eyed the candle, her tongue swiping across her lips as she nodded.

"Say it."

"Rosary."

Just like the last time, her unknowing use of the word I'd selected for her in my fantasy had my cock pulsing. We were connected in more ways than I'd ever thought possible.

"Use it if you need it. This might hurt. If the pain ever surpasses the pleasure, I want you to let me know immediately." Fisting my fingers in the hair at her nape, I tugged sharply. "And with each drop of wax that runs down your feverish skin, I want you to imagine it's my cum. Marking you. Claiming you. I want you to know who you belong to."

"Caleb."

"That's right. *Me.* You are mine, Miss Fallon. And right now, I can do anything I want to you. The most depraved acts of my imagining, and you'd beg for each and every one. You live to serve me, don't you, darling girl?

"Yes."

I grinned. If she had any idea it was the other way around, that she was the one who owned me, she gave no indication of it. That was probably for the best. She'd already ruined me. I don't think I'd survive if she actually flexed her power.

Focus trained on her face, I let the first drops fall across her breasts, watching the splashes of wax as they turned from clear liquid to white trails. My cock jerked, cum leaking from the tip just at the sight.

Sunday moaned. Arching her back as if she was trying to give me better access to her body. "I need more."

"Aye, me too. Now be quiet. I didn't say you could speak. Unless you're using your safe word, don't talk out of turn."

She clamped her lips shut and nodded.

I drizzled more of the liquid wax onto her, fighting the urge to touch myself when the thin rivers slipped down over the crest of her belly. My hand jerked, and wax landed on the peak of her swollen nipple.

Sunday cried out, a wanton, needy sound. "More."

Not giving a damn that she disobeyed me, I did it again on her other breast, both of us panting as we did our best to stave off our rapidly building climaxes. I could arrive untouched if we continued with this game of ours.

"I'll give you so much you won't know your name in a minute, Miss Fallon," I gritted out.

"You. I need you."

"Aye, and you'll be having me. In every fucking hole you have."

Setting the candle down, I reached for her. I slid one arm beneath her thighs and wrapped the other around her back. She was up and cradled in my arms before she knew I'd lifted her.

"What are you doing?"

"I'm having my way with you, right here on the altar. It's the only proper way for me to worship my Sunday."

Her breath hitched. "Yes. God, please."

"That's Daddy to you, Miss Fallon."

Setting her at the edge of the altar, I spread her thighs wide, noting the slickness with satisfaction. "You look positively edible. In fact, I think I need a taste." I reached between her legs, sliding two fingers through her folds, curling them up and into her before pulling out. She protested, her hips chasing me as I raised my fingers to my lips, licking them clean while I held her gaze. I groaned. "Delicious. My favorite nectar."

I reached back down, gathering more of her arousal, this time offering my fingers to her. Rubbing the tips along her bottom lip just as I had with the crown of my weeping cock. "Taste yourself, Miss Fallon."

She parted her lips and took my fingers inside, her tongue along my skin sending jolts of pleasure straight to my length.

"You're right. It's so sweet."

"Honey."

"God, Caleb, please fuck me."

I pushed her onto her back, offering her wet cunt a light slap. "What was that?"

"Fuck me, Daddy."

I shook my head, tutting under my breath. "You're not supposed to be speaking, Miss Fallon. I'm torn between giving you what you want for correcting yourself or punishing you further until you learn your lesson."

I sent up a silent prayer she wouldn't test me further because I needed it just as badly as she did. Everything in me hurt to sink inside her. But my plans involved much more than simply fucking her into oblivion. I wanted to possess her. To leave my mark on her soul. That meant she needed to be fully prepared for me to claim her in a way she wouldn't ever be able to forget. Our moments were fleeting, as the world had already begun to crash down around us. Tonight had to count for everything we'd never get to do again.

Glancing to my left, I searched the wall for the bottle of oil I knew had been stored there.

"Where are you—"

"Hush, Miss Fallon. Or you may never get that orgasm you're hunting."

She whimpered.

I lifted the bottle, dipping a finger in to ensure that it hadn't turned in the years it had been left sitting, but no. It would serve. Returning to her side, I held up the candle once more.

Her chest heaved as she guessed my purpose. I tipped the pillar, little splashes of wax landing between her legs, up along her thighs, and finally right on top of that perfect little cunt.

Sunday cried out, her back bowing off the altar. With the liquid wax properly disposed of, I blew out the candle.

"Open your legs wider, my darling one. Let me have you."

Her tight nod did unnameable things to me. Such a simple gesture, and yet it drove me wild. Candle still held aloft, I picked up the oil with my other hand, tipping it until the slippery liquid poured along her already dripping center. We were going to need plenty more of it by the time I was through with her.

Taking the candle, I ran the bottom along her seam, guiding the glistening drops where I wanted them to go. Then I pushed inside her, long, slow, as far as I could, loving the sight of her pink lips constricting as I did. I worked the candle in and out, knowing she could take it because I was larger and she stretched around me perfectly.

Her sweet cries filled the air around us, her body working to pull more inside her. I was teasing her, purposely holding back, and she knew it.

"Stop playing with me."

"Never, Miss Fallon."

I poured more lubrication across her, taking my fingers through the slickness and bringing it back to the last place on her body I hadn't fucked. Slowly, I sank one finger inside her arse, grunting at her soft moan. I worked her open, adding a second digit and timing my movements with the thrusts of my other hand. Only when she was writhing and dripping for me did I pull the candle free of her cunt before positioning it over the tight ring of her arse.

She sucked in a sharp breath, then whispered, "Yes, please."

Watching in tense fascination, I breached her with the wax pillar, imagining it was my cock and nearly spilling myself as I did. Fuck, I couldn't take this much longer. I only fucked her arse with the candle for a moment before pulling the damned thing out and tossing it aside. I was done letting her get pleasure from anything other than my body.

She was breathless, writhing, her eyes closed as she tried to suck in the air she so desperately needed. Grasping her by the hips, I drove into her pussy in one hard thrust.

"Caleb!"

Her perfect cunt gripped me so tight, her muscles already fluttering with her impending climax. I'd kept us both on edge for so long; I knew this would be quick and dirty. But I didn't care. I just wanted to hear her scream my name again, the sound of it echoing around the empty church. Casting away the memories that haunted me and rechristening this holy place as ours.

I fucked her ruthlessly, holding her wide open as I drove in and out. Full round tits bounced with each thrust, the sight erotic and tantalizing as her walls tightened around me and she came with a sob.

*More. I need more of this. Forever.*

"Caleb, I want you in my ass. You promised."

Lord have mercy. I pulled out and poured a liberal amount of oil into my palm, slicking it over my length before lining up against her tiny hole. "Tell me if it's too much."

"Stop talking and give me what I need, husband."

That did it. I was a man possessed as she used that name for me.

I pressed inside with the control of a saint, watching her for any sign of pain. But she writhed and moaned, her eyes rolling back in her head, and God help me, the woman came again as I sheathed myself to the hilt.

"So tight and hot. Fuck, Sunday."

"I need you to move. Please, I need more."

"I'll give you everything, Mrs. Gallagher. All you need do is ask."

"Caleb."

I began thrusting in earnest, pumping my cock into her and barely able to see straight from the pleasure. But I was a greedy man, and I didn't want to finish without hearing her climax one more time. Reaching down, I pinched her swollen nub, giving her a bite of pain to help her reach her pinnacle.

"Fuck, Caleb."

She detonated once more, her muscles squeezing me like a fucking vise and sending me right over the cliff with her.

She was mine. I was hers. And as I came down from my high and the world returned to focus, instead of seeing the remnants of a life I'd ruined, of the town I'd devastated, I saw only her and the life we'd created.

Sunday was my second chance.

I couldn't change what I'd done, but I wouldn't live in the guilt any longer either. This woman, this incredible, infuriating woman, had reminded me that forgiveness was possible. Even for someone like me.

What better proof of the divine could there be?

# CHAPTER
# TWENTY-FIVE

## THORNE

*Two weeks since Sunday's abduction*

I sat up on the verge of orgasm, heart racing, skin tingling from the echoes of whatever the bloody hell that was. My cock was a length of steel, my balls tight and full, heavy with unsatisfied arousal. I could smell her still, taste her, feel the softness of her skin and the slick evidence of need between her thighs.

"Sunday," I moaned, palming my dick. "Fuck, I miss you."

It had been ages since I'd felt her like that. I'd been trying to meet her in her dreams since the night she'd left, but she'd been closed off from me. Until tonight. My imagination was vivid, but even on its best day, I couldn't have conjured up *that*. Which meant it was real. I'd connected with her.

That bit of hope skated through my veins, burning me from the inside out. I closed my eyes and laid back against my pillow, searching for her through the fog of lust still gripping me. If I could break through while I was conscious, maybe I could pinpoint her location.

Her scent came to me again, but I couldn't get farther than that. There was nothing more than the tease of lilacs until even that was gone and I was alone in pure darkness.

"No! Goddammit! Come back!"

I fisted my sheets, frustration and unfulfilled hunger for her boiling to the surface. I was such a twisted fuck, wanting her body even though she'd been taken and was likely in grave danger. But my world had been hell these last few days since returning to the ruin that was Blackthorne Manor, and she was my solace. I needed to lose myself in her. Even if it was only in my mind.

Reaching for the phone beside my bed, I searched for the video I'd taken what seemed like an eternity ago. That night burned bright in my mind for more reasons than one.

Pressing play on the screen, I held the phone with one hand and wrapped my fingers around my length with the other. It wouldn't be as good as the real thing, but at least I could bring myself off with her name on my lips and her voice in my ears.

"I can't believe I agreed to this," she giggled, her beautiful face flushed as she watched me set up the phone before returning to her.

"How else will I satisfy myself if we're parted? No one makes me feel the way you do, dove. I only want to watch you."

"Stalker."

"A stalker would do it without your knowledge. I want you looking into the camera when you come. Knowing I'll be touching myself when I replay this."

My cock pulsed in my hand as she bit her lower lip and got onto her hands and knees on the bed, staring straight at the phone, her full tits swaying, hips lush and curvy flaring out behind her. I hadn't turned this video on once since taking it but seeing it now, I was so glad we'd done this.

I pleasured myself with languid, lazy strokes as she laid back on the bed, parting her thighs for me. Seeing myself there with her, knowing how much she wanted me, had precum leaking from my tip already.

"Fucking hell, Sunday," I said on a tight groan as her back arched and my head disappeared between her thighs.

I'd gotten the angle just right, so the Noah on screen didn't block a single part of her perfection. Other than the dip of my head as I devoured her, all I could see was my mate, writhing in pleasure. Evidence of her approaching orgasm was there, caught by the camera, things I hadn't seen in the moment. The tight, rosy nipples and flushed cheeks, her furrowed brow and parted lips. She was closer than I had thought from the instant my tongue slid across her.

I nearly came as her hands slipped over her breasts and she began toying with her nipples. I hadn't seen that while I'd been busy between her legs. Fuck, it was hot.

"Noah," she moaned. "You make me feel so good."

The hand fisting my cock moved faster at her words, my grip tightening as I chased my own climax. "That's right, dove. I always make it good for you."

A shadow fell over our forms just before Alek's voice filled the room. "Well, well, is there room for one more at this party?"

Sunday smiled, then moaned again, holding out her hand to him. "Always." Then she scraped her nails along my scalp and tugged my hair. "Noah, I'm hungry too."

I shuttled my palm over my length, remembering vividly what came next. With my other hand, I tapped the fast-forward button, moving past the part where Alek took over, working her with his teeth and tongue while I moved to her mouth.

Watching her suck me, recalling the way her throat convulsed around me as she took me to the root, I groaned again. This time I didn't care how loud I was. I pumped my dick faster, desperate to come.

"What the fuck is going on in here? Who are you fucking?" Kingston burst in, breaking the bloody lock, eyes blazing, fury on his face.

"Jesus fucking Christ, Kingston. I'm a bit busy at the moment."

I covered myself with the sheets, staring daggers at the enraged wolf.

"I heard sex."

"Does it look like I'm having sex?"

A cry of pure pleasure echoed from where I'd dropped my phone, the video still playing.

He cocked a brow. "Porn? Wow, I didn't peg you for a porn guy."

Sunday's ecstasy-filled voice filled the room. "Alek, fuck—"

"Wait . . . you have *Sunday* porn? And you didn't share? I thought we were bros."

"When have you and I ever been *bros*? I barely tolerate you."

"Well, we're about to get real close. Scoot over, Thorne."

"Are you serious? No."

Kingston reached into his gray sweats and gave his dick a cursory stroke. "Jake misses her too. It's not like we haven't jerked off in front of each other before. I watched you and Alek double team her."

"That was different. She was right there with us."

He gestured to the phone. "She's right there. It's only weird if you make it weird."

God, I was aching. I needed some relief. I needed her. With a sigh, I propped the phone on a pillow between us.

"Fuck, she looks hot. Where was I when you took this?"

"Off running with your pack. Bad choice, mate."

"Well, if I knew I was missing secret threesome time, I sure as fuck would have stayed in."

"You missed more than one of these. But I'm certain I was in the same boat when I had to hunt."

"No offense, dude, but my dick is in my hand. I don't really want to have a heart-to-heart with you right now. Rewind the tape and let's do this."

I started the video over, and soon the two of us were focused on what Sunday was doing, not each other. I would have thought wanking with Kingston in my bed would be odd, but honestly, once I felt that build of pleasure at the base of my spine, I didn't care who was with me. I was searching for one thing and one thing only.

"God, yes," Kingston gritted out, his groan only adding to the tense need in the room.

"Fuuuck." I couldn't stop it now if I wanted to. On the screen, Alek was fucking her deep, and I was spilling my cum all over her tits, ragged moans leaving all of us.

"Sunshine, fuck, yes, Sunshine." Kingston jerked on the bed, but I didn't tear my gaze from my beautiful mate on the phone.

She came with an unintelligible cry, her back bowing, and I was lost. My orgasm raced through me, wave after wave, as I painted my chest and stomach with the pent-up release I'd needed so much.

Both of us breathing hard, we watched our girl come down from her high. She stared straight into the camera and said, "I love you."

Kingston's breath hitched, and I knew he was experiencing the same twisting feeling in his chest I was. "I miss her."

"Me too."

He glanced at me, his lips twitching as he looked down at my cum-covered torso. "Been a while, huh?"

"Piss off."

Then he got to his feet, using his shorts to wipe up his own release.

Curiosity got the better of me as the two of us cleaned up. "Can I ask you something?"

"Sure."

"Didn't those hurt?" I pointed at his dick. "The piercings?"

He smirked. "That's kind of the point, Thorne. But they feel really fucking good now."

I winced. "Maybe for you."

"Hey. Wank mates don't kink shame. You get off on blood play. I like pain."

"Fair enough."

"So . . . you gonna send me that video?"

"Only if you promise we will never talk about what just happened in my bed."

"Deal." Then he grinned. "Although, I bet Sunday would get off so fucking hard if she knew. Might be worth letting her in on the secret."

"If we ever see her again," I murmured as I pulled on a pair of boxers.

"Don't fucking talk like that. We're getting her back. She is ours. If I have to stake that fucking priest myself, she's coming home with us. We aren't losing her. We've lost too much already."

The mood in the room changed instantly in the wake of his fiercely determined statement. God, we'd lost more than we'd won at this point. I'd forced myself not to think of Rosie, used my need for Sunday to distract me from the hole in my chest left by the loss of her and now my sister.

Kingston put his hand on my shoulder. "I know. I'm grieving too. But being sad doesn't help anyone, especially those it's too late to save. All we can do is find a way to end this."

"Saving the world seems like the best sort of vengeance, doesn't it?"

"Fuck yes, it does."

"It's a good thing we have a date with an archangel, then. If it's biblical intervention we need, he will be the one to provide it."

"Ah yes, our good buddy Gabe. Can't wait."

We stood there in silence, letting the determination to get our mate back sit heavy between us. Then I cocked my head and stared at Kingston.

"You really thought I was fucking some girl in here?"

He shrugged. "It seemed out of character, especially since you're . . . you. But I heard sex noises."

"And so you decided to what, come running? Is that like your mating call or something?"

"I figured it was either porn, or I'd finally have a reason to castrate you. Win-win."

I shook my head, blowing out a breath. "You really are a wank stain, aren't you?"

"I know you are, but what am I?"

"For fuck's sake, how old are you?"

Kingston hooked his arm around my neck and pressed a smacking kiss to my forehead. "I'm old enough to fuck our girl and jerk off with you in your bed."

"I hate you." He was never going to let me live this down. I still couldn't believe I agreed to it, but, well, here we were.

"Love you too, Thorne."

"Get out of my room." As he headed for the door, I called, "Oh, and Kingston? The next time you hear sex noises coming from behind a *locked* door, stay the fuck out."

He smirked. "Never gonna happen." Then the arsehole blew me a kiss and shut the broken door as he left.

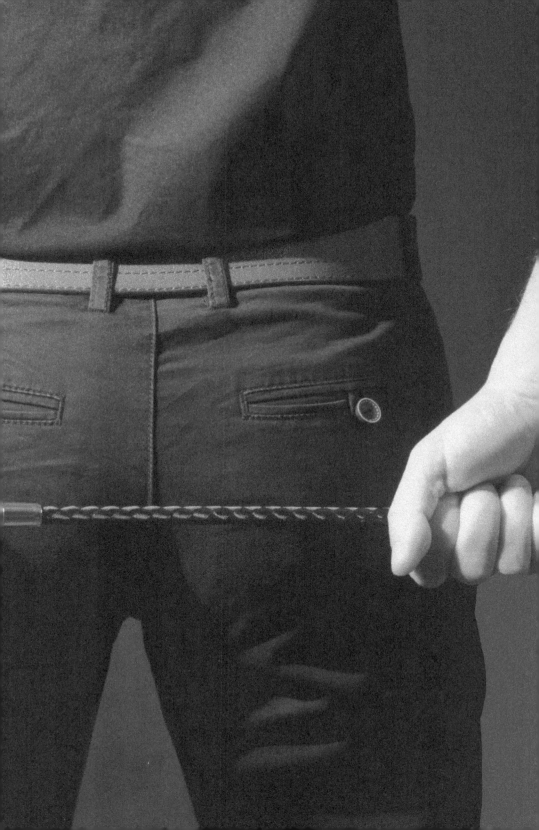

# TWENTY-SIX

## KINGSTON

"Are you sure this winged fuckboy is going to show his face?" I asked, staring daggers at Cashel. I shouldn't have been so edgy, not after blowing my load only a few hours ago, but I was a shitshow as we waited on our last chance at saving the fucking world.

It had been two weeks. Two fucking weeks since Caleb had stolen Sunday. All along, that ass had been right under our noses. Plotting. I never thought it would take us so long to find her. If I'd known . . . I don't think I would have been able to keep myself together as long as I had.

And after the week I'd had, the cracks were showing. I wouldn't make it much longer without her. She was the glue that kept my broken pieces together. Without her, I'd fall apart. Shattered. Broken. Useless.

"You're not very patient, are you?" Cashel asked, his expression unamused. "I summoned him only five minutes ago. The Messenger of God is not going to drop everything for this."

"You scheduled the meeting. He shouldn't have anything else planned."

The air shifted, the pressure change making my ears pop and my skin crawl as Gabriel materialized in the center of the room. Biker leathers and gleaming hair included. I still couldn't get over that.

"Patience is a virtue."

"So is promptness." I actually had no fucking idea if that was true, but it seemed like it should be.

The angel raised a brow. "Not when you're the one doing someone else a favor. Mind your manners, little wolf. This is not the most pressing event in my diary."

Recognizing the cover of the book in his pocket, I couldn't resist myself. "Oh, hey. That's one of my favorites. Isn't it wild how it was the mom stalking them all along?"

"No. I haven't finished yet. Hence the reason it's in my pocket." Gabriel scowled at me, his expression thunderous and, for the first time, truly terrifying. "And to think I believed you might retain one redeeming quality."

"Oh, he has them, I promise," Thorne said, coming to my rescue. "At least one. It's just buried deep."

"It would have to be."

"I still haven't found it," Alek said.

"Fuck all of you . . . except maybe you, Thorne. You have good porn."

Alek raised a brow, and Thorne's expression went murderous.

"How do you know what kind of porn he has?" Alek asked.

"Are we here to discuss the finer points of pornography, or are we here for another purpose, Cashel? I have an entire Apocalypse to plan for."

I didn't wait for the vampire to respond. "Well, Gabe, we need you to find Sunday."

"Gabriel. My name is not Gabe."

"Po-tay-toe, po-tah-toe, buddy. I need my mate back. And if you want to stop your doomsday, you need to help us."

"Was the Belladonna coven unable to lift the spell cloaking her?"

"Do you think we'd be here right now if they did?"

"It's not a spell," Moira said from the doorway. She looked haunted. Like she was still suffering after the failed attempt to find Sunday. To be fair, we all were. "It's something . . . evil. It felt like death."

"Come here, child. Let me look into your mind and see your truth." Gabriel's voice took on an almost hypnotic tone as he spoke. He held out his hands, and Moira tentatively approached.

Taking her palms in his, he took a deep breath before stiffening. Moira's eyes rolled back in her head and she went limp.

"What the hell are you doing to her?" Alek snarled, his berserker rising to the surface. That had been happening more and more frequently these last few days. His control was on a hair trigger. It wouldn't take much more before the beast snapped free of his leash.

Gabriel's lips twitched. "Oh, this isn't my doing."

"Stop it this instant," Thorne demanded.

"Quiet. I never get to witness visions as they're received. Let me enjoy it."

Moira blinked as she came back to herself, her gaze locking on Gabriel's, all the color drained from her face, her fire-engine curls now a deep plum. But it was the angel who spoke first.

"Death was right. Your Sunday is beyond my reach. My grace can't break through something like this." Despair flitted across his face. "It is done. We have lost."

"What the fuck does that mean?" I bellowed.

"There's something else blocking her from me, beyond any mortal or witch ability. The only time I've come across a power like this was when I laid the seventh seal. This is out of my, as you say, wheelhouse."

"Are you fucking serious?" Thorne's outburst surprised me, but I echoed his sentiments.

"I'm sorry. This level of darkness . . . it speaks to the work of Lucifer. The only being who has ever been able to best me."

"Best you?" Alek folded his arms over his chest.

"The fallen took my wings in battle. Nearly ended my existence. So yes. Best me."

"So Lucifer is in charge, then? God is the bottom in this situation?" I asked.

Gabriel shot me a disparaging look. "No. But my Father is unable to meddle in events such as these. He is bound by destiny."

"Useless fucking angel," I grumbled to myself as I took up pacing in front of the large fireplace. "Angels and demons, goddamned witches, Apocalypses. All I wanted was my mate, maybe a baby or twelve. I didn't sign up for the end of the world."

Moira snorted, color restored and seeming to have made a full recovery from whatever the fuck that was. She proved me right as soon as she opened her mouth. "Twelve? Good luck convincing Sunday's vagina about that. Your kids will be walking themselves out at that point."

"I wasn't asking for your opinion. Did you miss the part where I was muttering to *myself*?"

"Maybe you should try that in a room that isn't filled with other people then, sweetie."

"What about your gods?" Thorne asked, interrupting my sidebar with the witch and giving Alek a beseeching look. "There's more than one deity we can turn to, surely."

"Don't you think I would have mentioned it by now if it was a possibility? We may be blessed by our gods, but they have no power in this realm."

"Balls."

"Maybe that's exactly the problem," Moira offered.

"What?" I asked. "Does this have anything to do with your little" —I waved my finger around to indicate her eyes—"hallucination."

She glared at me. "It was a vision, dumbass, and of course it does."

"So what's the fucking problem?"

"Men. You're all so focused on the fight, you're not thinking with anything other than testosterone. This is why you have me around." She turned her gaze on the angel. "You're excused."

Gabriel's brows rose to his hairline. But he gave her a smirk. "Best of luck to you all. I'm certainly rooting for you. I do so love a happy ending." Then he vanished, but not before flinging the paperback he'd had straight at my face. I guess he didn't want to finish now that I'd spoiled it.

"Okay, Moira. We're all listening. Balls firmly in check. What does team ovary have for us?"

She grinned. "I'm so glad you asked."

"Well, I'm waiting, witch."

"Sunday's mom is probably Lucifer, right? Well, if good old Luci is part of this, as Gabriel seemed to think, why would we go to an angel for help?"

"Because he's all fucking powerful," Alek said.

"No, he's not. He said as much. But you know who is as close to Lucifer as we can get?"

I let out an exhausted breath. "Moira, just spit it out."

"Lilith."

"Is that who your vision was about?" Alek asked.

"Yes. I think it means we're supposed to go to her, that she's the one with the answers we've been looking for. And it makes sense, right? Since she *is* the original demon. I bet she can find Sunday for us if Luci is behind the veil hiding her. Who better to counteract the powers of hell than a creature made by them?"

I smirked, cutting a glance at Cashel. "Hey, pops, can we borrow the plane?"

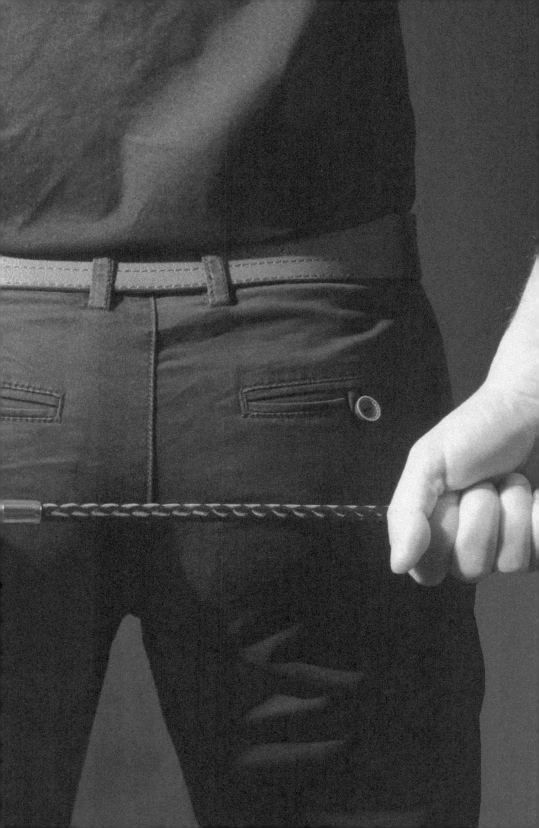

# TWENTY-SEVEN

## SUNDAY

A shiver ran through me as I carefully crouched in front of the hearth to light the fire. This storm seemed never-ending. Rain pelted the windows; wind howled with the force of a banshee, rattling the very walls of the house. Of course, Caleb slept through it because the sun was technically still up, but try as I might, I couldn't.

It had been so loud at one point that the rain sounded like bullets, and I'd been convinced the glass panes were seconds away from shattering. I'd been up ever since, moving around the house, trying to keep myself busy.

There wasn't a whole lot to do. I could only refold a blanket or organize the pantry so many times. Chewing on my bottom lip, I made a mental note to ask Caleb about our supplies. Things were a little sparse, and with the way this storm refused to die out, it wasn't likely a boat would be docking here anytime soon.

My stomach growled as the flames finally caught in the fireplace, the wood crackling and heat radiating into the room. *See, I don't need a man to do everything for me. I can take care of myself.* But, as I glanced at the one remaining log in the basket, I said a little prayer of thanks

Caleb would be here to go get more. I didn't want to go outside. Not if I could help it.

A sort of calm had settled over us over the last day. Something had shifted after our time in the church, a sense of belonging we hadn't been able to admit to before. I only wished my other mates were here too, sharing a home and a life with me like they should be.

The cottage was way too small for the five of us, well, six once Elodie joined us. Even so, I could perfectly picture Kingston in the kitchen, a towel draped over his shoulder as he made dinner. Alek sprawled on the couch, our baby in his lap while he sang softly. Noah in a chair by the fire, a book in his hands.

My heart twisted, and I pushed to my feet. I needed to keep moving. The quiet gave me entirely too much room to think. And thoughts weren't safe right now.

Switching on the kettle, I pulled a tea bag from the container and placed it in my favorite mug, waiting as the water came to a boil.

I smelled him before he touched me, that incense and spice scent that had haunted me since the night we first met. Something released inside me, pent-up tension I'd held coiled tight without even knowing. His hands slid around my waist before resting on my belly, cradling me gently.

"She's shifted since last night. You're carrying lower now." There was an edge of worry in his voice.

"She's growing so fast. I can breathe better, though, so at least there's that. She was up in my ribs only last night."

"Hmm." He didn't say anything else, but something told me this change in the baby's position wasn't good news.

I poured the hot water over my tea as he continued holding me. My thoughts were heavy, Caleb's concerns adding to the emotional weight.

"You're upset about something. I can see it in your posture, *a stor*. What sort of worries are tumbling around in your head?"

He pressed a soft kiss over the mark he'd given me, the small gesture sending a wash of desire through me.

"I'm not upset."

A little growl rumbled in his throat. "Do we need to talk about you telling lies, Miss Fallon?"

"It's not one of those commandments, is it?"

"It is in this house. Out with it."

I smiled at the snarly command, knowing he only forced the issue because he wanted to make it better. Unfortunately, there was no way he could give me what I needed. Not if we remained here.

I contemplated telling him the truth, that a part of me would always feel incomplete without the rest of my mates, but I didn't want to ruin the mood. Instead, I opted for another topic weighing on me.

"I'm worried we're going to run out of food. There's barely enough left to get us through the week."

He rested his chin on my head as he pulled me closer. "Aye, that's something I've had on my mind as well. This storm is vicious, and the supply boat won't be able to traverse the water until it calms."

"What are we going to do?"

"I'll figure something out. Don't go worrying yourself sick. I will always take care of you, Mrs. Gallagher."

I let out a light giggle. "You keep calling me that, but I don't see a ring on this finger."

"You started calling me husband first." Releasing his hold on me, he stepped away, and I instantly missed his touch.

I turned toward him, my gaze following as he picked up his scarf and tugged on one of its tassels, pulling free a few pieces of yarn. Discarding the scarf, he came back to me, a small, secretive smile ghosting across his lips.

"What are you up to?"

"If it's a ring you're wanting, this will have to do until I can find you a proper one."

Taking my hand, he tied the soft black yarn around my finger, knotting it tight so it wouldn't slip. "There. Now you do one for me." He offered me the other strand, his eyes twinkling with pleasure.

I could barely see through the tears that were filling my eyes. I managed, though, tying my ring around his finger and sealing it with a kiss on his hand.

"I now pronounce us husband and wife. I'm going to kiss my bride, if you have no objections."

I laughed, the tears running freely down my cheeks now as he took my face between his hands and claimed me as his with a tender kiss. I could feel his smile against my mouth, sense the happiness this one small moment gave him.

Not only him, me as well. It was perfect. A little slice of heaven we'd carved out just for ourselves. I knew it was fleeting, that reality would creep back in sooner rather than later, but I didn't care. If anything, that only made me appreciate it more. Something in me knew moments like these were numbered.

I shivered, the unwanted thought sending tendrils of dread spiraling out from my belly.

"You're cold. Let me put another log on the fire." Caleb stepped away, his brows furrowing when he took in our nearly empty wood-pile. "I guess I'll be going out to collect more firewood."

Relief flooded me. "Such a good husband."

He grinned, nearly boyish and full of pride. "You bundle up on the couch. My girls need to stay warm. I'll return soon, and we can continue celebrating. Technically it *is* our wedding night. How does that sound?"

Fuck, my heart was going to burst. This was the man he was meant to be. The provider, the devoted husband and father. I loved seeing him like this.

"I love you, Caleb," I murmured as he walked to the door, my thumb rubbing over the fuzzy ring on my finger.

"And I you, wife."

My cheeks hurt from smiling as he whipped the door open and hurried outside. The draft that swept in was practically arctic. The gust was strong enough to send a vase toppling over on the table and toss the coats hanging by the door halfway across the living room.

Leaves and rain blew in, littering the floor, and a bone-deep chill hit me from even the short burst of the raging storm.

"Well, Sunday, you wanted something to keep your hands busy. Looks like you're on cleanup duty." I wasn't sure it was worth it since Caleb would open the door again when he came back inside, but it gave me something to do.

I righted the vase first to stop the water from spilling onto the hardwood. Then I moved to grab a towel but stopped when I spotted the coats. They were directly in the path of the door, and with his arms full, I didn't think Caleb would see them. As amused as I was by the image of my proper priest slipping and falling on his ass, I was more excited about what he might have in store for our *wedding night*.

I waddled to the pile of coats and scarves, bending down as gracefully as possible—which wasn't graceful at all—and scooped up two of the heavy wool coats. After hanging those, then a few more, I reached down to pick up the last remaining scarf, my heart lurching as the memory of Caleb's attachment to it hit me. The last thing I wanted was his family heirloom getting even more tattered.

The amulet Natalie gave me swung free from its place beneath my shirt as I leaned forward and grasped the fabric. The baby kicked hard, pain slicing through my side and making me gasp as I straightened, but then everything around me went black, cold, and deathly still.

Hoofbeats pounded in my ears, so loud I cried out in pain, and the voice from my dream, the one speaking to my mother, said, "I'm coming for her, Sunday."

On instinct, I threw the scarf away from me, straight into the fire, needing to block out any connection that evil had to this place. To Caleb. To us.

I watched it burn, slowly catching fire. The smoke curling from smoldering fabric was not the usual gray I expected but a pale red, sickly and wrong.

The door opened, Caleb stumbling in with an armful of wood, his hair wet from the rain. "There are few times I'm thankful I'm a vampire. This is one of the—" His gaze locked on the fire, eyes widening as he dropped the wood.

"Caleb, I'm sorry . . . I—"

"No!" He lunged past me, reaching in and attempting to grab the now fully engulfed fabric, but it was nothing more than ashes in his hands. He turned to me, his eyes wild with panic. "What have you done?"

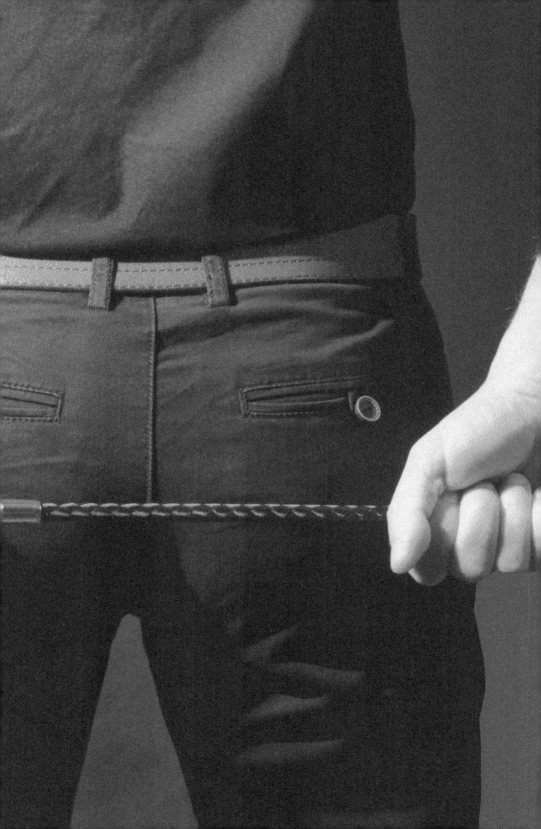

# CHAPTER
# TWENTY-EIGHT
## CALEB

I was going to be sick. My heartbeat, which had been an infernal beast since the moment I recognized it had resumed, faltered. Spots danced in front of my eyes. I should have never left her alone. The damned fool had just signed her own death warrant. Everything I'd done. All of it. For nothing.

"Caleb, I think you need to sit down."

"I'm already on my bloody knees."

"Please, come sit on the couch. You're scaring me."

I stared at her with unchecked terror bleeding from me. She'd killed us both. In one flick of her wrist, we were lost.

"I'm scaring you, am I? Do you have any idea what you've done?"

"I'm sorry. I . . . Caleb, something was wrong with that scarf. I know it was special to you—"

"Special to me? Sunday, that wasn't a fecking scarf. It was Death's Shroud, and it was the only goddamned thing keeping you safe. No one could find you so long as that remained by our door."

Standing, I worked to keep my limbs from shaking as anger and fear coiled like a snake ready to strike. We had no weapons, no methods of defense against the beings that were sure to find us now.

I paced the floor, my brain working on overdrive as I tried to find some solution to this disaster we found ourselves in.

"What are you talking about? It was just an old ratty piece of fabric." She reached for me, but I flinched away. I regretted the move instantly, especially once I looked into her eyes and saw the hurt there.

"No, Sunday. It wasn't. It was a magical relic that was the only thing standing between you and the hordes of creatures looking to kill you and our child. With it intact, it would conceal your where-abouts from any means of investigation. Without it . . . " I didn't bother finishing the sentence. Without it we were fucked. End of story.

"You were using magic to hide me? Why didn't you tell me?"

I let out a bitter laugh. "Until recently, you wanted nothing more than to get away from me. You can't honestly tell me if you'd known, you would have left it."

"So that's why they didn't come for me . . ." she mused, more to herself than me.

I knew exactly who *they* were. Kingston. Alek. Thorne.

"I wasn't trying to keep you from them," I said, my voice softer now. "It was everyone else."

She stared at me, her face unreadable for a second before it gentled. "I know. I understand you felt it was your only choice. That you were putting my safety above everything."

*Including her happiness.* She didn't say it; she didn't need to. The implication was heavy in her words. Damning. I'd gone from her husband back to her kidnapper in one fell swoop. Some wedding night this was shaping up to be.

"What do we do now?"

Taking a harsh breath, I raked my hand through my damp hair and stared into the fire, the ashes of our one means of protection mocking me. "We wait. They'll be coming for us. It's only a matter of time."

"Then let them fucking come."

"You don't mean that."

"I do. I absolutely do. I am so damn tired of just sitting here being scared all the time. If they're going to come, let them. At least then we can fight."

"Sunday, you can barely put on shoes by yourself right now. How can you be expected to fight in your condition?"

Her eyes went hard. "Don't underestimate me, Caleb. I'll do whatever it takes."

I moved to her, taking her hands in mine. "I know you will. But there is one of you and legions of them. No matter how fierce you are, my darling one, it will not be enough. Why do you think I went to the literal ends of the earth to keep them from finding you?"

She opened her mouth, her protest notched and ready to be unleashed, but before she could take aim, the power went out, cloaking us in darkness. But this was no natural outage. The fire, which had been blazing beside us, was little more than smoldering embers in an instant.

My stomach dropped. I thought we'd have a little more time. Hoped we could prepare. Instead I was crippled with fear.

"They're here."

The sound of glass shattering from the bedroom had me blurring to her, placing myself in front of the most important thing in my world. It was all I'd needed to slip into the role of her protector. The role I'd been born for.

We may not survive this fight, but I'd be damned if we weren't going to take every last one of them with us.

"Sunday, stay here. Do not breathe a word."

"Cal—"

I spun, gripping her face and kissing her with all the intensity in my blackened heart. "For once in your fecking life, Sunday, do as I say."

She bit her lip and nodded. We didn't have time for more than that.

Slipping away from her, I crept into the bedroom. Instead of the intruders I'd expected, all I found was a rock lying in a pool of glass and water, the wind whipping the curtains as it wailed outside. A flash of lightning illuminated the room, revealing it to be empty save the furniture and me. Foreboding gnawed at my gut, and even as I turned to head back to my wife, my everything, I knew I was too late. I'd fallen for the oldest trick in the book.

A crash from the living room had my pulse pounding, sending me barreling through the door and into the pitch dark space. But I was a vampire; I should be able to see even in the darkest of rooms. Faint shadows moved toward me, inky stains in the air. Shadow Court fae. They must be using some kind of glamour to keep me from seeing clearly.

But my sight wasn't my only asset. I just needed a hint of where they were, and I could blur to them before they finished taking a step.

Thankfully—if not surprisingly—Sunday had taken my request seriously. She hadn't made so much as a peep since I'd left her to investigate the room. Her silence would come in doubly handy now, as it would allow me to isolate the threat against us before they could get to her.

*There.*

The hitch of a breath and the barest scrape of a shoe over wood. I had the bastard in my hands, his throat at my lips, and my fangs tearing him apart before he could look at me. He was nearly drained in a matter of seconds. With a clatter, his weapon fell to the floor, and I dropped his now limp body. He wouldn't survive.

A sharp burn slashed across my back, the silver blade searing my skin as another fae warrior attacked me. I barely had a chance to do more than wonder why the fuckers were coming after me instead of her before he sank his blade into my side.

I grunted in pain. Shoving him away as I pulled the dagger free and turned it on him, ending the fae's life with no remorse in my heart. Freshly fed, my wounds healed almost instantly, but the sting from the silver remained and would for a few nights.

Adrenaline raced through me, sending my pulse spiking, and I turned to the spot I'd last seen Sunday. As I stared, a distinctly human shape materialized behind her.

"Sunday, look out!"

Her eyes went wide, hands turning to claws as she spun around, attacking even before she could see the threat.

There were muffled cries. Hers and his. The sharp scent of blood accompanied a soft gurgling sound as her attacker stumbled back, hands holding his entrails. I tore his head clean off his shoulders with a feral roar and watched him fall. But the blood in the air wasn't only mine or the fae's. I knew her scent better than anything, and the instant the last fae died, whatever magic they'd used to steal our light went with him.

I was at her side in a heartbeat, but it was too late. She sagged in my arms, her head tipping back, exposing the slash at her throat. Precious blood coated her, spilling to the floor. Her lips moved, but no sound came out. Reaching for me, hands already transitioning back to her human ones, she cupped my face as a tear slid down her cheek.

"No. Don't you dare. Don't you dare leave me like this."

I cradled her head and lifted my other hand to my mouth, ripping the skin at my wrist and shoving it up to her lips.

"Drink, damn you."

She was cold and still, not latching onto me, but I held my arm to her and willed the blood I was offering to do its job.

"You can't die, not after we finally came together, *a stor*. Please, please stay." My chest constricted as a deep ache built there, already feeling the loss I couldn't bear. "We have to write our story. Don't you remember it? Once upon a time . . ." I couldn't stop the sob from escaping, breaking my voice into shards of raw emotion. "You promised me. You said you would do whatever it takes. So live. Live for me."

Hope flickered as a faint tickle feathered over my wrist. I couldn't be certain the touch came from her, and I held my breath, terrified of moving in case it was only my desperate imaginings. But then it came again. More insistent this time. Intentional.

"That's it. That's my good girl. Take what you need. Take it all if you have to."

As she began slowly healing, I brought us both to the floor, cradling her to me and watching the life come back to her face. Her pulse filled my ears, along with the constant thrum of the baby's heart. They were both going to survive. I hadn't lost them.

Something in the back of my mind whispered, dark and sinister.

*Yet.*

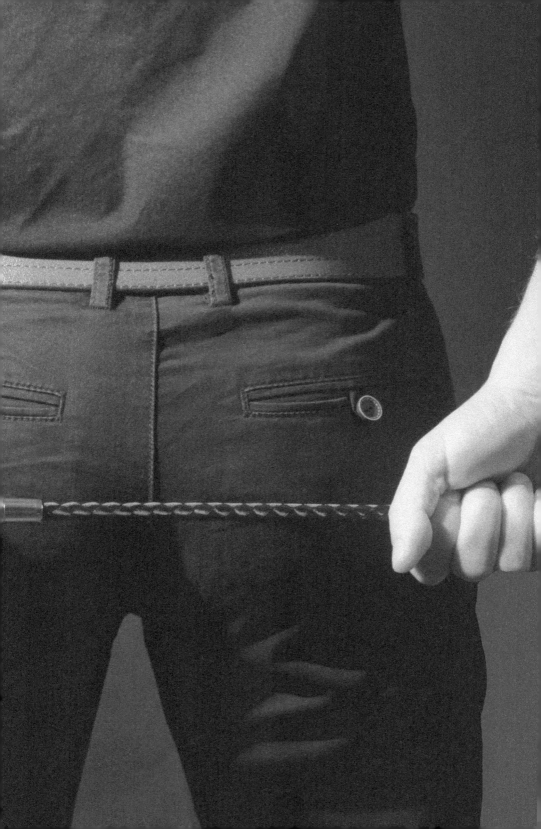

# CHAPTER
# TWENTY-NINE
## SUNDAY

The stench of death and rot hit my nose, and I gagged, my stomach cramping as it tried to rid my body of the vile assault. I held my hand over my mouth, fighting the urge to vomit. My other hand pressed to my belly, heart lurching as once again, it was flat. Loss washed over me.

Where was she? Not safe inside me any longer. Someone had taken her.

A low laugh rolled through the air, and I felt its echo in the earth beneath my feet. Lifting my head, I took in the burnt orange sky, little streaks of light falling as if even the stars themselves were trying to escape the wasteland the heavens had become. And across the charred remnants which had once been my home stood my mother, her eyes swirling like galaxies, dressed as I'd never seen her before.

She wore blood-red armor, a cloak the color of midnight that flowed behind her on an invisible breeze, and a helmet with two black horns curving up and back, my infant daughter clutched in her arms like a trophy.

"You thought you could hide from me."

"No."

"It doesn't matter. I've got what I want now."

"Give her back to me."

"She was never yours." The smile on her face was chilling and so confident I was struck with terrible fear.

As I stepped toward her, figures climbed out of the ground between us, bodies in various states of decay, coated in dirt and gore. What I'd mistaken as deep crevices had really been graves. I gagged again, and my baby wailed.

Everywhere I looked, I was surrounded by the faces of the dead. Callista, with her decapitated head clutched to her chest, red lips twisted in a sneer. Chad, his jaw missing, steps slow and lurching, as if his bones were still broken and only supported by what remained of his fleshy suit. And then others whose deaths came as a surprise. The Blackthorne's faithful butler, Martin, Professors Moriarty and Sinistra, and Phe and Ronin Farrell, who were nearly unrecognizable beneath the boils and sores covering them from head to toe.

"What have you done?" I whispered, my mouth tasting of ash.

"Me? Darling daughter, haven't you figured it out yet? This is *your* doing."

"No. I never hurt these people."

"Oh, but you did. You need to face the facts, my sweet. You played the game and lost. Your chess pieces were sacrificed to keep you safe to the bitter end, but now it's over. Only one can win. And I have always known I would be the last one standing."

Fury ate through my fear, and I lurched forward, intent on ending this here and now. But I didn't make it more than two steps before falling to my knees.

"No. God, no."

Lying between us, slaughtered, brutalized, mere husks of their former selves, were my four mates. Mouths open on silent screams, milky eyes staring up at the sky, expressions frozen in abject terror.

Dead.

All of them.

My gaze found Caleb's left hand, the ring I'd tied on his finger still there. Deep, aching grief swelled inside me, and I screamed his name on a ragged sob.

Hands pressed to the dry, dead earth, I hung my head and cried as my mother laughed from above me. My tears fell onto the ground, and from under my palms, blood welled to the surface, flooding the world around me, washing away the horde of zombies, the bodies of my loves, everything, and taking me under in a sea of red.

I gasped, choking on the metallic liquid that burned like fire as it slid down my throat. I shouldn't have been able to feel the tears racing down my cheeks, but I knew they were there.

It was over.

We'd lost.

Just as I opened my mouth to swallow more of the boiling substance and force the end to claim me quicker, a hand reached out, grasping mine. The brush of yarn on my palm was familiar, and I knew without seeing who it was.

"Please save me, Caleb. I don't want to be here anymore. I want to be with you."

His voice was a whisper in my mind, and I gave myself over to eternity with him. "I've got you, *a stor*. I'll never let you go."

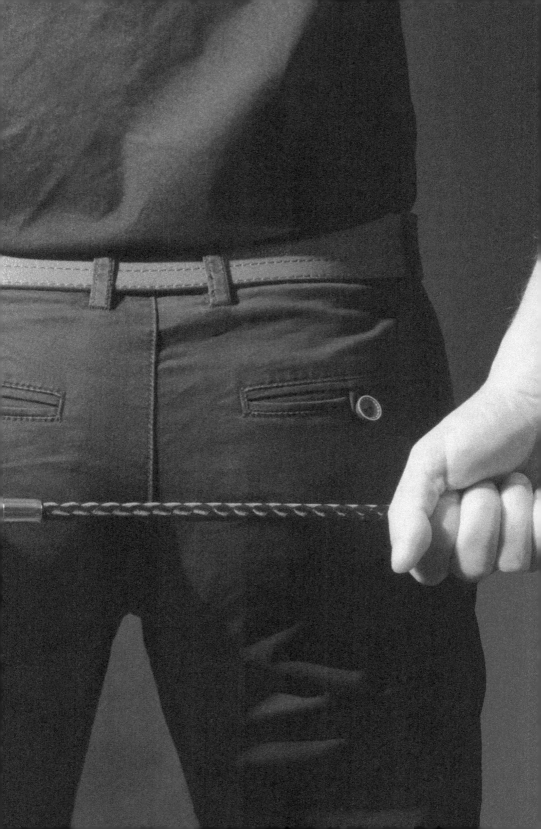

# THIRTY

I laid next to her in the bed, the bloodstained clothes she'd been wearing now in tatters on the floor. I couldn't look at them without terror shooting through me all over again. Her blood, her precious life-giving blood, had been spilled by that fae bastard. And I knew this would not be the last time. It had only taken them minutes from the time the barrier went down to find us. More would be on their heels. Better prepared. Relentless.

My palm gently circled the swell of my wife's belly as I watched the baby move within her. All this over an innocent child. Because I knew now, this wasn't some evil creature. She was mine.

Sunday let out a soft whimper, her brow furrowing as she cried out.

"Shh, *a stor*. I'm here. I've got you."

I pressed a kiss to her brow, but it did little to soothe her. She struggled in my arms, her moans turning distraught.

She was having another of her nightmares.

Gripping her chin between my thumb and forefinger, I kissed her lips, breathing, "Come back to me, wife."

Tears streamed down her cheeks as she began sobbing in her sleep, crying my name, then gasping, choking, desperate.

I linked our hands, holding tight to her, and she whispered, "Please save me, Caleb. I don't want to be here anymore. I want to be with you."

My voice was tight with pain at the defeat in her words. "I've got you, *a stór*. I'll never let you go."

I kissed her again, this time willing her to come out of whatever nightmare she was trapped within. Her body went lax, a contented sigh leaving her before she gripped the back of my head and deepened the kiss. I loved how she moaned into my mouth and writhed on the bed.

"Caleb, I need you."

"Yes. I need you too."

She moved into my touch, her body chasing the pleasure I was giving her. I skated my hand over her curves, dipping between her legs and finding her wet and ready for me.

"Always so responsive for me." I looked up, expecting to see her hooded gaze, but was startled to find she was still completely asleep. My cock throbbed at the realization that she wanted me this much, even in her dreams.

Somewhere between crying out for me and kissing me back, I'd taken her out of the darkness and somewhere much more pleasant. I grinned. "That's it, Miss Fallon. Join me in Eden."

I continued slowly fingering her tight, wet cunt, my thumb rolling across the rise of her clit and causing even more slick arousal to spill from her as she moaned. Fuck, my balls ached with the need to come all over her.

"More, Caleb."

Her eyes were still closed, her body as willing as ever, and I couldn't resist making her fantasy come to life. I added a second finger, then a third when she continued asking for more. I wanted to give her everything she needed. To make her come in her dream and in reality.

"I need you inside me. Why are you waiting? Please, Daddy."

*Christ.* How could I resist her when she begged so sweetly, asking for the very thing my body was screaming for me to do?

Shifting until I was kneeling between her spread legs, I grasped her by the hips, lifting her up so that I could run my swollen tip through her slick folds.

"Yes. More, Daddy. Inside me. Please."

"Fuck."

I was shaking from the need to sink inside her. I couldn't help myself. I placed my weeping cock at her entrance, watching for her eyes to flutter open, but all she did was moan again and roll her hips, taking me into her in one smooth movement.

"Holy fecking Mary mother of God," I groaned.

She cried out, and then those pools of blue were on me, eyes I'd been desperate to see open, wide, and filled with hunger. "Don't stop."

"I wasn't intending to."

She arched her back, pressing me deeper and making us both groan.

"This is my new favorite way to wake up."

"Mine too."

"The reality is even better than I imagined."

I chuckled as I thrust back into her. "That's always the case between us."

"Oh, God, just like that, Caleb."

Smirking, I did it again and again until her walls fluttered around me and I was barely able to hold back my release.

"Are you going to come for Daddy?"

The way she clamped down on my cock had me seeing stars. "Yes. Yes. God."

I deepened my strokes, and she screamed my name, hands fisting the sheets as she came.

"Where do you want it?" I fought for control as the climax hammered at the door.

"Inside me. Where it belongs."

I was coming before she finished speaking, her husky words sending me into beautiful oblivion as I pulsed inside her. I did belong there. Forever.

I kissed her sweat-dampened forehead before rolling off to lie beside her. Panting, she turned to look at me.

"What brought that on? Not that I'm complaining. I was very much a fan of everything *that*."

"You don't remember? You were calling out for me."

"Was I? Good job, past Sunday."

I huffed out a laugh, running my knuckles over her cheek. "Well, it didn't sound like a good dream. You were crying, begging me to wake you up. Do you really not recall?"

She shook her head on the pillow. "No. Nothing."

"I was worried you were reliving what happened last night."

"If I was, it's gone now. All I remember is us in the Garden of Eden, making love, safe and happy." She reached up and caressed my jaw, love shining in her eyes. "You saved me, Caleb. That makes at least three times."

"I'm not keeping a tally. I could never repay the debt I owe you for what you've given me."

She kissed me and then laid back, laughing to herself as she did.

"What are you giggling about?"

"I just realized that you literally fucked the nightmare out of me."

Pride swelled in me, along with amusement. "I suppose I did."

Her soft giggles stopped, and she looked at me, love and wonder shining in her eyes as she pressed a hand to her belly. "That's it."

"What is?"

"Eden. Her name is Eden."

I covered her hand with mine. "So it is."

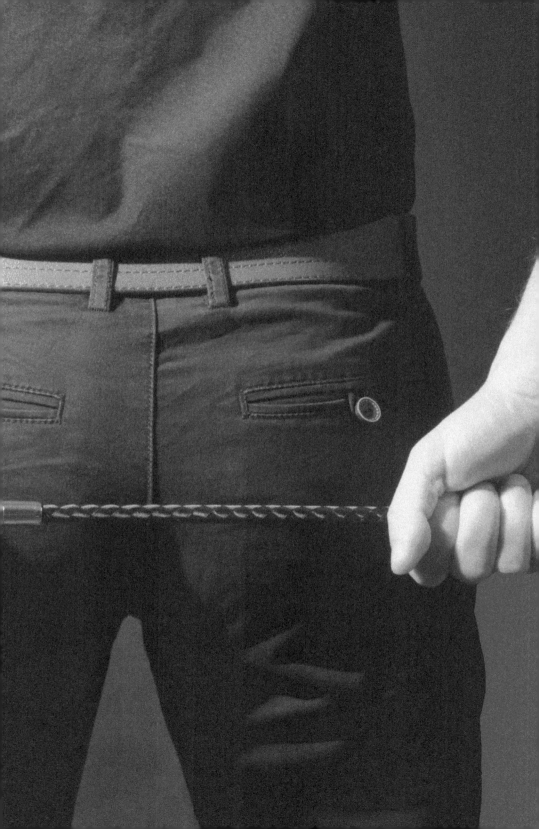

# THIRTY-ONE

## ALEK

My heart lurched as Moira opened the door to her room, echoes of Sunday still present even now. Her scent hit me, muted but still there at the fringes. Even so, after weeks of nothing, it nearly brought me to my knees.

"Who thought I would ever be so glad to come back to this dump," Moira said, breezing into the room and dropping her bags on the floor.

Ash was next, followed by me, Kingston, and finally Thorne. Ash immediately moved to Moira's bed, Kingston and Thorne to the one that used to belong to our mate, leaving me to lean against her old desk. A flash of sparkling pink caught my eye, which, upon closer inspection, ended up being an abandoned hair elastic. I picked it up and lifted it to my nose, breathing deep.

*Kærasta.*

Without stopping to think, I gathered my hair and tied it up in a knot with her hair tie. The piece of me that had been reduced to a howling thrashing beast calmed immediately at that small connection to my Sunny.

"You're such a sap," Kingston said, but there wasn't a hint of his usual disparaging tone. I thought perhaps if his hair was longer, he would've done the same. It was on the tip of my tongue to offer to braid his fur. This was what it'd come to. Savoring whatever scraps of her remained.

"Doesn't it seem like this was a lifetime ago? Us here at Ravenscroft?" Thorne ran his fingers over the blanket draping her bed, pain flashing on his face.

"It was. We were not the same men . . ." I had to swallow, my throat too tight to give voice to the rest of my words.

"Life began with Sunday." If Kingston had been in wolf form, he would have been droopy-tailed and whining.

Moira made a gagging noise. "Spare me your dramatics, boys. Besides, you'll be with her soon if my vision means what I suspect it does."

"Why didn't we just go to *Iniquity* directly?" Thorne scowled at the small tear in the bedspread as though the slight imperfection offended him.

"Because there's a chance you wouldn't get to Lilith in time. Trust me, if we do things my way, you'll end up right where you're supposed to."

"We're waiting, witch. The end of the world is literally in your hands right now." Kingston was more worked up than he had been since she first left us. His body nearly vibrated with tension and tremulously leashed anxiety.

I knew it was the same for Thorne and me, though we were likely better at hiding it behind the masks we'd spent our entire lives constructing. Something told me competence and control would not last us much longer. We were all coming apart at the seams.

I was surprised I'd held back my berserker for so long. I knew that would change the second I had an actual enemy in front of me. Berserker or not, there wasn't a whole fucking lot I could do to empty air. But the priest? I could do any number of things to him as soon as he was in my sights.

And I intended to do every single fucking one.

"Alek? Yoo-hoo? Hey, big guy, you think you could rein in the murder eyes?" Moira waved a hand in front of my face, pulling me back from the razor's edge I hadn't realized I was balanced on.

So much for that mask of mine.

"Apologies. My thoughts carried me somewhere . . . dark."

"I can see that." Then her expression softened. "You'll see her soon, Alek. I feel it."

Swallowing past the frustration and heartache, I nodded. "So how are you sending us in?"

Her grin was mildly terrifying. "Why, by magic, of course. Sweetie, can you whip out one of my special smoke bombs?"

"On it," Ash said, pulling open the bedside drawer and tossing random items onto the comforter until she found a crimson orb roughly the size of a softball.

"You three stand in the middle of the room."

"You're not coming with us?" Thorne asked.

"The vision only showed the three of you. Now stop interrupting. Hold hands. You have to be linked together."

Kingston gave her a dubious look. "What are we, kindergarteners?"

"You don't want me to answer that."

I grabbed Thorne's hand first, then Kingston's, shutting him up. "We don't have time for this. Sunny is waiting for us."

Kingston sobered and gave a tight nod. "Do it, Belladonna."

Ash handed her the ball and stepped back. Moira took a deep breath, looking each of us in the eye. "Go get our girl back."

It was the last thing I heard before the room turned into a wall of pink mist. I was still coughing, tears streaming down my cheeks, when we were instantly transported from Moira's room into what I could only assume was some sort of sex dungeon.

"I didn't consent to an audience, Lilypad."

I nearly swallowed my tongue at the sound of Crombie's voice from the large x-shaped cross he was strapped to.

Lilith stood in front of him, her body encased in a tight black leather corset, nearly her entire arse on full display due to the cut of the small boy shorts she wore. Then there were the boots. Thigh high, shiny, laced up from heel to top. Fuck, this woman would fit right in with Strega and her ilk. Dominant, a little scary, and not afraid to make you call her Mommy.

Kingston cleared his throat. "Is this a bad time?"

"Yes," Crombie spat, visibly on . . . edge. Looking like he'd been right on the cusp of climax before the three of us so rudely interrupted.

Lilith turned her gaze over her shoulder, one eyebrow raised. "He can wait. What's one more ruined orgasm in the grand scheme of things?"

"Everything. It's everything," Crombie groaned.

"How did you three get in here?"

"Moira."

Lilith smirked and shook her head, her long raven locks shimmying over her back. "That witch and I are going to need to talk about setting proper appointments."

"And fucking boundaries." The fae prince was clearly naked, though Lilith's form blocked him from full view. "Can you wrap this up, Lilypad? I've been waiting for this punishment all day."

Lilith winked at me and then lifted her hand and pressed down on a small black device. Crombie's moans were immediate, and I couldn't tell if they were from pleasure, pain, or a mix of both.

"Behave, poppet."

"I'm going to remember this when it's my turn," he gritted out, breathing hard.

Kingston and I exchanged a look. "She's a switch?" he mouthed. I shrugged, because what the fuck did I know about the succubus' sexual appetites, other than they were insatiable.

"She is, though that's none of your concern. My prince does have a point. What brings you here?" She turned to face us completely, her tits bared by the cut-out top of her corset. I had to force myself not to avert my gaze. She didn't need to know she made me uncomfortable. That would only give her more power over us all.

Kingston was blushing. "Nice jewelry."

Lilith plucked at the bar through her nipple. "This old thing? Thanks. Yours too. It would seem we have a matching set."

The shifter glanced down as if checking to make sure he was still clothed. "Does that mean I win a prize or something?"

Lilith's tinkling laugh was immediate. "You couldn't handle my prizes, wolf. Trust me."

Thorne cleared his throat. "We need your help."

"My help? Darling, you'll have to be more specific. What is it you need me to do?"

"Help us find Sunday."

"Ah, so you've finally figured it out then. I wondered when you'd come to make a bargain with me."

"Bargain? Who said anything about a bargain?" Thorne shifted from foot to foot.

"I don't do anything for free."

Crombie laughed from behind her but didn't say anything.

"Name your price. I'll gladly pay it," I said, stepping forward.

Her eyes flashed with pure pleasure. "Oh, yes you will, handsome. But lucky for you, deals with me are enjoyable for all parties involved, I assure you."

Crombie muttered something I couldn't make out, but his comment was immediately met with another press of Lilith's little black button.

"For fuck's sake. Stop. I'll behave."

"You're not going to ask for our souls, are you?" Kingston asked, speaking over Crombie's pitiful begging.

"Oh, sweetheart, that's not what I do. I'm much more interested in your . . . pleasure."

I swallowed, my adrenaline spiking at all the forms that could take. We were walking a dangerous path here.

"We're not going to fuck you," Kingston snapped.

"No, you bloody well aren't," Crombie vehemently agreed.

Lilith ignored him, tilting her head and giving Kingston an amused once-over. "Did I ask you to?" Then she trained her gaze on me once more. "You'll do just fine, Viking. I'll take every last drop of your climax in exchange for what you want."

"I won't be unfaithful to my mate."

"Of course not. She will be right there with you. And you will give me everything."

"I don't understand."

A wicked gleam flashed in her eyes. "Thorne and Kingston are both well acquainted with my rooms. Aren't you, boys? Tonight, each of you will require one, and Alek, you will give me access to your power while I grant you all your heart desires. It's more than a fair exchange if you ask me. You won't even know I'm there." She winked again.

I held her stare for a moment, the feeling that I was about to step onto a different kind of battlefield making me hesitate. I didn't know the rules of engagement here. I was in over my head. But if it would bring my Sunny back, how could I refuse?

"You did say you'd gladly pay, Aleksandr. This is my price. No souls on the line, no betrayal of your precious mate. Just a taste of your undiluted god-infused power. It's been so long since I've had a deity at my mercy."

Steeling myself, I nodded. "Done."

"Thank fuck. Can we carry on now? My blue balls have blue balls," Crombie's voice was laced with pure frustration.

"Kinky," Kingston muttered.

"Are you sure about this?" Thorne asked, his eyes showcasing his concern.

I nodded. "For her, there's nothing I wouldn't do."

"Show him the way, boys. I'll be right with you. I just have something to finish up here." She stalked across the room, hips swaying as she opened a chest and pulled out a black rod of some kind.

"Oh shit, that's my kind of magic wand," Kingston murmured.

Curiosity had me asking before I realized I was doing it. "What's it do?"

"What's a violet wand?" He shook his head, chuckling under his breath. "Never mind, buddy, I'll explain later. Let's go."

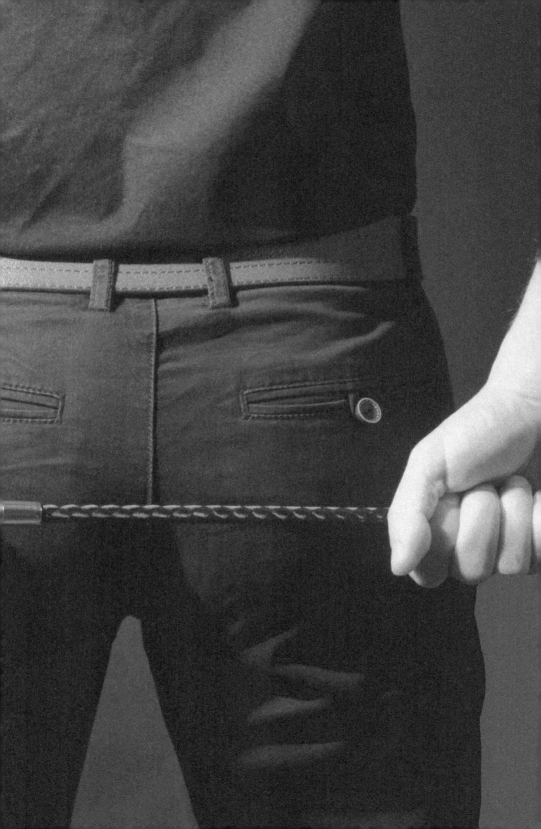

# THIRTY-TWO

My brow furrowed as I walked through the door to my assigned room at the club and into total darkness.

"If this is your idea of a sexy fantasy, demon, you need to broaden your horizons," I muttered.

I took two more steps forward when a spotlight came on, illuminating a chair at the end of a . . . stage? The rest of the room was obscured by smoke, but I could hear them out there. People. Soft whispers and the clinking of ice in glasses.

A brush of fingers across my back had me turning toward the sensation, but my Sunny's voice in my ear stopped me.

"Don't. Let me touch you, elskan min. It's been so long. I miss you."

"Kærasta." The word was a harsh rasp of need and yearning. Now that I knew it was her, I wanted nothing more than to look at her, touch her face, kiss her lips, and ensure she was real.

"Sit down, Alek. Let me take care of you."

"I want to touch you."

"You will. But not yet. Now it's my turn to make you feel good."

She pushed lightly between my shoulder blades, herding me to the spotlight. As I sat down, I became even more aware of the people watching us, though I couldn't make out a single face. Then she slid a piece of silk along the side of my neck, and I forgot all about them.

"Trust me."

I did. I'd do anything for her. Even if it went against my instincts to be on guard and aware of my surroundings. She secured the blindfold over my eyes, and I was awash in her scent, her long hair brushing my cheek as she straddled my thighs.

My hands drifted over her bare knees, up to her hips, and I groaned at the feel of thin lace lingerie. "Sunny, they can see you."

"Doesn't that make it more fun?"

Slow, sexy music filled the air, changing the mood from tense and unsure to sensual and intimate. My fingers gripped her hips, holding her down as the heat of her cunt pressed along the outline of my hard cock.

She slid out from my hold, and I moaned. "Stay."

"Shh, I'm right here." She leaned forward, her full breasts pushing against my face as she ran her hands through my hair, tugging gently as she removed the elastic and let the long locks fall free. "I missed your hair. The way it feels dancing over my skin as you thrust into me."

"Let me see you, and I'll have you under me quicker than you can say my name. I promise."

Her low, husky laugh told me that wasn't happening. At least not right now. "I hope you aren't attached to this shirt."

"What?"

She gripped the neck of my henley, and the sound of tearing fabric accompanied a sharp tug from her. Then her hands were on my chest, and I was helping her brush away the remnants of the shirt.

"I would have taken that off for you if you'd asked."

"It's more fun my way."

I laughed, recognizing my words as she tossed them back at me.

"Fair enough, Kærasta. Have your way with me then."

"I fully intend to." Her hand drifted between my legs, palm brushing my swollen length through the soft joggers I wore. It would be so fucking easy for her to take me in her grasp, to shove down the waistband of these pants and stroke me long and hard right here in front of all these people.

"Please. Show them I'm yours."

Her fingers tickled down my ribcage, slowly tracing the runes bearing her name. Marking me as hers. "What if I don't want them to see? What if that's just for me?"

"Then get us out of here, because I need to be inside you, Sunny."

Her soft laugh was my only answer. I couldn't see her behind the blindfold, but I was aware of the air moving over me. The press of her palms on my thighs, the brush of her torso between them. She was kneeling . . . I think.

Silken hair swept over my stomach, and I groaned. Warm lips against the flat of my abs had me tensing with the urge to rip the blindfold off as she teased her way to the place I needed her most. I wanted to see my woman take me in her mouth.

"I can feel your hands flexing, Alek. You can touch me if you want. It's okay. But I'm not going to let you up from this chair until I get what I came for."

"And what's that?" Fuck, my voice was nothing more than a rasp.

"Your cock in my mouth."

"Odin's teeth, then do it, woman. Stop teasing me and suck me off."

She slid her hand inside the band of my pants and gripped me in her fist.

"Fuuuuuck."

The warm air of her breath blew over my throbbing length a second before the perfect damp heat enveloped me. The feel of her mouth around me was second only to that tight pussy I fucking dreamed of.

Instinctively, my hand went to cup the back of her head, fingers sliding into the thick hair and tightening as I rolled my hips, sliding even deeper.

She moaned, the little vibrations sending each and every nerve ending inside me shooting off like hundreds of tiny fireworks. I was damn near incoherent as she hollowed her cheeks and began to bob up and down, her hand working me at the base, thumb rolling along the thick vein on the underside of my cock.

My hips rocked even as I tried to hold myself still, but I wanted her so badly. No. I needed her.

"Sunny. Fuck."

She pulled off, and I missed her lips immediately. "Do you want me to stop?"

"No. Please."

"But if I make you come, they'll all see you fall apart."

My cock pulsed in her palm. "Let them see."

"Should I move? Show them exactly what I do to you?"

"I'm not ashamed of how you make me feel."

She scraped the tips of her nails along the bottom of my shaft, and I nearly came then and there. My dick jerked as my balls tightened, full and aching. "Nor should you be. You're a fucking work of art, Alek. Perfect." She moved again, her lips now at my ear, her voice a throaty growl. "Mine."

Then she was gone, and I let out a strangled cry of frustration, reaching for her and finding nothing but air. But her scent was everywhere, surrounding me, as the blindfold fell away. The club was gone, replaced by some sort of private room. Not a bedroom, something closer to a boardroom. A conference table sat behind me, and floor-to-ceiling windows ran the length of the wall in front of me. My Sunny stood there, her hair a wild tempest around her, a sinful smile painting her lips, full, lush curves on display. My gaze roamed her body, taking in the swell of her breasts with rosy nipples begging for my mouth, soft skin I needed to touch, and a thatch of hair at the apex of her thighs marking the spot I wanted most. A treasure I had to explore with my tongue.

She crooked a finger, beckoning me.

I was out of that fucking chair so fast, the glass groaned in protest as I slammed her body up against it with mine.

"Somebody missed me." Her giggle went straight to my cock.

I kissed her. Hard and deep. Fucking her mouth with my tongue. Claiming her until nothing existed by the feel of her against me. The taste of her on me. "Let me in, Kærasta."

She wrapped her thighs around my waist and notched me right at her entrance without any effort. Like I was made to slide straight inside her. So I took the gift the gods had granted me and did just that, bottoming out in a single, hard thrust.

"Alek." She dipped her head back, the soft thud making the glass vibrate against the hand I had pressed against it.

I glanced out the window, taking in the writhing, dancing bodies of the club patrons. Anyone could look up and see us. Pressing a kiss to her shoulder, I gripped her hips and stood straight before pulling out of her and placing her on her feet.

"What? Don't stop. I was enjoying that," she protested.

"Turn around. Hands on the glass. Watch them as I fuck you."

She bit her lower lip and nodded, doing as I instructed. I threaded my fingers through the hair at the base of her skull, gripping and tugging hard, pulling her head back and making her gasp.

"Do you like knowing they're right there? That at any moment, one of them could look up and see exactly what I'm doing to you?"

"Y-yes," she stuttered out, her fingers clenching on the glass as she pushed her hips back against me, begging me to fill her.

Keeping hold of her hair, I slid my other hand down her belly, pressing on her swollen bundle of nerves.

"Me too."

I sank inside, and the ragged moan she released had me already on edge.

"Tell me what you see," I whispered, releasing my hold on her hair and wrapping that hand around her throat as I fucked into her.

"I see Kingston. He's watching you take me."

"Do you like it? Knowing he wishes it was him in here, filling you so well?"

"Yes."

"What else do you see?"

"Caleb. In his balcony, unzipping his pants."

"Where's Thorne?" I asked, taking her earlobe and biting down.

"Sitting in the corner. Running a finger over his bottom lip, staring at us like he wants to eat me."

"You love to be watched, don't you, Sunny? I can feel it. The way you clench around me. How fucking soaked you are."

"Yes. God, Alek. Make me come. I want them to see you take me over the edge."

I tightened my grip on her throat and played her clit like an instrument, coaxing the most perfect sound from her as she came. But I didn't stop my assault. If anything, it only made me work her harder as I continued my relentless thrusts.

My name was little more than an incoherent moan as her orgasm peaked a second time, this time bringing me with her.

"Sunny!"

Her name was a growled roar as the glass cracked and shattered beneath my hand. My arms banded around her, holding her trembling body tight against mine, keeping her from falling with the shards as they rained down on the dancers below.

"That was," she panted, "incredible."

"Every time with you is incredible. I love you, Sunday. So fucking much it hurts. I can't stand being apart from you." As my whispered confession left my lips, a part of my heart was already screaming in protest. I knew our time was over. "Don't leave me. Please. Stay. I need you."

Already she was fading. The weight in my arms becoming little more than a memory.

"I love you, Alek."

I dropped to my knees, mourning her with a fresh wave of grief as powerful as the ocean. Closing my eyes, I turned my face toward the heavens and let the tide consume me. I could almost hear the water crashing into the shore, feel the breeze on my skin, cold drops of rain hitting my face. This was it. Lilith had driven me mad.

"Alek, you all right, mate?"

My head snapped up at the sound of Thorne's voice. I looked around, taking in the raging sea and the thick gray clouds. "Where are we? How did we get here?"

"I was hoping you could tell us that," Kingston said. "One minute I was a wolf, running through the woods chasing Sunday, and the next I was on two feet, standing in front of a door. When I opened it, I saw you on your knees on this beach."

"It was the same for me," Thorne said.

"Oh, really? You were a wolf, chasing Sunday, ready to give her your knot?"

The vampire rolled his eyes. "No. I was feeding from her as I fucked her. Then she was gone, and there was the door."

I pushed to my feet, knees wobbling, body swaying. "I . . . something isn't right. I feel so weak."

"I always knew those muscles were fake," Kingston said.

"That would be the succubus. You're going to be feeling the side effects for a while," Thorne said. "I've let her feed deeply once before. You'll recover."

Kingston cut Thorne a sharp glance. "We're going to have a conversation about that."

"Later. Any guesses where the fuck we are?"

"If I had to guess, I'd say Ireland," Thorne said. "One of its islands, perhaps?"

I let my gaze glide over the beach. That tracked. We could technically be anywhere in the world, but at least it was real. "Lilith did say in exchange for my . . . payment she'd help us find Sunny. Ireland makes sense given what Asher told us."

Kingston huffed. "Rolling hills. Fucking green everywhere. And . . . you know, the priest is about as unoriginal as they come. We'll probably trip over a leprechaun on our way off this beach."

Thorne's shoulders stiffened, a new awareness shining in his eyes. "Come on, you can search for your pot of gold later. Sunday's here. Can't you feel her?"

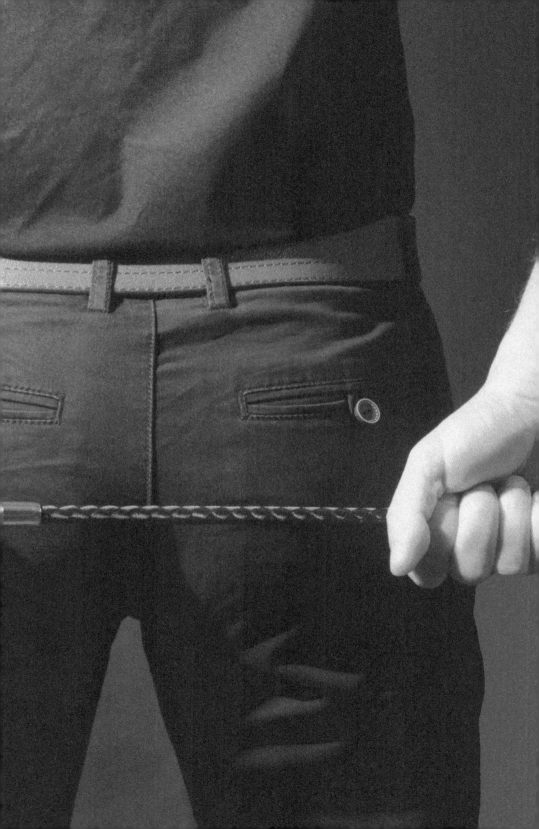

# THIRTY-THREE

### SUNDAY

I was going stir crazy in this cabin. The raging storm, combined with the tension of knowing what I'd done, how I'd destroyed the one thing hiding us from our enemies, was a heavy burden that never seemed to let up.

The one silver lining was that the storm seemed to be clearing. It was still too wet and muddy for me to wander off without Caleb. I had no intention of reenacting the old "help, I've fallen, and I can't get up" commercials. But at least I could stand in the entryway without having the door slammed shut on my metaphorical tail. The wind had been so strong last night that a window shattered in the living room. Now it was boarded up, keeping the daylight out.

Closing my eyes, I tipped my head back and breathed in the salty air. For a place that started off as my prison, it sure was beautiful here. Taking another deep breath, I drew in the scent of pine, snow, and . . . citrus. If I didn't know better, I'd say I was smelling my mates, but that was only wishful thinking. Just because the cloak had been destroyed didn't mean they were going to suddenly show up. I mean, I was still carrying on full conversations with them in my head. Smelling them was only the next stop on the crazy train. Hallucinations, here we come.

But I swore I felt something pulling me, some invisible thread tugging at my heart. It made tears spring to my eyes, and a sob caught in my throat. Fuck, how could my heart break all over again? I thought it had been shattered already.

"Sunshine?" Kingston's broken voice hit me hard, making my knees weak with the disbelieving anguish in that one word.

"Good grief, get it together, Sunday." Even as I admonished myself, my eyes scanned the horizon. And when my hopeful gaze landed on three familiar shapes running my way, I went down like a rock.

Noah's arms were around me before I hit the ground, his lips at my ear, mate bond telegraphing his relief straight to me. "I've got you, dove. It's okay."

I pressed a shaky palm to his cheek, feeling light-headed as I sank into him. "Are you really here?"

He feathered kisses over my face. "We're really here. We came for you."

I blinked away tears only to have my eyes immediately well with more. Twisting, I blindly reached for Kingston, fisting his shirt and pulling him to me. "Alek, get your ass over here."

Kingston wrapped me in his embrace, his mouth claiming mine in a sweet and tender kiss, the tremor in his lower lip sending a knife through me. "Fuck, baby. I missed you."

Then my Viking reached down and scooped me into his arms, taking me away from the others but still staying close. "I was afraid I'd never hold you again, Kærasta," he whispered before nuzzling his face into my neck.

I sobbed, the dam breaking free and letting loose the weeks of panic and grief I'd been trying to hide. They were here. All four of them. We were finally all together.

The moment should have felt perfect. It was the one thing my heart had secretly wished for since I'd first met each of them. But my stupid traitor of a brain wouldn't shut up.

They were here, but things were far from resolved between us.

Squirming, I silently asked for Alek to release me. But of course, the big lug wouldn't. He pretended he didn't notice the cues until I finally demanded. "Put me down."

His lips brushed my jaw as he took a deep breath, inhaling me, his beard tickling the tender skin just beneath my ear. "I never want to stop touching you. Not after being apart."

"Well, too bad. I'm not a child. Stop holding me like one."

"No."

I narrowed my eyes but couldn't maintain any sort of serious expression. I was too damn happy to see them. "How are we supposed to have a serious conversation if I'm not even standing on my own two feet?"

"Trust me, dove. I think we all know just how serious you are."

My gaze dipped at the soft censure in his voice, but he glanced at Alek and offered a slight tilt of his head. My Viking begrudgingly set me on my feet, but his palm remained on my lower back, massaging tense muscles. I'm not gonna lie; it felt amazing.

"How could you just leave us like that, Sunshine?"

The raw pain in Kingston's voice nearly gutted me. I had to stay on the defensive, or I would never make it through this conversation unscathed.

"Technically, I was kidnapped."

The air around us crackled with tension. If I had been looking, I know I would have seen the promise of retribution blazing in their eyes. Caleb had a reckoning coming. I hoped he was ready for it. But Caleb wasn't here. I was. So for now, I was the one on the witness stand answering for my perceived crimes.

"You took your bag. You were leaving either way," Noah pointed out. "You had Moira cloak your scent from us."

So I guess we were doing this here, then. Why did *I* feel guilty? I was running from them for a reason. The kidnapping notwithstanding, I would have left to save my baby no matter what.

"Maybe you should ask yourselves what would have made me leave." As if she knew I was talking about her, Eden stretched, pushing hard against my kidney and making me flinch.

Noah was there in a heartbeat, his hand on my shoulder, eyes blazing with worry. "Are you all right?"

"Yes, it's just my daughter and her daily kidney punches."

"*Our* daughter." He grinned, his expression not one of a man plotting to do terrible things to an innocent baby, but of a father, filled with love.

"Christ, Sunday. You're fucking huge."

I gaped at Kingston. "How very dare you. I am pregnant with your spawn, asshole."

He had the grace to blush. "No, I just meant. It's only been a few weeks, but to look at you, it seems like it's been months." His smirk was prideful. "Are you sure there's only one? Did we get multiples on the first try?"

I was so fucking confused. Why were they acting like she mattered to them? "I don't understand."

"Well, you see, my sperm are as Alpha as I am . . ."

"No. I don't . . . You . . ." I sighed, trying to put my words together before I said something I couldn't take back. "I left you all to save her. From *you*. I heard what you were planning to do with Cashel. I won't let you kill her."

"This is what comes from eavesdropping," Noah muttered. "You missed the most important part of that conversation."

Alek staggered, sitting down hard on the ground. I whipped around, well, as fast as I could turn this cruise ship of a body around. "Are *you* all right?"

He waved a hand. "Just a little tired. Carry on. You were just getting to the important parts."

I finally looked at him. *Really* looked at him. My demigod was unwell. His skin was pale beneath his natural tan. His eyes dull, face waxen. "Alek, what the hell happened to you?"

"It's just the cost of admission, Sunny. I'll be fine."

"Cost?" I turned to the others. "Explain. Right now."

"Look at you, already perfecting your mom voice."

"Kingston . . ."

He schooled his expression but couldn't do anything about the amusement sparkling in his eyes. "Lilith brought us here. Through the doors in her rooms. Alek paid the price for us all. She fed on him. Deeply."

"You mean, like the door that took us to the forest when we . . ." My cheeks burned at the memory of the first time we'd come together, when he'd given me his mark.

"She gave us all our fantasies . . . but my power was what she was after." I hated the exhaustion in Alek's voice.

It hit me then, the truth of Lilith's special rooms. The price she'd demanded for their use was high for a reason. "No, not fantasies. She gave you your heart's deepest desires. You wanted to mate me, Kingston. Which is what happened the first time you stepped inside the room. Caleb . . ." Feeling the building tension, I kept that revelation about our night together to myself. "Never mind." My nights with Noah were less obvious. We'd spent more time in the lower level of *Iniquity* than any of the others. "Noah, what did you want?"

"You. It's always been you." My heart gave a happy lurch. "And this time, when we went through, the three of us had one common desire above all else. To find you."

"And so Lilith brought you here."

"Power like that is beyond Lilith's ability. That kind of magic . . ." Kingston began, but his brow wrinkled as the words seemed to escape him.

"Reeks of the divine, doesn't it?" Noah mused.

It certainly seemed to. So simple and yet pure. If there'd been anything else they'd wanted more, the magic never would have worked. It was almost like a test. And they all passed. Still, I couldn't help but wonder, would they have been able to find me if I hadn't destroyed the shroud? Just how heavy-handed had fate been? And just which deity was getting their hands dirty?

"It also hurts like the whip of a wyvern's tail to the face," Alek grumbled, pulling my attention back to the present. His eyes were ringed with dark circles, his voice labored.

"Come inside. You need to lie down." I held out a hand, but Kingston stepped in front of me.

Alek gave a weary nod, which only sent another bolt of panic through my heart. Kingston helped him up, and we all shuffled into the cottage.

"What is this place?" Kingston asked once he'd helped Alek settle on the couch.

"Caleb's home. Our home, I guess."

Their expressions all went violent at the mention of his name. Fuck. Things were going to get ugly as soon as the sun went down.

"Bit small for the five of us, don't you think?" Alek's rasp made his joke fall flat.

"I guess you'll just have to do something about that when you're back on your feet, Viking."

He grinned at me, but it was pained. "I think I will."

"You three won't be staying here. Not unless we're all on the same page."

Noah's eyes narrowed. "Of bloody course we're staying here. We're your mates, Sunday. I won't be without you again. I can't."

"No one seemed to give a fuck about that in the library. Not one of you objected to your father's plan. I may not have heard everything, but I was there for that part. And trust me, your silence said a whole hell of a lot."

"If you'd continued listening, you would have heard all of us tell him no. Alek first and the rest of us shortly after."

My gaze shot to my berserker's. His silence had hurt the worst because he'd promised me he had my back not even an hour before they'd begun plotting. To know he'd kept his vow . . . it repaired something I hadn't even realized was broken.

"Told you, Sunny."

My anger and sense of righteousness were fading by the second. I knew I should hold on to it, but deep down, I didn't *want* to be angry at them. It felt unnatural.

Kingston approached me, dropping to his knees at my feet and placing both hands on the swell of my belly. "I won't let anything happen to our pup, Sunday. Ever."

My lower lip trembled. "Her name is Eden."

Kingston's smile was like a ray of sunshine breaking through the clouds. He pressed his lips to my stomach. "Hey there, Eden. I'm your daddy. I can't wait to meet you."

Noah's brows were knit in worry as guilt radiated from him. "I . . . fucking hell, Sunday . . ." He swallowed. "I don't know what to say. I failed you. Both of you."

"What?" I took Kingston's hands and pulled until he was standing.

"There never should have been a moment's doubt in your heart. If not for the things I've done, the times I abandoned you, you never would have had a reason to run. You would have known you were safe with us. I took that certainty away from you, and I'm so fucking sorry."

"Noah, stop." I wrapped my arms around him, resting my head on his shoulder, my lips brushing against the mark I'd given him. "I forgive you. For all of it. Now you need to forgive yourself."

He let out a tremulous breath, his hands sliding up my back as he held me as close as my bump would allow. "I love you, *both* of you. I won't let anything happen to her."

Tilting my face up, I waited for his kiss. I needed it. Kingston came behind me, dropping his lips to my mark as Noah gave me what I wanted.

A small whimper left me as my heart burst with joy. This. This is what I'd been missing. A part of me had been slowly dying without the rest of my mates. For the first time in weeks, it felt like I was whole.

"That certainly didn't take long. I'd expected you lads would find her, but this reunion is a bit sooner than I'd thought." Caleb stood in the doorway, sleep rumpled and sexy as hell.

Part of me—the horny part—was raring to go. Ready for all my mates to take care of every need I had. *If ever there was a time for makeup sex, am I right?*

But Kingston and Noah had other plans. Before I could open my mouth, they were across the room, slamming Caleb up against the wall. Noah wrapped a hand around Caleb's throat as Kingston pinned his shoulders, his fingers shifted into claws.

Kingston's wolf was close to the surface, his eyes a glowing amber. His voice a feral snarl. "Really, Priest? Because from where I'm standing, it took for-fucking-ever to find her. Now, what the hell do you have to say for yourself?"

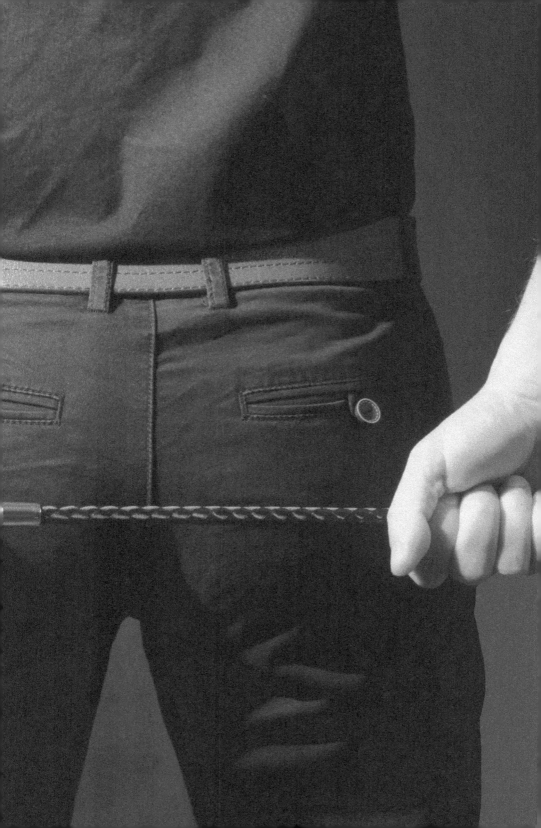

# THIRTY-FOUR

CALEB

Instinct screamed for me to take these young lads down. I could. It would be easy after how well I'd been fed over the last few weeks. With one swipe of my hands, I could leave them bleeding out on my floor. But this wasn't about dominance. It was the moment I finally gave Sunday everything she ever wanted. The only way forward was for me to allow them their pound of flesh.

When I didn't immediately answer his question, Kingston dug his claws in deeper. "Give me one reason not to tear your heart from your chest and throw it in the fucking fire."

"Uh, I can give you two."

I looked at my wife, keeping her distance, worry flickering in her beautiful eyes. "It's okay, *a stor*. This is no less than I expected."

She bit down on her lip but nodded. Knowing as well as I that we needed to work things out ourselves. There'd be no peace between us otherwise.

"Ask your questions. I've nothing to hide."

Thorne sneered. "If you had nothing to hide, why were you literally hiding? You took her by force. Drugged her. She's clearly in your thrall. Why else would she be playing house with her kidnapper?"

"You misunderstood me. I *had* things to hide. But no longer. Everything I did served a purpose. The greatest purpose, you might say."

"Oh, we know all about your Society. How you've been stalking Sunday since she was born. Fuck, man, that's creepy." The wolf dug his claws into my shoulders a little deeper. "Thorne's right. You couldn't get her to stay with you, so you held her captive. Such a fucking vampire thing to do."

Thorne cut him a glance. "I'm standing right here, mate. Also, still a vampire."

"Yeah. I said what I said."

Sunday stepped closer, her hand protective on her belly, eyes on mine. "I'm not in his thrall, Noah. Let him go. He's not a threat to you. He's not even fighting back."

"You wouldn't even know if you were, dove. He can't be trusted. Not until we know for certain what his intentions are."

I laughed. "Things would have been so much easier if that were true. My thrall doesn't work on her. Trust me, I tried. You think she's compliant? You should have seen her when we got here. Fought me nearly every step of the way. Nearly succeeded in killing me too."

"That's my girl," Alek said, his voice heavy with sleep. The Novasgardian had seen better days. He'd barely pushed himself to a seated position, his elbows resting on his knees as he regarded us.

It stung a little to see Sunday go to him, sit at his side and hold him. But the happiness flowing from her was undeniable. For a moment, she'd been solely mine, but now she was whole.

The wolf slammed me against the wall. "More meaningless words."

"You wanted answers. I'm giving them to you. Why demand them if you refuse to believe me?"

"Why should we believe you when every word out of your mouth has been a fucking lie since the day we met you?" Kingston growled.

"Not every word," I said, my eyes meeting Sunday's. Sighing

heavily, I turned to Thorne. "If you don't want words, then see for yourself. Look inside my mind."

Thorne offered me a curious look. "You would do that? Drop your shields?"

"Aye. Anything to move us past this. I have many sins I've already atoned for, but you need proof. I will give it to you. Just know there will be things you don't like."

"I'm certain of it."

He stared into my eyes, and I lowered the walls I'd so carefully constructed after my time with Aisling. Her ability to terrorize me, infiltrate my head, make me do and believe things I'd never have entertained had traumatized me deeper than even fighting in a war had.

I gave him everything I had freely, holding nothing back. Noah Blackthorne was the third person alive to ever know all of my depraved secrets. I could see the weight of them in his eyes as he stepped back. Accusation. Acceptance. Jealousy.

The reason for the last made sense as his gaze dropped to the frayed band on my finger.

"You married her?" His words were a soft, pained whisper.

"He fucking did *what*?" Alek's voice seethed with barely restrained fury. Thorne's words pulled him from his semi-fugue state. I wondered fleetingly what had caused him to be so weakened, but reason told me it had to do with their arrival.

"Sunshine?"

"He's mine, just as you are."

"Yeah, but we didn't get to fucking marry you." Kingston was trembling, his claws sliding deeper into my shoulder.

"That's easily remedied," she said.

"Not legally."

Her face twisted, the ferocity in her expression calling to me. "The laws of men have no bearing on my heart, Kingston. Ours are the only opinions that matter. A piece of paper doesn't make us husband and wife. Our vows do."

"I'll officiate a ceremony as soon as you assure me you're not going to make good on your threat to tear out my heart." I locked gazes with the shifter and waited. This was going to end one of two ways—forgiveness or death.

"All of us?" Alek asked, seeming pleased with the idea.

"Aye."

"He's telling the truth, Kingston. He didn't manipulate her mind. He loves her as we do. He'll die for her."

Kingston shuddered, finally pushing off me. "Fine. But I'm due for a fucking first."

"Excuse me?" Sunday's arched brow was an elegant rebuttal.

"He got to mark you first. *He* got to tattoo you. And this mother-fucker got to marry you. When do I get to be your first, Sunshine?" Kingston's eyes glittered.

"We've had firsts together," she breathed.

"Not like that. I want one that counts. That you can never forget." And then he grinned, looking frighteningly pleased with himself. "You're taking my last name."

"Am I?"

He left my side and went to her, pulling her to her feet and against him. "Yes. You are. You're taking my name, and I'm going to make sure you take my knot again during your next heat." His hands dropped to caress her swollen belly. "I love you like this, and I'm gonna be the first to put twins in you."

I forced myself not to groan at his possessive statement. But the thought of her going into heat again now that I didn't have to deny myself anything sent a thrill of promise through me. I could see it was the same for the others. It was something we were all looking forward to. Assuming the world didn't end, of course.

"Our days on this earth are finite. I am sorry we married without you, but I have gone my entire existence without *her*, and I couldn't waste any more of my life not being hers."

"Any of us would have done the same, given the chance. We don't have to like it, but we won't blame you for it either." This time when Thorne looked at me, there was nothing but understanding in his gaze.

"You speaking for all of us now?" Alek asked.

"Am I wrong?"

The berserker looked from him to me, his gaze weighted but no longer filled with anger. "No."

Sunday removed herself from Kingston's hold and walked toward me, her eyes on Noah, but her path directly to where I was still against the wall.

"Caleb's right, you know. None of us have much time left. I don't want to waste a second of it."

He caressed her face. "So don't. You deserve to have whatever you want. You deserve everything, dove."

She kissed him softly and then wove her fingers through mine. Looking over her shoulder at Kingston and Alek. "Then give it to me."

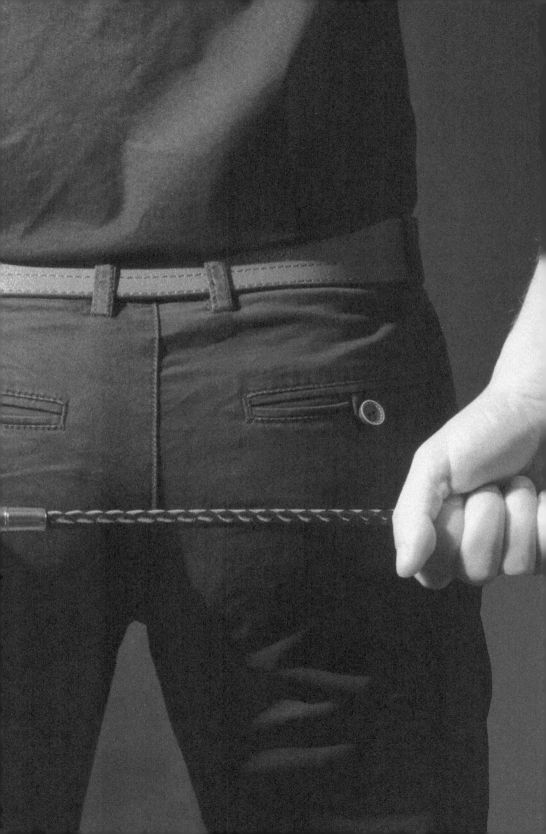

CHAPTER

# THIRTY-FIVE

THORNE

With five softly uttered words, the atmosphere in the small space went from one kind of tension to another one entirely. My gaze locked with Sunday's, and the hunger I'd been unable to sate since she left came roaring back with a vengeance. I didn't care who I had to share her with. I needed inside her, to feel her around my cock, to taste her sweetness and hear her moans fill the air. To love her in the most intimate way I could.

Fuck me, but I was painfully hard already.

I knew I wasn't alone. Even Alek was up and moving with more life than I'd seen from him since we set foot in this place. Kingston had his shirt off and was already working on the buckle of his belt.

Assessing the room, I cast a dubious glance at Alek. "Close quarters," I muttered.

He grinned and cracked his knuckles. "I can do something about that."

Sunday let out a sultry giggle. "Save your strength, Viking. You're going to need it for what I have in mind."

Without taking his eyes from her, he reached out and shoved the couch as far away as it would go, effectively making space for us in front of the fire.

Caleb tugged her away from me, pulling her against his body as his lips claimed hers in a show of passionate need none of us had witnessed from him before.

"Looks like the priest has been defrocked," Kingston said, eyes narrowed, jealousy burning in their depths.

"Quite." I knew she wanted us all. She'd married the man, for fuck's sake, but still, he'd had her all to himself for weeks. Debauched her in ways even I couldn't have imagined—on a fucking altar, for Christ's sake.

I turned toward them, about to take her back and shut him down, but Kingston spoke first.

"Sorry, Padre, you're on a timeout. She's ours right now. You wait your turn."

Sunday's breathless laugh as Kingston grabbed her and pulled her away from Caleb was a thing of beauty. Instead of fighting the decree, Caleb crossed his arms and leaned against the wall. "You know how I love to watch."

While the four of us had been distracted, Alek turned the woven rug into a large fur, creating a soft, welcoming nest to lie on.

"Come, dove. Let us love you."

Kingston and I led her to the fur, where Alek was already on his knees waiting for her.

"Where do you want me?" he asked, giving her a wicked grin.

"I want to go for a ride."

Fuck, the need in her voice had me opening my belt in preparation for my chance to sink into her.

Alek chuckled as he tore his shirt over his head and tossed it aside. "I've been dreaming of the day you rode my beard, Kærasta."

Her eyes widened as she looked down her body. "Uh . . . Not that I don't want your mouth between my legs, but I'm pretty sure I'll smother you with the size of this belly."

"If I can breathe, I'm not doing it correctly."

I laughed because it was true. Dying with Sunday coming on my face was one of the best ways I could imagine going.

"Perhaps a compromise?" I offered, gesturing to the couch. "I'm certain a beard ride can be arranged when our girl is more . . . comfortable."

She beamed at me. "Thank you, Noah."

I winked. I just wanted her to get everything she desired. And I certainly didn't mind watching her come. This ensured both.

Alek took her hand and brought her to the sofa, helping her drape her body over the cushions. Head resting against a pillow propped on the armrest, hips pulled to the edge, she allowed Alek to adjust her position to his liking. In a few smooth movements, he had one of her feet on the floor, the other propped beside her. I could see everything from where I was standing. If she was nude, she'd be glistening.

"All right, Kærasta?"

She offered a breathless, "*So* all right. I have you back with me."

With a snap of his fingers, their clothes were gone, and Alek took her mouth, kissing her hard and deep, pulling a deep groan from her before dropping between her legs. He wrapped a hand around the thigh of the leg on the couch and lifted it up, spreading her wide.

"Fuck, this view is even better than the video, eh buddy?" Kingston whispered.

Sunday's eyes flew open and met mine.

*Busted.*

"Shut. Up." I growled.

But he wasn't wrong. Not even close. Her entire body was a visual feast, her curves ripe and begging for attention. Her nipples dark and straining. Skin flushed. Hair wild. I was going to devour her when it was my turn. My fangs descended as the arousal mixed with thirst, and I palmed my aching cock.

"How are you not jerking it already, Thorne? Fuck. I can smell her dripping with need."

Kingston's arm was moving rhythmically in my periphery, and I was sure if I glanced to the side, I'd see him stroking his dick.

"What's the rule, Kingston?"

"We don't speak to each other when our dicks are in our hands."

"Precisely."

"Commentary is fair game, it's the heart-to-hearts that are banned."

I shot him a stern look. "No."

"What is this, Fight Club? I didn't agree to that."

"You're bloody well going to, mate."

Completely over his shit, I opened my trousers and grasped my aching length. Sunday cried out, her hands gripping Alek's hair as she came.

"Fuck, she's so hot."

"Stop talking."

I watched, mesmerized, as the pleasure rose and crested over and over on her face, feeling its echo along our bond. Her full lips parted, eyes hooded, skin flushed. I was going to fucking come right now if I didn't soften our connection. But God help me, I didn't want to. I could feel everything she was experiencing. The only thing that would make this better was if I had my cock sheathed in her tight cunt.

"Now you can go for that ride, Sunny."

Alek moved away from the couch, then laid back, his head angled toward us as Sunday took his hand and straddled herself over his hips. She would face us from this vantage while Caleb sat in a chair off to her left. I wasn't sure which of us was luckiest . . . no, that wasn't true. Alek was the lucky bastard she sank down on. The groan he let out as she sheathed him inside her filled the room, and his fingers dug into her hips, urging her on.

Kingston grunted. "Fuck, baby. Your tits look so good right now."

Alek reached up, taking one of the swollen globes in his large palm and kneading. Sunday keened. Scraping the tip of his nail along her peaked nipple, he made a pleased sound low in his throat. "Oh, they're sensitive too. She likes when you play with them."

"Aye, they're full and perfect," Caleb murmured. "I love how they feel on my face."

The wolf shot him a death stare. "You're still in timeout. Shut up."

Caleb raised a mocking brow but didn't reply.

"Really?" I asked, shaking my head. "You're far worse than he is."

"Whose team are you on, Thorne?"

"Hers," I said, watching the way her eyes fluttered closed as she rolled her hips. "Always hers."

"Fuck, I'm close, Alek." Her voice was a thin, almost panicked cry.

"Yes, Sunny. Chase your pleasure. Use me."

"Come with me? Please?"

Alek closed his eyes, brow furrowed for a moment as he must've been processing her request. If he was anything like me, he'd been fighting the urge to climax from the instant she took him inside her.

She came with a harsh moan, her palms flat on Alek's chest. I felt the pulse of her pleasure all the way in my balls and had to swallow back my own cry.

Kingston didn't bother fighting it. He came beside me with a growled, "Fuck, Sunshine."

"Hey," she panted. "That's mine."

"Don't worry, baby. There's a lot more where that came from. And this way, I won't blow the second I slide inside. Trust me. It's a good thing."

Alek sighed as they came down from their shared high, and Sunday rolled her hips. I was eager to get to her. Patience wasn't my strong suit, no matter how much I made it appear so.

Caleb remained quiet, but he was far from unaffected. His hooded eyes burned with hunger as he stared at our mate, his thumb brushing over his bottom lip.

Sunday must have felt the intensity of his regard because she looked over at him. "What should we do next, Daddy?"

"On your hands and knees. You have two other mates in desperate need of you."

"Just two?"

"Apparently I'm on timeout."

She smirked. "For now."

Alek pulled free, slapping her bottom and leaving a bright pink handprint as he moved to the couch, ready for a front-row seat of his own.

She positioned herself with her round arse to us and her face toward Caleb. She glanced over her shoulder. "Well? I'm waiting. Which one of you will give me what I want next?"

"Dibs!" Kingston called, already fully naked as I was still tearing off my clothes.

"I'm more than happy taking her mouth. I've missed those lips."

She grinned at me and took her lower one between her teeth. "Come on, Noah. I need you."

Fucking hell. Yes, she did. That sensual rasp of hers had me at her head, on my knees, ready and willing to do anything she wanted. I fisted my hand in her hair, tugging until her brilliant blue eyes met mine.

"I've missed you."

"Miss you too."

"Show me how much, dove."

She licked the drop of precum off my tip, and I groaned, hips canting forward just a bit, searching for more. Then she swirled her tongue along my crown, and my eyes rolled back as I groaned, enjoying the soft scrape. Without warning, she gasped, and her entire mouth enveloped me all the way to the root.

"Jesus . . . fuck," I gritted out, the feel of her swallowing me down so unexpected and almost too much to bear.

Kingston groaned, loud and long. "Fuuuck, baby. You grip my cock so fucking good."

*Ah. So that's what happened.* The momentum of Kingston's thrust as he slid in had forced her mouth forward. He was setting the pace.

Something about that was strangely erotic. Like he was making her fuck me with her lips.

I'd had to raise my mental shield when Alek was taking her so I didn't find my own release too soon, but now I needed that connection with her again. I tapped into her thoughts, the wash of her emotions sending heat and pride through me. Her mind was a jumble of pleasure and love. For me, for Kingston, for all of us. I sent my own want back to her, but over all the lust, I also made sure she knew it was nothing compared to how much I fucking loved her.

I could also feel her desire, the unspoken need for more.

"Kingston, her mouth is full. She can't tell you what she needs." I opened my eyes, locking gazes with the wolf.

"I fucking know what my mate needs, Thorne. You don't have to speak for her." His green eyes bled gold as if his wolf was right there, ready to take over.

"Then give it to her. She wants you to take her arse. She's dying to be claimed in every hole."

Without another word, Kingston placed his palms on her round globes and spread them open, spitting between her cheeks and making her whimper around my cock. Body tense as he stared down at her, he pressed his thumb inside.

She groaned, the vibration racing down my length and settling in my balls.

I slid my palm across her back, glancing down at her dark hair as she bobbed her head and made my fucking toes curl. I didn't even care that I wasn't going to fill her cunt. I was still a large part of what was giving her pleasure. That was all I needed.

"That's it, baby. Rock back into me. Take what you need."

Sunday's impending orgasm built, and I could feel it spurring on my own. "Christ, she's about to come. Harder, Kingston. She wants you to fuck her harder."

"My fucking pleasure."

Her climax hit as Kingston slammed into her, shoving her further onto my dick. The way her hair brushed my thighs had me shuddering with barely leashed control. "I can't . . . shit . . . Sunday." My words made little sense as I came down her throat, riding the wave right along with her.

Kingston's harsh bark of release filled the room along with mine. I slipped out of Sunday's mouth, her breaths coming in harsh pants as she came down from her climax. A drop of my cum dripped from the side of her mouth, and I used my thumb to brush it over her lip and back inside.

"Show me, dove." I stared down at her as she tilted her face up.

Fuck me, she looked sexy as hell as she opened her mouth and let me see the cum filling her.

"Now swallow," Caleb said from behind me.

Her gaze flicked to him, and she did as she was told.

"Good girl."

Kingston banded an arm across Sunday's chest and pulled her up so her back was pressed to his front. "Love you, Sunshine," he whispered, kissing her mark as he held her, still planted inside her.

"Love you too. So much."

The wolf looked at me, his grin smug. "That mind stuff is a fun trick. We should use it again sometime."

I shook my head, not sure where along the way Kingston and I became a fucking tag team, but there it was. There was no denying the massively successful results of our . . . partnership.

"Can Caleb come out of timeout now?" Sunday asked. "I'm not quite done."

The priest was already on his feet, unbuttoning his shirt as he stalked toward her. "Toss me a pillow, Nordson."

Kingston and I stepped away, giving Sunday and Caleb space as he laid her down on the fur and slid the pillow beneath her hips. He leaned down, feathering his lips over hers, then he knelt between her thighs and lifted both her legs until they rested over his shoulders.

"Watch closely, lads. This is how you make love to your wife. Feel free to take notes. Class is in session."

"I've missed you too, Father Gallagher," Sunday moaned as he slid into her.

Kingston and I shared a look.

"Fucker's got more game than I gave him credit for," he grumbled.

"There's a reason she loves him," I admitted, knowing all too well what sorts of acts those two had gotten up to while we'd been apart. Kingston would lose his mind if he realized all the things Caleb had introduced her to. It was a kindness, my keeping their secret.

Sunday writhed under his attentions, her brows pulled together, a blissful expression on her face as Caleb sank deep, rolling his hips slowly. It was a stark contrast to the frenzied fucking the rest of us had been engaged in. Then again, the arsehole hadn't been suffering without her for weeks on end. It was easy to go slow when you weren't making up for lost time.

"I love hearing her cry out like that. I don't care who makes her moan." Alek stared on with the intensity of someone watching a miracle be performed.

And *she* was a miracle, our Sunday. By all accounts, her existence should be impossible. But she was here, and ours, and she loved every bit as fiercely as she was loved. It took a hell of a woman to require four men to satisfy her. I was only glad to be counted among them.

Caleb turned his face into her leg, kissing her ankle as he deepened his strokes. "Are you ready to come apart, my darling?"

She whimpered. "Fuck, yes, Caleb, please."

He nipped her foot. "You know what to call me when I'm inside you."

"Please, Daddy. Let me come for you."

"Yes. Now, wife. Come for me."

I groaned as her blinding orgasm washed over me too.

Caleb tensed, his pace faltering as he gritted out, "Where do you want it, *a stor*? Inside or all over you so they can see?"

"All over me."

"Fuuuck, that's hot," Kingston groaned, palming his already hardening cock again. Jesus, the wolf was as insatiable as our pregnant mate.

Then again . . . I glanced down my body and was sporting my own growing erection.

"Is it bad that I want her again right now?" Alek asked, his fist slowly moving up and down his length.

"We all do," I assured him.

Our eyes were locked on the sexual tableau before us as Caleb pulled out, giving his cock two quick strokes before spurting all over Sunday's belly.

Kingston's moan joined Caleb's as he squeezed his jutting shaft. "Fuck me, it's going to be a long night."

Sunday opened her eyes, her body still splayed beneath Caleb's, glistening with sweat and cum. Her smile was beatific. She looked like a sensual goddess, and I was ready to worship.

"Are you ready for another round, love?"

She bit down on her lip and nodded.

"Good, because it's my turn to be inside you. You might be his wife, but you're my fucking obsession, and I will never be done with you." With one look, Caleb gave up his place between her thighs. I knelt down. "I'll warn you now, if you expect me to spill myself anywhere but in you, you're going to be disappointed. My cum belongs deep inside your perfect cunt."

"Yes, Noah. God, yes."

"I always knew you would be the death of me, dove. But I couldn't imagine a better way to go."

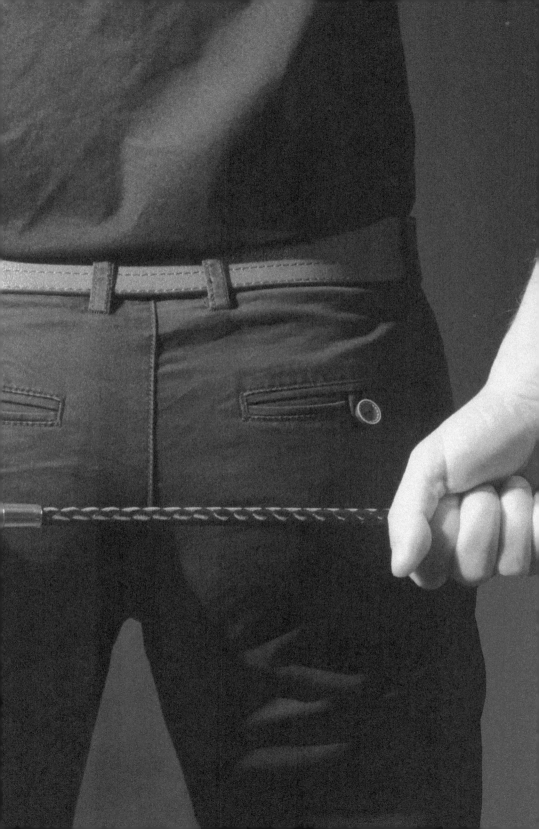

CHAPTER

# THIRTY-SIX

## KINGSTON

T he fire had died down in the hour since we'd all finally fallen into an exhausted, sweaty puppy pile. Caleb took off about fifteen minutes ago, claiming we needed more wood, but the pile behind me proved that was a lie. I knew the priest was giving us some space to reconnect. I should appreciate it, but it was his fucking fault we needed it to begin with.

My Sunshine was draped across a sleeping Alek, eyes closed as she trailed her fingers over the runes etched into his side. Thorne was behind her, tucking her into him with a protective palm over her belly. She had the sweetest, most sated smile on her lips. I knew exactly how she felt. Whole. Satisfied. Connected. It was the same for me. Being with her fixed everything that was wrong in my fucked up life.

Despite the comfort of having her back, I couldn't quite find the same peace as the others. Too much had happened. Was still *going* to happen. I was more aware than ever of the ticking of our very own doomsday clock. Two minutes from midnight and all that. The end of the world. The ruin of everything that ever meant shit to me. I was going to lose it all. Again. Unless we figured a way out of this.

317

"You're staring," she murmured, her blue eyes finding mine.

My lips twitched. "I'm afraid if I close my eyes, you'll go away again."

"Kingston . . ." Her irises flashed with apology as she reached out the fingers brushing over Alek's side to take my hand. "I'm right here. I'm not going anywhere."

I had to swallow through a tight throat. "I want to believe it. Fuck, baby. Losing you was hard enough the first time, and it never gets any easier. Once was enough, but I've done it over and over. Are you ever going to just stay mine?"

She sat up slowly, Thorne grumbling in protest, pulling her closer to him. "Where are you going?"

Sunday turned to face him, a smile in her voice. "I need to get up for a little bit. You stay. Rest. We're all exhausted."

He propped himself on one elbow and pressed a kiss to her shoulder. "Don't go far."

"I won't. There aren't many hiding places in here anyway." That seemed to placate him because the vampire laid back down as she moved to get to her feet. I was there, offering my help, the sensation of finally touching her skin soothing me.

I reached out and grabbed a lock of her hair between my fingers, twirling it with a smirk. "I left something in your hair."

The wry twist of her lips had me fighting a laugh. "You left a lot of something all over me. All of you did." She wrinkled her nose. "I need a shower."

Kissing her softly, I sighed as the tightness in my shoulders loosened with that simple gesture. "I'll come with you. Help you wash all those hard-to-reach places."

She laughed and pressed her hand to my chest. "Yeah, no. You go in there with me, we're going to do everything *but* shower. I need a little intermission." I opened my mouth to argue, but she stopped me with another sweet kiss. "Please, King. I'm a big girl. I can wash my own ass."

"Can you?"

She looked a little sheepish. "Probably."

"Will you at least promise to call out for me if you need help? I cross my heart Jake won't go anywhere near your pretty kitty."

An exasperated laugh escaped as she shook her head. "I've missed you. More than you could know."

"Not as much as I missed you."

"Oh yeah? Did you hold imaginary conversations? 'Cause I did. I did it with accents and man voices and everything."

I blinked at her, laughter tumbling out. "I'm sorry what? I'm gonna need proof of this, Sunshine. Show me your best, Kingston. I'm dying to hear your impression of me."

Thorne sat up, his brows lifted in amusement. "Yes, please do share. I'm intrigued."

Her cheeks burned pink. "You'll laugh at me."

"I can guaran-fucking-tee it."

"You're really not going to let this go, are you?"

"Not on your fucking life, baby."

She huffed, cheeks crimson as she spun around, giving both of us her back. "I can't do it if I'm looking at you."

"Whatever you need, dove. The stage is yours."

I wasn't prepared for what she did then.

She cleared her throat. "Go on, Sunshine. It's okay to tell Jake how much you missed him." Shifting into Thorne's snobby accent, she continued. "Oh, piss off, Kingston. I didn't have to name my cock to make sure she missed it." Without a beat, she slid into Alek's clipped British. "Please, we all know she loves my Novasgardian footlong best." Followed by Caleb's lilting Irish. "You're all a bunch of fecking children. Miss Fallon, be a good girl, and tell them all it's mine you love most."

Doubling over, I laughed so hard my stomach hurt. "You . . . Fuck . . . I can't . . . breathe."

Even Thorne was wheezing with laughter. "Bloody hell, is *that* what we sound like to you?"

Her shoulders stiffened, and she beelined for the bathroom, ignoring both of us.

"Baby, wait. That was incredible. Don't be embarrassed. You've got us totally nailed. We're nothing but a bunch of dick happy assholes."

"Leave me alone. I'm going to try and wash the mortification off now."

Thorne was on his feet, right beside me as we both went to her, doing our best to smooth over her ruffled feathers.

"Come on, little wolf. Don't be like that. You intended for us to laugh. Otherwise you would have said something else."

I dropped a kiss to her shoulder. "Would it make you feel better to hear our impersonation of you?"

"Not a good idea, mate."

"Why? Is your American accent shite?" I asked, slipping into my version of a posh British accent.

"Yes. But I'm sure I can do a solid arsehole wolf impression." Thorne cleared his throat and slipped into some bastardized version of a cowboy surfer. "Whoa, dude, you want me to whip out my cock and count my piercings for you? I'm such a badass. Yippee ki-yay, motherfucker."

"Bloody hell, would you like some tea and crumpets with your top hat and monocle, Mr. Blackthorne? Cheerio, govna. Pip pip and all that sort of thing."

"Fuck you, wanker. You can't even string a proper sentence together. I do not sound like that."

"You sure about that, buddy?"

Sunday lost the battle at that point, laughing so hard she snorted and tears streamed from her eyes. "Okay, I feel better now. At least I know my impersonations are better than yours."

"Oi! That was a perfect Thorne."

"No, mate. No, it wasn't." Thorne clapped me on the shoulder. "It was a good Dick Van Dyke."

"Does that make me Mary Poppins?" Sunday asked, looking at us over her shoulder as she resumed her stroll toward the bathroom.

"Yep. Practically perfect in every way, baby."

Her sweet grin had my heart lightening. I didn't look away until she closed the door, my pulse thumping erratically with each step she took. Logically, I knew she was safe. That it was only a shower, but people were dropping left and right around us lately. I'd feel better if I was in there with her. I took a step, but Thorne stopped me with a hand on my arm.

"She'll be fine. Why don't you make her something to eat, take care of her in a way that won't make her feel smothered?"

Taking a long breath, I fought the tightness between my ribs. It was always there lately—the pressure, the fear—but every passing moment seemed to build faster and faster. Time was running out, and I couldn't ignore it.

A distraction sounded good.

"Yeah, okay," I agreed, swiping my boxer briefs off the floor so Jake and I weren't flopping around in the wind as I did my thing in the kitchen.

Thorne followed my lead, grabbing his pants and pulling them on. He didn't hover; instead he took a seat on the sofa and picked up the book Caleb had left on the table. I was pretty sure he was pretending to read and giving me time to get my head straight before Sunday came back.

I opened the cupboards one after another, finding nothing but scraps. One piece of bread, a can of peaches, one of fucking green beans. How the hell was Sunday supposed to survive on this?

"What the fuck, Caleb?"

Thorne turned his head, casting me a curious glance. "What's he done now?"

"There's no goddamned food in this house. The ass is going to let her starve."

Frowning, Thorne peered into the empty cabinet behind me. "I find that hard to believe. He must have a plan in place. A way for supplies to reach them here."

"Can you two keep it down?" Alek groaned from his place on the fur. "I'm trying to recover here."

"Cry me a river, god-boy. I'd love to see how you react when there's no food for your eight-course breakfast."

Alek lifted his head. "What?"

"Now he fucking cares."

"Can't he just magic us some food?"

Stumbling to his feet, Alek swayed, then pulled himself together. Lilith had really done a number on him. The Viking still wasn't at full strength, but he looked a little better. "Magic food can't sustain us, not for long. It's not truly nutritious."

I slammed the cabinet closed. "Fuck."

"Calm down, wolf. I'll go find the priest. Figure out what the plan is. You just . . . make tea or something. I'll be right back." Taking one of the coats by the door, Thorne walked out into the night.

"You doing okay?"

I looked over at Alek, not appreciating the empathy in his icy gaze. "I'll be fine. You should go back to sleep. You look like crap."

Instead of fighting me, Alek climbed on the couch and closed his eyes. "I'll just rest a little while longer. Wake me when the food's ready."

"What food, asshole?" I muttered, shaking my head. But the Viking was already knocked out.

Spying the kettle, I set it on the stove and waited for the water to heat up. I grabbed a couple tea bags and dropped them in one of the chipped coffee mugs. I'd never made a cup of tea before. How did you know when it was done? Did I leave the bags in, and what were the strings for? Why were there tags? Did it need to be as strong as coffee?

Poking one, I gave it a little growl of frustration. It smelled like wet leaves and dead flowers. Why would anyone want to drink this crap?

As soon as the kettle began whistling, I filled the cup and took the light brown water to the bedroom. I hated how little I was providing her but was desperate to do something for my mate.

She'd left the bathroom door open a crack, the scent of soap mixing with the steam of the hot water as it crept into the room. I smiled as I heard her. She was humming softly. My song. The one I wrote for her.

Fuck. That did things to me.

The melody abruptly cut off as she let out a whimpered groan. I was off and running to her like a fucking gold medal was on the line. I burst through the bathroom door, not doing a damn thing to conceal my absolute panic.

"Sunday? Fuck, are you okay?"

I whipped open the curtain, finding her standing beneath a spray of steamy water, hands curled over her belly as she hunched over.

"Oh, my God, is it time? Is the baby coming?"

Once her shock at seeing me passed, she laughed. "No. It's just a contraction, I think. It's pretty common. Especially after what we've been doing."

"Contractions? That means the baby. I know what contractions are, Sunshine. You need to lie down. I'll get some towels and . . . fuck . . . we need to sterilize a knife or some scissors. Something to cut the cord."

Her eyes were wide by the time I was done rambling. "Kingston. We're not starring in Little House on the Prairie. I don't need a knife coming anywhere near me or my belly. Just calm down. It's too soon for the baby to come. It's just a little blip."

"A blip."

"Yeah. Now go on. I'll be out in a minute."

I couldn't stop the building panic. The thought of her having this baby with just us to help her through it sent my mind reeling. Anything could happen. I would *not* lose her. I'd already lost too many people. Phe and my dad. Rosie. But Natalie said . . .

"Kingston? You look like you're going to puke."

A tremor worked its way through my limbs, and nausea clutched my gut. I might puke if I didn't get a hold of my emotions. I couldn't breathe. Every intake of breath hurt like I was trying to swallow a dagger, and it was shredding my insides the whole way down.

"Kingston? Fuck. Hold on."

She shut the water off and climbed out, grabbing a towel and hastily wrapping it around her body as water dripped from her hair.

"Let's sit you down. You need to breathe, okay? In through your nose..."

She was holding onto my arm, pulling me into the bedroom. But I was barely aware of what was happening around me beyond that. The walls were closing in. My vision went fuzzy at the edges as my pulse pounded in my ears.

Why couldn't I fucking breathe?

"Look at me, baby. I'm right here. Look into my eyes." She pressed her palms to my cheeks, bringing my gaze to hers.

"I can't lose you," I gasped. "Not you too. I already lost Phe and my dad."

"What? Kingston, what are you talking about?" Her grip on my cheeks tightened, her face paling slightly.

"People are dropping like flies. The world is ending around us. I can't say goodbye to anyone else. I can't lose you again."

I was full-on shaking now, my voice taking on a bit of a hysterical edge. I'm pretty sure I was on the brink of a full-blown mental break. I just could not seem to get my shit together.

"I'm not going anywhere. I've got you. I'm right here." At some point, I must've sat on the bed because she crawled on and got behind me, wrapping her arms around me and holding me to her as tightly as she could. "Breathe with me. That's it, baby. You're okay."

I focused on her, the sound of her voice, the rise and fall of her chest against mine, the way she called me baby. She'd always been the center of my fucking universe, but in that moment, she proved it. She was the only thing keeping me together.

Eventually my breaths evened out and the tremors racking my body ceased. "Fuck, I'm sorry."

"Shh, it's okay. You don't need to apologize."

"I guess I've sort of been holding it all in. Things kind of caught up with me."

"It sounds like it. You want to tell me what that was all about? What happened to your sister?"

"They died. My dad, Phe, Rosie, Martin . . . Moriarty and the fucking Seer. It's the Apocalypse. All of it."

She let out a shocked gasp. Her hands, previously firm on me, trembled, showcasing just how deeply my words affected her. "They're gone? All of them?"

"Yeah. All within a few days of each other."

"Fuck . . . I . . . How is this just coming up now? Wait, don't answer that. I know." She shifted behind me, then got off the bed. "Okay. Shit. I . . . I need to get dressed, and then we should talk about this with everyone."

Still shaky, I got to my feet while Sunday pulled on a pair of leggings and one of Caleb's sweaters. I still felt a bit like the rug had been pulled out from under me, but at least I could draw a full breath. I hadn't realized how much all of it was still weighing on me. I hadn't really given myself time to think about it at all. It would take a lot more work for me to move past my dad and sister dying and what it meant for me and the rest of us. The closure I needed wasn't within reach. Not yet. But once this was over, I'd mourn them properly.

Linking our fingers, Sunday squeezed my hand. "It's going to be okay. I've got you."

We walked out into the living room, where Alek sat on the couch with one arm draped over his eyes. Sunday glanced around, clearly seeking out the others when the door opened, and both Thorne and Caleb walked in.

"Perfect timing. We're having a family meeting," Sunday said, still holding on to me.

I was pretty sure her strength was the only thing keeping me upright at the moment.

"Family meeting? What the hell happened, dove? We were only gone for twenty minutes at most."

"It was long enough. Did you know she's having contractions?" I snapped, gaze focused on Caleb.

"One contraction," she corrected. "Just a baby one."

"One is too fucking many when you're off in the middle of bumfuck nowhere stranded on an island without a hospital or doctor in sight. You saw it yourself when we walked through that ghost town of a village, Thorne. Warg Island has been deserted for a long fucking time. No people. No one to help. Not to mention no fucking food." Remembering what had set me off to begin with, I spun around to point a finger at the priest. "Some *Daddy* you are, Caleb. What the hell kind of protector are you? She's going to starve, or bleed out, or . . . or . . ." That panic began rising in me again, but I pushed it down.

"I'm totally fine, King . . ." Her protest trailed off into a soft grunt as she stiffened next to me. The stubborn woman was trying to hide it, but I could see the discomfort on her face.

"See? See? There she goes again. We need to get her off this island. Thorne, call your dad and get the jet. We're not sticking around for the baby to pop out. We are not prepared to handle this on our own."

"Pull yourself together, wolf. Do you really think I haven't planned for this? A boat with supplies will arrive in the morning, along with the midwife I procured for Sunday before we ever set foot on this island. There was a delay because of the godforsaken storm. You know I would never do anything to put her at risk."

I raised my brow but didn't list out the sheer number of things he'd done to prove that very statement wrong.

"I still want the jet."

"Me as well. I don't like the possibility of our being cut off if something goes wrong." Thorne reached into his pocket but came up empty. Realizing he must have dropped his phone, he searched the floor, jolting the couch and waking Alek, who sat up with a confused grunt.

"Like the end of the world?" Caleb offered dryly.

"Not funny," Sunday said.

He shrugged. "Aye, but it's the truth. We stay here. We will have everything we need."

"Sunshine deserves more than some midwife you pulled off the street. Doc can take care of her. He's delivered more shifter babies than I can count. I vote we go."

"As do I."

"I'm telling you. It's safer for us here."

Alek stood, his face lined with fatigue. "You're outnumbered, Priest. I'm the size of two men. I count as two. That's four votes to your one to take Sunday back."

Caleb looked to Sunday. "What do you want?"

Before she could answer, Thorne's startled cry pulled all of our attention.

"Bloody hell."

"What's wrong?" Sunday asked, taking a step toward him.

"It's Moira. I've missed about ten calls and have nearly four times as many messages."

"Is she okay?" Sunday's voice was pitched high with concern.

I didn't want to point out that with that many attempts to reach out, the odds weren't looking good. Especially with the way our luck had been lately. Even if Moira was all right, someone we knew likely wasn't.

"I've no clue."

Dread sat like a stone in my gut as I left Sunday's side and snagged my jeans off the floor. Pulling my phone from the pocket, I stared down at the multitude of notifications on the screen. I had just as many as Thorne. She'd been blowing up our group chat. Scrolling, I read the most recent ones, trying to bring myself up to speed.

Moira: Answer your phones, assholes.

Moira: HELLO??? Answer me! It's urgent.

Moira: What the fuck are you doing? Okay, I have a pretty good idea what you're doing, but this is an emergency!!!!!

Moira: Fine. Since none of you seem to care, I'll just leave the message here. *Iniquity* was attacked. Lilith is missing. The headmistress is dead. Oh, and according to Ash, that bitch hadn't had a human soul in her body for a long ass time.

Moira: Something evil had been walking around in her skin pretending to be her for no one knows how long, and that is beyond scary as fuck.

Moira: I had another vision.

Moira: They're not Horsemen. They're HorseWOMEN.

Moira: And they're coming for you.

## CHAPTER
# THIRTY-SEVEN
### SUNDAY

One thing had become terrifyingly clear. We knew absolutely fucking nothing. Knowledge is supposed to be power, but the more we learned, the less we knew. It was like we'd been given a box of puzzle pieces but no picture, no roadmap to show us how everything fit together. We were working blind here. Ikea furniture assembly would be less confusing.

It had been two days since Moira's bombshell about the Horsemen being women and on the hunt for us. Two days since Kingston's panic attack and revelations about people we cared for being targeted. Only two days since I'd gotten my men back just to have the rug ripped out from beneath us again.

Fuck.

My.

Life.

At least the sun was shining? *Yeah, because being murdered during the day is so much kinder than in the shadows. You fucking idiot.*

My constant protectors followed behind me as I took in the fresh air and slowly walked along the dirt road that led toward the bluff. I needed to move, to refocus on something other than . . . everything else.

Tightness built in my belly, that same breathtaking squeeze that had sent Kingston into his uncontrolled spiral. I didn't know much about pregnancy, but I knew I was supposed to have nine months to be where I was right now. Even as a shifter. I was a little over six months pregnant. But anyone who looked at me would expect me to pop out this kid within days. Hours, maybe.

Pressure in my hips was near constant now. A sense of urgency I hadn't expected raced through me as well. My body was preparing for the one moment Natalie said would end in my death. How was I supposed to wrap my head around that?

Denial. That's how. I would keep shoving my head as deep in the sand as it would go and pretend that this was just a normal baby and things were going to be fine.

Yeah. I wasn't buying it either, but it was the only thing keeping me from going the way of Kingston.

I just wish I'd had more time. More time to come to terms with this. More time with my mates. More time to adjust to the idea of being a mom. Or . . . not being a mom. Just more fucking time.

Tears burned my eyes. Dammit, I was a hormonal mess.

"I've got her," Alek murmured from behind me.

His large hands slid over my shoulders, pulling me back against his tall frame. I closed my eyes and just . . . breathed.

"I'm so glad you're feeling better," I whispered, not trusting my voice.

He pressed his lips to the top of my head, loosely wrapping his arms around me and holding me steady to his chest.

"Don't worry about me. It's our turn to take care of you. Fall apart if you need to. We'll be here to pick up the pieces. You're not carrying the weight of this by yourself anymore, Sunny. You don't have to hide it from us."

"I know . . . I just . . . You all risked so much to come here, and I'm going to lose you anyway. I don't want any of this. But . . ." I placed my palm on my belly, and his hands slipped over the swell in tandem, cradling us both. "Saying I don't want it means I don't want her. That's not true. I'm so confused, Alek."

"It's okay to be conflicted. You can love your daughter and hate the circumstances around her birth. It doesn't mean you are any less devoted to her."

"It feels like it."

He kissed my temple. "You've been spending too much time with Caleb. You've adopted his guilty conscience."

"He has a lot to be guilty about," Noah said under his breath. I'd forgotten they were behind us, standing sentry.

I turned, pulling myself from Alek's arms and mourning the loss of his touch all at once. "And you don't?" Noah looked chastened, but I continued. "You saw everything in his mind. His past, his penance. I forgave him, and that's all that matters."

Kingston smirked, laughing as he held up a hand to me for a high five. "That's my sexy Alpha baby mama. Put the bratty prince in his place."

"Watch it, wolf, or you'll be next."

He lowered his hand, still smirking. "Worth it. I like it when you spank me."

Noah cocked one dark brow. "Spankings? Really, Kingston?"

He shrugged. "They call it a spank bank for a reason. And I am secure in my masculinity. I can let her own my ass all she wants."

"Do you call her Mommy as well?"

"Mistress," he and I corrected at the same time.

Noah's mouth hung open as he glanced between us. "Bloody hell, where was I?"

"And me? Are you holding out on us . . . *Mistress*?" Alek brushed my hair back from my neck, leaning down and kissing the sensitive spot between my earlobe and my jaw. I shuddered as a ripple of pleasure raced through me. Even now, so pregnant I couldn't walk faster than a sloth, one small touch from my mates could make me needy.

"Do you want me to be?"

"I'd let you have your way with me. But we both know it would just end up with me topping from the bottom."

Kingston inhaled. "Our mate likes that idea. Fuck . . . pick her up, and let's go break in one of the new bedrooms Alek magicked up for us."

"Don't get too excited. Sunday has an appointment with the midwife in a few hours."

"Plenty of time."

"Not for what I have in mind," Alek murmured. "I finally have my stamina back. No more frenzied couplings for me."

I melted into him. "Tease."

One of his large palms cupped my breast and squeezed. "Consider it foreplay, Kærasta. You know we'll take care of you as soon as we get you alone."

"We're alone now."

My three mates laughed.

"And know that you and the babe are safe," he added.

I rolled my eyes. "We are fine." But deep down, I wasn't sure about that at all. Everything was different from what it was supposed to be. How could I confidently say I was healthy, that the baby was doing well? Just because Doc had taken one look early on and given us the proverbial thumbs up didn't mean it was smooth sailing from there.

He was also the one who pointed out the birth itself is where things could get tricky. Despite my words to Kingston otherwise, I had no way to know that the pains I'd been having *weren't* indications I was about to go into labor any day.

*"What else have you been keeping from us, dove?"*

The unexpected caress of Noah's voice in my mind made me jerk. I narrowed my eyes at him. "Get out of my head, Noah. It's rude to eavesdrop."

Hurt flashed on his handsome face, and I immediately regretted my harsh tone. "Don't keep secrets from me."

"Secrets? What secrets? Sunshine . . . you promised."

I raised a brow. "Oh no, just because you guys have this special new bromance going on doesn't mean you get to gang up on me. I'm allowed to worry about things without having to announce it to the world."

"But we're your mates," Kingston protested.

"And you are the kings of overreacting. Not everything requires a battle strategy and war council meeting. Sometimes I just have to sit with my thoughts and figure shit out before coming to you."

"This is a literal war, Sunny. We are fighting for a future."

Anxiety tightened my lungs. I couldn't breathe. Goddammit, these men and their stupid . . . making sense. "It's *my* body. Regardless of anything else, I'm the only one who decides who I talk to about what's happening to it. If I don't want to talk about it, I don't have to. And *you*"—I glared at all of them—"don't get to make me feel guilty about it."

Mood effectively killed. I waddled past them as they stood speechless. But I could feel the apology from Noah tickling my mind. He wasn't going to infiltrate my thoughts again, but he wanted me to know he was still there. Still joined with me. As a mate should be.

I knew they were worried. Fuck, so was I. We'd only just gotten each other back and barely had a chance to enjoy any of it before we'd been flung back into the deep end. We were all just doing our best to stay afloat.

I swallowed back a sigh, knowing I owed them an apology. Later. Once it would feel less like a retreat. I may not have been in the right back there, but it didn't make what I'd said wrong either. They needed to respect my space. Just because there was one of me and four of them didn't mean they got to steamroll me into decisions.

They flanked me as we walked back to the house, now so much larger thanks to Alek's magic being at full strength again. No one spoke; no one rushed me or scooped me up to hurry us along. They simply strolled slowly with me. Kingston on my left, Alek on my right, Noah behind me. My very own secret service. Although, it was no secret what service they provided.

Noah's hands wrapped around my hips, stopping me in my tracks as we rounded the bend toward the home we all now shared. "Stop, dove. Someone's there."

Kingston lifted his chin, taking a long inhalation. "It's the woman who came on the boat."

"The midwife? She's early." Alek linked our hands and held tight. "Why is she early?"

"Food. She brought us food. I can smell it."

I laughed at Kingston's eager tone. "Always motivated by food."

"You know I love to eat." He winked at me, and I had to fight against the little flutters that set off between my legs. "My favorite is a sweet sundae all smothered in cream."

*Stop it, Sunday. You do not want to get all hot and bothered before a stranger has to dive between your legs to inspect your vag. That is not the kind of first impression we're aiming for.*

Ignoring Kingston, I answered Alek. "I'm not sure. Let's go find out."

I started moving forward, not realizing Kingston had remained behind until he shouted, "Really? Not even a smile? That was some prime wordplay right there. Top-notch shit."

I could just make out the sound of Noah's voice, so I stopped and peeked over my shoulder in time to see him patting Kingston on the back. "It's all right, mate. Solid attempt."

Kingston sniffed. "Sometimes I don't even know why I put in the effort when no one even appreciates it."

"I appreciate you."

"You do?"

"Yeah, you make me look good."

"Fuck you, Thorne. You've seen what I'm working with."

"Now, Kingston. We've already discussed this."

I laughed all the way to the house as their banter filled up the space between us. But my laughter died as Alek and I went through the gate. The woman stood at the front door, facing us with a gentle smile on her lined face. She looked like a mom. A sweet, soft mother who just wanted to take care of us.

"Sunday?" she asked, her blue eyes sparkling with kindness.

Alek gripped my hand tighter. "Who are you?"

Why was he asking her that? Clearly she was the midwife. These protective men were driving me batty.

"I'm Victoria. The midwife? Caleb summoned me. I thought he would have told you." Her accent surprised me. An American midwife in Ireland. That sounded like a sitcom. Or a rom-com. Good thing this lady wasn't in her twenties. I was so not okay with a hot nanny situation.

Releasing Alek's palm, I stepped forward and offered my hand. She grinned and looked down at her arms, full of bags and a picnic basket.

"Sorry. You've got your hands full." I let her inside, feeling the weight of my men's gazes on my back the whole time. They were going to be overprotective about this, of course. I bet Kingston would hold my legs open for me while she checked my cervix too. Hell, he'd probably insist he was the one who did it as he reported back to her.

"I know our appointment isn't technically until sundown, but instinct told me I needed to come early to introduce myself and see if you needed any help. You're much farther along than Caleb said. Usually we have more time to get comfortable with each other. But from the looks of things, we'll be to the main event soon. And you've had no care?"

She settled her bags and the basket on the kitchen table as Kingston came up behind me, his fingers trailing over my arm and down to twine with mine.

"Does she know?" he murmured.

"Does she know what?"

"You know . . ." He raised his free hand and mimed claws. "Rawr."

I shrugged, trying not to laugh at him. That was the cutest thing he'd done in a long time. "Caleb wouldn't bring someone here who didn't understand our kind."

"But she's human."

Victoria turned around, training her focus on us. "I am. But I'm also up to speed on your particular . . . situation. Don't worry, I know what I'm getting into."

Kingston grunted but didn't seem any more inclined to trust her now than he did at first. This was going to be a fun afternoon. I could tell. I was already anticipating having to shove Kingston's snout away from my crotch.

"Bad dog. Sit."

He leaned in and nipped my shoulder. "You're gonna pay for that later, baby. I promise."

"Looking forward to it."

"We should wait for Caleb to wake before I begin my initial exam. In the meantime, I brought you all some goodies. I figured you could use a little treat after being stuck on this island during that awful storm."

"There are treats?" Alek asked, coming toward us with a curious tilt of his head.

"I like to bake. Apple pie, salted caramel brownies, hot cocoa. I can't help myself. I'm a mom. I have this deep need to care for people."

"Apple pie?" Alek repeated, his eyes glowing.

Victoria smiled indulgently. "It's still warm. Or it should be if you hurry."

The guys exchanged uncertain looks. None of us were very comfortable with strangers at the moment, even ones vetted by Caleb.

Not taking any offense, Victoria lifted a plate of brownies, selecting one from the pile and taking a big bite. "They're safe. I promise."

Alek needed no further convincing. He was up and digging through her basket in a flash, pulling out the pie tin. "Mine!" he snagged a fork and dove straight in without offering anyone a slice. Then, with an embarrassed grin, he looked at us. "Sorry. Did you want some?"

Noah stood with his arms crossed, eyes narrowed. "Forgive me. I'm not hungry."

"That's fine. I'm not offended. I brought wine for Caleb. I know how you vampires love your reds."

He raised a brow. "You're thorough, but this seems a mite out of your purview."

"Part of the reason Caleb brought me here was to provide care and comfort for Sunday. He never mentioned there'd be so many of you. But I'm nothing if not adaptable. You have to be in my line of work. Babies love to make their own plans."

Seeming satisfied, Noah backed down before taking the bottle out of her bag and pulling the cork.

"Yes, I have four mates. Caleb wasn't sure they'd . . . make it in time, though. This is Alek, Kingston, and Noah."

"And which one is the father?"

"I am," they all said in unison.

Victoria started.

"All of us," Noah clarified firmly.

Her mouth fell open in a little O, but she corrected herself and looked to Kingston. "Why don't you help yourself to a brownie? I saw you eyeing them. I'll serve the cocoa."

He gave her a look brimming with suspicion as he stalked over to the pyramid of desserts and selected one off the top. Holding her gaze, he gave it a sniff before finally taking a bite. His eyes widened. "These are pretty good."

Victoria snickered. "I'm so glad you think so."

Noah plated a brownie and handed it to me, some of the tension leaving him as he grew more comfortable having this stranger in our home.

As I took a bite, Victoria leaned in and whispered, "They're actually vegan and very good for you. Don't tell the boys."

"Secret's safe with me," I promised, taking a bite of my own.

"Have a seat. We can get to know each other better before we get down to business." Victoria poured rich hot chocolate out of a thermos into our mismatched mugs, then distributed the delicious drinks to each of us, herself included.

As she pulled one of the dining table chairs into the living room, she smiled and raised her cup. "To new friends and a new world for all of you."

We joined her, all of us watching as she lifted the mug to her lips.

"What is that, cinnamon?" Alek asked, taking a second sip and draining his entire cup.

"Jesus, Nordson. Show a little decorum," Noah chided before taking his own large taste. "I think it's chili powder."

"Really? It tastes like hazelnut to me, or maybe maple?" Kingston took a deep gulp as well, slurping loudly.

"You'd think they hadn't eaten in weeks," I muttered, sharing a look with Victoria.

"They grow fast, but men are all little boys at heart when it comes to sweets. You'll see."

Bringing my cocoa to my mouth, I let the liquid coat my tongue. "No. It's . . . caramel. Coffee and dark chocolate, maybe? What's in this?"

"Oh, just a little of this, a dash of that. It's a secret recipe."

Alek's eyes grew heavy, his shoulders relaxing from his place next to me on the couch. My poor Viking had been pushing through his recovery for me. I knew it. He pretended he was back to normal, but the truth was on obvious display. He'd used his power to give us a bigger place to live; now he was paying the price of doing too much too soon.

I shifted my attention, ready to ask Kingston to help Alek to bed, when I noticed his head drooping. Before I could comment, Noah's mug slipped from his fingers and crashed to the floor, shattering with a loud clatter. The guys didn't move. They were dead to the world.

Dread settled heavily in my stomach as tingles of foreboding raced along my spine.

"Be a good girl, Sunday." Victoria's voice sounded different, familiar somehow, but I couldn't quite place it. Everything around me was growing foggy, and it was nearly impossible to keep my eyes open.

She leaned forward and brushed some hair off my forehead. Her face swam in my view, rearranging itself but not quite settling into one distinct person.

She morphed from Victoria to Madame le Blanc to . . . my mother.

I gasped. "You."

"Oh, good. It seems the time for games is finally at an end. Sleep, dearest. There will be time for us to have a little mother-daughter chat when you wake up."

As darkness took hold, the pounding of hooves filled my ears, and three women materialized behind my mother.

That's when I knew. The horsewomen weren't coming.

They were already here.

And my mother was one of them.

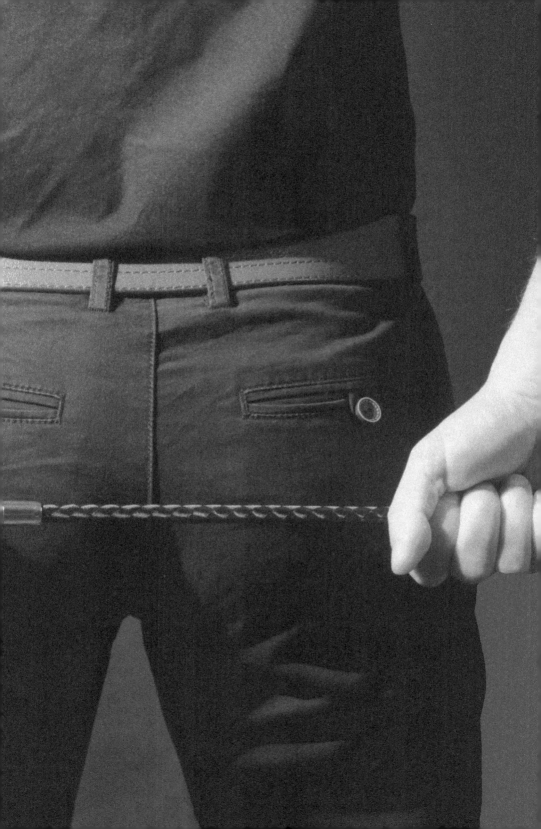

# THIRTY-EIGHT

## CALEB

S oft and warm, Eden laid on my chest, her tiny body nestled against me. Safe. Whole. Perfect.

"You look so good with her in your arms," Sunday said, standing in the doorway of the nursery, a smile curving her lips as the sun beamed in through the window. "I didn't hear her wake up."

"Well, she kept you up all night. It's my turn. You need your sleep, *a stor*." I ran my hand over Eden's downy soft hair, inhaling her scent. She smelled like all of us, but most prominent was her mother's lilac and honey. Pressing my lips to the baby's head, I let the feeling of pure happiness wash over me.

I knew in my heart I was dreaming. This was too good to be true. A future that didn't exist for any of us, especially not someone like me. But fecking hell, I wanted to hold on to this fantasy for as long as I could.

"Come here to me, darling. I want both my girls in my arms."

"Okay, Daddy."

There was a playful smirk in her words, the double entendre more meaningful now than ever.

"She's asleep, you know. You can put her in her crib."

"Aye, but I don't want to let her go."

She joined us on the daybed, curling into my side and making this moment truly perfect. I wanted for nothing. I held all I'd ever prayed for in my arms. A loving wife. A healthy baby girl.

Nothing could make me happier.

"Caleb . . . I have something I need to tell you."

I tensed, cursing myself for jinxing it.

"What's wrong?"

She laughed. "Nothing's wrong. I just . . . have a surprise for you."

Raising one brow, I gave her a stern look. "What have you been up to, Mrs. Gallagher?"

"I think you should ask yourself that question, husband."

"Me? What have I done?"

Her lips trailed over my heart as she stroked Eden's back. "You told me you wanted a big family."

Pulse racing as her words landed, I caught her hand in mine. "Sunday . . ."

"What's the saying? Irish twins?"

I laughed, my chest filling with thousands of tiny joyous bubbles. "Are you sure?"

"Would I risk telling you if I wasn't?"

"Not after last time," I said, grinning at the memory of her reddened arse when she'd played a similar trick on me only a month after Eden's birth.

"Are you mad?"

A shocked sound escaped me. "Mad? Why would another babe make me angry?"

She nuzzled closer, her fingers dragging across my throat where my shirt collar was open. "Could you pretend it makes you angry, Daddy?"

"Oh. Oh, aye. I can."

Sitting up, she stretched, her breasts pressing against her thin shirt, tempting me. "Put the baby in her crib, Caleb. We need to celebrate."

I gave my wife a kiss and gently untangled myself from her so as not to jostle Eden. Laying her down, I couldn't help but gaze at her, running the tip of my finger over her little button nose.

"We make beautiful babies, *a stor*."

"We do," she agreed, coming up behind me to rest her face between my shoulder blades, hands already working my belt open.

Turning to face my wife, I put on my most stern voice. "What do you think you're doing, Miss Fallon?"

The smile she gave me sent a bolt of lust straight to my dick. "Being naughty, Father Gallagher."

"That you are. I think it's time for you to get on your knees."

"I thought you'd never ask."

I knew the dream was fleeting. That this stolen moment would disappear when reality pulled me back. But for now? I was going to cling to it for all I was worth.

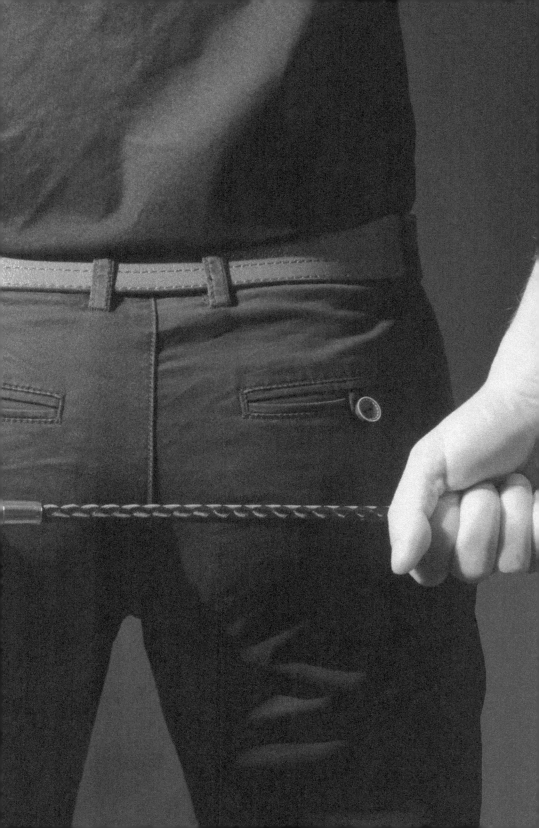

# THIRTY-NINE

## THORNE

"Noah!" Rosie's screams pierced through the chaos erupting all around me, her cry for help echoing in my mind as I stood outside Blackthorne Manor, watching smoke pour from the broken windows.

The house was on fire. We were under attack.

"Noah, please, save her!" My father crouched next to Mother's too-still form, agony on his face. "She needs you. Don't let her die."

Heart pounding, I blurred to the door, rushing through the billowing black cloud, choking on its acrid scent. All around me, people ran for the exit, hitting me as I worked against the current of escaping staff. With every step, the air grew heavier until it was unbearably hot and I could feel the hair on my arms curling as it was singed.

"Master Blackthorne, don't go that way. There's no way out." A serving girl I'd never seen before grabbed my hand and tried to pull me toward the front door. Her skin was reddened from the heat, and ash streaked her face.

"Let go of me. I am not leaving without my sister."

"Suit yourself."

The girl took off without another word, pushing against the crush of bodies to get out of the house.

I continued my descent down into Callie's lab, spotting my aunt's specter hovering outside the door.

"I tried, but I . . . there's nothing I can do. Noah. You have to save her."

A beam fell, narrowly missing my head as I jumped out of the hallway and into the lab, where my sister was caught beneath a large pile of rubble. I could just make out the satin of her headband and one of her pale arms reaching toward me.

She'd been knocked unconscious. Her body eerily still and lifeless.

"No." I wasn't losing her. Not this time.

I dropped to my knees beside my sister, tossing wood and books from the fallen shelves as I excavated her body. It felt like it took me forever to free her, the air growing thicker with smoke, the heat of the flames inching ever closer to where I curled protectively over her.

"Come on, Winnie. Time to go." The childhood nickname slipped out. I hadn't called her that in years, not since I'd learned how to properly pronounce my Rs and Ls.

She softly moaned, the sound sending hope through me. She was alive. I could save her.

Scooping her into my arms, I stood and turned toward the escape but stopped as a hooded figure came into view just beyond the open door. The robe and scythe needed no introduction. I knew exactly who this was.

Death.

Here to claim my sister.

"You can't have her."

Soft, ghostly laughter floated through the room as pale hands reached out from the long arms of the robe, rising to pull back the hood.

I steeled myself, expecting all manner of grisly visages. But not one of them came close to the truth of what was hidden beneath those black folds.

A woman. A beautiful one with long curling blonde hair. Bright guileless blue eyes. A smattering of freckles dotting her cheeks. As I stared at her, her lips twisted up in a smile that chilled me to the bone. It was the most terrifying thing I'd ever seen. There was no reason a woman who looked like she belonged in a primary school should be able to make me feel this way with a simple lift of her brow.

I followed her gaze as she glanced to the ceiling.

"Time's up, Noah," she said, a breath before the stone above me collapsed into the room, crushing me with hot rubble.

A wall of flame engulfed me, and the last thing I heard was Rosie's agonized scream of my name before the world went blissfully dark.

"Noah, please, save her!" My father crouched next to Mother's too-still form, agony on his face. "She needs you. Don't let her die."

Confusion swirled in me as I glanced around, finding myself once again standing out on the lawn, watching my house go down in flames.

"But I . . ."

A twitch of shadow pulled my focus. A black-robed figure was walking across the yard, heading toward the house. As I watched, it stopped, turned its head, and looked at me before disappearing inside.

Death was beckoning.

I was a slave to answer her call again and again.

"Rosie!"

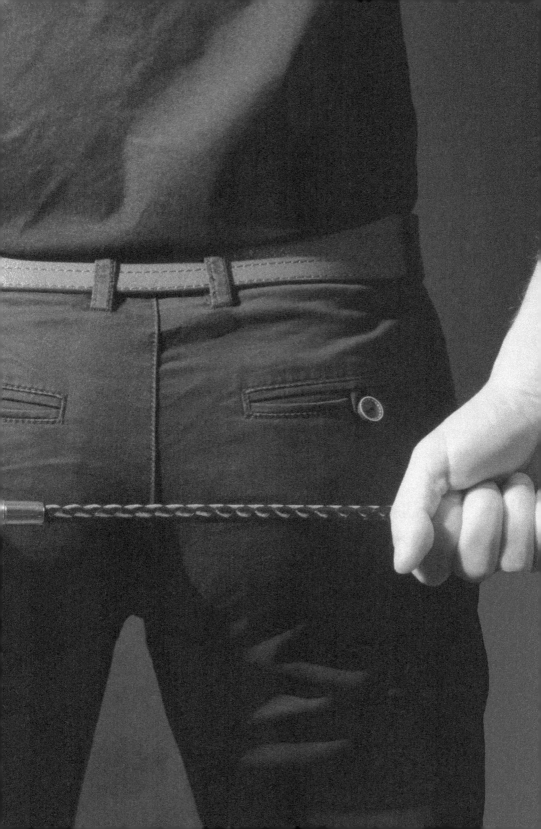

## CHAPTER

# FORTY

### KINGSTON

"Happy birthday, Pooh Bear!" Mama beamed at me as she brought the cake in from the kitchen. "Twenty-five. I can't believe it." Her eyes shone with tears as she looked at me. "You were so small I could hold you—"

"Diana, leave him be," my father barked. "He's a grown man. He doesn't need you to remind his wife how frail he used to be."

Sunday laughed, lifting our daughter higher in her arms as she leaned over to press a kiss to my cheek. "Trust me, there's nothing frail about him now." She took my free hand and held it to her swollen belly. "Him or his minions."

I looked at every person seated at our huge dining table. Mama and Dad, the triplets, Trouble, even Doc and my cousin Dylan. Thorne, Alek, and Caleb sat on the same side as Sunday and me, all of us considered family now.

"Dill pickle? Would you be a lamb and go get me the cake knife? I left it on the counter." Mama smiled sweetly at Dylan.

"Of course, Mama D. Be right back."

Dylan pushed his chair out and stood, coming around behind

Sunday and dropping a kiss on Eden's head. As he walked into the kitchen, I heard him cough once, twice, a third time.

A heavy thud had everyone out of their chairs.

"Here, take the baby, would you, Trouble?" Sunday asked, passing off Eden to my youngest sister so she could race into the kitchen on my parent's heels.

"Oh my God, Dylan!" Mama cried. "Ronin, Doc, quick. I think he's dead!"

Panic gripped me tight, clawing its way through my chest as Tessa started to cough.

Noah picked up our daughter while Phe smacked Tessa on the back, trying to help her catch her breath.

"What the fuck is going on?" Alek asked, eyes wild as Throne doubled over, shoving the baby at him.

The Viking took Eden and held her to his chest as she stared at him, her eyes calm and searching. Before I could make sure Thorne was okay, a crash sounded from the kitchen, breaking glass and wet gurgling noises sending me running toward my parents.

I found them on the floor, Mama and Dad already gone, staring unseeingly at the ceiling as pink foam dribbled from their mouths. Doc was on his hands and knees beside Dylan, gasping as he fell forward and rolled on his back. He was clawing at his throat, his eyes bulging as he suffocated. He died right there, looking at me.

"No. Jesus, fuck, no."

I scrambled out of the kitchen, a warning on my lips as I lurched into the dining room. It was a scene straight out of a horror movie. Dead bodies littered the floor, their faces purple and mottled, eyes discolored, blood leaking out of every visible orifice.

There was no way something this horrific could happen so fast. Nothing was making any sense.

And then Eden cooed, and my head snapped to the side where Sunday stood, booping our daughter on the nose and bouncing her on her hip.

*When did she get out here?*

"That's my good girl. Good job, Edie."

"Sunshine? What the fuck?"

"Oh, you're so pretty but not terribly bright, are you, Kingston?"

My fucking chest felt like it was caving in. "Did you . . . do this?" I couldn't bring myself to look at the bodies. Not again.

"*We* did, lover. Now hold your daughter, and you can join the rest of them." As she shoved the baby at me, Sunday's body changed, morphing from the woman I loved to someone I didn't recognize.

Her hair was as red as the blood dripping from my Mama's mouth, her eyes a pale, devilish green and so malicious I instinctively stepped back.

She pouted. "And here I was thinking we were getting along so well. You've done beautifully thus far, Kingston. Playing the role of a fool perfectly. Now be a good boy, and finish the job. Nothing left for you here anyway. So go on. Die and join your family. You know you want to."

The stranger handed me my daughter, and I pulled her in, clutching her to my chest.

Within seconds it felt as if someone had shoved their hand inside and started playing doctor with my guts. My lungs seized, my heart struggled to beat, my stomach knotted and cramped. I doubled over, dropping to my knees as I gasped for air. My chest was heavy, thick with fluid I couldn't cough out. I was drowning.

I looked down at the baby in my arms, unable to reconcile that she was part of this. That she was somehow responsible for the death of everyone else I loved.

As my eyes met hers, she evaporated, turning into a pale green mist the same color as the other woman's irises.

The stranger knelt beside me, her hand on my cheek. "You mortals are all the same. Give you a child, and you turn into utterly malleable toys. So fun, but so predictable." Then she sighed and stepped back. "She was never real, Kingston. Only a means to an end. Just like you. A pawn to move across the board and sacrifice to get what we wanted."

"Wh–why?" I croaked, though it was more of a desperate wheeze as my vision went hazy.

She smirked. "Because that's how the game is played, lover boy. We always win." Her smile stretched, and her eyes filled with glee. "Check."

# FORTY-ONE

## ALEK

"Why am I back here, Lilith? You're supposed to be helping us save Sunday. I can't do that bound in your dungeon."

I couldn't see her through my closed eyes, but I knew if I opened them, she'd feed again. A seductive chuckle right next to my ear had my skin crawling. "Oh, darling, what are you talking about? You never left this room. Sunday is gone."

"No. She's in Ireland. I'm with her. We're together."

She dragged her fingers through my hair and fisted the locks, tugging my head back. "But you're not. You're here with me. You have been the entire time. Oh, and the fun we've been up to. I don't even mind that you called me Sunday every time you came. The poor sweet lamb. She thought you were so devoted. That you'd protect her. Instead, you betrayed her simply so you could relieve your pent-up desire."

*No. I would never be unfaithful. It's only Sunny. No one else. Ever.*

"Try to convince yourself otherwise, Aleksandr. But the truth is right here between my thighs."

"Release me, demon." I tugged on my chains, snarling as rage and frustration coursed through me.

A moan filtered to my ears, but I couldn't bring myself to open my eyes. No matter where I looked, I saw Sunday taking her fill of me. It was shameful how hard my cock was even now. I knew I was simply being used, fed from like I was the succubus' personal fucking buffet, while she tormented me.

"I don't know why you're being so surly. I'm giving you everything you could ever want. It's your fault you're not enjoying it. You could be there, fucking her with all you have, writhing in pleasure just like the Alek you see, but instead, you're acting as if I'm forcing you to watch some heinous documentary. Give in, Alek. Enjoy yourself. You know you want to. You know I make it good for you."

"Enough!" I roared, struggling in earnest. I turned my thoughts inward, searching for a sign of the rage-fueled beast to come to my aid. But my berserker was nowhere to be found. All that remained was soul-deep panic and unwanted arousal.

"Oh, don't go looking for him, handsome. I took him first. Thanks for that, by the way." She took me by the chin and forced me to look at her. "I will never get my fill of you. Mmm, you are ever so delicious. I could feed on you for centuries." She trailed a long, talon-like nail down my chest. "In fact. I think I will. And when you finally have nothing left to give, I'll take all that sweet Novasgardian power you've been feeding me and pay your family a visit. Collect that twin of yours. Oh . . . I bet your father tastes even better than you."

"Noah! Kingston! Stop her!" I had to tell them. Get them out of here so they could find another way to Sunday.

"Oh, pet, they're long since dead. I drained them dry in moments. Poor dears. They never stood a chance. Not like you. A god in your own right. You and I are going to have fun for years to come. You belong to me now."

"The only woman I belong to is Sunny."

She laughed. "No, darling. Not anymore. But let's play this game. If I were to let you go right now, she would never take you back. Not after you betrayed her. Not after you filled me time and again with your seed while you left her to rot on some godforsaken island. You failed your mate, in word and in deed."

I retched, my stomach revolting at the idea of fucking her. I hadn't known. I wouldn't have done it if I'd known. She'd tricked me, made me believe I'd been with my Sunny. My Kærasta. I—

She clapped her hands together and let out a pleased giggle. "Oh, how much messier could this get for you? Perhaps you put a little godling in my belly?"

"No," I groaned.

"How would you explain that to your Sunday? Do you think she'd forgive you? Take you back?" She hummed. "No. I don't believe she would. It will crush her."

"Lilith, how could you do this? We trusted you. *She* trusted you."

"A deal with a demon never ends well for the person taking that risk. You should know that." She gripped my chin and forced my head up. "Open your eyes, Viking. Since you've been so, so good to me, I want to give you a little present. Something to ease a bit of that heartache. As much as I've been enjoying the decadent flavor of your fear and despair, I want to sample your hope."

"Are you mad?"

"Alek, please help me." Sunday's panicked cry called to me. "Oh, God. It hurts."

"Sunny," I hissed, giving in and opening my eyes.

"Oh, you're simply too easy. Honestly, I'd hoped for more of a challenge." The demon stood before me, her dark hair a mass of waves, clad in the same corset-outfit she wore when last I saw her. "For my next trick . . ." She snapped her fingers, and her body changed into Sunny's. Her eyes were beautiful but haunted as she stared at me and spoke in my mate's voice. "Why would you hurt me like this, Alek? All I did was love you."

I was going insane. I couldn't take this. "No. No, Sunny. I didn't. I wouldn't."

"But you did." The dark croon wasn't Lilith's sultry tone or even my sweet Sunday's. It was colder. Darker. Pure evil.

The woman in front of me snapped her fingers again, revealing a third form. She was still all woman, but clearly demonic. She had small black horns sprouting from her hairline, and her eyes . . . they were an eerie, milky white. No pupil, no color. She smiled, revealing two sets of fangs.

"Who are you?"

The sound of hoofbeats filled my ears, so loud I winced.

"You might know me as Famine. But my friends call me Sabine. And you and I, dearest, we're going to be such good friends."

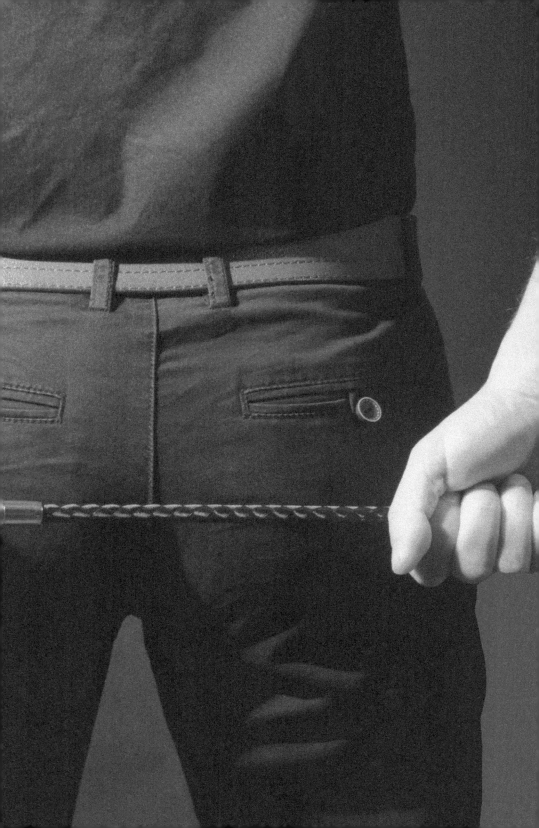

# FORTY-TWO

E verything hurt. My head, my hips, even my eyes. Fuck. Why
was the bed so cold and hard?

"Caleb?"

My voice was a harsh rasp, and it echoed. That one small detail
pierced through my mental fog. An echo? Where the hell was I?

I forced my eyelids open, squinting out of instinct, but there was
no light. It took my eyes a second to adjust, but when they did, I
recognized my surroundings instantly.

I was in Caleb's church. Left upon the altar like some kind of
sacrifice.

That's when everything came rushing back to me. The midwife.
The cocoa. My mother. She'd drugged us and brought me here. Panic
exploded inside me. Where were they? Were they hurt?

Slowly sitting up, I slid off the altar and assessed the church,
searching for my captor. I had to get out of here. Get to my mates.
Help them.

I took one step toward the door when the first crippling pain
bent me in two. This wasn't like the others. I gasped as the ache
ripped through me, building in intensity rather than dying down.

"Fuck," I moaned. I held onto the edge of the altar as I rode out the contraction, trying to breathe through it.

*No. Not now.*

Once the tightness finally crested, I straightened and made my way toward the doors. I didn't have long. A few minutes at most before the next one would hit. But I'd use every spare second I could to get out.

"Where do you think you're going?"

My mother's voice came from behind me, and it took significant effort to turn myself around to face her.

"What? You didn't appreciate the symbolism of the altar? I thought it quite fitting myself. You, my flesh and blood sacrifice, giving way to the one that will save—or in your case, I suppose— end it all?"

"Fuck you."

I returned my focus to the door and my goal of escape. But even as I headed down the aisle, another agonizing wave of pain gripped me, making me cry out as I hunched over and grabbed the nearest pew.

"Oh, it does hurt, doesn't it? I remember it well. Screaming in pain as I brought you into the world. It's all for the same goal, Sunday. It's why I lowered myself to take your useless father into my bed. Just remember, she will come no matter how hard you try to keep it from happening."

I bit back a cry, trying my best to ignore her taunts as I struggled to remain upright. The pain was excruciating. So much worse than I could have expected.

*How did women survive this? Why did they ever have more than one child at all?*

Once the contraction faded, I tried to take another step, but the wave began right on top of the last. Tears sprung to my eyes. It hurt so badly.

I allowed myself a second of selfishness to chase the thought. Hallucinations had gotten me through my weeks on the island.

Maybe they'd come to my rescue again now. In my mind, we were in a hospital. Noah in the corner, trying and failing not to appear like he was seconds away from losing his shit.

Kingston would be a fucking football coach, his energy at a twenty as he tried to chant us all through it. I heard him perfectly. "That's it, baby. Come on, you can do it, push! You got this."

As for Alek, I imagined he'd be on the bed behind me, his big body curled around mine, lending me his strength and offering me a hand to squeeze.

"Caleb," I whimpered, wishing he was here to help me through this with his soft murmurs of encouragement and love.

"He won't come for you, dear one. None of them will."

One after the other, the pains hit me like a rough sea crashing against the defenseless shore. Agony had me groaning and sweating as I shuffled forward, barely making progress.

"You really should lie down. It's only going to get worse. You can't leave. Not like this."

"You can't have her. I won't let you," I said through gritted teeth.

"Sweetheart, do you think you'll be alive to stop me? As soon as your water breaks, it's over. I'll have won."

As if she'd made it happen, a gush of fluid trailed down my legs, covering the floor. "No," I moaned.

Not like this. It wasn't supposed to happen like this.

Her laughter followed me.

"I really don't know where you think you're going. You might as well lay down and accept your fate. This will all be over soon."

I wanted to fight, but the pressure in my hips radiated down my thighs. It hurt so much. I hadn't prepared to feel like I was being split in two.

I fell to my knees, catching myself on my hands before my entire body hit the ground. "Please, please, please . . . it hurts." I wasn't talking to her but chanting to my mates, wishing they were here.

Flames burst to life on every candle in the church, casting the sanctuary in a warm glow. "Let there be light," my mother said. She was clearly enjoying herself. Why wouldn't she be, I guess? She was minutes away from everything she'd wanted coming to pass.

"Come on, let's get you comfortable. The show's about to begin."

I tried to push her off me, but I was too crippled by pain to be very effective. She wrapped an arm around me and led me back to the altar.

"No," I protested weakly.

"I know, I know. You don't want the altar. Fine. Be boring. But there's more space over there."

As we walked, she talked as though we were a couple of dear friends gossiping. "You know, I always wanted a daughter. Aside from the whole pregnancy thing. Ugh, that was an inconvenience. Your father really put a damper on my plans, though, abandoning you the way he did. He wasn't supposed to take you back to your grandfather."

"He's not the only one who abandoned me."

She shoved the altar to the side with one hand and then helped me down until I was lying on my back. She did all of this without missing a beat.

"Oh, that? Sunday, please. You know I couldn't stick around. I'm War, for crying out loud. What was I supposed to do with a baby? I had so many plans. You have to give me credit, though. You were my greatest. Nearly twenty-five years I waited for all the pieces to get into place. That's a long time, and I am notoriously impatient. Now stop interrupting your mother. I'm baring my soul to you. Consider it a deathbed confession, though you'll be the one dying."

I gritted my teeth, unable to stop her as a new contraction held me in its clutches.

"There was a time I worried I wouldn't be able to get my hands on you again, but once I found that dreadful headmistress of yours, everything changed. No one even realized I'd taken her body. It gave me the access I needed to you, and as an unexpected bonus, I was in on every single detail of that idiotic Society's plans for you. They were so cute. Trying so hard to stop us."

I was going to be sick, and I couldn't tell if it was because of my labor or her fucking monologue.

"Your grandfather jumped at the chance to get rid of you when I suggested Ravenscroft as your new home. I took on your care, and all the rest lined up. It's rather poetic, don't you think? Me choosing Gabriel's puppet and the sons of the most powerful members of the Society as your *mates*. I hand-selected them for you, daughter. Hit them each with a love spell they never saw coming. So don't say I never gave you any presents, because I know how much you enjoyed them. You're welcome, by the way."

She laughed darkly, her wicked gaze on mine as I tensed through another contraction.

"And oh, how trusting you were. It was so easy. Almost too easy, if I'm being honest. You are incredibly suggestible, you know. You must get that from your father. 'Drink zee potion, Miss Fallon. It will keep you from getting with child. It will stop your heat.' Ugh. That insufferable French accent almost gave me away."

"Th-the suppressants?"

"Oh, they weren't suppressing anything. That potion sent you into an uncontrollable heat cycle, only able to be satisfied once all four of them made their . . . contributions. That was the one sticking point, sadly. You needed them all for the magic to take hold and our little, what is it you've named her? Eden?" She waved a hand as if it didn't matter. "Regardless, she wouldn't have come to be without all of them. Four horsewomen, four mates. That's the deal. It was a requirement of the game. One to represent each of us. Because even if I were to *win*, we all want to be a part of the end of the world. Between you and me, they really struggle with FOMO."

I cried out as the twisting and tightening began to burn. God, I was really starting to hate the sound of her fucking voice.

Despite that, I had to know about something.

"Game?"

"Oh, yes, we've nicknamed it the mate games. Clever, right? One by one, we get our shot at kicking off the Apocalypse. We each came up with a strategy, selected our game pieces, and set up the board. But as the oldest, I got to go first. It's truly a pity you'll never get to see theirs come to fruition because clearly I'm going to win. But I don't mind saying that they did come up with some fantastic alternatives which really showcase their unique skill sets."

"Wh–why?"

My mother tilted her head, an almost pitying expression on her face. "Why not? This *is* what we were made for. To bring about the end times. We do it because we must. And if we fail, the men are waiting in the wings for their chance."

"Minerva, would you quit your monologuing and just deliver that baby already? Some of us have a plague to spread when you fail." A woman stood in the aisle, her red hair flowing nearly to her waist, tone filled with impatience.

My mother sighed, a long exaggerated huff brimming with impatience. "Would you give a girl a chance to enjoy herself? I've only been waiting for this moment for a few decades." She glanced at the woman, and my gaze followed hers. Two more had joined the first, and I knew, even through my delirium, these were the Four Horsewomen. "Did you take care of her mates?"

"They're trapped. None of them will escape the dreams we wove for them. And if they do wake, they'll be insane." The woman who spoke was dressed in all black but seemed as pretty and innocent as a kindergarten teacher.

"Diabolical. That's what you are."

"What can I say? I like meddling with minds."

One with two tiny horns snorted and crossed her arms. "You say that like you're the only one with any skill at it. Your targets knew you were interfering. Mine actually believed I was that stupid succubus. He fell for it all, hook, line, and sinker. Didn't have a clue none of it was real. Silly sausage thinks he cheated on her." She pouted. "He was so broken."

I screamed as a deep pressure hit me hard, the urge to bear down and push taking hold.

My mother rolled her eyes, giving me a conspiratorial wink. "Is that my cue, daughter? Are you ready?"

She brushed some hair off my forehead as I panted through the pain.

"Well then, let's get this over with, shall we? Come on, Sunday. It's showtime."

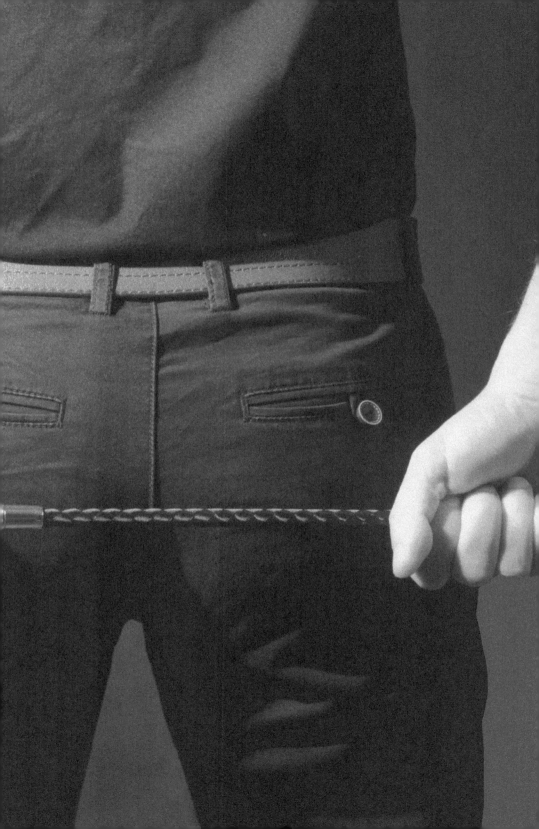

# FORTY-THREE

CALEB

W arm rays of sunshine on my back radiated through me, comforting me in a way the night never could. Eden's belly laughs filled the air as I caught her feet mid-swing and pulled them up to my chest.

"Again, my wee one?"

Her answer was a series of coos and claps. She was all pink cheeks and smiles, her bright blue eyes the same color as her mother's. I let her go, watching as the wind whipped her chocolate curls in her face. She looked so much like Sunday that it made my heart ache. I could not possibly love this child more. She was perfection. My absolute joy. My slice of heaven on Earth.

"But it isn't Earth, Caleb. And she isn't real."

Gabriel materialized beside me, and I stiffened but refused to look his way.

"It's real enough for me."

"You can't stay here, and you know it. You feel it."

His words prompted a slight sting in my chest. I lifted my hand, grimacing as I rubbed away the burn.

"No. It's not time."

"It *is* time, Caleb. You know what you need to do. You're the only one who can put a stop to this."

"No." Panic had my stomach churning, and I turned my focus back to the swing. But Eden wasn't there any longer. The playground had vanished along with her, and the bright summer sky turned a menacing burnt orange. Thunder rolled in the distance, a heavy wind whipping through the trees.

"She needs you, Caleb. This is happening whether you're ready or not. But the outcome is up to you."

"Angel, I need more than that. I can't . . ." Words failed me.

"You must."

A scream tore through the sky, the burn in my chest growing worse, more painful than any time before.

"Sunday!"

I shot up in my bed, her name on my lips. The room was cast in darkness, except for the slight glow behind the windows where the sun still clung to the sky. It wasn't quite dusk, though it was close.

"She's not here."

Gabriel stood in the corner, leaning against the wall, his eyes luminous even in the shadows.

"Then where the fecking hell is she?"

"You know where she is."

I glanced back to the far window, staring at the black curtain as if I could see the outline of the steeple beyond it. The angel was right; I could feel the pull of her from here.

"The church."

He didn't bother replying.

"Will you go with me?"

His eyes were filled with compassion as he slowly shook his head. "I cannot go where you're going, Caleb. The battle ahead is yours alone."

I hadn't expected him to, but knowing I had to face this alone terrified me.

"Do not be afraid. I will not leave you empty-handed. I came bearing gifts." He gestured beside me on the bed where an ornate sword now lay. "It always served me well."

"You're giving me your sword?"

"Technically it's not mine. And I'm not *giving* it to you. I'm letting you borrow it."

"It's not going to burst into flames and turn me to ashes, is it?"

Gabriel raised one brow without saying a word.

So the answer was yes. Lovely.

Another scream ripped through the air, and as I jumped to my feet I realized the one I'd heard in my dream had been real.

*Sunday.*

"Go, Priest. I'll collect the others. End this."

"What do you mean? Are they not with her?"

"They're trapped in their own minds, just as you were."

Grabbing the sword, I offered a sharp nod before racing out of the room, the only thoughts in my mind those of my wife.

I ran outside, the sky bleeding from orange to red as I watched. I'd been trapped in my dream world, living a fantasy where I had everything I ever wanted while Sunday was in pain. Laboring alone. I'd promised her she wouldn't have to do this by herself. That I'd be at her side, seeing her through, doing what I could to keep her safe.

A third agonized scream came from the church, and I nearly fell to my knees as the answering burst of pain shot through my chest. Every window shattered as though an explosion had ripped through the interior. The shards of glass dropped to the ground, raining down like tears.

"Sunday." My voice betrayed me, coming out a harsh rasp rather than the shout I'd been attempting.

She was dying. I could feel it.

Instead of wasting time bothering with the door, I threw myself through the closest broken window, landing in the sanctuary with the stealth of a cat. The sword Gabriel had given me was heavy in my hand, but the moment I caught sight of the four women standing in front of my altar, I understood why he'd delivered it unto me. He wasn't going to smite me with the blade. I was going to need it to get through *them*.

The nearly overwhelming scent of Sunday's blood hit me, and I staggered. She'd lost too much. Way too much.

She was bleeding out.

The time for stealth was over.

"Get the fuck away from my wife."

The four women turned as one, their expressions ranging from haughty defiance to amusement.

"Well, look who finally decided to show up to the party. You always were one to take your sweet time, weren't you, Priest?"

"Who the bloody hell are you?"

Before my eyes, she transformed into the visage of Headmistress le Blanc, then changed back to the formidable beauty she'd been. "Oh, can't you see it? I think she's my spitting image." That's when I noticed the resemblance.

"You . . . you're Sunday's mother."

She curtseyed. "War. I'd say it's nice to make your acquaintance, but the things you've done to my daughter . . ." she tutted, "they're enough to make a priest blush. Oh, wait."

Sunday screamed, the tortured sound cutting through my heart as surely as this sword could.

"Stand aside, or I will make you."

She laughed. "You and what army? If you hadn't noticed, you're a bit outnumbered."

I raised the sword, flames bursting to life, searing the hairs on my arm. I didn't care. I'd endure the pain to save my family.

"And that's our cue," the redheaded one said, stepping to the side.

"Wait, what?" War shot a narrow-eyed glare her way. "You're not going to stick around and help me?"

"It's not really our party, Minerva. If you win, great. But if you fail, we get our turns. So . . . best of luck to you."

"Does that go for all of you?"

The one dressed all in black gave her a simpering smile. "I'm not prepared to go up against the Sword of Michael. I just had my nails done."

"You faithless bitches."

"Takes one to know one, sis. You *were* the one running around free for the last twenty-five years while we were left to rot in hell. It's our turn to cause a little chaos, don't you think? But do call us if you manage to end the world."

Hope flickered to life. They were abandoning her. All I needed was to smite this bitch, and I could stop everything. I could earn my soul, keep my wife, and if I was lucky, my child.

Lifting the sword, I blurred down the aisle, only to be sent flying back by one powerful swing of her arm. I crashed into the wall hard enough my teeth rattled at the impact, the weapon falling from my hand.

"You didn't really expect that to work, did you? I'm War, darling. I literally wrote the book on this."

"Then why did it take you so bloody long to bring on your fecking Apocalypse? Isn't that your entire job?"

"What? You think this is our first attempt? There have been thousands. But there are rules. I can only do so much. It is the mortals who must take the bait. You want to know why I failed? I think the question you should be asking yourself is why did *you*? I've been stopped countless times until now. So tell me, Priest. Who's the one falling down on the job? Me, the one fulfilling my purpose, or you, the one letting it happen?"

I stumbled to my feet, reaching for the hilt of the sword. Sunday was going to die if I didn't end this now.

"Oh, I think not." The blade flew to her outstretched hand, and my heart sank. I'd failed.

One well-placed strike was all it took as she ran me through, pinning me to the door. Then she twisted the blade for good measure, sending pure agony ripping through me.

"That should hold you. Be a good boy and stay."

Blood dribbled out of my mouth as she patted me on the head before turning on her heels and flouncing up to the altar where Sunday was struggling.

"I can't do this," Sunday chanted. "I can't. It's going to kill me. I can't. Please stop it."

"You can and you will. That's the entire reason you were born, Sunday. And as your simple priest just reminded me, we all have our parts to play. So stop your fucking crying and push!"

"No!" Sunday let out an agonized wail as her body curled in on itself.

"Stop fighting it. Do not make me reach inside you and pull that child out because make no mistake, Sunday, I will fucking do it. Nothing is going to stop me from getting what I came here for."

I pulled on the hilt of the sword, working to free myself in a vain attempt to get to her even now. But I was stuck.

Helpless, I watched Sunday's face pull into a determined grimace as she bore down, a panicked cry leaving her lips as she pushed. I knew it the moment our child came into the world. I would have regardless of the consequences. I felt her. Before I could revel in the wonder of it all, a pain unlike anything I'd ever known seared my chest as the final seal shattered, and all that love and completion I'd sensed was eclipsed by darkness.

War reached between Sunday's thighs and lifted the baby—our beautiful Eden—into the air. How could someone so small and inno-cent bring about the end of everything? Eden sucked in her first breath before letting out an ear-splitting wail, the sound sending a thrill through me because I wanted her to live.

But then the earth gave a violent shake, the ground rolling in waves as War strolled down the aisle with my daughter in her arms.

"That's it, little one. Herald the end and announce my victory to the heavens above. You're just the sweetest little harbinger, aren't you?" War looked at me, a wicked smile on her face. "You certainly made the end beautiful, didn't you? All that temptation was too much to resist. Thank you for giving in. I couldn't have done it without you."

Blowing me a kiss, War stepped out of the church, leaving me impaled on the door. With her gone, any magic she'd used to keep me in place vanished, and I was finally able to pull myself free.

"Sunday!"

"Caleb? Did you see her? Wasn't she perfect? You need to go get her, Caleb. Please. You need to save her."

God's teeth, there was so much blood. The floorboards were soaked as her life spilled out of her. "No, my darling, I need to save you. I have to stop this bleeding. Fuck, there's so much blood here. I can't . . ."

"Save her, Caleb. Please. I need to know her father is taking care of her before I go."

"You're not going anywhere. Not now. Not ever. Do you hear me, Miss Fallon? You're mine, and I'm never letting you go."

A smile ghosted over her lips, but she was losing the battle. Her skin was pale and clammy, hair stuck to her cheeks, her eyes glassy. She was barely hanging on.

"Oh no, you don't, wife. You don't get to make me fall in love with you and then turn around and leave me."

"Took you long enough to admit it."

"Yeah, well. Some of us take longer than others to stop lying to ourselves."

She laughed, but it was a sickly rattle. "We keep meeting like this, Father Gallagher. But this time, there's nothing you can do. You can't always be my savior."

"Says who?" Without giving her a chance to answer, I tore open my wrist and shoved it against her mouth, making her drink my blood.

Except it wasn't enough. The damage to her body was too great. She was hemorrhaging faster than I could stanch the flow with my vampiric healing. For every swallow, she lost three. I knew then what I would give. What I *had* to give.

Everything.

As quick as I could, I pulled my wrist from her lips and ripped open my flesh, slicing deep into my vein, quickening the rush before returning to her. My pulse was pounding, pumping my life force out and into her. Filling her. Saving her.

And with each beat, killing me.

Then again, the only reason my undead heart ever beat in the first place was for her. It was fitting that it not only started with her, but that it would end with her.

Sunday was the one constant in my misery-ridden life. The one bright spot. She'd been right about one thing—Eden needed her parents. But she didn't need me. She needed Sunday. Who better to teach her to love than the woman who taught me I could?

I knew the instant Sunday started to heal because she fought against my hold, trying to shove my wrist away. She wanted to stop me, to keep me from giving her more than I could afford to lose.

I shook my head. "No, *a stor*, your wounds are too grave. You have to keep drinking."

Her eyes opened, Death's shadow still there, waiting. I saw the moment she realized what I was doing. Panic flashed, making her pupils flare wide.

Leaning forward, I brushed my lips to her forehead.

"Take it. Let me be your hero this time. You've already saved me more times than I can ever repay." A tear trickled down her cheek as my heart slowed and hers grew stronger. "I've never been as happy as I am with you, Mrs. Gallagher. Being yours was the greatest part of my long life. I need you to know . . ." My voice broke as I tried to put together the right words. All of them seemed trite compared to the gravity of what she'd done for me. "I need you to know I wouldn't sacrifice a single moment we've shared. Being your husband, being loved by you, it was . . . my salvation."

She tried to push me away, but she was still bleeding, her battered body not healed enough for her to fully recover. Only one of us was making it out of this church alive. It wouldn't be me.

"Shh, my love. You need this. I need to give it to you. I understand now what my role in all of this was. You have been mine to save since the night you were born. You need to let me do what I was born to do. This is the reason, you see? Why He tasked me with this path. God didn't forsake me. He knew that you would have need of me. All this time I thought I was damned, but I was destined for something greater."

She reached a weak hand up and trailed her fingers over my face. I shivered as my limbs grew numb.

"He needed me to become a monster so I could protect you from them. A human man wouldn't have been able to bring you back. But a vampire?" I smiled. It was getting harder to talk, my mind growing fuzzy. "It's fitting, isn't it? Saving you with my blood. An unholy communion. A sacrifice I willingly make. Drink this in remembrance of me."

I laid down beside her, my wrist still pressed against her lips, my forehead resting against hers. My breaths were uneven, my voice little more than a rasp, but there was so much more I wanted to say, things I needed her to know.

"I only wish I'd had the chance to hold her. Even once. I . . . I never thought . . . You gave me a child, Sunday. You gave me every-thing." I was so fecking cold. Why was I cold?

"Caleb, please. Don't." Somewhere in this mumbled confession, my wrist slipped to the hard floor between us. "Don't die. Oh, God. Don't leave me."

Her tears splashed on my face, the salt of them washing over my lips. It brought me peace knowing I'd die with her taste on my tongue.

"Sunday?"

"Yes, Caleb?"

"I love you."

"If you love me, then stay."

I smiled, or tried to. I wasn't sure my lips were obeying. "Tell me you love me, Miss Fallon."

"I love you, Caleb."

"Good girl." It was barely a whisper, and it was a battle now to simply keep my eyes open. But there was still one more thing keeping me from giving in to the darkness waiting for me.

I wanted to touch her, but my arms wouldn't move. As though she knew, she reached for me.

"*A stor* . . . will you tell her about me? Tell Eden our story, and . . . make sure she knows how her da loved her so. Don't . . . don't let her . . . forget . . ."

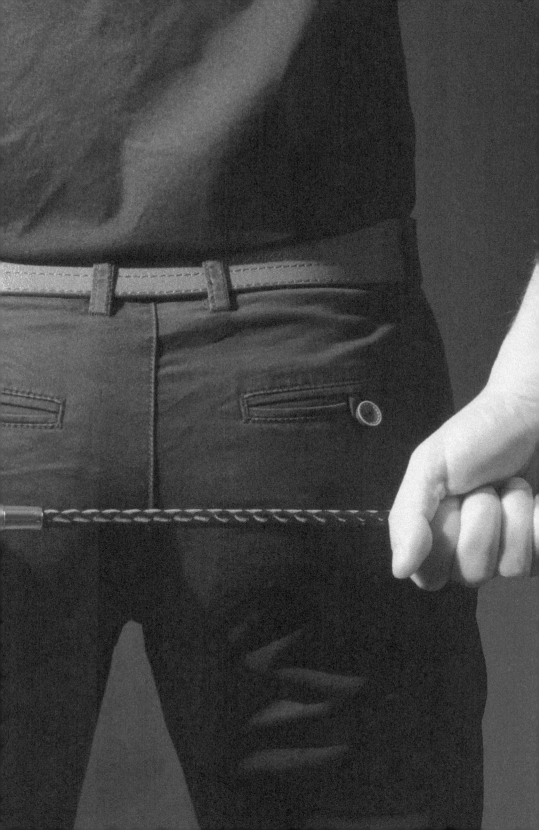

# FORTY-FOUR

### THORNE

"It's time."

Gabriel's voice plucked me from my nightmare, ripping me away from the hellish loop of fire and death. I sat straight up, gasping and coated in sweat, to find Kingston and Alek doing the same.

An overwhelming sense of dread fisted my heart as I glanced around the living room. Sunday wasn't here. She'd been right there on the couch with us.

"Where is she?" Alek asked, standing and wobbling slightly before righting himself. "When I get my hands on that midwife ..."

"I don't think she was a midwife." Kingston's voice was nothing but a low growl. "I knew we shouldn't have trusted that bitch and her baked goods. You never take candy from strangers."

"But we watched her eat them, the cocoa too. We should have been safe," Alek pointed out.

"She must be immune to her poison, or whatever the hell it was that knocked us the fuck out." Kingston scrubbed a hand over the back of his neck. "Did you guys have the hallucinations too?"

"Hallucination? I thought it was a nightmare." My relief at being free from the horror of it was short-lived. Real or not, I'd be haunted by my sister calling out for me for the rest of my life.

"Same damn thing."

Pain and despair sliced through the bond between Sunday and me. Excruciating. I groaned and held my head in my hands, feeling as though I was about to be sick.

"Now's not the time to get a fucking migraine, Thorne. Get it together," Kingston spat. "We need to find our mate. That cunt took her." He stormed into the bedroom, calling Caleb's name. "Mother-fucker." A raging shifter returned, his body trembling with the need to fight. "He's gone too."

"Maybe he's with her?"

"Why didn't he wake us?"

"You think he was in on it?"

"No," I moaned, my head throbbing as their conversation continued over me. "He was wholly committed to Sunday. I saw it. Whatever scheme played out here, he wasn't part of it."

Another bolt of pure agony ripped through me. Fucking hell. She was having the baby. That had to be what this was. Otherwise, she'd have her defenses up to keep this from affecting me. I had to block this out. I wouldn't be able to do anything if this continued.

"She's in labor. We have to help her." I somehow gritted out the words as I worked to raise my mental barrier.

"It's too soon. She's only six months pregnant." Fur rippled along Kingston's arms as his wolf fought to break free. Learning his mate was giving birth to his pup had likely triggered a primal instinct.

Alek fared little better, the berserker flashing in his eyes, his muscles rippling. "We all saw her. She looked like a woman at full term. There's no precedent for a child like ours."

"Or . . ." Kingston snarled before continuing, "Whatever *she* gave Sunday brought on labor."

"Does it matter the reason? We can't just leave Sunny to face it alone. What the fuck are we waiting for?" Alek stormed to the front door, but the moment he touched the knob the ground began to shake violently. "I didn't do that. That wasn't me."

I knew. I felt it in my bones, even through the block I'd raised. Relief from Sunday, exhaustion, fear, and beneath it all, pure love. "Congratulations. We're fathers." But there was no joy in my words. I dropped my walls and let myself feel her. "No. Dove, you can't do this," I whispered.

"What? Thorne, don't fuck around. What's happening?" Panic laced Kingston's voice.

"We're losing her."

Alek ripped the door off its hinges, his eyes bleeding black and flickering with lightning.

It was on the tip of my tongue to point out we didn't know where she was, if she was even still on this island, but as soon as I caught sight of the unnaturally crimson sky I knew she must be. Clouds gathered just on the horizon. Thick black and purple masses with flashes of neon green illuminating them.

We were at the epicenter of the Apocalypse. It was here, and we had done nothing to stop it.

Kingston leapt past Alek, his massive black wolf charging toward the church. He must've caught her scent just as I had. So much blood filled the air. Most of it hers.

The three of us took off in that direction, only to come up short as the doors flung open. A violent swirl of copper mist gathered just beyond the chapel. Kingston growled, a low warning rumble as the hair at his ruff lifted and he tensed.

"Odin's beard," Alek breathed. "Is that . . ."

"A horse."

"I've never seen a horse look like that."

Kingston growled again, his body tensed.

A dark-haired woman stalked out of the church, a tiny wailing bundle nestled in her arms. My heart stopped.

"Eden." As her name left my lips in a reverent whisper, my pulse kicked back into gear. "That bitch has our baby."

Kingston moved first, and we followed suit, racing for the woman as she smoothly mounted her horse. He snarled and took a running leap as soon as he was within striking distance, and for a moment, I thought perhaps it would be this easy. That we could cut her off at the pass and save the day.

I'd been a fool.

With one wave of her hand, she sent Kingston flying as an invisible force knocked him out of the air. He tumbled, crashing into the small fence around the churchyard. It cracked in half at the impact, and Kingston whimpered as he came down hard on the broken bits of wood and wire.

She directed her attention to us, smirking as she leaned forward, running her free hand over the steed's neck with a tenderness that didn't fit her terrifying aura. Her lips moved as she whispered something into the animal's ear, and instantly it shot forward at a speed that shouldn't have been possible.

"Fuck. Look what you did, Kingston. She's gone, you bloody fool." Fury ripped through me. If that wolf hadn't lunged before we arrived with him, we could've stopped her.

"Thorne." Alek's voice was filled with censure as Kingston struggled back up onto his paws. "If it's anyone's fault, it's yours. You knew what was happening, and you allowed us to sit with our thumbs up our arses. If you had told us what was happening sooner, that vile harpy never would have gotten her hands on our daughter."

"This is not my fucking fault. Without me, the two of you would never have even realized something was wrong."

Alek grabbed me by the collar, fisting his meaty hand in my shirt. "Tell me it was my fault one more fucking time. I dare you."

A menacing growl filled the air, calling our attention away from each other and to the wolf with burning eyes who was ready to fight.

Anger and adrenaline coursed through my veins, creating an unquenchable need for violence. I could hardly see straight through the red film coating my gaze. All I knew was the need to taste their blood. To make them bleed.

To make it fucking hurt.

Intent on doing just that, I bared my fangs right as Kingston came barreling toward us.

# FORTY-FIVE

## KINGSTON

I slammed into the two idiots fighting with each other instead of the madwoman running off with our fucking kid. It was obvious to me she was responsible for their sudden shift in target. I'd felt the whisper of her compulsion try to latch on to my mind, but as an Alpha, that kind of magic rarely worked on me. My will was the only law my wolf recognized, especially if I was in its form. I didn't think the others knew about that particular immunity of mine, so I was going to have a fucking field day when this was all over, rubbing their faces in my obvious superiority.

First, though, I needed to get these fuckers to focus. Nothing like a blow to the skull to get the message across loud and clear. They went down, both of their heads cracking against the rocky earth. I landed on top of them, my paws raking over their chests as I held them pinned to the ground.

Shifting so that I could speak to them, I snarled, "Get your shit together."

Thorne's lip curled, his fangs flashing, but then his eyes focused, the fight bleeding out of him.

"Bloody hell, what was that? I wanted to tear you limb from limb."

I didn't have time to explain it to him. Alek's irises had gone black, filling the whites of his eyes until he was more berserker than man. The last thing we needed was for him to hulk out on us and lose the goddamned plot.

"Alek, come on, man. We aren't falling for her trick, are we? She wants to keep us busy fighting each other. She has our kid, and nothing about this says she's just taking her for a play date."

The Novasgardian strained beneath me, but when he blinked, I knew it wasn't me he was battling. It was the warring urges inside him. As a berserker, it was probably twelve times harder to pull himself back from the need to destroy.

"That's it, big guy. Focus on your Sunny. On our Eden. They need us. The mean lady hurt them, and now we need to make her pay for it, okay? You can do it."

Alek's breaths came in heavy, rumbling pulls, but the darkness in his eyes receded as he came back to himself.

"You've got it. You can smash the shit out of her when we get there, okay? I'll be right beside you."

"So will I," Thorne said.

Together, we brought Alek back from the brink. We were a unit now. And if that horseback riding bitch wanted a fight, she was gonna get one.

We stood, Thorne lingering for a second, his focus on the church. I knew exactly what he was thinking because I felt it too. Sunday was in there, and the pull to go to her was nearly impossible to ignore. He was torn.

"Caleb's got her."

"There's just so much blood," he whispered, voice tight. "But you're right. Come on. She'll never let us live it down if the Apocalypse isn't stopped."

I wanted to argue that none of us would be alive if that

happened, but honestly, I think he was clinging to hope of a world where we were still together even as chaos reigned.

"Where did she go?" Alek asked. "Where's Eden?"

Glancing past him, I jutted my chin. "If I had to guess, I'd say we're gonna find her right over there. You know, where the clouds look like Satan's fucking vagina."

The roiling clouds had coalesced into one pulsing, writhing mass. It looked seconds away from coming alive. Or opening up. I'd bet my left nut it was some kind of portal.

"Buckle up, boys. I'm about to go full Cujo on her ass."

"We're not going to stop you."

Alek cut Thorne a glance and nodded in agreement. "She won't make it easy. Whatever you do. Don't fucking stop until you're sure she's dead."

"Wasn't planning on it."

I shifted, letting my wolf take over as the feral urge to defend my pup rushed to the forefront. I didn't care about the end of the fucking world. I cared about getting my daughter out of that evil bitch's hands. I'd stop her, or I'd die trying.

Lifting my face to the sky, I howled. Alek took up my cry with a savage shout of his own as we raced down the path that would lead us to the beach and the hellish clouds that were already spiraling down. I knew only bad things waited for us if it made contact with the land.

As soon as my paws hit the sand, I saw the horsewoman standing under the building storm, one hand raised as though calling it to her. This was our moment. She wasn't paying attention to anything other than the raging funnel above her. The baby was nestled in her other arm, screaming at the top of her lungs, face red and angry. A tiny beacon calling to me.

*Give her hell, baby. Daddy's coming.*

Alek snarled and manifested a fucking huge ax in one hand as he stalked toward her. But before he made it five feet onto the shore, she turned and stared us down, exasperation on her face. A face I knew very well. I could have been looking into the future, my Sunshine staring back at me ten to fifteen years from now.

*What the actual fuck.*

"You couldn't just leave well enough alone, could you? You just had to play the heroes. Well, boys, here's a little pro tip from me. In matters of War, the heroes rarely survive."

"I guess that depends what side you're on," Thorne spat.

"Oh, sweetheart, there's only my side."

She snapped her fingers, and the entire beach shook. Sand exploded upward, momentarily obscuring my view of her. When it settled, three towering giants stood between her and us. Fucking great. Of course she'd have some sort of monsters for us to fight.

I dug my claws into the beach, ready to do my level best to tear through them and rescue Eden. Thorne looked to me and then Alek.

"Together, then?"

Alek nodded, his grin bloodthirsty and manic as he raised his weapon and raced toward the creatures. "Valhalla awaits!"

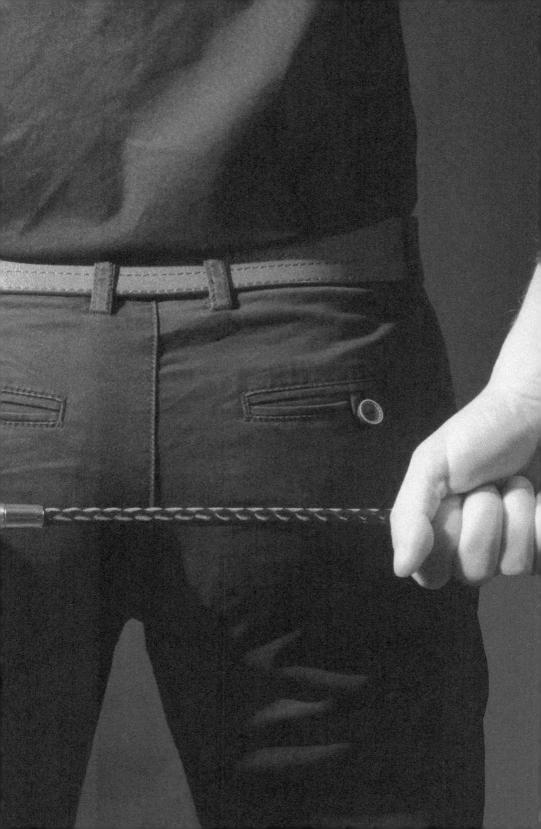

# FORTY-SIX

## ALEK

Purpose unlike anything I'd ever experienced surged through my veins as I gave in to my beast. I was the son of Odin's chosen warrior. A berserker in my own right, yet I'd never seen true battle. Born in a time of peace, I was a weapon newly forged. Untested.

Until today.

Today I would finally realize my glorious purpose. If I died, it would be with vengeance singing in my blood and Sunday's name on my lips. I would earn my place in Valhalla amongst my ancestors.

As one, the three of us ran headlong toward the sand constructs. Kingston leapt into the air, Noah braced for a fight, and I went airborne. A sharp yelp of pain from the wolf briefly tore my focus from my target. The monster had Kingston in his hand, gripping tightly as the wolf squirmed and fought to get loose. Then he was hurled into the torrential waves, so far away I couldn't see him.

In the next second, Thorne cried out. His giant shoved him to the earth, attempting to flatten him beneath one massive palm. I could hear the snapping of bones as the air was forced from his lungs.

My opponent would not be so lucky. I was much harder to kill.

Unable to spare the others any more of my attention, I refocused on the looming creature before me. I landed on its bent arm and kept running, using the friction of its sandy skin to aid in my efforts. It was big but slow, and it couldn't knock me free before I was already up, standing on its shoulder.

"I never liked playing in the sand. But I suppose I could make an exception. Just this once." I jumped, spinning in the air so I was facing its back, ax raised high before bringing the blade straight down on the crown of the beast's head.

My weapon slid clean through, gravity lending me its aid as I rode the air all the way to the ground, cleaving it in two and landing in a crouch that would make even the Marvel superheroes proud.

"Alek, go!"

Thorne's ragged shout spurred me on.

Already the giant was reforming, but I was too fast for it, my sights locked on the horsewoman holding my daughter. She looked like some kind of sorceress as she called the tunneling cloud down to the earth. I knew it was what she was waiting for. The only reason she was still here.

We were running out of time. If that evil mist touched down, all of this would be over.

The effort it took for her to pull the cyclone from the sky showed on her face, brows pulled together, lips twisted into a grimace, eyes hard and determined. By the look of her, she was prepared for battle. Likely to defend this magic she needed. Scarlet armor protected her chest and back, and a cape flowed behind her, black and moving with a strange oily grace as though it had a mind of its own.

A high-pitched whinny hit my ears. I cut my gaze to the side, spotting the copper-colored horse barreling toward me, plumes of smoke coming from its nostrils. It must sense the impending danger to its mistress, but I hadn't come this far to be trampled by a gods-damned pony. Hellraised or otherwise.

Swinging hard and fast, I sliced through the animal's neck, felling it with one sweep of my weapon. The horse dissolved into that same sickly red mist it had come from at the church, and the evil woman screamed in rage. Her hold on the storm seemed to falter. Her strength dwindling, perhaps?

"Give me my child, häxa."

She smirked then, taking a fortifying breath. "She was never yours. None of you. She belongs to me. She exists because of me. Her destiny has always rested in my hands."

I spun the ax over and over as confidence infused me with each step toward her. "We'll see about that. She has Novasgardian blood running through her veins. You didn't account for her papa being a berserker."

The woman bared her teeth in a hiss and renewed her efforts on the storm, a low, terrifying cackle leaving her as the cyclone finally touched down.

"It doesn't matter. You're too late."

The second her tempest connected with the earth, the clouds swelled and stretched, pulling apart like taffy as evil green light spilled through the strands. The misty shadows solidified on either side, creating an arch. No . . . a gateway.

It was nearly instantaneous, the storm transforming into a shimmering portal right before my eyes.

With one cruel smile, the horsewoman lifted my daughter and threw her into the pulsing green light.

"It is done."

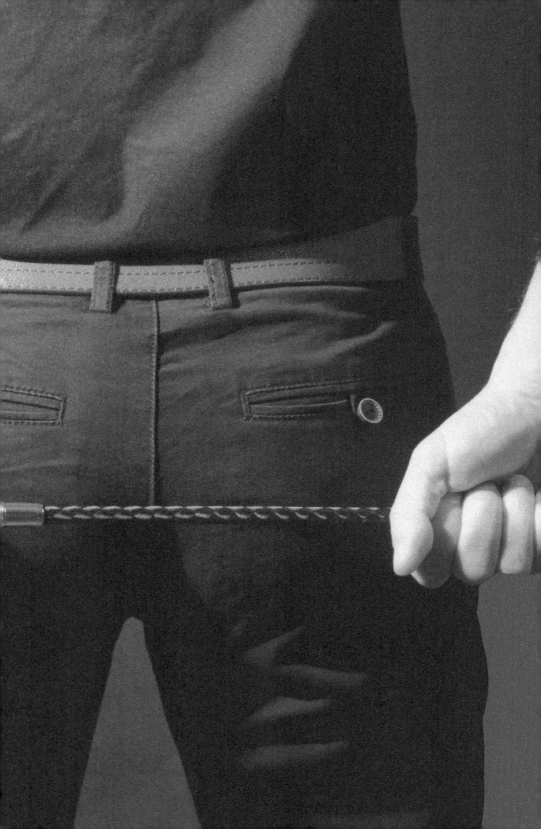

# CHAPTER
# FORTY-SEVEN
## SUNDAY

"A*stor* . . . will you tell her about me? Tell Eden our story, and . . . make sure she knows how her da loved her so. Don't . . . don't let her . . . forget . . ."

"Caleb!" His name was torn from me as a hiccuping sob as his eyes rolled back in his head. "No, please, no." Tears flowed freely down my cheeks. I knew he was gone, but I refused to let myself believe it. With his eyes closed, he could have been sleeping.

I needed him to only be sleeping.

He'd given his life to save me. Caleb was always saving me, even when it seemed like the opposite, even when I didn't want him to. My heart gave a painful lurch as it broke there and then. Deep, racking sobs rolled through me as I lay across his chest. His silent chest.

I cried for the life we should have had together. For the loss of everything he would have been to Eden. Sitting up, I brushed his hair back from his forehead, knowing how much he hated that stray curl that just wouldn't stay in place.

The reminder of my daughter gave me the strength to pull myself together. I couldn't be selfish right now. She needed me. I should have been in agony after the traumatic birth. Hell, I should have been dead. But thanks to Caleb's sacrifice, I was stronger than ever. Fully healed and buzzing with the need to avenge him.

His death could not be in vain.

Leaning down, I brushed my lips over his, letting one last tear fall. "I'll get her back for us. I promise she'll know how much you loved her."

Part of me expected him to frown and chastise me, but it was only that bitch hope, fucking with me again. He was gone. But Eden wasn't.

I refused to let myself look back as I got to my feet and stalked down the aisle. I didn't bother wiping away my tears. They were reminders of what I had to do. Why I had to do it. I would find strength in my pain.

I was going to go destroy a fucking horsewoman and stop a goddamn Apocalypse, and no one, not even my scheming whore of a mother, was going to stop me.

The vow was followed by a frenetic buzz beneath my skin. It wasn't painful, but almost curious. As if a part of me had woken up, stretched, and was now looking for direction. Similar to the feeling I got when my wolf finally broke free.

My wolf. I could shift again.

With a sharp kick to the doors, they flew open, slamming outward and breaking the ancient hinges. The sky roiled with eerie red clouds, lightning arcing across them and filling the air with the scent of ozone.

A whipping wind blew across my skin, turning me toward the beach. Just past the bluff, the clouds gathered into a gargantuan cyclone. That was my target. I knew it without question.

Without a second thought, I gave my wolf the reins. The shift was seamless, easier than it had ever been. If I'd been focused on anything other than absolute annihilation, I might have stopped to wonder what it would be like after so long. But there was no need.

My wolf was ready, eager, and as filled with the need to go save our pup as I was.

I sprang forward in a full-out sprint toward the cliff, instinct driving me straight to the edge. In one powerful leap, I shot off, not bothering with the steep path. The jump should have been impossible. Not just for a human, but a shifter too. But for me, in that moment, it was as easy as stepping over a puddle.

My paws hit the sand with a bone-rattling thud, the shock waves rolling through muscles already moving again as I bolted toward the figures standing next to the tornado. I scanned the surroundings, needing to take in as much as I could to prepare for this confrontation. But what I saw nearly took me out at the knees. Kingston was in the water, bobbing face-down, too still. I wanted to go to him, but I couldn't. Not when I caught sight of Noah's broken and bleeding body a few yards away in the sand. If not for Alek's brutal war cry, I might have given up then and there.

Still surging ahead, I watched in mounting horror as Alek swung his battle-ax and leapt off the ground, throwing himself between my mother and a shimmering green portal. My breath caught in my throat at the sight of the too-tiny bundle arcing in the air.

Alek's eyes widened as he reached out for Eden, and as I looked on, I came to a stop, shifting back to my human form and screaming at the top of my lungs. He caught her with one hand, curling her protectively against his chest like some superhero version of a football player, but any relief I felt vanished as they both disappeared into the swirling green vortex in a flash of light.

Time stopped as I dropped to my knees, my scream one incoherent wail. Finally seeming to realize I was there, my mother turned to face me, her lips lifting in a malicious grin.

"How touching. You arrived just in time for my big moment. You're such a good daughter, being here to witness my victory."

I stared her down, letting pure rage collect in my heart with every passing second. My vision ran red as I flicked my focus to

Noah's prone form, to Kingston, drowned and lost to me. She would pay.

A hum built inside me, moving through my veins like quicksilver, burning white-hot as copper-colored smoke blurred in my periphery. My mother's brows rose as she assessed me.

"Ah, look at you. Finally decided to claim your birthright? You could have brought the world to its knees long ago if you'd only been stronger. Your humanity has always been your weakness."

I didn't understand what she meant until my body was engulfed by the mist. It was coming from me. It transformed as quickly as it appeared, solidifying into something else entirely. Something I'd desperately needed. Armor now cloaked me, black plates detailed in red. Thick and weightless all at the same time. And at my side, sheathed in a holster, was a heavy sword.

My hair floated as though I was underwater as I strode toward her, fury propelling me forward.

"You took everything from me."

She smirked. "You never really had anything, remember?"

"And now you won't either."

Behind her, the portal was still a swirling vortex. I could hear inhuman shrieks growing louder with every step. Hell's army preparing to unleash themselves on an unsuspecting planet.

Not on my fucking watch.

"I will not be your pawn any longer."

Even though I'd never preferred the sword—it was too bulky a weapon for my tastes—I pulled this one free without issue, continuing to let instinct drive me.

Her laugh was mocking as she spread her arms wide. "Oh, you think you're going to hurt me with that? Go ahead, Sunday. Take your best shot if it'll make you feel better. Run me through. I'll show you what real power can do. Your pitiful weapon is no match for me."

My wrath was all-consuming, a furious, righteous anger. It bubbled in my veins, a molten flame forging me with its purpose. With a battle cry that would've made my Alek proud, I released every ounce of fury I had, pouring it from my broken heart straight through my fingertips. The blade burst into blinding flames as I shoved it clean through her armor until it poked out her back.

She gasped. Eyes wide, mouth opening and closing in shock. "Michael's sword. How?"

"I know people," I grunted before pulling the sword free and watching the blood trickle out of her mouth. "Fuck you, Mother. I hope you burn in hell." I raised my booted foot and kicked her square in the stomach, sending her falling backward into the portal she'd worked so hard to open.

I wished I could say I enjoyed it. Watching her body be consumed by the demonic vortex. But it happened so fast, there was no time to do more than blink.

She was there and then just . . . gone.

As soon as she went through, the black sides of the gateway turned to smoke, spiraling into the green light like water down a drain until the entire thing closed. Snuffed out as if it had never been.

The waves calmed from raging peaks to gently lapping at the shore, the sky now a backlit canopy of beautiful twinkling stars.

The sword slipped from my fingers as the rage fueling me died out. I sagged to my knees, my chest feeling like an open wound. I should feel victorious, but all I felt was soul-crushing grief. They were gone. All of them.

Everything I'd ever loved, ever wanted for myself, for my future, was fucking gone. Stolen from me before I had a chance to enjoy any of it.

What good was a world without them? I should have let it burn. I should have let all of it fucking burn.

"Fuck, Sunshine. You are a goddamned badass. Will you wear that armor the next time we role play?"

Kingston's voice punched me in the gut. Now wasn't the time for my mind to play tricks.

"Baby . . . come on. I was just joking."

A sob broke free as I spun around, seeing Kingston, naked as the day he was born and covered in bruises, walking toward me on the beach. I started crying in earnest, my tears blurring the rest of his journey to me.

"It's okay. You got her. You did it." Strong arms wrapped around me, pulling me out of the spiral of pain and into his warm body. "You did it, baby. You saved the whole damn world."

"Bloody hell. Remind me never to build a sandcastle ever, please. I'm going to have nightmares about being pummeled by those fucking golems."

I twisted in Kingston's hold, relief washing through me at the sight of Noah, his wounds healing as he joined us.

"I'm going to be finding sand in places it shouldn't be for weeks."

Rushing him, I slammed against his body and held him tight. "You're alive."

"I'm much harder to kill than most, dove."

I bit down on my lip, tears burning in my throat as I thought of another man who'd once said the same.

"A-Alek..."

"Is right over there." Kingston pointed to the path behind me, the one that wove its way around the beach and to the village. "Looks like he's got someone who'd like to see her mommy."

My breath caught at the sight of my berserker heading straight for me with our daughter in tow. It was a dream, him with all that golden hair blowing in the breeze, a sleeping infant cuddled against his neck.

I was frozen in the spot as I worked to put together the pieces. "I...I watched you fall. You went into the portal."

"Ah, Kærasta. I thought you had more faith in me than that. Mischief is my specialty. I just knew that bitch would need to think she succeeded if we were going to stand a chance."

"You tricked her?"

"Quite successfully, I might say. Hubris is always the downfall of the truly evil. They never believe anyone can get anything past them.

Give them what they want, and they'll fall for it every single time. My father taught me that."

I blinked, tears welling. "I could kiss him."

"You should kiss me instead."

God, yes, I should.

Kingston grabbed my wrist. "Hey, wait your turn. I was here first. I get dibs on all kisses."

"The only one with dibs right now is Eden. I need to hold her . . . please?"

"God, it's already started. We've all been replaced, fellas. Say goodbye to being little spoon."

Alek moved in so I could scoop her out of his arms. A relieved shudder worked through me at finally getting to touch her. I truly lost it then, my tears breaking free and everything hitting me all at once.

"Don't listen to him, my sweet girl. My precious baby. You're perfect. I knew you would be. They tried to tell me you were evil, but I knew you weren't. Me and your da-daddies." I pressed kiss after kiss to her head, drawing the scent of her deep into my lungs and memorizing it.

"She is perfect. Just like you, baby." Kingston's voice broke, and he took a shuddering breath, doing nothing to wipe away the tear streaking down his cheek. "I was kidding. She's the best little spoon in the whole wide world." He nuzzled my neck while Noah reached out to run his fingertip over Eden's nose, and Alek rested his palm against my lower back.

"I can't believe it's over and we're still standing," Noah said.

"Really? I never had any doubts," Alek said.

"Of course you bloody didn't, Viking."

Then, as if finally realizing we were still missing someone, Kingston stiffened and looked around. "Sunday, where's Caleb?"

## CHAPTER
# FORTY-EIGHT
### SUNDAY

For the first time in twenty-four years, the sense of dread that followed me everywhere was gone. I hadn't truly been aware of its presence until my mother showed her face, but now that she was defeated, it seemed like it should've been obvious. Despite the lack of that invisible weight, there was no relief. Only a new, heavier ache. One that was threaded through every fiber of my being. An emptiness. A hole in my chest where my heart should be.

I placed my palm on the weather-worn headstone engraved with the Gallagher name.

*Caleb.*

It was his blood running through my veins. Stitching me together when all I wanted to do was fall apart. But he was gone. His body lay cold and unmoving in the church where he'd sacrificed everything to save me. I hadn't found the strength to go back there. To face the reality of what he'd done. That time would come, but I wanted—needed—a quiet place to mourn and say goodbye. It was only fitting that place was where his family was buried. Where we would lay him to rest. But right now was for me.

Just a few stolen moments to myself where I didn't have to

pretend. Where I didn't need to mask the soul-crushing loss of him. Of all of them.

We'd won, but at what cost? Victory felt hollow in the wake of all that had been taken from me.

Because if my mother had succeeded in anything, it was robbing me of the certainty of their love and commitment. How could I look at any of my mates right now, knowing all of this had happened because of me? That they'd all lost people important to them because of my mother's stupid game? Not to mention the fact that they'd never even had a choice. They'd been forced to love me. Tricked. Used as her pawns.

On instinct, I placed a palm over my belly, but of course, Eden wasn't there now. She was safe and alive. Beautiful.

It had been hard to leave my daughter, but Kingston hadn't let go of her once since setting foot in the house. The way he loved her was clear in every gentle touch. She would be well looked after while I tried to come to terms with living in a world without Caleb. My confessor. My husband. My savior.

I had far too much on my mind to be in that home with Caleb's scent everywhere, knowing that none of them would be with me without my mother's intervention. That was what hurt the most. Caleb sacrificed himself for a love that didn't even exist. He gave everything.

For a lie.

My breath hitched and knees buckled as I fell onto the moss-covered ground and let the soul-deep sob break free. I fisted the earth, digging my fingers into the dirt but feeling nothing. And as the tears fell, instead of a cathartic release, I lost more of myself. My gaze landed on the black yarn wedding band Caleb made for me. Something in me shattered as I took in the already fraying fibers. One day it would fall apart. What would I have left of him then?

Eden.

I'd have her.

I'd do exactly what he asked. I'd tell her our story. Make sure she knew every single day how much he loved her. What a good man—father—he was.

The flutter of wings and a soft rustling breeze had me blinking open my eyes, expecting to find some kind of bird who'd come for a closer look at the woman drowning in her grief.

"Your burden is heavy, Sunday Fallon."

Through my tears, I stared at the man sitting perched on Caleb's father's headstone. He was painfully beautiful, his golden blond hair glowing even though the moonlight was barely peeking through the trees. His dark leather pants and jacket seemed out of place on him yet somehow completely worked.

"Who are you?"

His lips curled in a smile. "A friend. One with a vested interest in you and your happiness."

I scoffed. "Well, you're a little late, pal. I'm fresh out of happy." Perhaps I should have been a little more weirded out by the sudden appearance of a stranger, but after the day—weeks—I'd had, this was barely a blip on the radar.

"Good deeds deserve to be rewarded."

Sighing, I sat on my ass and rested my head in my hands, pressing my forehead into the heels of my palms. "Don't you know the saying? No good deed goes unpunished."

"You think this is punishment? Believe me, it could be so much worse."

My laughter was loud and slightly unhinged as I wiped my nose and looked up at him. "How, exactly? I just found out the four men I love were tricked into loving me, and that's *on top of* one of them fucking *dying*. So excuse me if I don't believe it could get any fucking worse."

"You could be forced to live your life knowing your soulmate is out there and never being able to have them."

"Did you not hear what I just said?"

"Sunday, after all the five of you have been through together, why would you believe they don't love you?"

Getting to my feet, I brushed the dirt off my knees and hands. "Why do you care?"

"It's my job to care. To deliver the message."

"Then deliver your message and let me get back to my mourning, will you?"

"Do you know who I am?"

"Obviously not. I asked, and you didn't exactly give me a name. Should I? Are you God or something? Because if you are, I have a serious bone to pick with you."

He smirked. "No. I'm surprised Caleb didn't tell you about me."

God, that name. It hurt. But my breath caught as understanding hit me. "Gabriel. You were the one who sent me the sword."

"I can neither confirm nor deny any involvement in acts that could technically be viewed as tipping the balance, but yes, child, I am Gabriel." He stood and puffed out his chest as a warm glow radiated from him. "The Messenger of God."

"Tell him to go fuck himself."

The glow died. "I don't think I shall. That rarely ends well."

"So is that it, then? Are you here to smite me?"

He laughed. "Darling, why would I do that?"

"You know. Daughter of a horsewoman. Gave birth to the Apocalypse. Seems like I'm a pretty big wrinkle in your plans."

"Wrinkle? No. Part of the plan? Definitely." Gabriel folded his hands and gave me a considering look. "Your mother wasn't the only one with pieces on the board, you know. It might have been their game, but they weren't the only players."

"What the hell is that supposed to mean?"

The angel sighed. "I thought it was quite obvious, but clearly you're upset. Maybe it will bring you more comfort later."

I shook my head, not appreciating the subtle dig. "I guess I should be happy that my mom didn't actually end up being Lucifer. Horsewoman has to be a little lower on God's shitlist, right?"

"You were never on a shitlist. You were born to play a role, but the script was unwritten. Your choices led to this end. And, as you can see, she failed because of your strength."

"What strength? I'm in a graveyard talking to an angel at my wit's fucking end, trying to figure out how I'm supposed to put the man I love in the ground. This is about as broken as I could possibly be." My voice wobbled, but I took a ragged breath and steeled myself as much as I was able. "Caleb is dead. And regardless of why he loved me, I love him, and that's real. I love all of them . . ." Another shuddering sob tore through me before I could continue. "But they . . . they're trapped here with me. They don't know why they feel the way they do for me. They don't understand it's not real. And I'm so selfish. So fucking selfish because all I want is to pretend she didn't tell me the truth. I want to keep them and make believe it's real love because what do I have without them? What even was the point of all of this if we don't get to be together in the end?"

"I'd say saving the world from a fiery end is probably a worthy cause."

"Fuck your worthy cause. This is too hard." I wiped more tears away, welcoming my anger and holding it tight. "Where the fuck were you anyway? If you're such a good friend, if you had such a vested interest, why weren't you here with us? You could have stopped all of this. Why let this happen? Why make us suffer this way?"

He offered me a soft, understanding smile. I wanted to slap him as he took up position next to me. "You earthbound creatures. You'll never understand how powerful free will is. My hands are tied in so many ways. You think red tape is something only mortals deal with? Try dealing with celestial regulations."

"Is this all a joke to you?"

"Far from. If I could have stopped all of this and saved you the pain and heartache, I would have. I did what I could. Skirted the line so closely I may still be cast out of heaven. But I have something you need to find."

"What is that?"

"Faith."

"Faith in what? A God that would allow terrible things to happen to the people who wholeheartedly believe in Him? I have no use for a disloyal deity."

"Careful."

"Fuck off, angel, I'm not playing any more games. I am no one's pawn."

"If you would just listen to me, you'd realize I'm giving you the answer you need."

Turning my gaze on him, I frowned. "How could you know what I need?"

He held my stare, raising one perfect brow.

I blew out a breath. "Angel. Right. Fine."

Silence stretched for a second before he bumped me with his shoulder. "We seem to have gotten a bit off topic. I'm trying to give you a gift, but you won't let me."

"A gift? What kind of gift?"

He pointed to the sky. "The heavenly kind. Straight from the top."

"I'm listening."

"One request. Anything you want. Here and now."

My chest fucking broke open as possibilities raced through my mind, chief among them Caleb. Could he bring Caleb back to me? I nearly cried out in anguished relief at the thought. But then . . . would he still be under the spell? Would he even want me . . . us?

"Where is Caleb, Gabriel?"

His expression was serene. "At peace."

"Where?"

"Heaven. Specifically, *his* heaven. Would you like to hear about it?"

The fist around my heart squeezed, and it was a struggle to breathe, so all I could manage was a jerky nod.

"It's a perfect summer day. Not a cloud in the sky. He's currently pushing your daughter on a swing and counting butterflies. You're there too, sitting on a blanket beside a picnic basket, nursing your son. We gave him the life he dreamed of. Most don't get that. Caleb's sacrifice deserved something special."

It nearly killed me, hearing that Caleb was truly gone, even as it brought me so much joy to hear that he wasn't alone. Even if I was. Sucking in a ragged breath, I wiped the tears from my cheeks, steeling myself. I couldn't be selfish. Not when Caleb had finally gotten the only thing he'd ever really wanted. I had to let him go. I had to let them all go.

Fresh tears spilled from my lashes. "I want you to undo the love spell."

"Are you certain?"

No.

"Yes, Gabriel. I can't keep them trapped. Free will, right? Aren't you guys pretty big on that whole thing?"

"We are. It's kind of our motto."

"Free them. I need them to have the lives they were meant for, not ones they were forced into."

He booped me on the nose. "Consider it done."

"Just like that?"

"Not quite just like that. This may hurt."

My neck burned, both sides caught in a searing pain that only lasted for a second at most, followed by the same sensation on my inner arm. And I knew. They were gone. My mating marks. Our bonds. I'd truly set them free.

He reached out and caught a tear as it slid down my cheek. Holding it up, he inspected the droplet. "Have faith. If not in us, at least in them."

"I do. That's why I let them go."

"Well played, Sunday Fallon. And you were right about one thing. You're no pawn. You're the most powerful piece on the board."

"What?"

"The queen." Leaning in, he kissed my forehead, his nearness making me close my eyes. "And I believe that is what you call checkmate."

The air shifted around me, the pressure making my ears pop, and when I opened my eyes, I was once again alone in the dark, cold graveyard. My only company the long-buried bones of Caleb's past and a sorrow so deep I didn't think I'd ever recover. I squeezed my eyes shut against the pain, willing myself to contain the ache. Instead, I was stolen away by a wave of grief strong enough that it brought me to my knees again. I hung my head, weeping openly rather than holding it in.

"Our marks might be gone, but I will always love you. All of you."

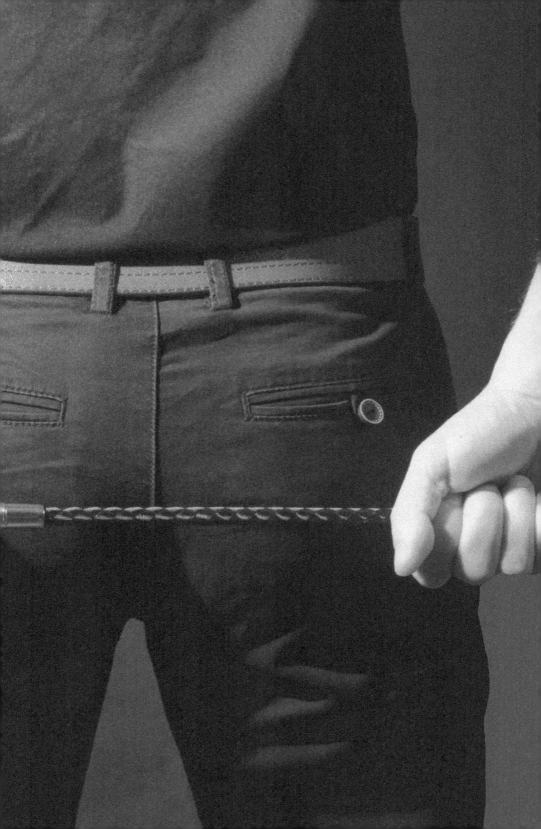

# FORTY-NINE

## CALEB

"Again, my wee one?" I asked, catching Eden's feet and playing our game with the swing. The one she loved so much.

Her eyes glittered with joy. She was my perfect little love, a version of Sunday and I with echoes of the others visible in her expressions. Her mother's sunny laughter. My eyes. Kingston's impish grin. Noah's intense stare. Alek's temper.

All I felt was peace and pure happiness. This was everything I'd ever wanted. Almost too good to be true.

"Darling, do you want a turn pushing her?" I called over my shoulder where Sunday sat feeding our son Nolan.

But she didn't answer. Frowning, I turned around, finding the blanket where she'd been seconds prior occupied, but not by her. A familiar smirking angel sat in her place.

"What are you doing here?"

"My, my, Caleb. You should be happy to see me. I bring tidings of great joy and all that."

"That is never the case with your news."

He gasped, pressing his hand to his chest. "You wound me. Maybe I should go without giving you your reward."

"Reward? For what?"

"You did it! You won. Bravo."

"Won what?"

Gabriel sighed. "I forget how quickly your mortal memories seep away up here."

"What are you talking about?"

He stood and walked toward me, placing an arm around my shoulders. "This is heaven. You're dead. There, now that you're up to speed . . ."

"Dead?"

"Come on. Get with the program, man." Waving his palm in front of the swing set, the vision of Eden disappeared, momentary panic setting in as I watched myself crouched over a dying Sunday in the church. And in the blink of an eye, I remembered every crushing detail.

Fisting my hand in Gabriel's jacket, I pulled him close, my voice a desperate growl. "Is she all right?"

"No."

"Will she be?"

"That depends."

"On?"

"Would you please unhand me?"

"Tell me," I snarled, pressing my forehead against his.

"You know, sometimes it really sucks being the messenger. No one ever just wants the news. They have to force their own agenda on you first." Rolling his eyes, he peeled my fingers back and shoved me none too gently away from him. "I cannot tell you what it depends on, Caleb. You know the rules. Choices must be made."

"Explain."

"She is strong. She'll survive. The world will go on for her as it will for everyone else."

"Does this mean it's really over? The Apocalypse truly prevented?"

"For now, yes. But the game never really ends. For others, it's only just beginning."

"So why are you here, then? You gave me a task. I failed. Leave me in peace."

"Failed? No. It's as I said. You're to be rewarded."

"But I didn't . . ." I shuddered at the mere thought of the original terms of the angel's bargain.

Gabriel raised his brow. "Didn't you? Choices, Caleb. They all matter. They all have consequences. And despite what I led you to believe, the one you made just so happened to be the right one."

"And?"

"As you can see, I returned your soul. If I hadn't, you certainly wouldn't be here. But that's not the choice I speak of now. Today I have a different offer for you."

"What choice are you asking me to make?"

He cocked one brow and stared at the scene before us as it morphed into Sunday weeping alone in a cemetery.

It hurt to see her so desperately sad. "Why are you showing me this?"

"You don't have to stay here. You could return to her."

"Yes."

"There are conditions attached to this bargain, Caleb. You have to decide. Stay in heaven, filled with certainty, and not a day will pass where you feel pain or sorrow. Just as it was before I lifted the veil and came to you. Or, go back to Sunday, to being a vampire as you were when you died. Never again feel the kiss of sunlight on your face, hunger for blood over all else, live as the monster you hated. But the pain will be worse because your soul has been returned. You will feel everything more deeply. Walk with the guilt of your past."

"I've borne the guilt of my sins with every breath."

"Not like this."

"Guilt is nothing new. I'm not afraid of pain. Not if I can have her. Them." My thoughts were immediately on Sunday and Eden. "The life I have here, that's what you're offering me? Only lived in the dark?"

"Perhaps. I cannot control where life takes you. We don't manifest your reality on Earth, Caleb. That's something we reserve for up here."

I swallowed through a tight throat as my decision crystalized. I stared at him, my resolve strong. "Then you already know there's only one choice it could be."

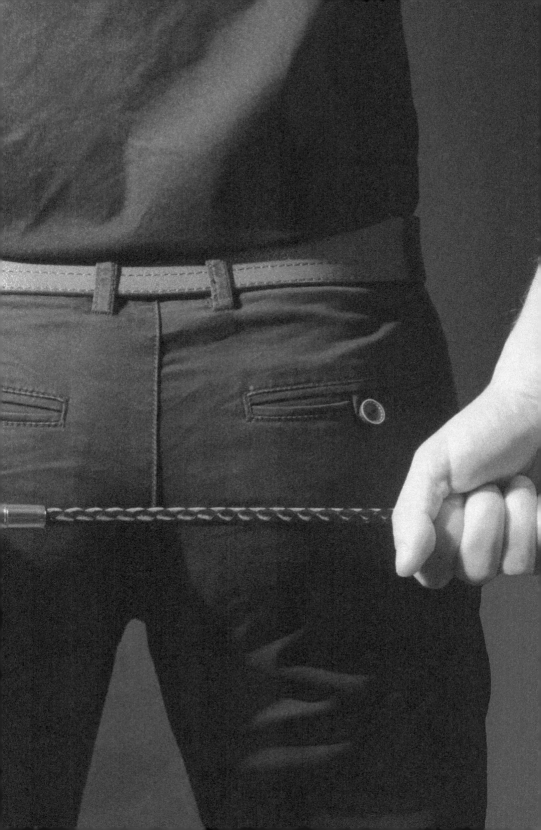

# FIFTY

## SUNDAY

"On your knees for me again, Miss Fallon?"

My stomach lurched at the sound of him, the scent of incense and spice floating on the breeze, the *feel* of Caleb's domineering presence. I didn't let myself think it was a fantasy. I couldn't. Snapping my head up, I blinked at the man standing at the mouth of the cemetery, his body bathed in moonlight.

"Ca-Caleb?" I scrambled to my feet and was up and running before my brain fully realized it had made the decision. I didn't hug him as much as collide with him.

He let out a muffled oomph as he caught me in his arms, holding me tight. "I take it you're glad to see me, then?"

"Shut up and kiss me."

"Now who's being boss—"

I shut him up with my mouth, our kiss tasting like tears and redemption. But almost as soon as it started, I broke us apart, remembering what had passed between Gabriel and me.

"You were in heaven. He said you were."

"Aye."

423

"Then why are you here?"

He cupped my face, staring down at me with eyes that searched mine for some unnamable reason. What did he want me to say? To do?

"For you, Sunday. I'm here for you." He slid his palm over me, assessing my form with a smile. "Are you healed? Are you all right? Is Eden . . ."

"She's beautiful and perfect. Kingston has her now. And I'm good as new. Your blood fixed me and then some."

"A worthwhile sacrifice if ever there was one. I'd do it all over again to save you."

My lip trembled, the memory of his still form beside mine too fresh. "I'd rather you didn't."

"Loving you means I will always value your life above my own. Being a father means Eden's needs supersede my selfish desires. Our daughter needs you far more than she does me, *a stor*. So, like it or not, I will always put you first. You're mine. You always will be."

"But why? He broke the spell. He set you all free."

Caleb's brows furrowed, and he pulled back slightly as if seeking a better view. "What are you going on about? What spell?"

Even though it nearly killed me, I untangled myself from his arms and stepped away. "The love spell my mother used. None of us would have been together without her meddling. It's why you thought I was your mate. It's why you broke your vows."

Caleb laughed. That fucker actually laughed.

"Well, I didn't think it was very funny."

"Miss Fallon, you cannot really believe a spell is responsible for all that transpired between us. That was fate, darling girl. And fate alone. I was destined to be yours."

"I wish that was true."

"It is." He lifted my hand and placed it on his chest, right over his heart. "Do you feel that?"

The steady *thump-thump* pulsed under my palm. "Yes."

"A made vampire's heart only beats once they find their true mate. If the spell was the reason I fell for you, surely my heart would no longer be beating now that it was over."

"But . . ."

"It's for you. Only you, Sunday. You're my mate. No matter what kind of plot your mother thought she'd been part of, that much is true. I would've chosen you regardless."

His gaze trailed over my neck and shoulder, eyes narrowing. "Where's your mark?"

"I . . . I asked Gabriel to free you all. To lift the spell and give you back your lives. He broke the bonds."

Pain and something a lot like anger blazed in his eyes. "How could you doubt us? Doubt me?"

God, this hurt. I couldn't rejoice in him being back. Not with the look of betrayal on his face.

Jaw set, he took my hand. "Do they know?"

"What?"

"Do they know what you did?"

"N-no. It just happened."

"Fecking hell. Come on."

"Wh-where are we going?"

"Do pay attention, Miss Fallon. It's time for you to face the consequences of your sins."

I tried to pull my hand free, but his hold on me was ironclad. I wasn't going anywhere except where he wanted me to.

"I did the right thing. How could you expect me to live the rest of my life with them—with you—if it was all a lie? Even if it was real for me, I couldn't live with myself if it wasn't the same for them. I'd rather spend my life alone than know the only reason you're all with me is some magical obligation."

He grumbled under his breath as he tugged me up the path, but his hand never released mine. The way he ran his thumb over my skin was so gentle and loving that I wanted to cry.

I saw them in the distance. Three figures racing toward us. A strange mixture of happiness and dread swirled in my gut. If Caleb was this upset, if they were frantically coming for me, what had I done? I'd made a huge mistake, hadn't I?

Noah's arms were around me before I could steel myself for his touch. "You're alive. Bloody hell, dove, we thought we lost you. The bond—"

"She broke it," Caleb growled.

"She what now?" Kingston stepped close, our sleeping baby girl in his arms. "I must've heard you wrong because my Sunshine couldn't possibly be that stupid. Also, hi. Good to see you're not dead anymore. Decided to pull a Jesus and do the whole resurrection thing, huh? Seems a little excessive, but whatever floats your boat, man."

"He meets the Messenger of God, and yet he's still as blasphemous as ever," Caleb muttered, rolling his eyes before bringing the others up to speed. "Her mother spelled us all in order to ensure we played our parts in her twisted game. So our naughty little martyr thought she needed to *free* us from her bond."

"Sunshine . . ." The hurt in Kingston's voice made a tear slip down my cheek.

"I couldn't let you live your lives like that. Bound to me by magic and lies."

"What the fuck do you think a mate bond is? It's fucking magic, baby. That's why it's rare."

"Sure, when it's real, but she faked it, made you believe . . ." My eyes found Alek's, my broody Viking absolutely ruined.

He shook his head, disappointment etched in every perfect angle of his face. "I already lost you once, Kærasta. How could you do that to me again?"

His intentional use of the endearment had me blinking back tears. If he didn't love me, truly love me, he never would have said it. The reproach, so tenderly delivered, absolutely gutted me.

"Once? Please. Try six or seven times. She rejected me more times than I can remember, and I've *always* come back for more. How could you ever doubt me, Sunshine?"

"Dove . . . surely you didn't actually believe *everything* had been a lie?"

Caleb squeezed my hand in a silent 'told you so.'

"I didn't know what to believe. She broke me. She took everything to get what she wanted. Including you."

"But you're the one who chose to cut us loose." Noah's brows pulled together. "Do you really not want us any longer?"

My heart shattered under the weight of their pain. "Please, you have to understand. If there was a chance, even a microscopic one, that what you felt for me wasn't real, I couldn't bear it. I could never allow you to go on loving me against your will if there was something I could do to fix it. If our roles had been reversed, if I was the one who'd been tricked into falling for you, wouldn't you have done the same?"

"Fuck no," Kingston said. "You know I'm way too fucking selfish to ever let you go, baby."

"Perhaps," Noah said a bit more softly. "Because I love you, I would want you to be free to choose me."

Alek continued to hold my gaze. "When can we fix it?"

"Alek, take the baby. Sunshine, I'll mark you again right the fuck now. Are you fully healed? I'm not going to be gentle." Kingston gripped my nape and pressed his forehead to mine. "I don't want to go without being yours, Sunday. Ever."

"You all still . . ." My voice broke, the realization of their truths hitting me with all the subtlety of a sledgehammer.

"We will never stop loving you, little wolf. You're ours, and we're yours." Noah pulled me away from Kingston and kissed me hard before murmuring against my lips, "At least we get to exchange marks again. That was quite . . . pleasurable, if I recall correctly."

"Since I don't remember the last time, I'm quite looking forward to a second chance," Alek said.

Wordlessly, I shook my head. I was suffering from emotional whiplash. Ten minutes ago, Caleb had been dead, and I thought for sure I'd lost all of them. Now . . . now they were proving just how short-sighted I'd been. But the relief I felt knowing it was real, that their love for me hadn't been some cruel cosmic joke, it was worth the pain.

"I love you all so much. I'm so sorry for hurting you. I promise it hurt me far more to let you go."

"That should have been your first clue not to do it," Kingston mumbled.

"Says the man who purposely seeks out pain," Noah said.

Kingston smirked. "Touché."

I bit down on my lip, shaking my head at their teasing even though my heart was still heavy. "Can you forgive me?"

"There's nothing to forgive. We can fix it." Kingston trailed his fingers over the place my mark had been.

"Aye, we can, and we will." Caleb, who'd been so quiet until now, finally joined us, his words strong and determined. "Perhaps this time we can find a way to all do it together."

"You asking for an orgy, Priest?"

"I was thinking more along the lines of a proper mating ceremony since you were all so put out by ours."

"Oh. Yeah, that sounds good too. Ceremony first, orgy after." Kingston held out his fist to Noah. "Priorities, right?"

I loved how playful those two were with each other now. The suggestion of a mating ceremony between us all, and the fact that it came from Caleb, meant so much. "I love that idea. We can do it right. No one feels left out. If I have any regrets about the way we did our marks, it's that."

"When? Now?" Alek took my hand and ran his thumb over my knuckles.

"Not now. I need a little time. Today has been . . . a lot. We should plan this. Celebrate with the people who are important to us."

"Like a wedding? You gonna wear a white dress, Sunshine?"

"Do you want me to? Pretty sure no one is going to believe I'm a virgin, Kingston." Eden let out a soft little snore, underscoring my words and making us all chuckle. I couldn't resist running a finger over her chubby cheek, smiling up at Alek, who shifted her so I had better access.

"I just want something I can rip off."

"That can be arranged. We can do it at the ranch. Bring some light to a place with dark memories?"

The look on Kingston's face had me near tears. "Fuck. Mama would love that."

"Are you crying, Kingston?" Noah asked, amusement in his voice.

"I'm not fucking crying. I have . . . allergies."

"Will the wolves be okay with vampires around?" Caleb asked.

"I'm their Alpha. They'll accept you, or they can leave. The five of us are pack."

"Six," I corrected.

He smiled and gazed down at Eden cradled and sleeping soundly in Alek's arms. "Six."

I reached out and took her from my Viking, my whole body aching with the depth of my love for this little person we'd made. She yawned, and her eyelids fluttered. Big, soulful eyes stared back at me, one a deep blue, the other amber. "Oh, look at you. You are the most beautiful thing I've ever seen."

"She's magic, Sunny. Our magic."

I glanced over at Caleb, who stood next to me, tense, his jaw clenched tight, brow furrowed. He was uneasy. Worried.

"Come meet your daughter, Caleb. She's as much yours as she is theirs."

He glanced at the others, then back at the bundle in my arms. "It's okay. I can wait my turn."

"It *is* your turn, mate. We've all gotten to hold her."

Noah's words had tears pricking my eyes again. Fuck these hormones.

"Well, if you insist." Caleb reached out, and I caught the slight tremor in his hands as he lifted Eden from my arms, holding her like he'd been fucking born to do it.

She began to fuss, her little face scrunching into a frown as a thready cry escaped her. I reached for her, but Caleb softly bounced in place, shushing her.

Alek took up Caleb's spot behind me, curling an arm around my waist and drawing me against him. Noah threaded his fingers through mine while Kingston did the same on the other side. Together we watched Caleb step out of the shadows where he'd spent so many years hiding and into the role where he truly belonged. As part of our family.

"Don't cry, my wee darling. It's all right." He locked eyes with me and smiled, pure happiness on his face. Then he turned his attention back to our daughter. "Your da is going to tell you a story."

My heart lifted as he began.

"Once upon a time . . ."

The End . . . or is it?

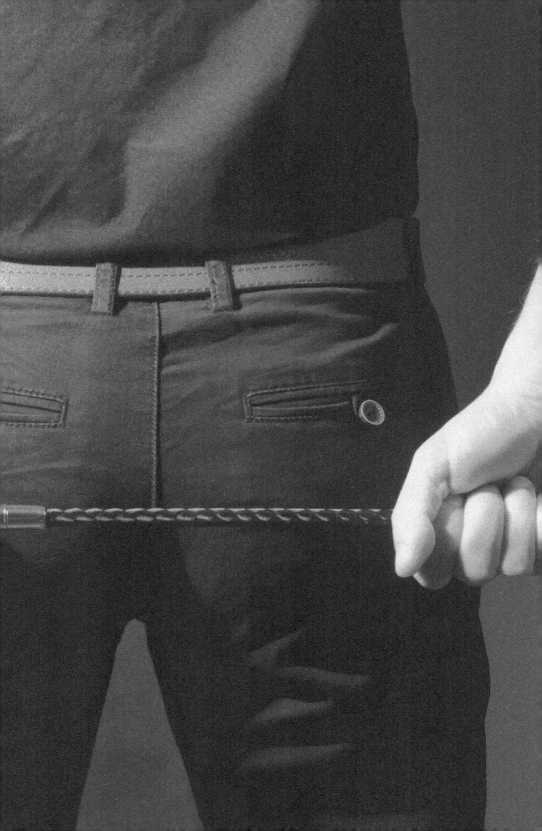

# EPILOGUE
## SUNDAY

*Two months later*

I didn't end up going with a white dress. But something told me Kingston wouldn't be disappointed.

"I've always said red is your color." Moira beamed at me in the mirror as she fussed with the silk buttons that ran from my bra line to the base of my spine.

I nervously skimmed my hands over the scarlet-colored satin, pleased with the simplicity of my dress. The bodice was perfectly fitted, showcasing my curves and flowing down my body in a pool of fabric. Elegant, striking, and leaving very little to the imagination in the most demure way. It would drive them all wild but stayed just on this side of the respectability line.

Which was important to me when I had four mates and three mothers-in-law.

The guys were holding on tight to the antiquated notion of not seeing me before this ceremony, which I found ridiculous. I mean, they'd seen just about every single part of my body in very intimate ways, but if it was what they wanted, I'd do it. I was actually surprised by how seriously they were taking this whole thing. It was like once Caleb planted the idea, they ran wild with it.

As much as I was looking forward to the part where we exchanged our vows and formally tied our lives together in front of our friends and families, what I was really looking forward to was the *after*. Even though it had been my decision to hold off on redoing our mating marks, I hadn't anticipated how much I'd miss that soul-deep connection to my men. I wanted it back. I was more than ready. The rest of this was a formality, a way for our families to also unite, but solidifying our bonds was the part that truly mattered to me.

A soft knock on the door had us both turning toward the sound, excitement humming in my blood.

"You. Stay." Moira leveled me with her stare before she crossed the room and opened the door.

A whiff of bergamot hit my nose, instantly making me long for Noah. But this particular scent wasn't him. It belonged to Westley.

"A gift for Sunday from my mother."

"Thank you, West. Is she here?" I asked, staring into eyes the same color as my Noah's.

He smiled and nodded. That one revelation made my heart soar. Noah had been so worried she wouldn't be ready to be in mixed company after being turned. That was part of the reason we'd waited two months. It seemed like forever, but we'd all needed the time to say proper goodbyes to those we'd lost and settle into our new normal.

But now, *everyone* was here. The remaining Farrells, the Black-thornes, and even the Novasgardians—though Quinn and I had a long talk before I extended her invite. I still didn't like her very much, but I had to respect the woman for the lengths she went to protect my mate.

"Well, are you going to open it, or what?"

I rolled my eyes at Moira, sharing a conspiratorial look with West as he handed me a flat velvet case. I opened it, revealing a familiar twinkling necklace.

The Blackthorne jewels.

"Pfft. Mine was better, but I guess the real thing is nice too."

"Salty, Mo?"

"Maybe. Just a little." She lifted her thumb and forefinger, holding them close together. "But only because now I can't magic you up something."

"We had a few details added to it especially for you." He winked and left us without another word.

"What does he mean, *added*? These are centuries-old jewels. What can you add?" Moira inspected the necklace and let out a little gasp.

It didn't take me long to figure out what set her off. Nestled within the various swirls of thorns that acted as links were three new gleaming additions that somehow looked as though they'd been there all along. A crescent moon, a cluster of stars, and a gorgeous snowflake. Symbols to represent my other mates. Noah, of course, was still represented by the rose that hung in the center.

"Okay, fine. It's better than mine," Moira muttered, adding under her breath, "Why didn't you think of that, Belladonna? You call yourself a witch."

She draped the jewelry across my throat and helped me do the clasp before letting my hair fall back down in a waterfall of loose curls. It was the missing piece to my ensemble, completing my look by adding *them* to it.

"You ready to get this show on the road, babycakes?"

I rested my fingers over the rose pendant, smiling at myself in the mirror. "So ready."

Moira slapped my ass. "All right, then. Sunday Amadeus Fallon, let's go get you mated. Again."

I'd like to say I remembered every moment of the ceremony, but once I saw them all standing at the other end of the aisle, I couldn't focus on anything else. Except, of course, for our sweet

Eden, who was nestled in Kingston's arms, her dress the same color as mine.

They knew how to clean up for their mate, that was for sure. Kingston, Noah, and Caleb all wore black suits. Caleb's was the simplest—and in my opinion, sadly lacking a white collar. Kingston's, of course, was the flashiest, with its velvet patterned lapels. Noah was every inch the British aristocrat with his perfectly tailored suit and matching pocket square. And then there was my Alek. He'd opted for something more traditionally Novasgardian and stood in the center of them wearing a mouthwatering set of leather pants, a simple white shirt, and a beautiful fur cloak. He'd also taken the time to braid and twist his hair. I was ready to climb him like a tree.

But it wasn't really how gorgeous they were that got me. It was the looks of absolute love in their eyes. We exchanged perfect words, made eternal promises, devoted ourselves, but I couldn't stop thinking about what came next. The real thing. The marks. The moments we'd take just for us with no one else around.

I'd taken Eden from Kingston as soon as we'd finished, knowing that I was going to have to say goodbye to her for the first time since the day she'd been born. As much as I wanted—needed—my alone time with them, I was anxious about being away from her. We'd fought so hard to have this, to have her. It seemed too soon to leave her with Diana, even if it was only a few days. But I also knew there was no one more suited to take care of her than Kingston's mother.

"I love you, sweet girl. We will be home soon." I nuzzled Eden, and each of her daddies took their turn kissing her before I handed her off to my new mother-in-law.

"Don't worry about a thing. Eden and I are going to have a great time together. I promise." Diana held her close, and the love shining in her eyes eased something in me. "Now go on. You five deserve some time to celebrate after everything you've gone through to get to this point."

I knew she was right. It was time. I stole one last kiss from my daughter and sought out Moira in the crowd. She and Ash were dancing and laughing and so much in love it made my heart squeeze. Everyone I loved was right here. Safe. Happy. Carefree. It was such a difference from where we'd been a few months ago.

Diana was right. We'd earned this.

Turning back, I looked at each of my men, my smile growing wicked and distinctly *not* demure.

"Are you ready to get out of here?" I asked them.

"Aye, *a stor*. I've been waiting to truly make you mine since the day you first set foot in my office."

Kingston snorted. "Creep."

I couldn't contain my laughter. "Let's go, then."

"The car is waiting. But if you need time to say goodbye . . ." Noah's gaze trailed to where Diana and Dylan were playing with Eden.

Alek scooped me up, throwing me over his shoulder in a fireman's carry. "Fuck that." His large palm gave my ass a rough squeeze. "No more waiting."

The squeal of surprise that left me would have been embarrassing if not for the benefits of my position. Namely, the fantastic view of his butt in those leather pants.

He put me down as soon as we reached the car, Noah holding open the door like the gentleman he was.

Caleb climbed in the limo first, while Alek set me down and got in after him. Noah took one look at Kingston, kissed my cheek, and went in next.

Kingston moved in close, resting one hand on top of the door and the other on the top of the car, caging me in. "I hope you're ready, Sunshine. I'm up first. I saw the way you looked at Eden. Don't worry, I know what you want."

"You do?" I asked, more than a little breathless, my heart already racing in anticipation. No one had let me in on their plans for *how* they were going to re-do their marks. Only that it would be intimate and the details handled completely by each of them. But if

Kingston's low growl was any sign, I was going to enjoy the surprise.

He chuckled, but the sound was filled with dark promise. "Fuck, yes. You want my knot. But not as much as you want me to put another baby in you. And I'm gonna give you both. I'm going to give you everything."

I swallowed, the flood of arousal hitting me all at once. Oh, shit. I was so fucking wet already.

He inhaled, and his eyes flashed amber as he pulled me away from the car. Leaning down, he stuck his head inside and said, "We'll see you there." Then he closed the door and turned on me, gaze hungry and feral and sending a thrill straight to my core. "You better run, baby."

"Run?"

He grinned, his big bad wolf shining through. "Run."

~

### KINGSTON

FUCK ME, that silky red dress had me sporting a hard-on from the moment she appeared at the end of the aisle. It had been uncomfortable as hell, my whole goddamned family watching me as I tried to hide it. But now? She was all mine until I marked her and claimed her again. I'd planned to wait until we arrived at the lake house. I was going to take my time, seduce her, make love to her. That flew out the window as soon as my wolf got a hit of the scent of her slick.

She wasted no time, turning and fleeing straight for the trees. My wolf was primed for the hunt, but I needed this to last. I wanted to chase her. Pounce and claim her. If I was to go right now, it would be over before it started.

I counted in my head, my body vibrating with the urge to shift. When I got to one hundred, I finally gave in, transitioning from man to beast in a single leap. I found the scraps of her dress a few feet into the brush.

*My very own Little Red Riding Hood. What do you have in your basket for me?*

It was so very easy to track her. It was almost disappointing, like she wasn't even trying to get away. But the smell of her arousal tempered the instinct to chase. Now I was overtaken by another, more primal desire. Mount her. Fucking breed her.

I was a regular fucking Boy Scout. Ready to get my merit badge for the three Ms of the wolf pack. Mount. Mark. Mate. I was really fucking good at them too.

Her voice echoed in my head as I lazily trotted through the forest, following her trail. *"What is taking you so long? Have you lost your touch?"*

*"Baby, I know right where you are, but I'm holding back. I want you on two legs for everything I have planned."*

I saw her, a flash of pale naked skin in the moonlight as she ran. I was salivating, desperate, aching.

Growling low and long, I let her know I was coming for her. Promising with every heartbeat just what I intended to do when I got my paws on her.

That slight hitch in her breath told me she felt it, that she craved it. The game was over after that. I was a blur through the trees, barreling into her and knocking her down into the dirt and leaves seconds later.

I inhaled her scent, running my muzzle along the delicate column of her throat, loving the erratic flutter of her pulse.

"Kingston," she whispered, fingers threading through my fur. "Please."

My teeth scraped across her shoulder, but I needed more. I shifted into my human form, desperate to kiss her, to feel her hands on my skin and know her body again.

"Fuck, baby. I love you."

"I love you too." She bucked beneath me, flipping us over so she was on top, straddling my hips. Her hair was loose, cocooning us in the scent of lilacs. She lightly scraped her nails over my chest. "I want to go first this time."

Jesus Christ. Yes. "Oh, God . . . please," I moaned, drawing it out, writhing under her. I was so hard it hurt.

Rising on her knees, she reached between us and lined me up at her entrance. With excruciating slowness, she sank down until I was sheathed fully inside her. I couldn't help myself. I let out a harsh growl, my wolf begging to be freed as I held her hips.

"God, Kingston. You feel so good."

"Yes. Use me however you need to."

She rocked back and forth, sliding me deep inside with each thrust. "I can feel your piercings so much more like this."

I smirked. "Jake aims to please."

Her laugh was low and throaty, and it skated across my skin like invisible fingers. Fuck, everything about this woman seduced me. I thrust up into her, wanting to be as close as fucking possible.

She moaned. "No topping from the bottom."

"Then fucking mark me, Sunshine."

Leaning down, her full tits brushing my chest, she feathered her lips over my throat, trailing down until she found *that* spot. The one that had me nearly coming right then and there. I let out a warning growl before her sharp teeth pierced my skin as she gave me what I was so desperate for.

I came with a surprised grunt, spilling in her as my fingers turned to claws, holding her in place. "Fuuuuuck, baby."

She released me, lapping at the wound and healing it with her saliva like only my mate could. Then she pressed a sweet kiss right over the newly healed mark. The sensation had my cock twitching and ready for round two.

"My turn." Her little yelp of surprise was fucking adorable as I flipped us over and drove deep inside. "You think I'd let you out from under me without giving you my knot? Before we're done, I'm gonna make you forget your own name."

"Then shut up and do it."

Her fingers were woven through my hair, and she punctuated her words by giving the strands a sharp tug.

"You asked for it. Wrap your legs around me. You're gonna need something to hold on to."

I let go of the thin tendril of control I'd been clinging to and let my rut take over. Like a tether connecting us, my lips found the spot on her neck that was a perfect mirror to my own. I drove into her with relentless thrusts, fucking her and worshipping her in equal measure. As her cries turned desperate, I growled low and bit down hard. Marking her and sending her straight over the edge.

She was still whimpering, her cunt fluttering and gripping me tight when it happened. The subtle change in her scent. The flood of slick.

*Heat.* My heart stuttered, my wolf perking up.

My mate was in need of me. Of the one thing I could give her that the others couldn't. My knot.

She came again as I swelled inside her, locking us together. I followed, the harsh bark of pleasure that escaped me echoing off the trees.

This. This was what I needed. What had been missing from my life. My Sunshine.

"Mmm, that was exactly what I wanted," she murmured after we finally were able to move and I pulled free of her.

"You're never getting away from me now, baby."

She kissed my chest, right over my heart. "Who says I want to?"

Desire burned bright in her eyes, summoning my own. "You sure you want to go join the others? We could den up here. I could keep fucking you until you're boneless and keep you in an orgasmic haze until we know for sure you've got my baby inside you."

Her little shiver of arousal had Jake perking up again. "Tempting, but you know they'll come looking for us."

"Fine. But you know I could take 'em."

She laughed. "I don't want to test that theory." Then she got to her feet. "How are we going to get there?"

I followed, smirking. "Baby, we're wolves. We do what we do best." Dropping a kiss to her mark, I whispered, "Run."

*Noah*

I HEARD them bounding toward the lake house as I stood outside. Anticipation rolled through my veins. Heady. Intoxicating. It felt like I'd been waiting for this night for years instead of only a few months.

I remembered the first time I saw Sunday. That instinct calling me to take her had been strong. I'd thought it made me obsessed. In reality, it was my soul recognizing my destiny. Obsession is a dark thing, twisted and ugly, but nothing about what we have is twisted. If anything, it's the purest connection in my life. And now, I'd give her my bond again, this time with no rush, no fear of losing her, no pressing threat pushing us forward.

Two wolves broke through the thick line of trees on the edge of the property, Sunday's beautiful white fur catching the moonlight as she raced ahead of Kingston. He caught up to her, leaping and knocking her to the ground, both of them playfully nipping at each other. But then she saw me, her eyes locking on mine.

It was nearly instantaneous, her transition from animal to woman, and it took my breath away. She stood, naked, beautiful, a goddess under the wide-open sky.

"Bloody hell, you're gorgeous."

"So are you."

Kingston gave her hand a soft nip and wandered off, leaving us alone.

"You going to stand over there all night?" I asked when she made no move to close the distance between us.

"Just enjoying the view."

"You come a little closer. I'll really give you something to enjoy."

Her brow cocked. "Is that so?"

"Do you doubt me, dove? I'd give you anything."

The slight quirk of her full lips had me thickening behind my fly. Yes, she could have anything she fucking wanted. Any way she wanted. All she need do was ask.

"I'll never doubt you again, Noah. I promise."

Pulling my hand from my pocket, I held it out to her. "Then come here, darling, and let me make you mine. For keeps."

Her cheeks flushed, and she moved toward me, weaving her fingers through mine and pressing her lips to my knuckles. "I like the sound of that." When we didn't head inside, she faltered, giving me a curious stare.

"We'll go inside later. I have a surprise for you just round back."

"You're the romantic. I've decided."

"Am I?"

"Yes. You're my romantic. Kingston is my dirty Alpha. Alek, my strong, steady rock. And Caleb is my strict yet tender daddy."

I cupped her cheek with my free hand, leaning forward and feathering my lips over hers. "I do love to sweep you off your feet." Doing just that, I lifted her, cradling her in my arms and blurring us to the back side of the house, where her surprise was waiting just as I'd promised.

"What took you so long?" Alek asked.

Sunday's head snapped to the side, a laugh falling from her lips. The Viking was seated in the bubbling jacuzzi, rose petals floating on the surface, arms spread across the edge, hair piled in a bun at the top of his head.

"You were supposed to wait for us," I said, exasperated.

He snorted. "So I got a head start. I just wanted to be ready for Sunny. Besides, it looks like she's ready for a soak. You're the only one still dressed."

"Yup, you're the romantic. Candles, rose petals, the whole nine yards." She trailed her fingertips through the hair at the nape of my neck.

"It's our honeymoon. What else would I do?"

"It's perfect."

"*You're* perfect."

She rolled her eyes, but a happy flush swept across her skin.

I carefully set her down, discreetly plucking a leaf from her tangled curls. "Go on in. Alek and I made sure the water was just right."

"Aren't you coming?"

"Not in this suit, dove."

She snickered. "We wouldn't want to get it wet."

"You're the only thing I want wet."

"Already done."

"God, I love it when you're cheeky." I spanked her, sending her scuttling forward. She shot me a heated glance over her shoulder before gracefully moving down the steps to Alek.

She settled into the water, her breasts bobbing enticingly at the surface as she sat on Alek's lap. I began undressing, eager to join them. Sunday's eyes were locked on my hands as they worked to free my belt. A soft moan escaped her lips as Alek massaged her neck.

Christ. I was already rock hard and aching.

She squirmed, and I deliberately slowed my pace. The look on her face was an indication she enjoyed watching me strip. I had all night. This wasn't frantic fucking. I wanted to make it count.

Alek swept her hair to the side, revealing the slender column of her throat. Dropping his hands, he cupped her breasts, kneading the full globes as he trailed kisses over her neck.

Sunday fought to keep her eyes open, pleasure making them heavy. But I could see how badly she wanted to watch the show I was putting on for her.

I unbuttoned my shirt and slipped the fabric off my body, baring my torso and loving the way she raked my form with her gaze. It turned me the fuck on knowing she was looking at me as Alek made her feel good. Then, unable to keep myself from her any longer, I shoved my trousers down my hips before removing every stitch of clothing I wore. I itched to touch her. To taste her. To mark her.

She bit down on her lip as I moved toward her, keeping my steps measured and deliberate before hopping into the jacuzzi.

"You're pretty good at that."

"Getting into hot tubs?"

"Stripping."

"I've had some experience taking off clothes."

Her laugh was a husky scrape of breath when Alek slid his palm over her belly. I could just make out the tanned skin moving between her legs beneath the agitated water.

"Oh, God."

"Yes, Sunny. You can be as loud as you want out here." Alek's lips trailed over her shoulder. "But if you're going to cry out for anyone, let it be the man who's touching you."

"Hear, hear," I said, taking Sunday under the arms and pulling her off Alek. "In case you missed it, that man is me, dove."

"Sneaky," she whispered.

"Smart," I countered, kissing her.

My lips claimed her mouth, and my hand replaced Alek's. I delved two fingers inside her heat. She moaned against me, her hips rocking in search of the orgasm she wanted so badly. I took a couple of steps back, towing her body with me as I continued to work my fingers inside her. Alek trailed behind us, his palms resting on her hips.

"She's going to need your help up," I warned him as I removed my fingers from her cunt.

"Got it."

Sunday cast a curious look between us. "What do you two have planned?"

I smirked in answer, pressing my palms against the stone edge and pushing myself up and out of the warm water. She moved to follow, but Alek held her back.

"Wha—"

She didn't get a chance to finish the question. Alek spun her to face him, then lifted her before setting her on my lap with her thighs spread across mine, her arse against my jutting length.

I shifted, notching myself at her entrance.

She slowly sank down on my cock with a sigh. "Oh. I see. Good plan."

"That's just the first part," Alek said, smiling at her as he waded closer. Settling between our legs, he dove in face first, licking her straight up the middle, his tongue brushing my cock the barest hint. There was little more than a second for me to register the contact before he had her writhing on me.

She dug her hand into his hair as he worked her while I rocked my hips into her. Every flutter, every fucking clench of her pussy had me on edge.

"Do it, Noah. Please."

I pulled her hair away from her neck, gathering the silky strands to one side, and then I bit down, giving that perfect skin my mating mark on the opposite side of Kingston's. She came, her hot, tight cunt squeezing me as she did.

But I needed to finish the bond between us. Needed that one final step before I could find my own release. I broke the seal around her skin, a trail of her blood trickling down her chest, and brought my wrist to my lips.

Using my fangs, I opened a vein for her and then pressed my arm to her mouth. "Drink, dove. Complete me."

Sunday latched on, needing little encouragement. My pulse raced, and with each pull, the bond was formed. I came, spilling deep inside her as her mind opened fully to me once more.

*"I missed you, dove."*

*"I missed you too."*

From my vantage behind her, I saw Alek lean back, lips glistening, eyes hooded. Spotting the line of crimson rolling down Sunday's belly, he lifted up, catching the bead of her blood and licking her clean. A groan of pleasure escaped him, eyes closed, expression euphoric.

When he opened his eyes, there were little flickers of lightning in the pure black depths. The berserker had come out to play. Holding Sunday's gaze, he swiped his thumb over his lips, smearing them with red.

Why was that so bloody arousing?

Sunday shuddered in my arms. She had taken her pleasure from both of us, and I felt every last wave. Then she released her hold on my wrist and leaned her head back against my shoulder before whispering, "More."

*ALEK*

SUNDAY'S HARSH RASP, combined with the barely banked heat in her gaze, had my already throbbing length weeping with need.

"You're up, mate."

I shot Thorne a look, making it clear I wasn't asking for his fucking permission as I scooped up our girl and lifted her out of the hot tub. The smug, sated grin on his face would have earned him a fist to the throat any other time. Instead, I carried her with one arm, using my other to flip the vampire off as I moved us to the cabana not far away.

"How do you want me, Alek?" Fuck, I loved her voice when it went all breathy and hungry for me.

"I love watching you bounce on my cock like it's your favorite ride in the world."

She peppered sweet kisses across my shoulder and chest and then flicked her tongue over my nipple, sending sparks shooting through me. "It is one of my favorites. So big and thick." She moved until her lips were at my ear. "No one stretches me the way you do."

Now who wore a smug grin?

447

Me.

I did.

Thorne couldn't see my face, but I knew he could hear every word she whispered. I only wished that cocky fucking wolf was here to hear it as well. He could do with a reminder that not all of us needed accessories to get the job done. Maybe I'd name my dick too. Xander had a nice ring to it. Or maybe Excalibur. That was a mighty magical sword, wasn't it? Mjölnir might be more appropriate, but that was too obvious.

I didn't release her as I sat on the bed-like cushion in the cabana, only adjusted my hold and shifted her so by the time I was on my back, she was astride me. Gods, she was beautiful. Dark hair tumbling wildly down her shoulders, curling over the tops of her breasts.

Her eyes glinted with lust as she raised up on her knees and reached for my length. I helped her along, my fist gripping the base and placing my head at her hot, slick entrance.

"I love you, elskan mín."

Then she slowly lowered herself until I was sheathed fully. I couldn't hold back my hiss of pleasure at the feel of her around me. She was so small, and I was so fucking big. It never got old, this feeling. The completion that came from having my mate take me. A hundred years from now, I'd still want her like this.

Sunny rolled her hips, and we moaned in unison. I gripped her by the waist, halting the movement.

"Wait, Kærasta. I need to see my mark on you."

Her eyes met mine, shining with arousal, yes, but also so much love it nearly stole my breath. "Do it. Please. I've missed having your name on my body, seeing mine on yours."

Calling on my power, I ran my fingers along the smooth flesh of her inner arm, branding it with my runes. Staking my claim. She shuddered and groaned as the magic ran through us both, her pussy fluttering around my cock.

"Oh, we should have done it like this the first time," she whispered. Apology instantly flitted through her eyes. "I . . . I'm sorry. You don't remember."

"Don't apologize for that. I'm yours. Now I get to make a new memory of claiming what's mine, and from the sound of things, get it right." I took her hand and drew it to my left side, right along my ribs. "Help me put you back where you belong."

She shifted forward just enough that my crown pressed against her womb, making us both suck in harsh breaths at the sensation.

"Do you remember what they look like?"

"Of course I do. That's not something I'll ever forget."

"Then mark me, Kærasta. Make me yours."

She kissed me. "You've always been mine."

"True. Even when I didn't remember who you were, my soul was yours."

Her eyes filled with glittering tears, and I reached up to brush them away as they fell. But I knew there was no sadness in them. It was relief pouring from her. We could finally share our love without danger at every turn.

Holding my gaze, she traced the runes down my ribcage. With each slide of her skin over mine, I called on the magic, bringing the mark into being.

As soon as it was complete, I gave her a savage grin. "Now, Kærasta. Ride me."

Her nipples were hard and tight, breasts swaying as she began a slow, seductive dance atop me. Soon we were both shaking with the need for release, but I didn't want this to be over yet. Not when every moment felt so good. I ran my fingers down her lower back, trailing them over the line of her spine until I reached the lush globes of her arse. When she moaned and tipped her hips to give me access, I continued my exploration, finding her puckered hole and applying pressure.

"You want more, don't you?" I gritted out.

"Yes. Please. More."

"Thorne. You're needed."

"I thought you'd never ask."

I could hear the water splash as he immediately jumped out of the hot tub where he'd been watching us. As much as Sunday and I both loved an audience, I didn't mind sharing this with him because it was a way for me to give her what she needed.

After all, he'd allowed me the same.

Using my power once more, I conjured a bottle of lubricant into my palm and tossed it to the vampire without a word. He caught it one-handed and instantly popped the top, pouring a liberal amount of the clear liquid into his other hand. He knew exactly what part he was about to play.

Sunday's eyes were all mine as Thorne pressed her forward until she was on hands and knees.

"Stay still. Let us do the work," I murmured.

I felt it as he slid inside her slowly. The brush of his cock through the thin wall separating us, the tightening of all her muscles, the rush of slick coming from her cunt. It was overwhelming and now even tighter than before.

"Can you take it all, dove?"

"Yes."

"That's my good little wolf," he said on a groan.

I had to swallow back a cry of my own as Thorne fully seated himself inside her arse. We panted in unison as he moved the fall of her hair away from the mark he'd just given her. When he leaned down to kiss her, she shivered and moaned.

Sensation ghosted across my skin, sending tingles arcing through me like little webs of lightning. It was as if I could feel everything she was feeling, my desire cranked up by the intensity of hers.

"Gods, you feel fucking divine, Sunny."

She was too far gone for her words, her face flushed, her mouth open on soundless moans, and Thorne and I began to time our thrusts, pushing in and out in tandem.

I gripped her by the hips, stopping her from moving and sending us all over the edge.

"Are you ready to come now, Kærasta?"

"Only if you both come with me."

"God, please. I can't hold on much longer," Thorne rasped.

Taking her face in my hands, I pulled her down, kissing her deep and shifting the angle of her arse. Thorne groaned, and I swallowed the sound of Sunday's moans as I reached between her legs and pinched her clit.

She went off like a bomb, detonating around us and pulling us both with her. I poured everything I had into her, grunting against her mouth as the orgasm sent me into white-hot ecstasy.

Thorne pulled out first, gasping for breath as he came down from his high. "Bloody hell, look at that. The sight of our cum dripping out of her has me ready to go again."

I had to agree with him. I could feel it dripping down my balls.

"You'll have to see to yourself, Blackthorne. You've both had your turn."

Sunday's breath hitched at the sound of Caleb's voice. She lifted her forehead from mine, feathering a final kiss over my lips before turning to look over at him. "Have you been here the entire time?"

I could see what the thought alone did to her. Goosebumps erupted down her arms, and her nipples immediately pebbled.

I sat us both up, taking one of the stiff peaks between my lips and sucking hard before releasing her with a pop.

"Of course he has. Father Gallagher loves to watch."

CALEB

"CLEAN YOURSELF UP, Miss Fallon. You're a mess." God save me, but my voice was tight as I cloaked myself in false disapproval. But I knew how she responded to me when I was stern. I wanted her wet only for me now.

She licked her lips and rose to her feet, her legs trembling slightly. She was still flushed from her last round with them, but I could see the desire burning in her eyes. "You should be used to it by now, Father Gallagher."

I bit back a grin, loving that she'd already picked up on what I had in mind for us.

"Will you be joining me in the shower, or . . ."

"I left instructions for you on the bed. Follow them. I'll meet you once you're done."

Her eyes widened slightly. I'd piqued her interest with that. Good. I wanted her eager. I wanted her naughty. The two were an intoxicating combination.

And then? I wanted her to be my good girl. To take everything I had planned for her and beg me for more.

"Yes, Daddy." She blew a kiss to Thorne and Alek, letting the backs of her fingers brush against mine as she wandered into the house. I tracked her movements, noting the sway of her hips and fighting a groan of need.

It took every ounce of will I had not to snatch her by the wrist and toss her over my shoulder, naked, dripping, fecking perfect, and simply claim her here and now. But I had plans.

I thought of the note I'd left for her. Simple and to the point.

MISS FALLON,

YOU'VE BEEN NEGLECTING OUR SESSIONS. PUT THIS ON AND COME TO MY OFFICE TO SERVE YOUR PENANCE. 10:15 ON THE DOT. DON'T BE LATE.

FATHER GALLAGHER

I could already picture the too-tight shirt, plaid skirt, and knee-highs. I'd only seen her wear them once, but it was seared in my memory. This time, I didn't have to resist. This time, I could give her everything.

This time she'd not only fecking take it, she'd revel in it.

My cock throbbed, hard and insistent behind my fly as I headed into the room Alek had helped craft with his magic. A confessional booth held pride of place as the centerpiece here, with a lone chair in the corner and a few candles flickering in their holders on the wall. My stark white collar was waiting for me on the cushion.

I hadn't worn one since the night Gabriel brought me back. Looking at it now, I felt none of the shame or grief I used to. Tonight, all I felt was anticipation as I slipped it into place.

I heard her footsteps coming down the hall, so I stepped into the booth, assuming my place on the confessor's seat and making myself comfortable.

This was going to be fun.

My fingers twitched as her scent hit me. I would forever be soothed by lilacs and honey. My heart was made whole by those two things innately *her*.

"Caleb?"

"You're late. It's time to make your confession, Miss Fallon."

"It is, is it? Have I been bad, Father Gallagher?"

"You know you have, naughty girl. Do you remember what to do?"

"Something about getting on my knees, but then that is the way you love me. Isn't it, Daddy?"

I had to bite back a groan. I loved it when she called me that, with her taunting tone. "Spoiled brat. I've been too lenient with you."

She snickered. "That would be more believable if it didn't sound like you approved so much."

If she could see my cock right now, I wouldn't be able to disagree with her. "In the booth, Miss Fallon. Tell me your sins."

"Where to start? There's been so many since the last time we did this. Pre-marital sex? Pregnancy out of wedlock? Sodomy? Hmm . . . that last one is a favorite of mine. And yours . . ."

I sucked in a sharp breath, already palming myself to relieve some of the ache. "Why don't you begin with your most recent behaviors? Don't leave out any detail. I need to know it all if I'm to absolve you."

"Well . . . I don't know how much you saw, but earlier I was being fucked by two men at once. Noah took my ass while Alek pounded my cunt. Is that enough detail for you, Father?"

I had to clear my throat. "Go on."

I could hear her wicked smirk in the words. I loved making her smile, wicked or otherwise. "Actually, the most recent would be in the shower five minutes ago. I touched myself. Made myself come. I had dirty thoughts . . . about you."

Fecking hell, I wasn't going to make it through this. If I hadn't committed to this scene with her, if I didn't know how much she loved this, I'd already have had her up against the wall and been buried inside her. Marking her as mine, claiming every part of her.

But this was her night. Ours. So I returned to the role I'd played so well. "You have a filthy fucking mouth, Miss Fallon."

"You love it."

*Damn right I do. Especially when it's wrapped around my cock.*

"Tell me what you were thinking about."

"You. Spanking me. That first time."

*Christ.*

"Did you like it, then? The feel of my palm on your round arse?"

Her breath hitched. "Yes. Does that make me a bad girl?"

"That depends. Is your cunt wet right now? Touch yourself. Tell me."

The rustle of fabric told me she was doing exactly as instructed. But even without that clue, her barely audible moan would have given her away.

"Y-yes."

"How wet?"

"Dripping. I ruined my panties. God, Caleb, I need you."

Without realizing it, she'd given me the exact opening I needed. Thank fuck. I was about two seconds away from coming in my trousers.

"What you need, Miss Fallon, is to learn some restraint. Clearly you never learned your lesson. So perhaps it bears repeating. Do you have any idea how many rules you've broken?"

"R-rules?"

"You were late. You wore knickers, even though I distinctly remember telling you never to wear them with me, and I certainly didn't leave any out for you. You called me Caleb. You know that name is reserved for when my hands are on you, Miss Fallon. And that's just the tip of the iceberg. Shall I go on?"

"Oh, God . . ." she moaned.

"Are you still touching yourself?"

"Yes."

"Don't you dare bring yourself off. Your orgasms are mine."

Her answering whimper had me up and out of my side of the booth, tearing open the curtain that hid her with no warning. There she was, legs splayed, white cotton knickers pulled to the side, fingers working her clit, lip caught between her teeth.

Petulant.

Perfect.

*Mine.*

"If you come, so help me, you will regret it."

She smirked. "Doubtful. I never regret an orgasm."

I took that as the challenge it was, knowing I had her beat before the words left my lips. "I won't let myself inside you for a month."

Her hand stopped, and she pouted, the look on her face making me warm to her.

"Is it my cock you're wanting, or quick release?"

"Your cock."

"Then get up. If you can prove your restraint, if you can take my punishment without coming, I'll give it to you."

She stood, her knees wobbling, knickers still firmly in place and begging to be ripped free of her hips. I ignored my need to give her what she wanted and strode to the chair, gripping it so hard the wood creaked as I brought it close.

"You want me to sit?"

I smirked. "No, I'll be doing the sitting."

Her eyes widened as she realized what I'd intended.

"That's right, Miss Fallon. I'm going to spank you. And then, if you prove yourself, I'm going to fuck you."

She blinked, her lips parting on a soft gasp. "I'm going to hold you to that, Father."

"Earn it, and you won't have to. I'll give it to you willingly. I'm nothing if not a man of my word."

Settling on the padded chair, I spread my thighs and cocked one brow at the woman who owned me. "Bend over my lap. You've a punishment to receive."

Fuck, I could see her nipples pressing against the thin white shirt. I wanted her naked and writhing. Moaning my name.

She knelt and bent over my thighs, those supple mounds nestling my rigid length as she arched her back. I ran my hand over the curve of her sweet arse, roughly tugging down the offending scrap of cotton.

"Spread your legs, Miss Fallon."

She let out a muffled whimper and obeyed. "Yes, Father Gallagher."

I spanked her. One hard, swift slap. "Caleb."

"W-what?"

I slid my fingers down her slick seam. "Need I remind you, Miss Fallon? You *will* call me Caleb when my hands are on you."

She wriggled her hips, searching for more. "Caleb."

"Aye, that's a good girl."

As a reward, I sank one digit inside her, clenching my jaw at the feel of her hot, wet cunt.

"Fuck, Caleb, please."

"Not yet, *a stor*."

"I need you. I need your mark."

"Be my good girl and earn it. Serve your penance."

She nodded, her arse tipping up. "I deserve your punishment. I'm ready."

With my free hand, I cupped her cheek, sliding my thumb over her full bottom lip. When she opened her mouth and drew it inside, I couldn't stop myself. I thrust my hips, searching for some friction, some promise of finding my own release.

It was time to move this along. No more toying with her. No more denying us what we both desired. I brought my palm down over and over, teasing her by slapping the puffy lips of her sex between strikes on her arse. And only when both cheeks glowed a bright pink and we were each breathing hard did I stop. I inhaled deeply, the scent of her slick filling the room.

"You did beautifully, *a stor*."

I could feel her heart thundering against my thighs. "Th-thank you."

I tipped her face up, noting the flush of her cheeks and the dilated cast of her pupils. "I'm proud of you, darling girl. I'm ready to give you your reward now."

Her flush deepened at my praise. "Yes, Daddy. Please."

As it always did when she called me that, my cock gave a happy jerk. Fuck, but I was ruined for this woman. It had always been her. Never had anyone tempted me the way she did. Even now, when she was mine.

She made to push up, but when she started to move away, I stood and took her wrist. I didn't want to lose that contact with her as she got to her feet. My heart gave a near panicked lurch as I gazed at the face of the woman I never thought I'd have.

"Caleb? Why do you look so sad?"

"Not sad, *a stor*. Reverent."

Sinking to my knees, I wrapped my arms about her waist and held her tight, my head pressed to her belly, her fingers threading in my hair. I never wanted to let her go. I'd lost her time and time again.

I knew exactly how to fix the one thing that was still broken between us. What we were truly here for. Our bond.

Releasing my hold on her, I helped her step free of her destroyed panties, then slowly did the same with her shoes and stockings. I didn't say a word as I worked my way up her body, removing each piece of clothing until she was bared to me.

"Your turn," she whispered, reaching first for my collar and slipping it off.

I took it from between her fingers and laid it back on the chair, then watched as she undressed me with as much tender care as I had done for her.

"I want to love you now, Sunday."

"Forever. Love me forever, please."

I cupped the back of her head and pulled her in for a kiss that rivaled every single other we'd shared. Without stopping, I lifted her up, carrying her over to the confessional, using the side wall for leverage as I pressed her back against it.

I sheathed myself inside her in one long thrust, filling her until she cried out and clamped down around me. On edge since the moment she stepped into this room, I was keenly aware of my release building, ready to break free. I didn't have long.

"I'm going to make you mine, wife. Are you ready?"

"God, Caleb, yes."

She tightened her legs around me and ground her hips into mine as she began riding me when I wouldn't move. She was going to bring me off before I could finish bonding with her at this rate.

I dipped my head, placing my mouth on the top of her left breast, directly over her beautiful heart. Then I struck, sinking my fangs into the soft flesh, loving the moan of pleasure that spilled from her.

It was heady, intoxicating, and it sent need careening through me.

I forced myself to stop, to pull back and growl, "Now. Mark me, Sunday. Make me yours."

Face still twisted with pleasure, she called on her wolf, her teeth lengthening to deadly points. Then she whispered her lips down the side of my throat before giving me exactly what I asked for.

There was a hiss of pain, but it was quickly replaced by pleasure so intense my knees threatened to buckle. I tightened my hold on her, trying with the frayed edges of my control not to come until she did. I wanted us to jump over the edge the same way I wanted to do everything with her. Together.

As our bond solidified, I let loose a groan, deep and guttural, and began fucking her in earnest. Our combined climaxes reached the crest at the same time. She dug her claws into my back, scoring my skin, amplifying the euphoria with pain, and I cried out her name as the wood of the confessional cracked and she brought me to my knees.

When she removed her lips from my throat and cradled my face in her hands, all I saw was my future staring back at me.

"I love you, Sunday. Forever and ever."

She smiled, looking radiant and damn near angelic until a wicked glint sparkled in her eyes.

"Amen."

# BONUS EPILOGUE

## ASHER

*Aurora Springs, Alaska*

That witch was going to be the death of me after all. A hiss escaped me as a burn shot through the mark she'd saddled me with years ago. A parting gift for my unfortunate misstep.

I checked the spot on the back of my hand; just a small star right in the center. What the fuck? Was the thing growing? Instead of a single star, there was now a small cluster. Dread curled in my gut. What did this mean? How could I stop it? Whatever it was, it couldn't be good.

A loud crash from behind me pulled me out of my spiral of doom. Two wolf shifters and a burly lumberjack were locked in a scuffle. I had to get the hell out of here before this turned into a full-on bar brawl.

I pulled my collar up higher as I left the Tipsy Moose behind. I hadn't even been able to enjoy my beer before those fucking Mercer twins started a fight. They had thirty other days to act like a bunch of assholes, and they chose the one night a month where I came into town for my supply run. It was my only chance to stop in for a taste of semi-normal existence, and it had been ruined by dick-swinging shifters.

Fucking typical.

The wind kicked up, sending the curly hair of my fake beard fluttering across the hollow of my throat and tickling me without mercy. Maybe one day I wouldn't have to hide my identity, but as of right now, I was still the supernatural world's most wanted hacker. That meant a life of anonymous sex, zero meaningful relationships, and way too much wig adhesive. It was all fake names, deep cover, and high security for me. Unless I wanted to get caught and become the captive of that vengeful witch.

Hard pass. She'd already done enough damage.

I scratched at my chin with an annoyed grunt, my irritation rising when I felt the adhesive give way. Great. My goatee probably looked drunker than I did—than I was *supposed* to be.

The whole thing was bullshit, my night wrecked, and now I didn't even have a good buzz to make any of the effort worth it. I should have just waited until I got home. Then I could have cracked open one of the bottles of Jack I'd bought and found oblivion in the best way I knew. Alone.

I hated the need for these disguises, but it was the only way to maintain any sort of social life when, as far as the people of Aurora Springs knew, Asher Henry didn't exist. And I needed to keep it that way if I wanted to stay alive. In a town of one hundred and seventy-three people, that was a special sort of hell.

Thus I became Joe Baker, resident hermit and curmudgeonly fisherman. No one bothered me. No one cared if I ever showed my face.

Well, almost no one.

Starting up my old beater of a truck, I waited for the heat to blast and fill the cab. Even in the spring, it was cold here. But going into hiding meant isolation in a small, nowhere town. What better place than the near wilds of Alaska?

I drove the forty minutes up the winding path to my mountain fortress, mostly muttering to myself and ignoring the sorry excuse for music playing on the radio. It was really just a bunch of static with a random guitar strum here and there, but what could you expect from a town with one fucking station?

If the night had gone according to plan, I would have slept it off at Joe Baker's houseboat or any of the other properties I owned under various names. But since tonight had shit the bed before it even started, all I wanted was to go home. That meant my log cabin in the woods. The one filled with technology so advanced not even the military had access to most of it, and no one in Aurora Springs, let alone anywhere else, would find it on any kind of map. Google Earth could fuck right off.

As I pulled past the camouflaged gate hiding my property from the prying eyes of wayward hikers, I frowned. The beams of my headlights flashed across strange tracks in the muddy earth of the dirt road.

"What the fuck?"

My pulse raced, adrenaline spiking as the path continued toward my house. Animal? Maybe. I'd encountered my share of wildlife here. They were the only creatures who breached my walls.

But as soon as I parked, I saw the culprit. A dirty lump huddled against my door. Stringy dark hair hanging in front of their—no, *her* —face.

Reaching under the seat of my truck, I pulled the revolver I kept hidden there out of its holster. You never knew what you'd come up against out here. I'd learned that the hard way.

I got out, breath tight as I raised the gun and switched off the safety. Then I cocked the hammer and said, "Don't fucking move."

Her head snapped up, and she pinned me with eyes the color of burnished gold. My heart stuttered. I knew those eyes. That face. I'd stared at them far too many times from the glow of my computer screens under the guise of "research." But she wasn't my assignment, shouldn't have been on my fucking radar at all. And yet I hadn't been able to look away even after—

"You're dead."

Her stats flashed in my memory:

**ROSLYN "ROSIE" BLACKTHORNE**
**AGE: 21**
**SPECIES: VAMPIRE-HUMAN HYBRID**
**(NEVER TURNED)**
**PARENTS: CASHEL AND OLIVIA BLACKTHORNE**
**SIBLINGS: NOAH AND WESTLEY BLACKTHORNE**
**STATUS: DECEASED**
**CAUSE OF DEATH: HOUSE FIRE**

"Not dead enough, it would seem." She got to wobbly feet, her eyes tired, face dirt-streaked and pale. "Asher, I need your help."

"Why the fuck should I help you? How did you even find me?"

A proud, exhausted smile flitted across her face. "You're not the only one with a certain skill set."

The knowledge that I'd been hacked sent a bolt of terror straight through me. If she'd been able to find me, who else could? I'd be so damn careful. There weren't any breadcrumbs, cyber or otherwise. I was as off the map as possible. Yet her presence here, the fact that she'd called me by my name, proved just how fucking wrong I was. *Christ, I was going to need to do a full security sweep.*

"Then why do you need me at all?"

"Could you put that thing down?"

I glanced at the gun I still had aimed between her eyes. "Shit. Sorry."

"And I need you because you have connections I don't."

"Such as?"

"People, papers, access to new documents."

"So you're on the run."

"Well, I can't exactly go around as the late Roslyn Blackthorne, now can I?"

"That's what this is about? You want a new identity?"

"I need to make sure Rosie stays dead and buried. God knows I went to enough effort killing her. No one can know I'm alive. Not even my family."

"What are you running from?"

Her expression went grave. "My husband."

～

*THE MATE GAMES CONTINUE IN DEAL WITH THE DEMON, THE MATE GAMES: PESTILENCE BOOK 1. PREORDER YOUR COPY NOW!*

# ACKNOWLEDGMENTS

Dear gentle reader,

We went into this series with the intention of writing something that ticked every one of our boxes. No kink was spared, no steamy scene unwritten (you're welcome). This series was our fangirl fantasy, the books we wanted to read, narrated by the voices we wanted to hear. We are so thankful they came to life in such a beautiful way and with so much support from the beginning.

To our alpha readers: Suzi, Sarah, Ruhla, Mo. Thank you for your time, your love of these characters, and your feedback as we wrote.

Sunday's Ravens. Thank you for your early adoption of our world.

To our publicity team, you rock! Thank you for your eagerness in sharing our books. We love seeing your posts. Keep 'em coming!

To our narrators and audio team: J.F., Jason, James, Aaron, Stella (you lucky b*tch), Jacob, Shane, Teddy, and Tyler the audio engineer wizard, you all gave these characters so much life and made the audiobooks an experience listeners will never forget. The laughs, the tears, the blushes...those are because of you. Because you loved these characters as much as we did and jumped into the deep end with us. It was a huge undertaking, but together we created something amazing.

To our husbands, thank you for not getting too jealous of all the time we spent hidden away writing about our other guys. Boardgames and brews are in your future, we promise. Just as soon as we're done writing the next book.

To our shipping department (Violet and Sophie) you are the best sparkle friends of all time.

To the Breeder Readers group. Thank you for giving breeding kink a special place on Facebook. You are our people.

And to everyone who slid into our DMs, left a review, and/or publicly shared their love of Sunday and her sausages—we mean mates—thank you. We could not have gotten here without you.

So...we guess all that's left is to ask the big question...who's ready for more?

xoxo,
Meg & Kim

# THE MATE GAMES UNIVERSE
## BY K. LORAINE & MEG ANNE

# ALSO BY MEG ANNE

**BROTHERHOOD OF THE GUARDIANS/NOVASGARD VIKINGS**

**UNDERCOVER MAGIC** *(NORD & LINA)*

*A SEXY & SUSPENSEFUL FATED MATES PNR*

HINT OF DANGER

FACE OF DANGER

WORLD OF DANGER

PROMISE OF DANGER

CALL OF DANGER

BOUND BY DANGER (QUINN & FINLEY)

*THE CHOSEN UNIVERSE*

**THE CHOSEN SERIES: THE COMPLETE SERIES**

*A FATED MATES HIGH FANTASY ROMANCE*

MOTHER OF SHADOWS

REIGN OF ASH

CROWN OF EMBERS

QUEEN OF LIGHT

THE CHOSEN BOXSET #1

THE CHOSEN BOXSET #2

# Also by K. Loraine

~

**REVERSE HAREM STANDALONES**

# ABOUT MEG ANNE

USA Today and international bestselling paranormal and fantasy romance author Meg Anne has always had stories running on a loop in her head. They started off as daydreams about how the evil queen (aka Mom) had her slaving away doing chores, and more recently shifted into creating backgrounds about the people stuck beside her during rush hour. The stories have always been there; they were just waiting for her to tell them.

Like any true SoCal native, Meg enjoys staying inside curled up with a good book and her cat, Henry . . . or maybe that's just her. You can convince Meg to buy just about anything if it's covered in glitter or rhinestones, or make her laugh by sharing your favorite bad joke. She also accepts bribes in the form of baked goods and Mexican food.

Meg is best known for her leading men #MenbyMeg, her inevitable cliffhangers, and making her readers laugh out loud, all of which started with the bestselling Chosen series.